'From the very first page, this first [book in] The God Fragments hurls you head[long into] the world that Lloyd wraps you in [with his] storytelling'   *SFX*

'I loved this book from start to finish' Adrian Tchaikovsky, Arthur C Clarke Award-winning author of *Children of Time*

'Beautifully designed and superbly executed' James Barclay, author of Chronicles of the Raven series and *Heart of Granite*

'A fun and fast paced romp in which a mercenary company's latest job goes horrendously wrong and they have to evade pursuit. A great cast and some very good action set pieces'
    Aliette de Bodard, author of *The House of Shattered Wings*

'Grabs you by the throat on the first page' Ben Galley, author of *Heart of Stone*

'Grips you from the beginning and doesn't let go'
                    Edward Cox, author of The Relic Guild trilogy

'The action is relentless'   KV Johansen, author of *Blackdog*

'[a] fantasy adventure in the modern style, comfortably mixing gritty realism with swords and sorcery. Imagine Steven Erikson's Malazan marines teaming up with Lara Croft for a mad dash across Joe Abercrombie's Red Country with an unplanned detour through the forgotten deeps of Moria and you'll be most of the way there'   Forbidden Planet International

'This is a great start to what I expect will be an amazing new series, and will appeal to those who, like me, felt bereft when Chris Wooding completed his Tales of the Ketty Jay series as well as fans of Scott Lynch'   Jo's Book Blog

Also by Tom Lloyd from Gollancz:

The Twilight Reign
The Stormcaller
The Twilight Herald
The Grave Thief
The Ragged Man
The Dusk Watchman
The God Tattoo

Empire of A Hundred Houses
Moon's Artifice
Old Man's Ghosts

The God Fragments
Stranger of Tempest
Princess of Blood
Honour Under Moonlight (novella)

STRANGER OF TEMPEST

TOM LLOYD

First published in Great Britain in 2016 by Gollancz
an imprint of the Orion Publishing Group Ltd
Carmelite House, 50 Victoria Embankment
London EC4Y 0DZ

An Hachette UK Company

1 3 5 7 9 10 8 6 4 2

A CIP catalogue record for this book is
available from the British Library.

ISBN 978 1 473 21318 0

Typeset by Born Group
Printed in Great Britain by CPI Group (UK) Ltd, Croydon CR0 4YY

www.tomlloyd.co.uk
www.orionbooks.co.uk
www.gollancz.co.uk

For Euan Richard Lloyd-Williams

Soldiers of Anatin's Mercenary Deck

	SUN	STARS	BLOOD	SNOW	TEMPEST
PRINCE	ANATIN				
17	Foren				
16	Sonnersyn				
KNIGHT	PAYL	OLUT	REFT	SAFIR	TESHEN
14	Karra	Dortrinas	Silm	Layir	Finc
13		Arut	Brellis	Aspegrin	
DIVINER		ESTAL	HIMBEL		LLAITH
11	Haphori	Rubesh	Crast		Flinth
10					
STRANGER	VARAIN		ULAX		
8	Darm		Toam	Sandath	
7	Brols				
MADMAN	CRAIS	KAS		BURNEL	
5	Fael	Hald		Shoal	
4				Ismont	
JESTER		ASHIS	DEERN	TYN	BRAQUE
2			Hule		Tunnest
1					

Interlude 1
(now)

For a damsel in distress, she was rather more spattered with someone else's blood than Lynx had expected. And naked. Very naked.

'Well?' she demanded.

Lynx could only gape a while longer. Finally his words spilled out in an abashed mumble. 'Um – come to rescue you, miss.'

'You'll have to wait,' she snapped at the knot of mercenaries crowding the doorway. 'I'm busy.'

'Guh.'

Lynx tried to say more, but something in his head had stopped working the moment she'd opened the door, and his tongue seemed to fill his mouth. A beguiling scent of vanilla and night jasmine fogged his mind. Beside him the hard-bitten veteran, Varain, sounded like he was choking, while the silent giant, Reft, was as wordless as ever.

It fell to Safir to remember how to use words and even the former nobleman hesitated before he offered a deep bow.

'We are at your command, my lady.'

That prompted a small smile. 'Glad at least one of you's seen a woman before.'

Safir inclined his head and gave a polite cough. 'Ah, my lady?'

'Yes?'

'Your, ahem, friend,' he said, pointing behind her. 'He's found a knife.'

Once Lynx managed to drag his gaze off the woman, he saw a half-dressed man with pale hair and chiselled features staggering woozily in the room behind. Blood dribbled from his broken nose down a once-fine white doublet and his silk stockings were ripped and sagging. As the man tried to yank his britches back up from his ankles he only managed to rip them further as he snagged one foot.

An emerald silk shift lay on the floor nearby. From the smell of brandy, Lynx guessed the man had staggered in and ripped it off her when she answered the door. A broken nose certainly seemed a fair start.

Eventually the man managed to haul his britches over his knees and waddle forward, brandishing a gold-hilted dagger in their direction. His long, oiled hair was now plastered over one side of his face, his lips swollen and bleeding as he tried to work his mouth well enough to call for help.

'Oh please.'

The woman sighed and stalked back into the room, ignoring the blade Safir offered. Instead she swept up a candlestick from a side table and lashed out with a ferocious backhand swipe. She caught the nobleman's wrist and Lynx heard something snap under the impact. As the blade tumbled from the man's grip she followed the blow up with a knee to his stomach. That threw him back against the ornate bedpost and drove the wind from any further attempt to cry out.

'Lady Toil,' Anatin called from behind Lynx. 'We're on something of a schedule here. Could we hurry this up?'

Lynx glanced back at their commander. The grey-haired man didn't seem in the least surprised that their fifteen-year-old kidnap victim was in fact a muscular veteran of about thirty, the glisten of sweat on her skin only highlighting her wide assortment of scars. Nor that she was beating seven shades of shit out of an armed nobleman.

Her long hair was tinted a deep red and had been carefully styled prior to her current exertions, her fingernails painted a similar bright shade to her raw, bloodied knuckles. Even naked she stood tall and moved with lithe purpose, quite unconcerned by the mercenaries watching like lust-struck little boys. Lynx realised he'd been holding his breath as he watched her and exhaled noisily.

'Lady Toil?' The woman laughed. 'I like the sound of that.'

She punched the nobleman on his already-broken nose and he flopped back on the bed, whimpering.

'You,' Toil ordered, pointing at Lynx. 'Clothes in that drawer, boots in the cupboard.'

Lynx blinked dumbly at her for a moment. It took a swat around the head from Anatin before he sheathed his sword and ducked his head, muttering, 'Clothes, right.'

'Good boy.'

'So who in the coldest black is he then?' Lynx added as he pulled open the drawer and tossed aside a silk dress to unearth something rather more practical.

A pair of short-swords lay under a plain tunic and trousers so he pulled them out and threw them over a chair. He shook his head as though he could dislodge the image of Toil that had been burned into his mind, stoking his anger to distract the lurching sensation from deep in his belly.

'This ray of sunshine?' Toil asked, holding the man's lolling head up. 'Can't you guess?'

'All I know's we've been lied to all the way here,' Lynx said. 'Those were proper soldiers downstairs, this ain't the house of some minor noble who didn't like being told no.'

Toil let the man drop back and hauled on her linen drawers and shirt. 'You're mercs,' she commented. 'You do what you're told and you get paid for it.'

'Lynx,' Anatin added in a warning tone, 'you of all folk got no right to start getting pissy now.'

Lynx gave the commander a level look. 'I signed up for a rescue, not an assassination. Right now I'm guessing this job's a whole lot more dangerous than we thought. You even told your Knights what the real mission is?'

Toil took a step towards him. Despite the fact she was unarmed and distractingly beautiful, she carried a threatening air that made him tense.

'You were told enough,' she said firmly. 'Get me out of the house, escort me out of the city.' Without warning a dazzling smile broke like the sun through clouds. 'Now be a sweetheart and fetch my pack and boots. We'll be running soon.'

'She's right, Lynx,' Safir added, stepping in to the room so Lynx's unit commander, Teshen, could look inside. Both the dark-skinned Safir and pale Teshen were Knights of the company and neither seemed disquieted by what they saw. 'I can put the pieces together, but now's not the time. We ride clear of the city, then we can fling blame about like angry monkeys.'

Lynx paused as he pulled the boots and pack from the cupboard she'd indicated. He looked over at the battered man on the bed while Toil continued to dress. Olive-skinned and blue-eyed, the man was clearly an Asann merchant prince and now he looked around the room, Lynx realised this wasn't some nobleman's city residence at all. More likely the elegant home of a merchant's mistress, albeit a rich one.

What'd be the worst trouble we could be in right now?

Lynx sagged. 'He's Princip of the Assayed Council, isn't he?'

'Not for much longer,' Toil said darkly, lacing up her boots. Once that was done she stood and belted her short-swords on. 'Anatin, you ready?'

The commander nodded towards Teshen and jerked his thumb at the corridor behind him. 'Get ready to move, assume there are more guards.'

'There won't be,' Toil interjected. 'He always comes with just a handful, but there will be patrols on the street.'

'So we go quietly,' Anatin replied. 'Teshen, check the street.'

'Quietly? Sure, I guess,' Toil said with a small smile. 'Now come here, you gutless little fuck.'

She grabbed the Princip of the Assayed – ruler of the entire city-state of Grasiel – by his bloodied tunic and hauled him upright. The man whimpered and snivelled, barely supporting his own weight, but Toil was a powerful woman and held him easily.

'Yeah, we could do quiet I suppose.'

Toil gave the mercenaries a savage grin and lurched abruptly right. Lynx watched open-mouthed as she took a brief run-up to the diamond-pattern window that covered much of the western wall. With a grunt of effort she hurled the Princip at the large central panel. The glass seemed to explode out into the night air and he pitched through – finally finding his voice as he flailed at the darkness. He dropped, the echo of his shrieks cut off by a sickening crunch from the paved street beyond.

There was a moment where no one even breathed. Then Toil leaned out of the window and gave a grunt of approval.

'See, all quiet now,' she said as she headed for the door.

It was late into the night and a quiet neighbourhood. Lynx was in the corridor and already running by the time he heard the first screams.

Chapter 1
(two weeks earlier)

Lynx opened his eyes and immediately regretted it. Dark stone walls swam before his eyes, outlined by a faint scrap of light that crept in through bars set into the door. His breath caught in his throat as panic set in and his heart began to judder in his chest. It was a cell.

The cloying stink of shit and rank old sweat hit him like a punch. Memories blossomed from the dark stars unfolding before his eyes as pain shot through his head. Voices of men long dead, cries in the night and the bite of pitted iron shackles on his skin.

He closed his eyes again, as though willing himself away from that place, but instead another voice came – a deep rolling accent of the far south-east that cut through the fear. A man he'd once known. A man who'd once saved him from fear.

Lynx fought the panic down and opened his eyes again, finally able to notice the sensation of a vice clamped around his head. For a while that was all he could feel and slowly he realised that this was no ordinary hangover. The throb seemed to be most obvious down one side and he tried to touch his fingers to his head. That prompted a whole new set of hurts as he discovered his wrists were bound so tight his hands were numb, his shoulders bruised and aching.

'Aye, they fucked you up good.'

Lynx turned his head and found a new set of regrets. The view hadn't improved, but now his neck had joined in the clamour.

His vision blurred as muscles fluttered in spasm and the mother of all hangovers kicked him in the head. For a moment all he could see was the memory of bottles on a table, and a small wheeze escaped his cracked and swollen lips. He focused on the pain, embraced it as a friend compared to his memories.

A small man with long hair sat on a stone ledge, biting filthy nails as he eyed Lynx.

'So who'd you kill?'

Lynx felt a lurch at the question and his cramping stomach obliged, heaving up what little remained inside while every other pain in his body clamoured for attention. A bright white flash lanced across his eyes, obscuring everything until his stomach finally settled.

Kill? Night's whispers, what did I do?

The small man's face curled into a cruel smile as he lifted his feet away from the spattering of puke. 'Must've been one hell of a night,' he commented.

'Don't remember,' Lynx croaked.

He paused and looked again at the man. There was something not quite right about him. Gap-toothed, check. Grimy, stinking clothes, check. Silver ring on his finger engraved with three diamond shapes – black, grey and white – hmm.

'That's . . .' Lynx said, almost panting for breath at the effort of speaking, 'that's my ring.'

'Nope, it's mine.'

'Give it back. Now.'

'Found this a while back,' the man said, 'and it don't have your name on it. More importantly, you're trussed like a hog and I could stamp your face in right now if I wanted. You're in no condition to give orders.'

'Why'm I tied up?'

The man snickered. ''Cos they had to drag you in, what with it taking half the guards to beat you senseless. Anyway,

I reckon you killed someone last night so you won't need a ring where you're going.'

Lynx spent a dozen breaths trying to order his thoughts. Even thinking hurt and left him panting for breath.

'That's my ring,' he said eventually.

The man hopped forward and bent low over Lynx, teeth bared in anger now. 'And I said it's fucking mine now, get it, fat boy? You don't like it, mister tied-up-and-puking, tough shit.'

Lynx blinked then very slowly closed his eyes. His head rang like a temple bell. Cuts and bruises on top of the hang-over that was really getting its teeth into him. Inwardly he shrugged.

With what strength he had left, Lynx grabbed the man's shirt and hauled him down. Their heads cracked together and stars burst before his eyes as the other man howled. With a jerk that made the world swim and his stomach heave, Lynx hauled his broad body up and the other's down so his greater bulk pinned the man. It wasn't easy with hands and feet bound, but he had a good enough grip that the squirming wretch couldn't move. Lynx was on the tall side, barrel-chested and with arms as thick as the other man's legs. It was true he had something of a paunch on him too, but he was strong enough that few were so stupid as to comment on it.

'What are you in for?' he growled.

'Bathtad!' squeaked the man, blood squirting from his nose.

'Answer me or I'll do it again.'

'Okay, okay! Theft, it'th theft!'

'So there you sit, half my size and thinking I'm in for murder – but you still take my ring?' Lynx's hands closed around the man's neck, not too tight, but enough to make it clear that even bound he could still throttle the man. 'You really that bloody stupid?'

'No! No, take it!'

8

Lynx felt hands fumbling under him and eased to one side enough to let the man pull the ring from his hand. In his haste he dropped it between them so Lynx shoved him off the bench and into the puke on the floor. Slumped on his side, it took him a while to find the ring, but at last he did and he jammed it on his left hand as best he could.

'Shit,' the small man moaned, 'bathtad!' With one sleeve pressed to his nose the man picked himself up and crawled on to the other bed. 'Didn't need to do that.'

'Pretty sure I did,' Lynx muttered, submitting to the cries of his body and relaxing back down on to the bed with one eye on the other man. His vision lurched and went from black to purple and pink as everything hurt at once, but as he lay still it slowly receded. 'You didn't figure I could move enough to get it back.'

'They hang you,' the man huffed, 'guards get ya stuff anyway.'

Lynx winced. 'Shut up.'

Shattered gods, did I really kill someone last night?

Praying his expression wasn't obvious in the gloom of the cell, Lynx stared up at the ceiling and willed the straight lines above to remain still. He couldn't remember anything from the previous night and the more he tried the more his head hurt. The ache was a cloud in his mind that obscured and confounded every effort.

Gods – what town is this, even? Where am I?

Before any clarity could come the cell door was yanked open. Lynx looked up, scowling at the shaft of daylight that cut across the room beyond. He screwed up his eyes and managed to focus on the figure at the door – a grey-haired man who frowned at each of the occupants, one hand on the butt of a club stuffed into his belt.

'Time to go,' he said in a gruff voice.

'Me, sir?' the smaller man piped up hopefully, scrabbling upright.

9

'No.' The guard paused and gave the thief an appraising look. 'What happened to you?'

A scowl. 'I fell.'

The guard snorted and raised an eyebrow at Lynx. 'He fell, eh? That's why there's blood on *your* face, eh?'

'Fell on my forehead,' Lynx muttered with a wince. 'Tried to rob me.'

'Bloody disgrace – you put a thief in gaol and the bugger just tries to steal stuff.'

Lynx decided not to comment. The man was probably joking, but he wasn't inviting others to the party and anyway, Lynx wasn't much of a laugh when hungover and hurting.

'Can you get up, madman?' the guard continued after a pause. 'After last night I ain't keen on cutting your bonds.'

Lynx grunted. His feet were bound too. Whatever had gone on the previous night, he'd been enough trouble to make them truss him up like a turkey. 'Not sure I'll manage the walk to the magistrate.'

'Your lucky day then, you ain't off to see her. You're getting out.'

'I am?'

'There's a fine to pay, then we'll be glad to see the back of you.'

'I didn't hurt anyone?'

From his right the smaller man snorted angrily, but Lynx ignored him and the guard shut him up with a glare.

'Only a man's pride. You were too drunk to do much more'n get a beating.'

'That's a mercy then,' Lynx said with relief. He glanced down at himself. He still had his jerkin, boots and trousers, but his sword-belt and jacket were conspicuous by their absence. 'A fine, though. Don't know what money I've got left.'

'Enough,' the guard said curtly. 'We're not all thieves round here. You can come and pick up your possessions now.'

Lynx nodded. 'Definitely won't get any trouble from me in that case,' he said, lifting his hands in a suitably pathetic manner.

'He gets off with just a fine?' the smaller man yelped furiously. 'He's mad, you said it yourself! Probably a murderer too! Just broke my damn nose!'

'Shut up,' the guard and Lynx said in unison.

The men exchanged looks and Lynx tried to remember what apologetic looked like. He was well aware he was still bound and in gaol. He wasn't sure if the guard was annoyed or amused, but either way the man didn't comment.

'Your nose ain't broken,' the guard said at last, ''cos you'd be squealing like a pig if it were. And none of us give a damn anyway – certainly not enough to trouble the magistrate over some thieving scrote who deserved it. Frankly, compared to the chair he fell on while trying to punch old man Greyn, your nose ain't worth anything.'

The interruption seemed to make the guard's mind up and he drew a knife. Lynx tensed instinctively as the man approached him then lowered his eyes, feeling foolish.

'Sorry, old habits.'

'Soldier?'

Lynx nodded.

The guard paused. 'What side?'

'Not one I care to defend these days.'

The guard nodded and cut through the rope around Lynx's hands. When the heavyset mercenary only groaned with pleasure and rubbed his wrists, he did the same for his feet and stepped back. Lynx sat up as best he could and propped himself against the wall.

'Thanks.'

That seemed to surprise the guard. He gave Lynx a suspicious look, then shrugged and backed away to allow him to rise and leave the cell. Lynx did so without haste. The nice man was letting him leave and Lynx had no intention of startling him, even if his protesting body suddenly became capable of it. He shuffled out and stood where the guard directed, trying not to fall over, while the man locked the door again.

That done, Lynx was ushered down the corridor and up a short flight of stone steps, emerging into a square guard-room where three armed man glared at him. Thin strips of light slanted down through the narrow windows on the far wall and Lynx faltered as he blinked away the bright trails in his vision.

'Over there,' the guard ordered, pointing to a pair of iron-bound doors on the left. A lock-room, Lynx guessed, with a messy desk placed at one side of it. He dutifully shuffled over as a portly old guard with impressive whiskers took station there. With a self-important huff the guard sat and opened a ledger, eyeing Lynx with disdain.

'Name?'

'Lynx?'

The guard paused. 'Real name.'

'Lynx.'

The guard placed a hand flat down on the ledger page. 'Listen, son, you're getting off with a fine. Now's not the time for playing silly buggers.'

'I realise that,' he said, adding 'sir' a little later than intended. 'Name I was born with got left behind years back, along with the damn fool who was proud of it. I've been just Lynx for more'n five years now. Suits me better'n anything from a place I don't care for any more.'

'And where's that?'

'So Han.' He knew it was coming, but still he felt the hairs on the back of his neck rise as the men around him tensed.

'You're one of them, eh?'

Lynx shook his head. 'Not since before the war ended – place can rot for all I care. I've left all that behind, is why I've gone by Lynx ever since.'

'Why Lynx?' asked the guard who'd escorted him up, appearing at the older one's side. Of all the men in the room, his was the only demeanour not affected by the place of Lynx's birth, which presumably meant he was an easterner. So Han's brutal campaign of conquest had gobbled up a fair chunk of the Greater Lakes, but had imploded before it could reach across the continent.

Lynx shrugged as best he could without provoking his hangover.

'They don't live in packs; prefer their own company and rely just on themselves, but they're not the biggest or toughest out there. I ain't trying to persuade the world I'm as dangerous as a mountain lion. That'll just get a man in more trouble than his drinking is likely to land him in.'

His attempt at a self-deprecating smile got little change from his audience so he quickly continued. 'Also, my eyes are a funny colour; folks used to say like a cat's when I was young.' Lynx turned to look at the man properly, blinking as he afforded him a look at his yellow-flecked brown eyes.

The older guard grunted, clearly unwilling to give too much of a damn about Lynx, even if he didn't like his name.

'Fine, Lynx it is, once of So Han. We've got a note of your marks already – if any bounty hunter comes looking for the man you once were, the description's clear enough.'

Lynx nodded. The scars on his back were extensive, one of the many joys of his homeland's army discipline, and he also had cat's claws tattooed on his forearm, legacy of another night's excess. Most obvious though was the complex character on his right cheek – a stylised script from somewhere to the south that translated to 'honour or death'. He preferred the sentiment to the tattoo, but it was far better than the prison designation it had suborned.

'No one's looking for me,' he said. 'I've done nothing but bodyguard work for years and made no enemies.'

'Well I suggest you keep on doing that – away from Janagrai too.'

Lynx winced as he suddenly remembered why he'd come to this town in the first place. 'Got something I need to do here first. Think my last employer's family are here.'

'Don't tell me you're dumb enough to go and start making demands for payment now?'

'Just returning what's theirs,' he said with a shake of the head. 'We got hit a couple of days back by bandits and Master Simbly took an arrow in the lung. I brought his goods, came to give them to his widow and tell her where I buried the man.'

'Master Simbly?' the guard growled. 'I know him, knew anyway. Where'd this happen?'

'Out on the lake road from Tambal.'

'Why would you be taking that route?'

Lynx shrugged. 'Said he was late and needed to take the shorter road. He'd heard the road was safe this season and I wasn't the only one with a mage-gun. He took passengers too, woman who said she was from somewhere down towards the ocean channel coast and her retainer. Some sort of militia officer she was, called Kelleby. Once we sent a few icers their way the bandits scarpered, but they'd already got in a lucky shot.'

The guard glanced around his fellows and someone behind Lynx spoke up. 'I've seen the woman; she's staying at the Witchlight too, waiting for passage onwards.'

Lynx nodded. The name rang a bell. He just had to hope the rest of his kit and Master Simbly's goods were still stored there, otherwise folk might start getting an unfriendly impression.

'Hach,' called the whiskered guard to a younger one loitering nearby, 'go and find her, check that out. Guess I'll be giving the bad news to the Widow Simbly.'

'I'll do that,' Lynx said. 'I was there when he died, that's on me.'

The guard's lips tightened as he stood up. 'If she wants to talk to you, I'll fetch you, get me? Hach will take you to the Witchlight Inn and take charge o' the goods so there's no argument.'

His expression made it clear he didn't want to hear anything more on the matter. Lynx kept quiet while the guard unlocked the strongroom and fetched out Lynx's sword-belt, tricorn hat and jacket. Hanging from the sword-belt was a wooden cartridge box, slightly curved to settle comfortably at his hip. Just the sight was enough to make Lynx break out in a sweat.

'I picked a fight wearing my cartridge case? Deepest black!'

The guard nodded. 'Aye, we noticed that too,' he said with a scowl. 'Didn't much appreciate it neither, just glad all those burners and sparkers are properly packed given the way you fell on them.'

Lynx winced at the thought. He had two fire-bolts in the pouch, alongside seven spark-bolts. The twenty-four ice-bolts – icers – could themselves have easily killed someone if he'd broken the seal around the magic-charged glass packed into one end, given the power of the mage-made weapons. But burners or sparkers could have set the whole building on fire and killed them all.

'Guess that was my year's worth of luck used up,' Lynx said once he'd checked the cartridges were still packed securely in their individual pouches. The guard didn't speak as he waited for Lynx to finish, though no doubt he'd done the same. There were some things you didn't skimp on or rush.

'Five silver fine, make your mark here.'

Lynx dug his purse out of an inner pocket and hefted it. A little lighter than he remembered but a night of drinking accounted for that. The fine made a considerable dent in what was left but he didn't argue, just wrote his name in a neat copperplate hand that raised eyebrows. That done he ran his hands over the scabbard and falchion within to check for damage, then buckled it to his waist. It took him a little longer to wrestle his grey jacket over his aching shoulders, though, and by the time he'd succeeded he was groaning in discomfort.

The guard looked him up and down. Black boots, once-white shirt, grey trousers and jacket, black tricorn.

'Shades of grey, eh? Some sort of mercenary statement, is it?'

Not the one you're thinking of, friend, Lynx thought as he shook his head, *just a sign to a brother that I'm wearing the ring.*

'Just doesn't show the dust of the road so much.'

'Aye, mebbe a bit deep for your sort, even if you write like a noblewoman. My advice is you move on smartish,' the whisk-ered guard added as Lynx straightened his hat. 'You've caused enough trouble in these parts.'

Lynx nodded. 'Any suggestions?' he said as he straightened up, determined to walk out with his head held high. 'I'm out of a job now.'

'Aye. I suggest you keep your head down for the rest of the day and leave in the morning, on foot if you have to.' The guard scowled. 'If it gets you gone, tip the landlord at the Witchlight when you reimburse him for the chair. Remind him he'll see the back of you faster if he hears any of his evening trade needs an extra hand.'

Lynx nodded and turned to the door as the bearded young guard, Hach, beckoned him forward and opened it. Sunlight streamed through, a beautiful spring day by the looks of it. Lynx scowled as the throb in his head intensified, screwed up his eyes and followed the man out.

Chapter 2

For a two-bit backwater town, Janagrai looked pretty good to Lynx – even through the grey tint of a hangover. He stumbled down the street under Hach's direction, squinting through the morning sun at the street of houses and shopfronts on either side. Above the sun was the hazy smear of the Skyriver, a vast striated band that encircled the world, barely visible behind a tattered curtain of cloud. Up ahead he saw a large marketplace where a handful of farmers had their wares laid out, while on the corner stood an L-shaped inn that had to be their destination.

Somewhere at the back of one of the shops a pair of dogs began to bark, the noise enough to set off some geese sat around a pond opposite the tavern. Lynx scowled – both at the unwelcome noise and the realisation of what those geese signified.

'Knights of the Oak, eh?' he commented to his guide. Lynx nodded towards the squat stone building behind the pond that, while not exactly fortified, wouldn't be much fun to attack.

As they passed it, Lynx saw the small stone canopy over the door which sheltered the craggy features and jutting tusks of their patron god – Ulfer, Lord of the Earth. A heavy shroud of creeper covered half the building's flank and a chaotic bloom of wild flowers filled the ground around it, both heavy with the hum of honeybees. Their scent drifted across the street and Lynx filled his lungs.

'Aye, Janagrai had one of the first waystations around, so they tell me,' Hach said. 'Why, you got a problem with one of the Orders?'

'None of 'em got a problem with me,' Lynx clarified, 'but religion and soldiers ain't a good mix in my opinion.'

'Thought your lot were in favour of that?'

Lynx grimaced. 'So Han? Oh yes. Always surprised me that the first Orders didn't come out o' the place. Authority of the gods themselves *and* overwhelming military might – bloody wet dream to most o' the Lan Esk Ren, but they don't like foreign priests much.'

'These ones keep to themselves mostly.' Hach shrugged. 'The townspeople are glad for 'em. We see a good number of wealthy travellers stop here.'

'No doubt. But it only takes one bastard to decide his god don't like how you're doing things. Then they start to look like professional soldiers who outgun the rest o' you on top of supplying most o' the continent's ammunition.'

'Something tells me you're this cheerful even without the hangover,' Hach said with a snort.

Lynx ducked his head in acknowledgement. 'Oh aye – Sun's own Jester, that's me most of the time. Mercenary work really makes a man happy and welcoming over the years.'

He tried to smile to back up the unlikely claim, but it proved difficult to muster. Quickly Lynx gave up in favour of concentrating on walking in a straight line.

They reached the inn and headed on inside to a relatively bright barroom where a man and woman were bent over a piece of paper on the bar.

'Morning, Master Efrin,' Hach called, his smile widening a little as he gave a half-bow to the woman. 'Mistress Pallow, looking lovely as always.'

Lynx frowned at the room as his eyes readjusted feebly from the brightness of outside. Despite the large open windows it still seemed blessedly cool and dim inside, but the faces ahead of him were a blur to start with.

'You've got some nerve coming back in here,' the woman snapped at Lynx, who rocked back on his heels. 'Didn't you cause enough trouble last night?'

Lynx raised his hand. 'I'm not here for trouble, but as your fine town's guardsmen,' he said, indicating Hach, 'are more honest than most I've met over the years, I can pay for the damage I caused.' He winced at the effort of thinking and speaking but made himself struggle on. 'And I need to see the wagon to my employer's widow. It's in your stable; I took a room here, right?'

'You did,' was the curt response.

'And I paid ahead? Just need to sleep this off, have some food and see what new work's going here.'

'We'll be looking in on him,' Hach added. 'The wagon belongs to Mistress Simbly and we'll need her to confirm the goods are all there before he's free of us.'

Mistress Pallow frowned at Lynx, but Hach's words had dampened her anger. 'Mistress Simbly? Ornan Simbly is dead?'

'Bandits,' Lynx confirmed, hoping his efforts not to be sick would be taken as feelings of sympathy for his late employer.

'I suppose you have paid ahead of time,' she said after a moment's pause. 'Go on then, it's the first attic room – top of the stairs. There'll be fried onions and potatoes for lunch so I won't need to wake you.'

*

Lunch came and went in a rather more literal fashion than Lynx was comfortable with, but the handful of hours' sleep he managed beforehand improved the state of the world dramatically. He was still a scarred, unwanted exile from a country

19

of bastards who'd spent years brutalising their neighbours, but he could at least walk in a straight line without feeling like the floor was going to punch him.

The afternoon passed quietly, the only break to self-indulgent wallowing being when Lynx found himself inspected by a tall and beautiful woman with red-rimmed eyes. She seemed the least likely candidate for Mistress Simbly he'd met in Janagrai, but he managed to conceal his surprise as he struggled up from his seat. Her husband had been an amiable fellow, but on the short side with something of a squint and thinning hair. His wife was of a similar age, it was true, but had she been wearing finer clothing Lynx would have thought her some local duchess.

The formalities were dealt with easily and with little input from Lynx, he was glad to discover. His account had been confirmed by the militia officer, Kelleby, and the goods in the wagon were as Mistress Simbly had expected. Though Lynx had been careful to take his pay before arriving in town, the bereaved merchant added to it in thanks for his honesty – enough to pay for a broken chair at least. She left about her own business soon enough and Lynx found only himself and Mistress Pellow in the common room, an hour or more before the evening trade was likely to begin.

'So you're looking for fighting work?' she called to him from behind the bar.

Lynx looked up. The woman hadn't exactly warmed to him, but her manner had thawed somewhat in the face of a newcomer who could string a sentence together. In his years of wandering, Lynx had seen that often enough. Villages and towns were so small most wanted news of the outside, but many were just glad to talk to someone new.

He shook his head. 'Not if I can help it.'

'We don't have many merchants looking to take on a stranger as escort,' she warned, 'not with the Knights' outpost in town.'

'If there's labouring work, I'll do that. Can balance books too, if you want it.'

'You? I've not met many mercenaries who can write their own name.'

'Wasn't born a soldier,' Lynx replied. 'Father was a shop-keeper in a town not much bigger than this. Can't say it's a job I'd like for the rest of my life, but I can remember it well enough.' He grunted and glanced at the long leather sheath beside him that contained his mage-gun. 'Can't say there's any job I'd like for the rest of my life, actually, but I guess it'd be better than the alternative.'

'From So Han, right?' she said with a pointed look.

Lynx paused. 'Aye, once upon a time.'

'So you served.'

'We all did, if you were of an age. All swallowed the same shit about the honour of our flag, defence of our people.'

'My brothers died in the Valleys campaign.'

Lynx ducked his head in acknowledgement. 'Lot of folk did. Glad I wasn't there myself.'

'So where, then?'

'Mind if we drop this? Ain't exactly a happy subject for any of us.'

'The Greensea?'

Despite himself, Lynx felt the memory like a claw inside his gut. 'For a time,' he said in a half-whisper.

'So you're one of them?'

The condemnation in her voice was enough to make his fists tighten, but Lynx was no stranger to it and he relaxed quick enough.

'Never one of them,' he said firmly. 'There was some real fighting to be done there too, at first anyway. I had no part in what came after.'

'Easy enough to claim, that.'

21

He looked her straight in the eye. 'You want to see the scars on my back, I'll show you. Ain't ashamed of what I did in that war, I'll tell you now. Won't bloody defend what others did either, but in So Han they don't whip a man for liking the killing too much.'

That stopped her short at least. This part of the Riven Kingdom hadn't seen the worst of So Han's violent spasms of conquest. There wasn't the hatred ingrained in the very earth that he'd find in the Greensea or the Hand Valleys if he was ever stupid enough to visit them.

So Han was the westernmost of the so-called warrior republics, nestled in the lee of the mountains off which most of the rivers in the area flowed. The Greensea lay to the south of So Han, a prosperous scattering of principalities around the shore of that inland sea, while the Hand Valleys was the long region to the east through which mountain rivers flowed and merged. The victories there had been swift and accomplished – the brutalising of the population seemingly a punishment for not proving enough of a challenge.

'You clearly learned your trade there well enough,' Pellow said, a smaller note of antipathy in her voice. Lynx could tell her enthusiasm for it was waning. 'You still live by the sword and the gun.'

'Sometimes it ain't so easy to escape your past,' Lynx muttered, 'and yeah, I was good at the fighting. Wouldn't say I enjoyed it, but I'm good at it still. It *was* a war at first, you had men out there looking to kill you and you knew your purpose. Might've been the goal was a crock of shit, but I didn't know that at the time, was just a stupid kid with dreams of glory. Been in a few more since . . . well, since I came east, but none of 'em you could much call a war. Handful of skirmishes over some small slight – no real cause to fight for or sense of purpose.'

She had no questions after that and Lynx found himself sitting alone, morose and brooding on times past.

Must be ten years since the start of the war, he realised sourly. *And look at the world now, just a little more broken and miserable than before. So much for the Shonrin and his grand vision. Hope he's enjoying his life stuck up that miserable bloody mountain.*

Lynx groaned and stood, stretching expansively. *One day, mebbe, I'll go and try to kill him, even if it does mean going back to that place.*

Finally deciding he was capable of something real to drink, Lynx shifted his mage-gun and other valuables with him to the bar. He knew what people were looking for in a guard, or anything else Lynx was capable of. Slumped in the back room was hardly the best advertisement, while at the bar he would be in view of all the shopkeepers and traders heading in for the evening.

Sit upright and look big, Lynx told himself as he found a quiet corner where he could sit at the bar, out of the way but in view for the curious. *Folk want a man who looks dangerous, but ain't causing trouble or drinking too hard. Not sure I'm capable of either of those right now anyway.*

After receiving a stern look his late mother would have been proud of, Lynx found himself nursing a battered tankard of beer while the evening trade filtered in. First the town's shop boys and apprentices clattered in, then their masters and mistresses once everything was locked away. Towns like this flourished on the travelling routes, Lynx knew, so he was unsurprised when the door opened again and the smell of horses and dust heralded more strangers to town.

He was careful not to stare at those when they arrived, knowing they wouldn't want to deal with hiring extra guards until they had rooms secured and the weight off their feet. Slowly the room became filled with a gentle babble of noise and the smell of stew. Lynx let it all flow over him, pulling out one of his most treasured possessions from the bag at his feet; a leather-bound book from the heyday of the Riven Kingdom.

It was an account, of sorts, retelling an adventurer's travels across the kingdom and as far as one man could travel into the east. It was a story unlike most Lynx got his hands on – a meditation on that supposed golden age as much as it was an account of the adventurer's journey, but also a descent into madness and back as he encountered the five gods and beings from no known mythology.

He let himself sink into the much-read tale and time passed without him being aware of it. Only the arrival of a bowl of stew and a corner of peasant's bread distracted him, whereupon he carefully put the precious book away and set about his food.

The noise behind him edged up a notch, the pair of serving girls under Mistress Pellow's supervision moving a step brisker to keep up with a busy day's trade. Belatedly Lynx remembered it was Feastday, the end of the week, when evening would see prayers or merriment depending on each individual's particular bent.

Most likely it's Ulfer getting the thanks here, given those Brothers of the Oak outside, Lynx realised. He glanced down at the bag where he'd just put his book with all the care most reserved only for mage-cartridges. *So here's to you, Lord of the Earth. Our man here seemed to like you when he met you, so that's good enough for me.*

'Hello, sailor,' came a breathy voice in his ear. 'Sitting all alone?'

Lynx snorted and continued to eat his stew. 'I don't pay for it.'

'What I'm paid for,' the unseen woman continued in an amused voice, 'you wouldn't want.'

Lynx turned and paused. He'd seen more than a few tavern whores in his time and most weren't anything close to pretty

– certainly not after a few years of a job that wasn't easy – so this woman had them all beaten.

He smiled at her, somewhat awkwardly given his lack of practice in recent months.

'Think I was a bit hasty there,' Lynx said as the woman tilted her head and let her loose hair cascade over one shoulder. With an easy smile, twinkling reddish eyes and smooth brown skin, she was a sight indeed – sufficiently arresting that it took him a moment to notice her clothes and realise she wasn't a whore after all.

'Still not what I get paid for,' the woman said, grinning quite unconcernedly at the desire in his eyes. 'But buy me a drink and you might be in the right direction.'

Lynx looked her up and down: a short-sword on her belt, a stiletto strapped to the outside of the archer's bracer on her left arm. What she didn't have was a uniform, just a sleeveless tunic that showed off her bare arms.

'Depends if you're recruiting,' he said, sounding gruff as he got a hold of himself and started to think straight. 'I've seen that one before – a woman merc there to tempt boys into joining.'

'Sorry, friend, but you ain't been a boy for a few years now,' she said, not in the least offended. 'Maybe I've had that effect once or twice, sure, but it still ain't what I'm paid for.' She offered her hand. 'I'm Kas.'

'Kas? What sort of a name's that?'

She shrugged. 'Kasorennel, if you must know, but you white people butcher names something awful, so the Cards mostly just know me as Kas. All except the boss when he's pissed at me. *Then* he remembers how to pronounce it.'

'Just Kas?'

'Yup. We all go by one name in the Cards. You know how it is, more'n a few with a past they're keen to avoid.'

Lynx nodded slowly. 'Yeah, reckon I can appreciate that. The Cards?'

'Our company.' She nodded off behind her, where the bulk of the room's noise was now coming from. 'Anatin's Mercenary Deck, but everyone calls us the Cards, o' course.'

Lynx nodded. There were more than a few variants on a deck of cards, more than he'd heard of no doubt, but if you spent enough time around soldiers you got to know several. The Mercenary's Deck was just a twist on the Soldier's Deck found in every army across the Riven Kingdom. In his experience, the sight of one was a good indicator that you were about to be fleeced for everything you had.

'Sounds like you'd all be great under pressure, then,' Lynx grunted as he returned to his drink.

'Hey, you ain't introduced yourself yet,' Kas said, nudging his arm without an indication she'd noticed his attempt at a joke, 'or offered me a drink.'

'I ain't interested in joining the Cards,' Lynx repeated. 'I'll buy you that drink, since you asked so nicely, but I'm not joining your company.'

Kas slipped on to the stool beside him, leg brushing his just enough to make him very aware of her warmth and scent. He focused on his drink. Friendly and beautiful she might be, but his experience of mercenary companies warned him off – however long it was since he'd been with a woman.

'From what I hear, you're not the most popular in town right now,' she said softly. 'And you're looking for work. Well, we're hiring. Is anyone else?'

Lynx took a long swig. She had an easy way about her, likeable. It didn't seem to fit that well with a mercenary and certainly wasn't making it easy for him to ignore her. A life on the road was a lonely one and Lynx knew all too well that most of those who walked alone were bastards, mad or broken in some other way.

Broken was something he was intimately acquainted with, but not so broken that the loneliness of the open road was always craved. Kas had an air of immediate familiarity about her, of friendship where there was none, and that made him both wary and faintly giddy.

The mercenary rapped her knuckles on the bartop. Her calloused fingers, marked with a half-dozen scars, declared she was either an inattentive cook or had been in the fighting game a while now. 'Another beer, please.'

A tankard was deposited in front of Kas and Lynx stared at it for a moment before sighing and reaching for his coin purse. She raised the tankard and knocked it against his.

'Cheers then, even if you still haven't told me your name.'

Despite himself, Lynx smiled. 'Cheers,' he echoed and took a long drink. 'Name's Lynx. Just Lynx.'

Kas stared at him for a moment. 'And you thought "Kas" was odd? Bloody westerners.'

Lynx nodded. 'I'll drink to that.'

Chapter 3

The evening wore on and despite everything Lynx found himself slowly relaxing and enjoying Kas's presence. They talked principalities they had travelled through, wars they'd fought in. She hadn't been old enough for the Greensea or any other So Han campaign, he was glad to hear. Instead she'd been growing up in a fishing port well to the south, away from the chaos up north until a fool called Sener Robern had started his strange crusade down there. It had been a few more years before Kas was dragged in, when a raiding party descended upon the port while the fishing fleet was out.

Her cousin had been one of those taken, but the villagers had been lucky and met the company Anatin served in as they followed the raiders. They'd hired the mercenaries with all they could and joined them in attacking the raiders' camp, their numbers tipping the balance. Kas bloodied her knife twice that grey morning and signed up with the company in the afternoon, with the rest being history.

Not long after, it turned out, she and Lynx had been on opposing sides of a fight. A struggle over import levies that one of the largest Militant Orders, the Protectors of Light, had waded into. The merchant guild had been forced to hire every mercenary they could get their hands on, but Captain Anatin had rightly judged the Protectors of Light to be the safer side to join.

'Nasty fight on the hill, that was,' Kas said grimly. 'Wasn't looking forward to the order to take the wall that day.'

'*You* weren't looking forward to it?' Lynx exclaimed. 'There were three thousand of you! I had a bloody good view from that wall and we sure as dammit weren't expecting to last the hour.'

Kas raised an eyebrow. 'Truly? Well, I'm glad I didn't have to kill you that day then.'

'You'n me both, was only a hundred of us left before that self-serving shit surrendered.'

She laughed. 'Restless Banesh, I'd forgotten that! We were all shitting ourselves; someone had said you had over a thousand in reserve there and elementals bound into the wall. We thought we never stood a chance, then it turned out your reserve had run away a week before!'

She finished her tankard and waved for another one. 'Right, time for a game I reckon. Come on, few friendly hands of Tashot.'

'I ain't playing cards when I'm outnumbered.'

'Oh balls,' she said with a dismissive wave, 'it's too early to play for high stakes. It's just a copper game for the next few hours. You fleece the locals before decent folk've gone to bed, you ain't so welcome in town no more. Trust me, we've had that happen enough. It'll be all childish fun until the respectable folk go and we've just got the boys who want to join up.'

'And then you get 'em running up debts to make sure they join?'

She frowned at him. 'Then, I see if I can find a decent man and take him to bed. We ain't card sharks, we're mercs. We drink hard and play hard. Coins not promises, okay? We start claiming debts scribbled on slips of paper, folk complain to the town council and they'll have those Knights of the Oak to back 'em up. That's trouble we don't need for a few shop boys. What money they bring to the table they might lose, but that's a life lesson for 'em.' She winked. 'And little boys ain't much fun to cheat, so unless one of 'em is too full of himself, the boss demands a fair game.'

Lynx was still half-stuck on the image of Kas finding a man to take abed and just found himself nodding along to what she was saying. Her next beer arrived and Kas slipped nimbly from her stool, heading a few steps back to her company before pausing to glance back at him.

'You coming?'

He sighed. 'Fine, I'll sit in on the game. Ain't joining your company, though.'

'No one's asking you to.' She smiled. 'We've got a job, though, which is more'n you've been offered so far tonight. Might be worth hearing what Anatin has to offer.'

'I've had enough of mercenary work,' Lynx growled.

'Ah, but this ain't battle, just escort work. Bit we'd need you for anyway. Us professionals will take on the rescue.'

Lynx signalled for another drink and stood as well. 'Rescue?'

She shrugged. 'Some girl got kidnapped, aye. Two-bit baron trying to force her into marriage. Father wants her back, simple as that.' She batted her eyelids at him and gave a mock simper. 'Ah, the romance, rushing to the rescue of a damsel in distress.'

Lynx hesitated. This really was the last thing he wanted, but he was more than aware of how short his welcome in this town would be, and the locals were keeping well clear after the previous night's foolishness.

'You said I'd just be escort?'

'A girl can dream,' Kas said, grinning. She started walking again and called over her shoulder, 'Don't forget your big gun now. We wouldn't want you to leave that behind.'

The rest of the company had caught her words during a lull and Lynx received a few smirks as he walked over, but most were focused on the game. The table was covered in a variety of goblets and tankards, half-finished platters of food, cigars and pipes – with a space in the centre reserved for a spread of large playing cards. Despite the amount of drink they had clearly consumed, those mercenaries still in play were devoting all their attention to the face-up cards.

'Make room, Varain,' Kas announced cheerfully, prodding at the shoulder of the nearest man. He scowled but, with all the precision of an army of cats, the mercenaries on the near side of the table shuffled around until there was space for two chairs to be added.

'Teshen, count us in,' she called to the dealer, letting Lynx squeeze his oversized frame into the modest space that had been made and draping her legs over his thigh as she sat herself.

The dealer passed over two stacks of copper coins of varying sizes and origins without looking at either of them. Kas tossed him a silver coin in response and Lynx did the same once he saw the coin dropped into a horn cup, realising that was the winner's pot.

At one end of the oval table sat a tall, greying man in a worn blue tunic that had once been of the highest quality. The man had the characteristic scar of a sparker burn running over his cheek and right ear. The cigar jammed in one corner of his mouth contorted the jagged white lines of scarring, but failed to hinder his cheerful narration of the game to the three shop's apprentices sat opposite.

Those three, Lynx saw, all bore a marked similarity to each other – cousins, he guessed. All dressed in similar grey shirts, their green jackets hung in a careful row on pegs behind. Their pale cheeks were pink from an evening of drink, the one still in the hand chewing furiously on his lip as he tried to ignore the mercenary's monologue.

Aside from Anatin – as Lynx assumed it was him talking so freely over the game – they were as varied a mix as you'd likely find in any mercenary company. A small, scarred weasel of a man with long sandy hair and a scrappy beard sat in the lee of one of the biggest men Lynx had ever seen – a very pale north-easterner he guessed, hairless as a eunuch but astonishingly trim for one of his size. Far taller than Lynx, he was at least as broad but had none of the press on his belt that Lynx was all too familiar with.

Two white women, one dark-haired and tall, one white-haired and squat, occupied the far side of the table with the shop boys, while a scowling black man puffed angrily on a cigar on the near side. Teshen, the dealer, was a burly long-haired white man who sat hunched and perfectly still, one hand hovering over the deck. Before him were five cards. One lay face down to appease Banesh, God of Chance and Change, while a Five and Jester of Blood lay with a Four of Stars and Eight of Tempest.

'What's it to be, my boy?' Anatin asked like a fairground conjurer dragging his act out. 'Five and a four sitting there looking up at you – got a Madman in your hand to make a squad? Jester o' Blood sitting beside 'em, that's Deern's own card right there, eh, Deern?' Anatin reached out and gave the weasely man a thump on the shoulder. 'He loves playing the Jester, his own card. We all got a weakness for our name cards.'

As though to demonstrate he raised the lapel of the jacket hung on the back of his chair. Stitched to it was a cloth playing card, sun- and rain-bleached but still recognisable as the Prince of Sun, highest value card in the deck.

Anatin's Mercenary Deck, Lynx reminded himself, glancing at Kas. She didn't wear a jacket, but Deern indeed wore a stylised Jester of Blood, while the big man beside him bore the Knight of Blood.

'Give it a rest, Anatin,' Deern grumbled. 'The boy don't need any more help. Goat-shagging yokel's been bleeding me all night as it is.'

'I'll keep talking 'til one of you does something more than stare at their bloody cards,' Anatin replied. 'Now, boy – what was yer name again? Fashail?'

The youth nodded.

'Right, Fashail, you better show more balls than Deern or you're no use to us. Modest bet on the table, options fer both o' you. Deern will go to the hilt if he's holding the rest o' Jester's own and he ain't done that. What's it going to be?'

'Who gives a shit?' said the unhappy black man abruptly. 'It's not his call yet.'

'Course it ain't, Himbel,' Anatin exclaimed, 'I just thought you'd fucking died or something, you'd been sat there so long. Thought Teshen had checked your hand and decided to put you out of your misery, all sneaky like.'

The dealer, Teshen, raised an eyebrow and snorted at his commander before returning to his vigil.

'Play, you black bastard,' Deern added. 'What you waiting for? That finger to grow back? Hairs to appear on ya chest?'

'I'm waiting for you to grow some manners,' Himbel spat back, the twist of a grin on his face. 'Some brains too. You *do* remember I'm the one who stitches you up after every bloody fight we get into, right? I know you're a gutless shite, but that ain't the only reason you scream louder'n the rest.'

'I fucking knew it, you filthy son of a whore!' Deern yelled, half-rising from his seat before the meaty paw of his huge friend grasped his arm. Deern flailed for a moment then was dragged inexorably back down.

'Aye,' Anatin commented, 'you listen to Reft and keep that naughty tongue in check. There's nice folks in this town who don't want to hear anything out of your mouth. We know there's bugger all chance of you bein' quiet, but you'll stow that crap until we've got the place to ourselves.'

Lynx gave Kas a look and she laughed.

'Aye, Deern's got a mouth on him – don't get any better the more either of you drinks. But he comes along with Reft so . . .' She shrugged and indicated the huge man, who was so big that even sitting quietly his value to the company was undeniable. 'Time to time Deern gets a punch, shuts him up for a day an' gives us some peace. You get used to not listening.'

'You're usually too busy—' Deern's spiteful little riposte was cut short by the big man again, Reft nudging his companion with one massive elbow hard enough to jolt the sentence loose in his mouth.

'Stow it, the lot o' you,' Anatin proclaimed, 'Himbel – make yer call or Teshen takes you out.' He cackled cruelly. 'Out o' the game that is.'

'I'll raise,' Himbel said at last, tossing a coin into the centre of the table where Teshen snapped it up quick as a snake.

Lynx felt a slight spark at that, noting well just how fast Teshen's hands had moved. *No burner-fodder that one. Old enough to be an elite during the wars, too.*

'I'll match,' the shop boy, Fashail, said, quick enough that Deern gave him a sly smile as he also tossed a coin down.

'Let's see that last card then, Teshen,' Deern snapped.

The dealer didn't respond, just slipped the top card deftly over his thumb and revealed it to the table before placing it beside the others. He blinked his cold grey eyes. The Prince of Sun itself.

'There I am,' crowed Anatin, 'come to fuck up your day once more, Deern!' He thumped his fist on the table for emphasis, causing his own goblet to jump in the air and spill.

'Be the only thing you're able to fuck these days, old man. Last time we went—'

'Oh just shut up, for the love of all five gods!' Himbel groaned, head sinking down over his cards. 'After this afternoon's rants about how beetles are the wrong colour round here, why cheese makes you stupid and the merits of female goats over So Han whores, I'm going to shoot you in the face if you don't shut the fuck up. Reft can do what he likes after, I'll die a happy man knowing I shut you up first.'

The collected mercenaries all chuckled while Deern cursed under his breath and tossed three more coins down.

'Shove these in your face, ya black bastard.'

'I'll kiss 'em as I collect your money,' Himbel announced, matching the bet with all he had left. 'How's about you, boy, you in?'

Fashail nodded, tossed his remaining money down and set his cards on the table. They all leaned forward and for a moment silence reigned.

'You little sod,' Anatin breathed. 'That's a sneaky kind o' luck right there.'

Both were picture cards, a contorted face with blood running from scratches down his cheek – the Madman of Blood – and a hooded figure with bloody tears – the Stranger of Blood. With the Jester on the table he had a run of three noble cards in Blood and that would win most hands.

Deern grunted and tossed his cards carelessly forward. Jester of Stars, sixteen of Sun – nothing that could beat Fashail's. 'Bastard.'

Anatin grinned at him then. 'So, noble run of Blood for Fashail beats Deern's pair. Don't worry, boy, his pair have taken a fair beating over the years. Can you beat that, Himbel?'

The company surgeon shrugged and turned over his own cards. 'So close,' Himbel sighed, shaking his head. Two of Stars, eleven of Snow. It gave him a run of four cards – five, four, Jester, two – but given the spread of suits, he needed five cards to count.

Teshen tossed the shop boy half the coins for winning the show, then as one the mercenaries craned forward again to watch as he turned Banesh's card. The God of Chance was represented in a deck of cards by the Tempest suit, so the card would only came into play if it was a Tempest. A third Jester wouldn't win it for Deern, but a Madman or a one would make Himbel's run into five cards. Lynx wasn't the only one to smile as the Knight of Tempest appeared – in play, but of no use to anyone.

'I'll remember this, boy,' Himbel said nastily, 'if you ever need stitching up.'

The shop boy looked startled, but the other mercenaries just snickered at their surgeon's words and if anything the man looked more cheerful now he was out of the game and able to concentrate on his drinking.

'Don't you mind him.' Anatin laughed, reaching over the table to thump Fashail on the shoulder. 'Himbel don't know how to be happy, it's been so long. He's only comfortable when he's losing, it's all he knows.'

'If you've all stopped kissing his arse,' Kas declared, 'maybe we can be dealt in now?'

She got a jumbled chorus of assorted curses and agreement from the mercenaries at the table, all of which she laughed off, while Teshen gave her a level look. Undaunted, she planted a loud kiss on the man's pale cheek. That made the dealer crack a small smile at last and with a shake of his long hair he started to shuffle for the next hand.

It took Lynx an hour to be cleaned out, he was pleased to discover. Unlike most such groups, the mercenaries seemed to have adopted their commander's love of the game itself rather than mad risks and aggressive bluster. He wasn't enough of a fool to play for higher stakes, but other than bitter little utterances from Deern and Himbel, it proved a pleasant accompaniment to an evening of drink.

The neat, muscular frame of Kas half-draped across him ensured it was a better evening than he could remember having in a while. As a man used to his own company and little else, he didn't speak often but no one demanded much of him and he was left in peace to observe their ways.

Eventually the number of players dwindled until the pot went to the tall, reserved woman at the far end. Only then did Lynx hear her name spoken, Payl, though by then it was clear she was Anatin's second in command. With a certain ceremony she gathered the coins from the pot and stowed them in a pocket while Anatin stood and called for more wine.

'Now, boys,' the commander said gravely to the shop boys, 'the stakes go up. You can play if you've got money in your pocket, but we'll take it off you like as not, ya hear me? So unless you want to join up or become broke, now's the time to head home.'

Payl, the winner, grunted at that and stood herself, draining her cup before gathering up her mail-stitched jacket. Only then did Lynx notice Fashail's eyes follow her and Payl give a nod in the direction of the stairs leading up to the inn's rooms. He smiled inwardly as the young man scrambled up, almost falling over his cousin in the process, and followed her.

'Someone else winning tonight,' Deern muttered, turning to the cousins. 'You two want to try for our money? You played a good few hands there, just poor luck an' that tends to turn when the stakes change.'

'Shut up, Deern,' the white-haired woman snapped, clipping him around the side of the head. 'They ain't got much and their luck ain't changing all night – I can see that easy enough.'

'You don't see shit with that head o' scrambled brains.'

Anatin raised a hand and the small man fell silent, rubbing the side of his head and scowling.

'How about you, Lynx? You're looking for work and we've always got space for new blood.'

'I don't do mercenary work no more,' Lynx said carefully. 'Not the best at taking orders these days.'

'You'd be in fine company with half o' these pox-ridden mules then.' Anatin laughed. 'Don't stop them needing to earn some coin. I hear you ain't so welcome in town and we're the only folk with work to offer.'

'Still not interested.'

'Tell him about the job,' Kas urged rather tipsily, prodding Lynx in the shoulder and pointing at Anatin. 'Not usual merc stuff.'

'True, it's a rescue,' Anatin confirmed. 'We're heading there now, out Grasiel way. Some small-time landowner didn't like getting no for an answer. We took some losses in our last job and could do with the numbers. You've seen action, Lynx, that much is clear. The young 'uns can sign on recruit wages, but experience and a mage-gun buys you a named man's wage.'

Lynx was quiet a moment. Grasiel stood at the heart of a region of interweaving river valleys, every landowner sat in their toy castle on a hillside and ruling over a tiny fiefdom. They spent half their time feuding with each other – it was places like that where he'd become sickened by mercenary work. Petty squabbles leading to stolen crops, poor folk burned out of their homes, or the brief skirmish between a few dozen pretend soldiers. A man of Lynx's skills and few morals could make a good living there, but not Lynx. He had no illusions about settling down with a farm and a family, that just wasn't in his nature, but there were still choices he had no intention of making.

'Where you escorting her to?'

'Chines. Father's a merchant there. Used to do the trade routes through Grasiel, it's where the baron saw his daughter. Barely fifteen, so I'm told, just a slip of something.'

'Fifteen? Won't be a virgin by the time he gets her back then.'

Anatin shrugged. 'Man's no fool; I guess he's just ignoring that bit. Wants his daughter home safe, is all – he's not a nobleman anyway, so probably ain't too bothered there.'

'Chines, eh?' Lynx paused. 'Means you've got to round Shadows Deep. You're not proposing to cross the ruins, right?'

'No reason we should. Any soldiers come out after us, we ambush 'em before we have to cross Shadows Deep. Life'll be pretty hard before I go anywhere near any ancient ruin. I'm no treasure hunter or errant knight and it's not like any Militant Order patrols those valleys, no presence we couldn't handle.'

Lynx sighed and shook his head. He really did need to move on and his purse was light enough that he couldn't just wait until a job crossed his path.

'Fine, I'm in.' He stood and gathered his bag. 'Unless I change my mind when the drink's worn off. See you in the morning.'

As Kas hopped up beside him and took his arm, Anatin chuckled filthily.

'I can live with hoping you're in a good mood come morning, aye. We're on the road an hour after dawn – ah, wait, one thing we got to do first. If you're coming on as a named man, that is.'

Lynx hesitated, old instincts kicking in as his hand itched for a weapon. 'Which is?' he said cautiously, making sure he could see the whole table of mercenaries.

'We work out where you are in the order o' cards,' the commander said, nodding towards the white-haired woman, Estal. 'Our seer assigns the cards to everyone in the company. Guessing Fashail will be, heh, something *under* the Knight of Sun given that's Payl, but you're a veteran so you might get a picture all o' your own.'

Estal reached out a hand to Lynx, who took it after a moment's effort to relax his muscles. That close he could see the scars at her hairline – not a sparker burn or anything, but a jagged wound that had to have brought her close to death. He'd heard of folk granted second sight after such injuries, but never before met one.

'Ah, now that's a soul to suit us,' Estal murmured, eyes closed. With her free hand she waved blindly until Teshen placed the deck in her hand. She spread the cards with her fingers, fanning them in a wide mess as Lynx felt his hand grow oddly warm.

'Yes, there you are.' Estal opened her eyes and released Lynx. They both looked down at the table at the cards under her hand. Both their eyes went straight to one particular card under her thumb and Lynx felt a chill run down his spine at the sight.

Estal raised the card to show the rest of the table. 'No doubt for this one – Stranger o' Tempest.'

Anatin growled. 'You going to be more trouble than you're worth, Lynx? That's the Vagrim card. Always messes up my hands when it's dealt.'

'Vagrim?' Deern snorted. 'That bloody myth? Hells above, bunch of old women the lot of you.'

Lynx met Anatin's eyes and attempted a mysterious smile. *You call it the Vagrim card, eh? More right than you'll ever know.* He avoided glancing down at the silver ring on his finger, the mark of the Vagrim to others of that nebulous, disparate brotherhood.

'See you in the morning then.'

Interlude 2
(now)

Tyn opened the door and the back of her head exploded. The mercenaries threw themselves back as more detonations fractured the night. White streaks of icers burst across the darkened room – punching through walls and leaving their wraith trails hanging in the air. Splinters rained down, beams burst open. Before Tyn's corpse could fall another icer smashed through her arm, half-frozen blood rattling against the wall behind.

Lynx wrenched himself around, trying to pull his mage-gun from the holster down his back. In the cramped hall he caught an arm instead, then someone else fetched him a meaty thump in the side and pitched him into the wall. A pale lance of fog erupted from the wall and zipped past his widening eyes. He flinched back and hauled his gun free, the weapon already loaded. On one knee he aimed out of the door but he couldn't pick a target in the gloom beyond.

More gunshots and swearing filled the room. Anatin yelled, Safir cursed in his own language – then the madwoman, Toil, began to cackle with laughter.

'The shitsticks're you laughing at?' growled someone behind Lynx.

'Less quiet now!' Toil said, her face shining with animation. 'More fun this way.'

'Only fun when we're not the ones trapped like rats!'

'Fucking shoot back then!'

Crouched nearest the door, Anatin pulled a mage-pistol and aimed. The confined room shook with the detonation, a hammer blow against Lynx's ears.

'Spark 'em!' Anatin roared.

Teshen jumped forward, mage-gun at his shoulder. The distinctive whip-crack of lightning lashed at Lynx's ears as the man fired and a bright flare of light erupted from the muzzle. Screams came from the street beyond as the savage hiss of the sparker grabbed those beyond in its teeth. More icers smashed their way through the outer wall in response, but fewer than the first volley.

'Out!' Anatin ordered and Reft barrelled his way forward, gun in one hand and a hatchet in the other.

Lynx followed, weapon ready, as Safir fired past the pale giant and Toil scooped up Tyn's gun. The assassin then dragged Tyn's cartridge case over what remained of the woman's head while the rest clattered out.

There was a mess of bodies in the street, one almost torn apart by the sparker and three others bloodied and writhing. Lynx searched for a target but glimpsed only the black and white livery of a Knight-Charnel scurrying away around the corner.

'Blackest hells, we got more Charnelers here,' he hissed. 'Looks like they're falling back.'

'Friends o' yours?' Toil said.

'How'd they find us?' Anatin shook his head. 'No – doesn't matter. We move, head for the gate.'

'Got Tyn's patch,' Olut announced, brandishing a square of cloth. In the pale light of the Skyriver, Lynx could just make out the depiction it bore. Jester of Snow.

Never a joke from her, he thought in a moment of reflection, *just the flame-burn that gave her half a smile.*

'Olut, Lynx, Safir, watch our backs. Teshen and Reft, lead the way.'

As the pair set off right down the street, Lynx automatically counted the rest of the group, checking there was no one left inside. Nine again, one added and one lost. Not far away was the corpse of the Princip, face down and still on the cobbled ground. The near-side leg and arm were both at unnatural angles, a black pool of blood forming around the mess of his head. In the room behind, Tyn's ruined face was still half-frozen, perfectly white around the coin-sized hole in her cheek and frost in what was left of her hair.

'Load sparkers,' Olut reminded the two remaining with her as the rest set off. She shoved a cartridge into the breech of her own weapon. If they did have a squad of Knights-Charnel in pursuit, their best chance was outgunning them. The soldiers would only be carrying icers for fear of collateral damage to the city.

Lynx replaced his cartridge and slapped his gun's breech closed as they set off, keeping up as best they could while watching behind the group. The empty street echoed with the sound of their boots. It sounded dull after the thunderous gunfire, but was more than enough to make pursuit simple. The houses were dark, but he glimpsed faces at the windows – fearful merchants peeking past their curtains.

They turned the corner and entered a wide avenue of tall three- and four-storey houses. Sandstone walls and pale brick fascias loomed on either side, shuttered shopfronts hid in the shadows of awnings. The street ran straight for fifty yards towards a square colonnade, in the shadows of which Kas waited with the horses. Safir held back, waiting at the corner to spy for pursuit while the remaining mercenaries scurried towards their horses.

Two figures staggered out from an alley and the whole group slewed right, guns coming up like a disciplined unit before one of the drunks yelped and fell backwards. The other stared open-mouthed at the mercenaries then turned tail and fled, leaving his friend on the floor, but before that one could move they had set off again. Just as they reached the alleyway a hiss cut through the night, then the thump of Safir's boots and flutter of his long kilt as he sprinted to catch them up.

'More Charnelers,' the man spat as he reached them. 'Five or six at least.'

'Ulfer's crumpled horn – a whole squad?' Anatin shot Lynx a dark look. 'Sure you didn't meet any trouble today?'

'None,' Lynx said calmly, 'and I checked for a tail before I got back. This ain't me.'

'In case none of you noticed,' Toil broke in with a fierce grin, 'tonight's all about me.'

'This is your doing?'

'Dumbshit mercs,' she muttered. 'You think I couldn't get out of there by myself if it was just the Princip and his guards? The man was negotiating with the Orders, expanding their numbers in the city to smooth over any obstacles to his control of the Council of the Assayed. There're patrols all over the city, slowly extending their grip.'

'Expanding their numbers?'

'They've more'n three times the soldiers than the Assayers. Soon he'll have the army he needs.'

That stopped Anatin. 'An army ready to take over? And we just tweaked the Lord-Errant's beard? Oh, bloody thanks for not telling me that before.'

Toil rolled her eyes as he mounted hurriedly. 'Shattered gods, man! Not all of 'em will be ready to ride out in the middle of the night.'

'Fuck does that matter?' Anatin snapped, sawing at the reins of his horse as he manoeuvred it around. 'They'll have full squadrons of cavalry, dragoons too most likely – most of our company are on foot! They left the city yesterday; it'll take no more'n a day before they're caught.'

'We should get a head start then.' Still she didn't mount, instead kneeling beside one of the pillars.

The mercenaries watched her for a moment then Teshen and Lynx slipped from their horses too and loaded icers. The ice-bolts had far better range and accuracy than sparkers, for all the chaos and destruction those could wreak. If they outnumbered the pursuing Charnelers, felling one or two might see them off. Before their pursuers could appear, though, a chunk of stone burst off the pillar above Toil's head in a white cloud. More gunshots rang out and the mercenaries ducked as icers whistled past all too close.

'Shit, another patrol!'

Lynx swung around left, his aim drawn by the white muzzle-flash of their attackers. Movement in the street was all he could make out in the dark, no white uniforms but even a district watchman might be a half-decent shot. The crash of his gun was echoed a moment later by the double-crack of two more. Further back down the avenue he saw a half-dozen figures scurrying to cover. One was winged and spun around, howling, the rest fell into nearby doorways.

'We'll get pinned,' Anatin growled as he snapped off a shot and reloaded. 'Rain fire on 'em all.'

'Burners?' Lynx shouted, appalled. 'You'll start a firestorm!'

'Only advantage we got,' the man yelled back.

Lynx glanced at his comrades. Reft was beside him, loading an earther into his gun. Toil clearly had fewer qualms about using fire-bolts in a residential street and already had her gun loaded.

'There are people in every house!' Lynx shouted.

'A burning house don't help us,' she replied, nodding at the street ahead. 'They're locals, just need to scare them off.'

Belatedly Lynx realised the patrol were too far for a burner to reach; the destructive bolts just didn't have the range, even if they didn't need accuracy. He swore and pulled a sparker, bearing right towards the street they'd run out of. Reft raised his gun and the deep boom of his earther roared out through the night – despite his great size, the hairless man was still jolted back by the shot. A dark path split the air ahead of them, night turning in on itself before it hit and Lynx felt the ground shudder under the impact. Cobbles exploded left and right as a furrow burst through the street fifty yards away. Screams rang out, glass shattered, stones and wreckage drummed against the buildings on either side.

A flash of movement came from the right. Lynx checked a moment then saw the distinctive shape of guns, the flash of white tabards, and pulled the trigger. A jagged tear in the dark spat out from the muzzle of his mage-gun; a bolt of lightning corkscrewed across the street to consume the nearest Charneler. Spiked white claws leaped in all directions, savaging another and slashing at the wooden awning of the nearest house.

Toil took that as her cue, not bothering to aim much as she fired the burner down the centre of the street. A dulled, animal roar burst from the gun as an orange streak raced forward, dropping short of the Charnelers. A great whump of yellow flame burst out from the pale tip of that streak and mushroomed out – fire reaching almost from one side of the wide street to the other.

'You'll be the death of us,' Lynx muttered as Toil stood and made for the horses.

'Not yet.' Toil smiled as she passed him. Anything more was lost in the crash of gunshots ringing out in her wake, then they all raced for their mounts and there was no time to argue.

'Later then,' Lynx said.

Toil swung gracefully into her saddle while the mercenaries around her clambered up. She reached out and gave him a little pat on the head.

'Aye, I have that effect on people.'

Chapter 4
(then)

Lynx grunted and sat abruptly up. A familiar flicker of panic ran through him until the room came into focus. He shook the sleep from his head and disentangled his legs from the blanket, reaching down between the bed and wall until he touched his fingers to his dagger hilt.

'So much for me thinking I was stealthy in the mornings,' chuckled Kas from across the room.

Lynx froze. The dark-skinned woman was standing at the washbasin, naked as the day she was born and wiping a sodden cloth over her body. A handful of scars stood out in light curtailed by shutters closed over the narrow window, their abrupt lines highlighting the lean, muscular shape of her body.

'I, ah, I'm a light sleeper,' he muttered, unable to drag his eyes away.

'That much I worked out,' Kas said, deftly bundling her hair up so she could wipe the back of her neck down. Lynx found himself transfixed by the trails of water running down to her buttocks.

'One day I want to hear that story.'

'Eh?' Lynx jerked back to his senses. 'What?'

She paused and pursed her lips at him. 'See anything you like?' Lynx could only cough, but that was enough to make her laugh out loud. 'Boy, you really are out of practice around women.'

'Around anyone,' he said, scratching his bulging belly and swinging his legs around so he was sitting on the side of the bed.

'Around anyone,' she agreed with a smile. 'But last night was a creditable effort at remembering what to do with a woman. Bit o' practice and you might be half-decent at it.'

A stupid grin stole across Lynx's face at that. There'd been more than a little drinking before they turned in, enough to cast a pleasant haze over his memory, but it had also washed away the awkwardness of unfamiliarity.

'Aye, you too.' He stood and crossed the two steps to where she stood, sliding one hand around the taut curve of her left buttock.

'Me? I'm more'n half-decent,' she insisted, playfully slapping his hand away. 'I'm fucking great, ask anyone.'

'Anyone?'

She coughed at his tone and turned to face him, one hand slipping around his thick neck to pull him closer to kiss. Lynx did so willingly, but as their lips touched he felt her fingers tighten around his balls. 'Anyone,' she repeated softly. 'Might not mean they know it first hand, o' course.' She looked down and tightened her grip a fraction more. 'Looks like someone enjoys that.'

Lynx followed her gaze. 'Depends who's doing it,' he said huskily. He slipped his hands around her waist and pulled her close. Kas pushed her hips against his and kissed him long and hard before she broke off and leaned back, giving him a sharp slap on the buttock for good measure.

'Hold up a moment, soldier!'

Lynx blinked. 'What?'

'Dawn's come, time for grub and muster.' She cocked her head at him. 'Plus, you'll be getting Anatin's lecture.'

'Why? He got his eye on you?'

Kas shook her head and pulled the damp cloth from behind her, draping it over his stiffening cock before slipping clear of his embrace. 'There's rules in the company, rules we all keep to.'

Lynx frowned. 'About sex? He didn't seem to mind last night. His second slipped off with a recruit, didn't she?'

'Aye, and he didn't mind then, but as of muster we'll be working. Rules change between work and play. The man likes to play hard – drinking, gambling, screwing, all the fun things in life – but that changes when we're at work.'

Lynx regarded her a moment, wondering if she was trying to let him down gently or something else was going on. From the look on her face, and the way she was making no effort to cover herself, it didn't seem like she was full of regrets.

'He'll expect us to explain it so he don't have to go on about it,' Kas continued after a pause. 'Payl will be saying the same to that boy, whatever his name was. Anatin finds someone breaking the rules, he'll shoot 'em himself. Once had a couple on guard duty who sneaked off to screw against a tree and we lost fifteen of the company that night.'

Slowly, Lynx nodded and turned to the washbasin. Standing there with his cock out and his blood high, her words weren't filtering in to his head too quickly, but the years had taught him to keep a closed face to the world until everything made sense.

'Why don't you explain it to me then?' he said quietly, rinsing out the cloth before starting to wipe his body down.

'It's simple enough, has to be for all of us to remember. No screwing while we work. We're mercs and we fight for a living. If we let personal shit get in the way, folk die. Anatin only likes grown-ups in his company; he's seen enough of dumbshit farmboys thinking the rules don't apply to them. Might be, the odd evening out on the road, he'll call leisure time for anyone not on guard duty, but that'll only happen when we're safe and secure, which ain't often on most roads.'

'And you all keep to it, no issues?'

'Hah, wouldn't quite put it like that. Mercs aren't the cleverest folk around.'

When he turned around again, she'd pulled on her small things and was untangling her trousers from the pile of discarded clothes. 'But *you* do?'

She paused and looked him straight in the eye. 'Aye, I do. Some folk'll fall in love first tumble they have – me, I can enjoy it for what it is and go back to work. Don't mean I've not got feelings, but it'll take more'n one night for me to fall for anyone.' She gave him a sly smile. 'Don't take it as a complaint though, half-decent's a pretty high standard.'

Finally Lynx did laugh. 'Suppose I'll take what I can get then,' he said, 'so let's start with my clothes.'

She tossed him his drawers and he pulled them on quickly, feeling less foolish now he wasn't completely naked.

'I meant what I said, though,' she added in a more serious tone.

'About what?'

'I want your story one day.' She brushed the tattoo on his cheek with her fingers.

Lynx tensed. 'Not much to tell.'

Kas nodded, pulled her leather jacket on and began to lace it up. 'If you say so, but most folk don't wedge 'emselves against the wall and flinch if they're touched in their sleep.'

He frowned and looked away, very aware he was showing all too much but just as aware he couldn't help himself. 'Aye, well, I'm used to sleeping alone.'

Kas nodded and sat to haul her long boots on while Lynx fetched the rest of his clothes. 'That you are. But some of these bruises I got the fun way last night, and a couple I got when I brushed your arm and your hand closed like a vice on me.' She held up a hand. 'I ain't demanding answers, just

50

saying I reckon you've got some history to you. One day I'd be glad to hear it.'

Lynx pursed his lips. Unseen by Kas he touched his thumb to the silver ring he wore and nodded. 'That's the thing about history,' he said gruffly, 'it's all in the past. Best place for it.'

'Not sure it *is* all in the past for you,' she said as she grabbed her weapons, 'but it's your history and you tell it as you want, Lynx. In the meantime, I'm for a piss and some food.' She slapped him on the backside one final time and grabbed him by the shirt, pulling him close for a last kiss that was a lot more tender than before.

'Thanks for a good night all the same,' Kas whispered. 'Don't dally, though. I'm not pulling rank; if a recruit's the last to muster Anatin might make an example of 'em and you get Reft, not your superior.'

'Get him for what?'

She grinned. 'Stay here a while longer and you can find out.'

*

Muster wasn't quite what Lynx expected. Over the years he'd seen quite a variety, from the arrow-straight ranks of So Han parade grounds to the sergeants-at-arms of mercenary armies corralling their troops with bullwhips. Today was a little different, mostly because the man in charge, Anatin, was still so drunk he couldn't even stand.

The courtyard round the back of the Witchlight Inn was a spacious square, with plenty of room for two-score-odd mercenaries to mill aimlessly around while carthorses were being hitched up to three large wagons. They were all painted red and blue, presumably the company's colours; two had canvas-covered frames, while the largest was a caravan with a rounded

51

wooden roof and a shuttered window at the side. It was easy to pick out some of those he'd played with last night, most obvious among them being the pale giant, Reft, who was even vaster than Lynx had remembered. The morning light seemed to make the man's hairless skin glow – he could almost have been a Wisp but for the slabs of muscle.

They don't speak either, Lynx reminded himself, casting his mind back to the one time he'd glimpsed a member of that underground-dwelling race and heard their story. *Never heard of a half-breed before, though. Is that even possible? And Banesh's Promise, was his human parent a giant?*

At Reft's side was his scowling companion, Deern, and behind them the white-haired seer, Estal. She paused in her conversation with an elegantly dressed easterner with an extravagant moustache to give Lynx a nod. The easterner followed her gaze and had a long, hard look at Lynx himself, but Lynx ignored it. With brown skin, flowing black hair and, for some reason, a skirt, the man was clearly an exile of Infri or somewhere like that, well away from anywhere So Han had brutalised. He had the lithe build of a duellist, though, and protruding over his shoulder was an ornately worked brass gun butt – no doubt he held a high rank in the company and was sizing up his new comrade.

On Lynx's right, slumped in an armchair that had been dragged outside, was their illustrious commander, Anatin, with his lieutenant, Payl, at his side looking sternly on. The man's hair looked greyer and lank in the morning light, his clothes stained. He gave a piteous whimper, just about audible above the general hubbub.

Lynx reminded himself a soldier didn't last long if he kept aloof from the rest of his company, so he ambled over to one of the shop boys who'd been part of the game last night, Fashail. He nudged the youth with his elbow. Fashail jumped and darted to one side, only belatedly realising he wasn't being jostled unceremoniously.

'Got told to keep out the way, eh?' Lynx asked, trying to remember how to look friendly. 'She does seem a stickler for the rules, that one.'

The only response he got was a grunt and downcast eyes.

'Had a good night?'

A nod this time and reddened cheeks.

'You got the talk about company rules this morning too?'

'I, yes, I did.' Finally Fashail looked Lynx in the eye. He was a fair-looking youth, tall and strong with a scattering of freckles on his tanned cheeks. He had no kit or weapons, of course, just a heavy jacket and a belt-knife.

'What—' Lynx didn't get any further as Fashail's companion for the night stepped forward.

'FORM SUITS!' Payl yelled across the courtyard. The mercenaries were jerked into silence with the exception of their commander, who shuddered and lolled sideways to be sick.

'Shattered gods, woman,' Anatin whimpered, 'you trying to kill me?'

'Suits?' Fashail muttered to Lynx.

The bigger man looked around, trying to fathom a pattern in what the rest were doing. Before he could, Kas appeared and pointed at the left-hand group.

'You're there, most likely,' she said to Fashail. 'You're a recruit and I'm betting you'll be part of Sun.'

'Sun?'

Kas gave a dirty laugh. 'Anatin's Mercenary Deck, remember? You just spent the night playing horsey for the Knight of Sun, I'm guessing you belong to her now. Go introduce yourself to Karra, Fourteen o' Sun – guess that'll make you the Thirteen.'

'And me?'

'Can't you work it out, Stranger?'

Lynx nodded, remembering the previous night. The mercenaries had moved into five groups so if the suit of Sun was on the far left, the far right would be the suit of Tempest. 'Stranger o' Tempest, right. Ain't many of us, by the looks of it.'

Kas shrugged. 'Couple of wounded aren't along for this job, but you've got the Knight of Tempest leading if you get sent off on a job. Teshen's worth a dozen, trust me.'

A door banged behind Anatin, the sound echoing around the courtyard, and the second of the shop boy recruits stumbled out into the morning light. A few paces forward and he slowed, realising every eye in the courtyard was now turned his way.

'Looks like we got a winner,' Kas commented as Anatin twitched in his seat. 'Late to muster, there's always one.'

Very slowly the commander tightened his grip on the armrests of his chair and levered himself up. He turned with the jerky deliberation of a reanimated corpse, hair hanging loose over his face, until he was staring straight at the newcomer.

'Name?' Anatin growled.

The young man quavered, fear making his words just a whisper. 'Ah, Hule. Sir.'

'What?'

'Hule,' he repeated, loud enough for the courtyard to hear this time. 'Sir.'

'Hule.'

For a while Anatin just glared at him, but eventually he levered himself around to Payl. He tried to adopt some sort of dignified pose, chin resting in one hand, but he was too drunk to keep his elbow on the armrest and eventually he gave up. 'Hule?'

'One of the new recruits,' the tall woman said baldly. 'You gave him to Deern. Two of Blood.'

'Two o' Blood.' Anatin seemed to spend a while considering that detail, but eventually he looked up again. 'Deern?'

Payl nodded. 'Aye, sir.'

'You heard them, worm!' Deern roared at the recruit once Payl gave him a nod. He stepped forward with an evil grin on his face. 'Get over here, time for your punishment detail!'

'Deern?' Anatin repeated, wincing at the shout. Eventually something seemed to click into place in his brain. 'Recruit turns up late, slams door right by my ear just to spite me, and . . . and, ah, other crimes too. And he's to get his punishment from the scrawniest fuck I ever met?'

The malevolent glee on Deern's face wavered, but not for long. 'Can pass it up the chain if you like, chief,' he said, pointing back towards the vast bulk of Reft behind him. 'Knight of Blood.'

Anatin cackled briefly, almost falling out of his chair and having to clutch at one armrest to keep himself in it.

'Don't want to kill the little bastard,' he muttered. Anatin made an effort to stand and got halfway there before his body folded sideways on itself and he dropped like a corpse on to the ground.

Lynx kept quiet, as comical as it was. There were a few smiles from the rest of the mercenaries, but no one was enjoying the sight too much.

I bet Anatin's the sort of bastard who remembers everything you say. No matter how drunk he is it'll all come back sometime.

'Take your shot, Deern,' Payl ordered, stepping around her commander. 'Punishment for being late to muster, recruit, one to the gut from your direct superior.'

Lynx noticed then the badge sewn to her breast, a simple playing card design denoting the Knight of Sun. A quick check around identified the others. Clearly there was only one Prince in the company – Anatin – but all five suits had a Knight to lead it.

There was a wild-haired northern woman wearing the Knight of Stars at the fore of the next group, while the unmistakable Reft wore the Knight of Blood. The moustached duellist displayed the Knight of Snow, and lethal-looking Teshen was Lynx's own commander – the Knight of Tempest.

Deern sauntered out into the middle of the open ground and beckoned Hule forward. The young man didn't move for a moment, before he realised he had no choice and edged closer. Once he was near enough, Deern took him by the shoulder and gave him a merry smile as he tapped him on the cheek. 'Next time it'll be Reft and he'll knock you into next week, understand?'

Just as Hule opened his mouth to reply, Deern hammered his fist into the youth's gut and Hule doubled over the blow. As the young man wheezed and an assortment of laughter came from the mercenaries, Lynx took the opportunity to join Teshen and the handful with him. Teshen gave Lynx only the briefest of nods as he reached them, one hand grabbing at someone behind him as he did so.

Lynx frowned at the movement until he saw the dark-skinned woman Teshen had caught hold of, her cheeks scarlet with rage and eyes full of murder. Lynx stopped as he saw her hand was around her sword-grip, only Teshen's fingers on her wrist preventing her from drawing the weapon. Her face meant nothing to him, nor the Jester of Tempest badge she wore, but he'd seen that look before.

'We going to have a problem?' he asked quietly.

The woman bristled as Teshen slowly shook his head. 'That depends,' she snapped, 'on where you fought. Who you raped and murdered.'

'No one,' Lynx replied. 'That was where me and the army disagreed.'

'Bullshit, all you So Han fu—'

Teshen's hand moved in a blur, two fingers coming to a sudden stop an inch from the woman's eye. 'Enough, Braqe,' he said softly. 'Walk away, go and talk to Kas.'

There was an intake of breath as Braqe readied herself to argue, but Teshen snapped her a look that made her think twice. Jaw clamped shut, the woman swallowed her rage and stalked away to where Kas now stood at the rear of Reft's group.

'Thank you,' Lynx said.

'Didn't do it for you,' Teshen said coolly, 'but you outrank her now and that'd make it my problem.'

'Fair enough.' Lynx hesitated. 'Will she give it up? I can still walk away.'

'But you won't, not now. As for Braqe, mebbe you'll have a problem, mebbe not. Mebbe Kas will persuade her otherwise. She hates your lot with all the fire of a zealot and nothing'll change that, but she's no fool, for all that she wears the Jester.'

Lynx sighed. 'Think I just remembered why I hate mercenaries.'

At that, Teshen raised an eyebrow. 'Think I just worked out why some of 'em hate you.' He nodded forward. 'Our prince stirs. If he can stand, it's time to go.'

True enough, Anatin was floundering on the ground in a way that made it clear he'd end up standing at some point, by accident if nothing else. Payl continued to ignore him, however, and did the count from memory – reeling off a list of names and apparently checking them against faces, given she didn't wait for anyone to reply when their name was called.

In minutes it was done and Anatin was precariously balanced on two legs. The entire company seemed to take that as their cue to grab what bags they had left and sling them into one of the wagons. One of the older mercenaries pulled himself up and began arranging the bags according to some system Lynx guessed was the same as the muster count. Lynx watched and waited for his own card to be reached, but when the man muttered it aloud he gestured for Lynx to keep hold of the bag.

Lynx narrowed his eyes, expecting some sort of joke, but the man didn't seem interested in laughing at him, just carried on with the remaining few until everything was stowed neatly. Only the fact that a few others also still had their belongings told him that this wasn't some sort of recruit hazing, but before he could ask what was going on the wagons were pronounced ready and a variety of horses were led out of the stables. He guessed Anatin had already been poured into the caravan, given the snoring that was coming from it, while Payl mounted a beautiful grey horse and waved the company forward, singling Lynx out once she'd done so and beckoning to him.

He trotted over to her, idly wondering if he was expected to salute, but the woman just started talking as soon as he was close enough to hear.

'We got a commission this morning. A Mistress Simbly who wants her husband's murder avenged.'

Lynx blinked and dredged up the widow's image from when he'd met her the previous day. 'Guess that doesn't surprise me,' he said, 'but don't we have a job?'

'The money's good and the wagons are slow.'

He nodded. 'So you're sending them on ahead. Guess that makes sense, it's not a long diversion if we're on horses. Maybe just a night.'

'There's a horse for you,' she said, pointing towards the stable. 'The one with the white forelock. You have battle experience?'

Lynx nodded.

'There'll be seven of us. Better you guide us and hold back than get in the way. I'm told we outgun them, but I don't want to get in any sort of fight.'

'I led a strike company, once upon a time.'

Payl regarded him in silence for a few moments. 'Commando, eh? You willing to take orders, then? From a woman too? There aren't any in your armies, are there?'

'Doubt it. Not been back in a while, though. But I'll take orders unless they're stupid or cruel, doesn't matter who gives them.'

She gave a half-smile. 'About as good as I'll get from anyone round here. Some of this lot struggle if I just use long words. Mount up.'

Payl turned away to find five other figures with horses, all in the process of tying their belongings to the saddles. 'You all ready?'

Lynx looked them over. They were an elite group, if their cards were anything to go by. Teshen stood at their fore, a grizzled veteran beside him wearing the Stranger of Sun. Behind them were Kas, a thin disease-scarred man who wore the Diviner of Tempest, and a broad woman with permanent crooked smile thanks to the flame-scar down one cheek. She wore the Jester of Snow.

None of them spoke, they just finished with their packs and mounted, waiting for orders. Lynx was the last to do so but he wasted no time in pulling himself up into the saddle and adjusting his weapons so they sat comfortably for riding.

'Right, let's be quick about this and back to the company,' Payl announced. 'Lynx, the lake-road towards Tambal, right?'

He nodded. 'Maybe less than a day's ride to where we were ambushed, if we push the horses hard. Road was bloody slow going by wagon.'

'If we get close enough by mid-afternoon we'll take the last part on foot, then. Kas and Teshen will sniff them out. We get it done by nightfall and start back in the morning. Get moving.'

Chapter 5

The seven mercenaries made good time under the warm morning sunshine as they retraced Lynx's route back towards Tambal. As much as he distrusted the Militant Orders, even Lynx was happy to admit he was among the many who benefited from some of their efforts. The largest Orders all maintained dozens of highways across the continent, on top of the network of vast, ancient canals humanity had inherited, and trade flourished as a result. It meant the Orders felt they had the right to stick their noses into the business of anyone using either, but outside the cities the rule of law was generally the simple maths of guns anyway.

The road itself was straight and wide until it reached the tip of a long lake, branching left and right around the calm clear waters. Lynx could see white-faced ducks out on the water and swifts darting through the air high above, but dominating it all was a slender tower of mottled grey stone. Payl called a halt there to let the horses drink and Lynx allowed himself a moment to stand at the lakeside and enjoy the view.

The tower rose directly out of the centre of the lake, perhaps half a mile offshore and huge by mortal standards – a relic of the Duegar civilisation that had doubtlessly been scaled and picked clean of artefacts centuries ago. There were strange protrusions and platforms jutting at random from its sides and narrow windows that seemed not to conform to any regular design. Given Duegar cities were built mostly underground, Lynx couldn't help but wonder at what was hidden beneath those idyllic waters.

There was a stark contrast between the two choices ahead of them. The wide well-maintained road of chalky stone continued left around the long edge of the lake, encompassing a dozen miles and a few villages, while the right-hand track was swiftly swallowed by the dark expanse of forest that engulfed the hills on that shore. Lynx knew they were taking the darker path, one that wound through the trees time and again to avoid the steepest ground before it left the lake behind and swung off east to the town of Tambal. It had been difficult going with wagons, but Master Simbly had at least been right that it remained a quicker journey than the better road.

His moment of peace was broken when footfalls idled up beside him; the plague-scarred Diviner of Tempest, Lynx guessed without turning, given the smell of tobacco hanging in the air.

A tight twist of paper was waved across his view. 'Smoke?'

Lynx shook his head. 'Bit early.'

The man shrugged and raised a coal pot, opening it and blowing on the embers inside before using it to light his cigarette. 'Suit yerself,' he declared with a satisfied breath. 'Name's Llaith.'

He tapped the embroidered badge on his breast, the design faded but done with skill once upon a time. It portrayed a black woman with white hair flying in the breeze, her cape quartered black and white, with a trident in her hands and a lightning flash in two corners of the card – Diviner of Tempest.

'Quite a sight, eh?'

'Aye.'

'It's Lynx, right? You're Tempest's newest?'

'For the time being.'

Llaith sucked hard on the cigarette and turned to Lynx. 'Oh?' he croaked through a puff of smoke.

'I needed a job that got me out of town,' Lynx said with a shrug. 'Ain't making too many promises on how long I stay after the job's done. Never had much love for mercenary work.'

The man gave a snort. 'I'll try not to get too attached, then,' he said, returning his attention to the tower in the lake.

Lynx turned, immediately wary, but the man's face betrayed no real offence so Lynx forced himself to swallow his caution. 'Might be hard,' he hazarded. 'I'm pretty lovable.'

That made Llaith chuckle. 'Don't you take Kas's affections to mean you're lovable. Our girl treats sex like she's in training for a shot at the title.'

Before Lynx could respond the pair of them received a cuff around the head. Lliath growled as his cigarette was jerked into the water, but Lynx barely caught himself in time, dagger half out of its sheath before Kas's laugh stopped him.

'Break's over, boys,' she announced, 'so quit your gossiping and get back in the saddle.'

'Piss on you, Kas,' Llaith muttered, 'you ain't in charge here, ya bossy bitch, remember? Diviner trumps Madman so far's I recall.'

Behind them all, Payl swung herself up into her saddle. 'Break's over, boys,' she announced without looking at Kas. 'Enough talking, all o' you. Get back to it and, Llaith, ditch that bloody coal before we're into the forest. If they smell it on the wind I'll shove a burner so far up your arse you'll be lighting your smokes with that instead.'

Llaith gave an amiable nod and produced a second cigarette with a conjurer's flourish. He lit it and emptied the ember pot on the ground before scrambling back into the saddle, well aware that Payl's stern eyes were watching him the whole time.

They pushed on in silence and Lynx found his eyes drifting towards the tower again and again through a screen of trees hunched over the water's edge. Its height was impossible for him to gauge, but certainly far taller than any structure he'd ever seen. The still and silent presence lurked on the fringe of his sight, while the dark forest on his other side seemed to draw him inexorably in.

There were few Duegar ruins in So Han. The bulk were to the north and east, dotted around the inland seas, inlets, sounds, rivers and Duegar canals that were the lifeblood of trade in the continent. Shadows Deep, which they would hopefully be skirting in a few weeks, was probably larger than every combined ruin in the whole of So Han and it was by no means the biggest or most wondrous in the world. Lynx had no desire to investigate any of them, those dead places of a lost race that remained dangerous both by accident and design. He'd known a few mercenaries who'd worked at one time or another with relic hunters, but only the crazed signed up more than once or twice, despite the rewards.

With regular breaks to rest the horses, they were well into the afternoon by the time Payl called a halt. Easily long enough for him to observe his companions without looking overly rude. Payl wasn't a natural leader, he thought; she'd been pushed into it and obviously disliked command, despite being good at it by Lynx's reckoning. Having seen Anatin helplessly drunk, Lynx could well imagine the worth of her sober and capable manner to counterbalance Anatin's uncertain flamboyance.

Kas and Llaith engaged in quiet, good-natured banter for much of the journey, mostly about the surly, muscular man called Varain who wore the Stranger of Sun badge, while Teshen rode ahead and barely spoke a word. The woman with the crooked smile was called Tyn, Lynx discovered once they halted. She had brought up the rear of the group the whole time, apparently preferring her own company.

At Payl's order, the seven dismounted and led their horses down an overgrown rabbit path until they were hidden from the road. There they hobbled the mounts and left them in Llaith's charge while Teshen and Kas produced recurved bows from their saddle holsters and set off through the undulating forest. Once the two scouts were at the crest of the first rise, Payl gestured for the remaining four to follow, Lynx, Tyn and Varain keeping close to her heels.

They were comfortably short of where the attack had happened so for a while they moved as quickly as the terrain permitted, but after an hour Payl raised a hand to stop her group. She crouched and squinted forward. It took Lynx a moment to pick Teshen out from the undergrowth, so he only caught the last of the man's gestures, but it was no signal code he'd seen before anyway.

'Kas has found 'em,' Payl called softly back. 'Lookout by the road, camp further down – Teshen will deal with the lookout.'

'What's the order?' Lynx asked.

Payl glanced back at him, her face unreadable. 'Employer wasn't too specific there, she just asked for justice.'

'We killing the bastards or not?' Varain growled.

'Piles giving you gyp again, Varain?' Tyn asked.

'You're the only pain in my arse, woman.'

She smirked. 'You'd love it if I was.'

'Quiet, the pair of you,' Payl said despairingly. 'Order depends on what we find there. I want to take them unawares, quick and bloodless if we can. Varain and Tyn, on my right. Once we've got the target, take their right flank and follow my lead. I doubt they'll put up a fight if they find a mage-gun in their faces. I'll keep a burner in the pipe just in case, rest of you load icers.'

Lynx allowed himself a small moment of relief as he pulled his mage-gun from the sheath on his back. Too many mercenaries would just kill everyone in sight – it wasn't like there was any law in these parts to object – but Payl clearly had no desire for blood.

He clicked open the chamber of his gun and slipped a slender brass cartridge from his cartridge case. One end was wadded tight, holding a porcelain bullet inside, while the other was capped with fired clay and marked with the runic shape denoting 'ice'. When he pulled the trigger, the hammer would crack the clay and break the magic-charged glass core against the porcelain. That would shatter into dust, which for reasons Lynx didn't understand was the best medium for the magic to explode forwards faster than any arrow. Icers had greater range and accuracy than other types – powerful enough to kill at almost half a mile – but lacking the terrifying destruction of a burner or sparker.

Lynx closed the gun up again, hands moving out of habit, and stood ready until Payl signalled for them to advance. Unwelcome memories intruded as the group slipped forward through the trees, moving quiet and swift towards Kas. His army career had been relatively short-lived, but the So Han elite commandos had fought this way – tearing a quick and efficient path through the unprepared militias they faced. From the outset, Lynx had learned in a baptism of fire as months of intense fighting had carved them a path hundreds of miles east across the continent. By the time the main army had caught up with their progress, most of the fighting was done and the defenders already shocked into capitulation.

Payl led the way, with Varain and Tyn slipping to the right so they were twenty yards away by the time she reached Kas. The bluff, light-hearted woman of the previous night was all business now, briefly describing the camp up ahead without a second glance at Lynx.

'Hundred yards, I count five. No watch, just the lookout on the road. Tents in a hollow, small fire burning. Bracken all around. Teshen or I could get within ten yards without being seen. There's a big oak up ahead, follow me and you'll be close enough.'

Payl nodded and gestured forward with her gun. It was a heavy, blockish weapon – one that could be used as a club without much risk to the integrity of the barrel. The shorter barrel limited the accuracy, but given fire-bolts exploded into flames when they struck, that wouldn't prove much of a problem.

Kas scuttled forward, all three moving at a cautious crouch. Lynx kept his eyes on Kas, doing his best to ignore the fact his view was mostly of her buttocks. Twice she paused, the second time for long enough that he almost raised his gun, ready to fire. She kept an arrow nocked and three more in her draw hand, but both times started forward again without a glance back. When they came to the oak Kas paused and looked right to check on Varain and Tyn. They were barely visible through the brush, but Lynx followed their progress forward until they had found a good position to wait.

The oak was ancient and low, split by a lightning strike further up so the top branches were twisted and withered. The lower ones had spread wide, a green canopy shrouding the ground around it for ten yards in every direction. Lynx could smell the rich, dark earth underfoot, mingling with the peppery scent of bracken hanging in the air.

Payl spared Lynx a final look and nodded towards the left-hand side of the oak. Seeing he understood, she gave Kas a pat on the shoulder and moved right herself, mage-gun levelled. Lynx skirted behind Kas before all three of them stalked forward through the oak's gloom until they reached the edge of the branches. No more than thirty yards away he saw faces, three turned away from him and one facing their way. Pale-skinned under all the dirt and tousled hair, the man didn't see them at first and when he did there was a moment of surprise that froze him to the spot. Before he could do anything Payl surged forward, her voice crashing through the peaceful forest.

'Move and you're dead!' she roared, aiming her gun straight at the man. Lynx and Kas both held their ground, obvious enough to be a threat as they each picked a target. 'Pull your weapons and I'll burn you all!'

There was a frantic flurry of movement off to the right. A tall man jumped up from a tent, bow in hand, and Lynx turned to line up a shot, but never had a chance to do more than that. The whip-crack of an icer split the air and a white streak slammed into the man's back. The bolt tore right through him, a cloud of blood and chill vapour bursting from his chest to hang briefly in the air as the man was hurled through it by the impact.

'Stay where you are!' roared Payl, holding her ground while Lynx and Kas advanced as fast as they could.

The echoes of the icer seemed to still be reverberating around the trees as they both added their voices to hers, repeating her orders as Varain and Tyn did the same. The hush of the forest was shattered by their shouts and Lynx could see the terror on the faces turning their way – bewildered and shocked into inaction by the noise and violence.

Here's the moment, a voice said in the back of Lynx's mind. *Here's where we'd have killed them all.*

For a heartbeat he was back in the Greensea, the forest region surrounding a great inland sea that had been So Han's first conquest. Rising from the undergrowth, flashing out through the dark, the commandos would converge as one man – gunshots echoing out, bloodthirsty warcries on their lips – and cut down the defenders before they even knew they were under attack.

Taking prisoners had been impossible – it would have crippled their lightning assaults – but there was little time to discern those soldiers trying to fight back and those still wondering what was happening. Before that could happen they were all dead, or watching swords and axes begin their final fall.

He stormed forward, aware he was outstripping Kas as the ghosts of his army days carried him on. From the right Tyn and Varain appeared too, still yelling madly, Varain closing the chamber of his gun as he came, another bolt loaded. Lynx stopped at the edge of the hollow, not wanting to get close enough for anyone to make a foolish grab at him. As he reached it what remained of their targets' resolve dissolved. Two fell to their knees, sobbing and crying for mercy. The others stumbled back in the face of the onrushing mercenaries, hands raised in surrender.

'On your knees,' Lynx commanded. 'Hands on your heads!'

They obeyed without question, the last two dropping down as if their strings had been cut. Varain slung his gun over one shoulder and drew a short-sword, holding it ready as he half-dragged the bandits all in a line and threw their weapons out of the way. It was a paltry selection of hunting bows, a spear, an axe and three long knives. Payl arrived last, carefully pulling the fire-bolt from her gun's breech and leaving the gun empty as she spoke.

'So, who's in charge here?'

The four quailed at her voice, but eventually the eldest of them, a woman with greying hair, coughed and croaked out a reply. 'Guess it's me now.'

'Wrong!' roared Varain, cuffing her around the head. 'We are, got it?'

There was a moment of silence. 'Ah, Stranger?' Payl said, almost apologetically. 'I meant which of them, you damn fool.'

'Eh? Oh. Right.' The veteran scowled and took a step back. 'Answer the question, then.'

'I . . . I am,' the woman said hesitantly, cringing slightly.

'Who do the bows belong to?'

She nodded towards the dead man. 'Vass.' A pause. 'And Obe here,' she added in a reluctant voice, turning to the youth beside her.

Two of the others were young enough to be her sons, but from the look of them Lynx guessed they weren't. Obe was one of those, the last of the prisoners being a woman not much older than the boys. He couldn't see much of the dead man, lying face down with a hole in his back, but he was bigger than any of them.

'Dead man looks fat,' Lynx said, 'fatter'n the rest of you anyway. I'm guessing he was the boss?'

A nod.

Payl took a step forward and looked Obe in the face. 'You ambushed a wagon a few days back? You shot a man.'

'Weren't me!' the youth exclaimed, wild-eyed with fear. He was a gangly one, cheeks marked with spots of Vass's blood. 'Vass did it!'

Lynx watched the faces of the others as Payl replied. 'The man who gives the orders took the shot? Not often how it works, that's what being in charge means. You get some other fool to do stuff.'

The older woman's face twitched as Obe continued to claim his innocence, the others just stared at the ground, but it was enough for Lynx and clearly Payl agreed.

'Look on the faces around you says different,' she continued, 'and given I'm second in command o' my company, I'm inclined to agree. My boss is still drunk somewhere most likely. He prefers me to do any work he don't have to do himself.'

'We never meant anyone to get hurt,' the woman blurted out, 'I swear it. We never killed anyone before, never needed to. Was a warning shot, just something to scare 'em into surrendering.'

'That makes you fucking stupid thieves,' Payl replied. 'Sooner or later you'll get hunted down if you let people live to tell the tale.'

She shook her head. 'We were going to move on soon. Just needed food or money first. Obe ain't the best shot; we weren't finding much to eat in the forest. Vass reckoned if we didn't kill anyone, we'd not be worth bothering with for a few weeks. Not before we moved on, not off the highway.'

'So it was a lucky shot?' Lynx demanded angrily. 'The man was sitting right next to me! You got him plumb in the heart.'

'We didn't know,' the woman insisted. 'We just saw he'd hit someone then you starting firing mage-guns and we ran.'

Lynx grunted, realising it was probably true, but before he could say anything more Payl gave him a look that told him to back off.

'Turns out you were right,' she announced. 'No one in Janagrai cared enough to want to run you off, the town watchmen weren't interested in heading into the forest and the Brothers of the Oak only care about their road. Shame you killed a merchant whose widow actually liked him.'

The woman looked her straight in the face, over the initial shock of their capture. 'What now?' she asked in a quiet voice, clearly dreading the answer.

Payl scowled and caught Varain's eye. The veteran nodded, standing just out of sight of the prisoners. 'Widow asked us for justice,' Payl said. 'By my reckoning that's whoever was in charge and whoever shot her husband. I've no doubt the rest of you'll be long gone by the time we get back round these parts.'

The woman gasped and sagged in relief, while Obe whimpered and Lynx saw a darkening stain down the thigh of his britches. Varain didn't give him long to accept his fate. In one practised movement he pulled a stiletto from his belt and slammed it into Obe's ear. The young man spasmed, eyes widening with shock and pain for one long moment before the spark went from his eyes and his body fell limp.

Varain jerked the dagger out again, blood spattering over the other youth's shirt, and let the corpse fall. There was a moment of fearful silence as they all looked down at the body of Obe, then Payl gave a sniff.

'Give them both a proper burial,' she ordered, looking at the remaining prisoners. 'We'll leave you your bows – you'll need them to hunt as you're moving on. None of you look dumb enough to come after us, but rest assured we'll kill the lot of you if we ever see you again.' She paused and glanced off in the direction of the road. 'Our scouts had the match of your lookout easy enough. If you think you'll be able to sneak up on 'em, day or night, it'll be your last mistake, I promise.'

'No trophy?' Varain asked as they started to retrace their steps.

Payl shook her head. 'Don't want to waste the time cutting back to town to deliver it. We got paid half in advance, agreed we'd tap her for the rest when we headed back this way in a few weeks. It ain't enough money to rush back for – nor for her to screw us over. Either there'll be more reports of robberies and we'll finish the job, or it's done and she'll pay up.'

They ghosted back through the trees with practised, ingrained stealth and as they were collecting their horses Teshen appeared in their midst as though by magic.

'You kill the lookout?' Varain asked him as he led his horse past the man.

The only reply he received was a scornful look, but it was answer enough. With a little of the day's light left they cut through the woods once they found a path they could follow and headed out across open country in search of the road the rest of the company would be on.

There was a curiously restrained air over the group as they made camp at nightfall, tents strung from trees and a pair of ducks dripping fat into the fire built at the heart of a small copse. The last sun of evening cast golden shafts through the leafy canopy, just the contented coos of pigeons and the distant, shrill cries of swifts breaking the silence.

'You're quiet,' Kas commented, settling down beside Lynx and giving him a gentle elbow.

He shrugged. 'I'm always quiet.'

'Not a problem with what went down?'

'Nope. Wasn't expecting anything else. They killed a man, almost killed me, no matter that they're not hardened raiders. There's no justice out here 'cept at the barrel of a gun. Most would've killed 'em all.'

She nodded. 'Still felt like an execution, though. We knew they never stood a chance.'

'Best fight to get into.'

'Aye!' She laughed. 'There's that. Saw you remembered some of your training. Not bad for a man who don't want to fight no more.'

Lynx scratched his cheek. 'Say what you like about my blood-hungry countrymen, the bastards know how to beat fighting habits into a man.'

'Watches!' called Payl from the far side of the fire where Varain was prodding the ducks expectantly. 'Someone pull a deck.'

Kas reached into her jacket and withdrew a stiff leather wallet embossed with a Madman of Stars, holding it up for Payl to see.

'That's how you pick watches?' Lynx asked. 'You lot really are card-crazed.'

She grinned and slipped the fat wad of cards from the battered holder. Fanning the cards briefly she checked they were in no apparent order then handed him the deck.

'Pull one.'

'Two watches,' Payl added, 'lowest cards win.'

Lynx quickly fanned the deck and extracted a card – the four of Sun. He sighed and passed it to Tyn on his left, not bothering to watch her draw before heaving himself to his feet. 'I'll take first watch, then.'

The deck went quickly round the group, ending up with Kas who laughed as she drew Payl's own card, the Knight of Sun. Llaith growled, having picked even worse than Lynx. He pinched out his latest smoke and grabbed a hunk of bread, not waiting for the ducks to be cooked through now he only had half a night's sleep coming.

Lynx peered out through the trees at the darkening sky beyond. Behind the clouds, the great arc of the Skyriver was a brightening smear across the sky. During the day it was easily forgotten, just a pale band in the heavens, but at night the dusty grey streak was a dull glow that matched the moon for light. At this time of the evening, the Skyriver was a regular arc from horizon to horizon across the southern half of the sky. Soon the world's shadow would start to trace a path around the inner edge and provide Lynx with a simple means of charting the night's progress.

'Clear enough sky,' he commented, 'I'll wake you at shadow's peak, Llaith.'

'No rush,' the man said through a mouthful of bread.

Lynx pulled his coat back on, having shrugged it off as soon as they had stopped for the evening, and grabbed his cartridge box and gun, loading an icer.

'Shout when there's food,' he commented before heading out to walk the fields surrounding them. If anyone bothered to reply, he didn't hear it, but he was already lost in the sleepy peace of evening. He realised as soon as he was away from the small camp that he'd have happily volunteered for the first watch. For a man used to being alone, it became an effort to spend a whole day around strangers and a few hours of quiet – just him, the creatures of dusk and the Skyriver – was more than welcome.

'*Too often did I seek the solace of the wild, forgetting the pleasures of human company.*'

Lynx patted his jacket where a slim book rested in a hidden pocket, the writings of the first Vagrim. It was no manifesto, the book of Vagrim, nor a philosophical text. Rather it was the thoughts of a man who had come late to education, but had hungered for more than the wisdom of battle that had been his only tutor for decades. It was plain-spoken and profound, however, written from the heart of a man who had looked deep inside himself and found more than he had expected.

And there's some pleasure to be found in this company, Lynx reflected, remembering both the touch of Kas's smooth skin and the disarming flash of her smile.

Here's hoping it continues. I've been on my own for too long, too many nights sleeping out with one eye open, one hand on my gun. Can't say I trust Anatin further than I can throw him, but I guess you never know. This job might be just as simple as it sounds. That'd be a nice change.

Chapter 6

The seven mercenaries caught up with the rest of the company on the old King's Highway towards Grasiel mid-way through the following morning. While Payl rode on ahead to catch up with Anatin, leading a small column at the front of the company, the others reluctantly divested themselves of their horses and fell in with the rest on foot.

The company marched in suits, Lynx and Teshen joining the rear of Tempest's column. Though the kings and kingdoms had long since been eradicated, many of the names remained – possibly as reminders of past failings as much as anything else. The King's Highway drove a near-straight path up through the inland seas of the continent, starting at Whitesea Sound five hundred miles to the south-west and heading north-east.

The Mercenary Deck would be travelling a hundred miles on it, stopping short of the rich and fertile region that stood between two of the continent's largest inland seas, Udrel and Parthain, to reach the merchant state of Grasiel. From there, once the rescue was complete, they would travel east then north, rounding the mountainous ruin of Shadows Deep to reach Chines. Lynx had visited that grand old city on the south-eastern shore of Parthain once before – a city easily remembered for the legacy left by a guild of stone mages who had ruled it for hundreds of years.

Grand towers, tiered arcades that wove a path above the streets, arches forming something akin to a dragon's ribcage over the vast lower plaza – Lynx had spent his days there marvelling at the sights, but doing less of a good job watching the back of the card sharp who'd hired him. Grasiel City, by contrast, was a younger and more vibrant place – wealthy but without old-kingdom grandeur, a hub for the mineral wealth of the mountains, spices and dyes of the south and the agriculture of the land between lakes.

Anatin set a fair pace each day riding at the fore of the column, but with the region knowing a rare period of peace, the company met it easily and there was a relaxed air as they made camp each evening. Too large to be bothered by any town militia or raiders, they needed only minimal sentries on watch and Anatin was happy for the rest to drink and gamble, so long as they could keep pace the next day.

To Lynx's surprise, Payl and Varain proved to have excellent voices and often both would be cajoled into regaling the company once they had finished eating. Thanks to the variety of backgrounds within the company – coming from all points of the compass and including natives from the shores of every sea and coast so far as Lynx could tell – the pair had learned songs from across the entire continent. Payl in particular sang comfortably in languages she could not speak, so good was her ear.

Lynx kept himself to himself during those first few days, watching the balance of personalities and slowly teasing out the power links between them. Anatin was a charming, unpredictable rogue who could be father one instant, tyrant the next. Payl was devoted to him completely – a reliable constant to balance the man out. If Lynx hadn't seen evidence to the contrary, he would have assumed they were lovers by the closeness of their relationship, but a different sort of loyalty seemed to exist between the two.

A handful – namely the seer, Estal, Teshen, the giant Reft, and Safir, the fallen nobleman who wore a skirt and called it a kilt – were mostly exempt from the usual rules of banter and griping by something unspoken among the rest. Kas rose above the ranks to serve as a point of reference for the entire company, sister to half and object of lust to many of the others, but never obviously exploiting the affection she was held in. Himbel, by contrast, made it clear he didn't give a damn what the others thought of him, while the foul-mouthed and rarely silent Deern seemed to revel in the discord he sowed.

The third day on the King's Highway saw the weather turn worse and a persistent drizzle greeted Lynx as he heaved himself up from his bed roll and looked out of the end of his tent. Sullen grey covered the sky, the first chill of autumn lingering in the air. At the smoking remnants of the fire, Anatin bellowed for the company to muster with an irate edge to his voice and Lynx wasn't the only one to hurry on his jacket, tricorn and boots.

'Bitch better be worth it,' Deern announced, emerging dishevelled and scowling from the tent he shared with Reft. 'If that lost girl turns out to be some lump of lard with a face you'd improve with a punch—'

'It wouldn't matter,' Anatin broke in loudly, ''cos you're being paid to get her out of Grasiel, not fuck her.'

'Hah!' said Himbel, one hand down his trousers, apparently readjusting himself without regard to his audience. 'That'd be one cruel joke on the father. Here's your daughter, congratulations – she's pregnant with the ugliest, most miserable brat you're ever likely to wish was drowned before it could talk.'

There was a smattering of laughter around the camp, but the sun was only just over the horizon and most were too tired to pay much attention or join in. After Deern cursed Himbel's parentage and a part of the continent five hundred miles from the man's birthplace, a busy silence descended on the camp as the tents and stores were packed and stowed in the carts.

Once they'd set off, Lynx noticed Teshen had fallen in beside him, the Knight of Tempest's hair hanging like a veil over one side of his face. He inclined his head, but had seen enough to know that if the man wanted to talk, he'd do it on his own terms. They were of a similar size, although Lynx was comfortably broader of chest and waist alike, but he knew in any fight it'd be Teshen's speed, not his own strength, that would prove the difference.

Not for the first time he wondered about Teshen's origins, but an unspoken rule in any mercenary company was to not enquire too much. Few of them had a happy tale to tell and Lynx had no intention of expanding on what he'd shared himself. With a Hanese face he was forced to explain a certain amount, but beyond that his past was his own.

Once the company had settled into the steady, shambling rhythm of soldiers on the march, Teshen began to say what was on his mind.

'You were a commando.'

It wasn't a question, but Lynx nodded anyway.

'Must've been young.'

'I could read and write.'

'Officer material, eh?'

'Something like that.'

'Good.'

Teshen was quiet a while longer, but finally he seemed to make up his mind about Lynx. 'This rescue, it's no full-scale assault on a castle; word is she'll be in the city where the baron's main holdings are, well away from his wife. Just a townhouse to deal with, but district watchmen not far off.'

'Diversion, then?' Lynx asked. 'Small team goes in and grabs the girl, rest of the company covers the escape?'

'Close enough. A commando could be useful.'

'You're leading the team, not Payl?'

'She'll be giving the orders,' Teshen said with a shrug. 'Those'll be to do whatever the fuck I say.'

Not your first covert mission then, not by a long shot. Sounds like yours is a more interesting tale than most, maybe even the sort that's dangerous to be told.

Lynx couldn't help but glance down, just a sideways look at Teshen's hands, but the man wore no rings of any sort, let alone the three diamonds of the Vagrim.

'Price of my card, is it?'

'Man with a noble card on his jacket gets paid better,' Teshen said in a non-committal tone. 'Even if he hasn't actually been given the badge yet. You're expected to be worth it. But getting Anatin value for money ain't my concern when I take a team in somewhere.'

'Fair enough.' Lynx nodded. 'Guess I'm in if you want me.'

'I know.'

Lynx shot him a look at that, but could make out nothing on Teshen's face and had no intention of pressing the matter. Instead he let his mind drift as the miles crawled by and the drizzle waxed and waned – never turning into a downpour but never letting up either. With his hat tilted forward and his jacket fastened tight, Lynx did his best to ignore it all, letting the world wash over him. The tang of mud and tramp of boots were easy to dismiss after years of wandering and soon it all faded from his awareness.

In his mind he explored places he had only read about in the one luxury he permitted himself, the books he would save and scrimp for – the books he would mourn for weeks when finally he sold his current one to make way for another. The roads he walked varied little and the principalities, city-states, republics and fiefdoms that dotted the continent rarely possessed a veneer of the unique. Money ruled and strength led. There was no justice outside the states and precious little within them, save for those who decided what justice was.

But in his mind he could walk the deserts of the east, where high stone formations preserved tiny wildernesses from the rest of the world below. On roads such as this one or chalky, overgrown tracks barely big enough for carts to use, he had stalked the souks of the mage islands and raced with the dusk hunts through their maze-like streets. With the rain falling all about him and his cheeks damp, Lynx conjured the legendary Jewelled Falls and felt his breath catch at the sight. There it was said the River Araiv emerged from a great forest to cascade down a hundred waterfalls and cast a hundred rainbows before it wound its way to the waters of Lake Witchfire to the north.

When the shout from up ahead came, he missed the words spoken and on instinct was reaching for his gun before Teshen caught his arm.

'Peace, Stranger,' Teshen said as Lynx flinched under his touch. 'Just knights on the road.'

Lynx shook himself awake. 'There a problem?'

'Nah – we just make it a habit to call out when we see any. They don't like mercenaries much, which is funny when they get paid to fight the same as us often enough.'

He heard it properly now as the call was passed back by those in the middle, unnecessary perhaps but anything to break up the day, and many Militant Orders were unpredictable at best.

'Charnelers!' came the muted voices down the line, one woman's voice raised above the rest; whoever that was, they were marching safe in the anonymous heart of the company.

The nickname was down to their avowed holy missions, that just so happened to be the basis for their power and wealth. For millennia they had gathered and stored the fragments of the five shattered gods which had been scattered across the known world by their apocalyptic final battle, raising great charnel fortresses to securely store the hoard. Lynx glanced down at the cartridge box at his waist. Each glass core inside the cartridges was charged with magic, each one of those had been created using a god-fragment to focus the power.

'Looks like they caught a sparrow,' Teshen commented as the column moved on. 'Who are they? Knights-Charnel of the Long Dusk? Could be worse, I guess.'

Lynx craned to see over the heads in front of him as a party of horsemen trotted towards them. There were six in the party, four men and two women; five wearing the quartered black and white livery of their order, with a shield device on their chest bearing a spear and a red setting sun. It was a sight Lynx knew well enough. The other rider was a small shape in a grey shawl, her bowed head covered by a white scarf. Barely more than a girl by her size, she rode at the centre of the knights – an escort of some form, but she didn't look rich enough for the better sort.

The Knights-Charnel of the Long Dusk were one of the largest of all the Militant Orders. Cities had built up around their three principal fastnesses, which were now hubs in the production of mage-guns and cartridges, and many of the roads Lynx had walked in his life were thanks to their wealth. Most likely half of Lynx's own ammunition had come from a Knights-Charnel sanctuary, the walled and guarded heart of their cities where mages lived under the generous protection of the Knights-Charnel.

'Better or worse than other prisons,' Lynx muttered, 'that ain't much of a ringing endorsement.'

Teshen shrugged. 'I've seen inside one. They might not live like kings, but they do better'n you and I.'

Lynx snorted. 'While they make their masters rich.'

'True enough.' Teshen seemed disinclined to say more on the subject; after all, they both knew it had been an old argument long before either of them were born.

The knights wore long coats down to their knees, asymmetrical so the badge stood centrally on their chest, and fastened with fat brass clasps down one side. Wide-brimmed hats kept the rain off and conspicuously decorated gun holsters hung at their horses' flanks, while each soldier wore a plain rapier on their hip.

The young captive straightened a little as they passed the mercenaries, finally lifting her head from its weary slump. Despite her white scarf, Lynx could see she had trails of brown hair, darkened in the rain and plastered across her face. She couldn't have been much more than fifteen or sixteen, taller than most perhaps, but Lynx realised with a jolt that was down to her parentage. Whatever the colour of her hair, her features dragged him straight back to his homeland – memories of girls he'd kissed in his youth or just passed in the street every day of his early life.

The girl's eyes widened as she saw him too, recognising something in him, and her lips parted to croak words Lynx couldn't make out. The knight at her side grabbed her arm and shook it angrily, but though she cringed she repeated her words and this time he heard it clear enough.

'Tau-na-se.' *Save me.*

Lynx hesitated mid-step. Hair stuck across her face by the rain. Anyone with their hands free would've moved it.

'Sorry,' he said in a low voice to Teshen.

'Huh? Oh shitting hells . . .'

Lynx had already stepped back and slipped between the last few mercenaries behind him, an icer flipped from the ready-pouch at the front of his cartridge box. In one movement he drew his mage-gun and slipped the cartridge into the chamber.

''Scuse me, gents,' he called out, casually holding the gun out with one hand so it pressed against the belly of the last rider.

The lead knight, already past him, glanced back and saw the weapon. He yanked hard on his reins to bring the horse round as his comrade stopped dead, looking with horror at the gun at his belly.

'What's the meaning of this?' roared the lead rider, a broad man with a fleshy face and thin mutton-chop whiskers, as he advanced on Lynx. 'Are you mad, sir?'

'Nope,' Lynx replied as Teshen barked an order for the company to halt and the call was taken up down the line.

A few had already stopped, watching in astonishment as Lynx carefully withdrew the mage-gun but kept it levelled at the last knight. He was a young man, clean-cut and handsome with sandy-blond hair – the very epitome of the noble warriors the Knights-Charnel made themselves out to be. Other than the naked fear on his face, that was.

'What the name o' pissing dark is goin' on back here?' Anatin roared, spurring his horse forward from the front of the column.

Lynx waited for the man to catch up, keeping his eyes on the knights but also trying to see past them to the young woman. There was fear on her face too, but as one of the nervous horses fidgeted he saw he was right. Her hands were bound to the saddle.

'Lynx, what're you doing?' Anatin demanded, reining in beside him.

'I want to talk to the young lady.'

'Is that it?' the leader of the knights said. 'You're from So Han, aren't you? Is this some honour thing? I've seen how your lot treat your women folk and I couldn't give a shit about a broken nation's honour. She doesn't belong to you. Your laws got changed, remember?'

'That much I know,' Lynx replied in a calm voice. 'Still want to talk to her.'

'Get on your way, mercenary,' the knight said, voice thick with contempt now, 'and we'll forget about all this. You, you're in command here?'

'I am,' Anatin replied stiffly.

'Well, I've marked your badge. Do you really want to make an enemy of the Knights-Charnel?'

'That I don't. Lynx, get the fuck back to the column.'

'Sorry, chief, but first I got to ask this girl something.'

Anatin swore loudly and drew his mage-pistol. Lynx could see him from the corner of his eye. The gun wasn't exactly pointed at Lynx's head, but it'd take just a twitch to put a shot right through his skull. 'You forgotten the whole idea of taking orders?'

'No, sir, but the girl asked for help.'

'So?'

'So I want to know why. She didn't call out for you all to hear, she spoke in Hanese. Now my people ain't exactly friendly or charitable, so that makes me wonder what she reckons I've got going for me that the rest of you don't.'

Before anyone could reply the young woman blurted out, 'I'm a mage!'

There was a moment of silence, broken only by the faint patter of rain.

'And there we have it,' Lynx said eventually. 'She's a mage. And So Han's got little going for it, but it's the one place round here where mages don't get rounded up by Knights to work as slaves in their ammunition factories. Mages got respect there, even the women, so my guess is she knew I wouldn't have grown up looking the other way when a slave party rode past.'

'She's a criminal,' the leader of the Knights snapped, 'and we're taking her to justice. It's none of your business, mercenary, and it's time for you to step back.' He paused. 'Your name is Lynx?'

'It is.'

The knight's voice took on an even haughtier, aristocratic tone as he drew himself up in his saddle. 'Well, *Master* Lynx. My name is Commander Ntois. You're a long way from home and I urge you to ask yourself how loyal your fellows are to a man old enough to be a veteran of the war. Your captain there appears to grasp what it means to threaten a man of my rank, or indeed any other ranked man of the Knights-Charnel.'

'Prove it,' Lynx broke in, nodding towards the woman. 'If she's no mage, free her hands and give her something to charge.'

'I'll do no such thing. She's a criminal!'

'Why? Even a mage wouldn't be able to kill all of you and make her escape.'

'My patience is at an end, Master Lynx.'

The mercenary turned so his gun was pointing at the leader's face. 'Mine too, Commander. It's time to release her and see if she can prove her claim. You ain't moving on until something happens.'

'Okedi,' Ntois growled. 'Check her binds are secure and ride on.'

Lynx felt something tighten inside him. *You choose to do what's right, even if it means you're dying that day.*

The man beside the young woman leaned forward, Lynx found his eyes drawn to the movement, but he knew it would be a diversion. As soon as Lynx glanced away, Ntois grabbed the mage-pistol at his waist. He had it drawn in an instant, but Lynx gave him no time and fired from the hip with his long gun. The deafening shot took Ntois in the throat and rocked him back. There was an astonished look on the man's face as the white rime of frost stole over his skin – whitening his flesh like an actor at the theatre. A gasp of blood-tinted mist exploded from the back of his head like a fleeing soul as the horses shied from the gunshot and the body slumped sideways.

With no time to reload Lynx swung with his empty gun and slammed the barrel against the wrist of the first knight to reach for his own. Turning he tried to strike at the next man but was kicked in the chest and stumbled backwards. The gun fell from his hands so he hauled his sword free, trying to get it up towards one of the knights before he was shot, but before anyone else died there was a shout from behind them.

'Hold or die!' Teshen roared over Anatin's squawks of rage. 'You too, Lynx, stay your blade!'

He did as he was told, turning to see Teshen with a mage-gun levelled at the knights and half of the Tempest mercenaries scrambling to follow his lead. The knights froze, one then three then a dozen guns pointing their way as more of the mercenaries swarmed forward, backing up their comrades on instinct.

'All of you, bloody stop!' Anatin yelled, scarlet with fury. 'Teshen, what the buggery d'ya think you're doing?'

'Keeping the man beside me,' Teshen said, still sighting down the barrel of his gun. 'It's what we do – and better'n letting some shit-licking zealots kill one of our own.'

'He bloody ain't one of our own much longer!' Anatin brandished his mage-pistol in the air. 'Not after pulling this shit. Cards, take a damn step back the lot of you. The first man on either side here to pull the trigger I'll fucking kill myself, got that?'

No one spoke, but no one fired either and Anatin sensibly let everyone take a breath before continuing. A few moments of silence did as much good as orders when someone's blood was high.

'Now, I'm going to stand in between the lot of you,' Anatin continued in a calmer voice. 'Any bastard shoots me and I'm going to get really angry, get it?'

Again there was silence so Anatin nudged his horse forward, forcing Lynx to step back and away from the knights. 'Lynx – the only reason I haven't shot you dead is that it would leave me with an empty gun and, like I said, I plan on shooting the first of the rest of you who fires.' He cocked his head at Lynx and pointed with his pistol at the dead commander. 'I do need to ask exactly what you were thinking there, given the Knights-Charnel are one of the biggest Militant Orders in the whole crap-steaming world?'

'He was drawing, didn't have a whole lot of choice.'

'Oh, right, guess that makes it okay then, does it?'

Lynx shook his head. 'She's a mage, they'd captured her like slavers and were going to kill anyone who got in the way of that.'

'And that, you soft-witted streak of dung, is the damned way o' the world round these parts,' Anatin spat. 'You might not like it, but picking a fight with a huge army who don't care for your opinion ain't much of an alternative.'

'Only one I got.'

'Commander,' said the female knight in a tight, angry voice. 'Now is not the time for debate. Your man's murdered one of our officers. Such an act demands blood in response.'

'Oh, please don't start dictating to me, Paladin,' Anatin snapped, 'not when you got thirty guns pointing your way.'

He pointed his pistol at the mage, who flinched until she realised he was just addressing her. 'Half these impotent halfwits can't shoot worth a damn, girly, so I'd sidle away from your friends there, but the rest are crack shots and now ain't the time for anyone to get uppity with me.'

'You would prefer vengeance to come from my Order?' the Charneler said in a quieter tone as the young mage tried to urge her horse out of the firing line. The paladin had a sword-scar on her face and a broken nose; no stranger to violence and not intimidated by Anatin's words, but she recognised the situation she was in.

'I've got no beef with the Knights-Charnel,' Anatin said softly.

'And I assure you, they will not have one with you if you hand this man over to us. Mercenaries are a disparate folk, the actions of one rogue need not reflect poorly on the remainder of the company.'

'You can't have him,' Teshen said, gun now aimed at the woman.

'Who the fucksticks made you commander here, Teshen?' Anatin bristled. He turned to the rest of the company. 'Hey, the lot of you – I said lower those guns! Do it now!'

Lynx saw their hesitation, but most did as commanded – although a few of the senior officers were reluctant to do so entirely. He saw Payl and Estal drop theirs from shoulder to waist, but they were experienced soldiers standing at a five-yard range.

'He killed the man fair,' Teshen said, almost ignoring Anatin entirely. 'You people don't get to string him up for that.'

'Is that what this is about, Teshen?' Anatin said in a quiet voice. 'You pick your moments, my friend.'

'Do you want to join him?' the woman asked coldly.

'Hey now, there's no reason for this to go that way,' Anatin declared.

'I think there is, Captain,' she said, arching an eyebrow. 'Hang him here or bind his hands and put him in our charge. No So Han piece of filth gets to kill a Knight-Charnel without righteous retribution.'

Anatin scowled. Lynx could see the mercenary thinking furiously, weighing the hand he'd been dealt.

'Take the bastard's purse first,' piped up a voice from further back in the company, 'since he's been murdered an' all, theft on top o' that ain't worth much at all.'

'Ulfer's crumpled horn, Deern,' Anatin sighed. 'You reckon now's the time for your joking?'

'Who's joking? We got more guns than 'em.'

'There will be no plundering of the dead,' the paladin said gravely. 'The crime is limited to one man at present, but the blame will encompass the rest of you should you steal from his corpse.'

'Aye, and there's my problem,' Anatin mused. 'How far the blame spreads.'

'You wish my oath? On my honour as a paladin of the Knights-Charnel of the Long Dusk, I give it.'

'You ain't getting him,' Teshen repeated. 'Walk away now, best we'll offer.'

'Teshen, step back. Please.'

'Sorry, not happening. He's one of ours now, new or not. We've all seen the value of *their* oaths,' he spat with a sudden vehemence.

Anatin sighed in exasperation. Lynx saw him glance up at the road and was already moving away when Anatin almost idly shot the paladin through the chest. Four more shots rang out in the next moment, three white threads darting out while a darker one ripped a wide furrow through the air.

The remaining knights were smashed backwards by the thundercrack detonations, two thrown clear of their saddles. The other two fell tangled in their stirrups but were dead just as quickly. The young man Lynx had first threatened was hurled ten yards through the air, body folded around a giant's punch to crash broken and mangled in the dirt behind.

In the stunned silence, Anatin glared round at his troops. 'Which arsehole loaded an earth-bolt there?'

'Apologies, my prince,' said the easterner, Safir, in a level voice. 'My mistake.'

'You almost took my bastard head off!'

Safir offered a florid bow, but Lynx saw the ghost of a smile on his face as he did so. 'I loaded in haste. To make amends I shall mention you in my prayers tonight.'

Anatin glared at the man and shook his head. 'I've heard you pray,' he growled. 'I don't want to get caught up in that list of accusations, just in case the gods are ever actually listening.'

'As you wish, my prince.'

Anatin gave up, muttering, 'Bloody mercenaries,' before he went to inspect the dead. 'Looks like we've got plunder, Deern.'

The smaller man gave a cheer and barged his way forward, but Anatin's boot caught his shoulder before he could reach the bodies. 'Shame you didn't shoot any of 'em though,' the commander added nastily, 'so get your slack-ringed arse back in ranks. Spoils go to those who did the fighting, same as always.'

Anatin stood in his stirrups and looked up and down the road before continuing. 'Be quick about it too. Shift the bodies and set the quality horses loose, take nothing identifiable. Cartridges and that standard-issue gun are fine but you leave those pretty mage-pistols alone – no, chuck 'em away as far as you can. Don't need to advertise what we have done here.'

The commander paused and sought out Lynx. 'You. I really ain't happy with you, hear me?'

Lynx nodded but Anatin clearly wasn't done.

'I don't think you do truly get how wrath-o-Veraimin fucking angry I am right now, 'cos I don't have the words yet. For starters, though, the main reason I don't shoot you here an' now is 'cos we don't need to leave behind a body that could get connected to us. As it is, I'll be having to drop comments at the next town about a troop o' Sons of the Wind our scouts spotted, see if we can draw some attention away from us.'

At last he remembered the young mage and turned in her direction. 'You, sparrow – you got a name?'

The woman bobbed her head. 'Sitain, sir.'

'You really a mage?'

She quailed at that, shoulders hunched as though she feared the answer as much as the killers asking it. 'I, I think so, sir.'

Anatin snorted. 'You think?'

'I've no training, no idea what I'm doing most of the time.'

'What sort o' mage do you think you are then?'

Another hesitation. 'Night, sir.'

'Night?' Anatin whistled in surprise, his anger clearly fading. 'Not many of you about, eh? Still, that could make you useful. Ever considered the employment opportunities afforded by joining a mercenary company?'

The look on her face was a picture. Sitain straightened up in her seat and looked Anatin in the eye for the first time. 'No, I haven't.'

'Fair enough,' he cackled, 'just look at the arseholes I have to work with! Even one o' my best either can't tell the difference between an icer and an earther or he chooses the weirdest time to mess with me.' The next instant his mirth was gone like a voice on the wind. 'Consider it now, for a few weeks at least. I'm guessing you can't go back home, that's where this lot found you, no?'

'It is.' She glanced down at the bodies on the ground around her, lips pursed against the blood and the pained, surprised stares of the dead. 'I'm seeing the career in a whole new light.'

'Glad to hear it. Lynx, she's now your responsibility. Do a better job for her than you have up to now.'

With that Anatin yanked his horse back around and headed back to the column, calling over his shoulder, 'Two minutes to search and hide 'em. After that we move out.'

Before Lynx could investigate the purse of the man he'd killed, he found Teshen's hand on his shoulder.

'I'll do that for you,' the man said in a pointed tone. 'Reckon he's the richest of the lot and I stuck my neck out for you, got to be worth a commission.'

Lynx tensed, old instincts rising to the fore and demanding he stick a knife in Teshen's guts. *I wouldn't have him pegged for some thieving bully, out to prove his dominance.* He paused. *So maybe he isn't, maybe he's just got a point and this is the price of stepping out of line.*

'Maybe so,' he admitted. 'Reckon I can guess what his purse'll look like. Reckon I'll have no complaints if half of that comes my way plus a share of cartridges.' He glanced at Teshen's hand and the man, with a half-nod, took the point and removed it from Lynx's shoulder. 'I'll get the horses going.'

He pulled a dagger and went to cut the knotted cord binding Sitain's hands to her saddle. She gasped as they were freed, wincing and rubbing at her wrists until Lynx offered her a hand to dismount.

'I can manage.'

Lynx shrugged. 'Go on then.'

Sitain fumbled at the horn of the saddle with fingers that refused to grip and she had to resort to slumping forward and hooking her wrist around the front. She gingerly eased one foot up until she could slide her body off without falling, but as her feet touched the ground her knees buckled underneath her. Lynx grabbed her waist just before she fell, ignoring the angry hiss he received.

'Enough now,' he said firmly, 'you did well just getting off by yourself. You made your point.'

As gently as he could he eased her down to the ground and then stepped back. Lynx looked her up and down as Sitain pulled the scarf from her head to reveal a mass of brown curls that certainly didn't come from So Han. Most likely she was some local farmer's daughter; she was dressed in hard-wearing homespun, while her hands and face were well tanned.

'I'm Lynx,' he said eventually.

'Lynx?'

'Long story.' He paused. 'Well, short story actually. Not very interesting either, but Lynx is who I am.'

She eyed him suspiciously. 'Deserter?'

Lynx shook his head. 'All years in the past anyhow, so let's move on. You're Sitain. Got a family name?'

'Yes.'

He gave her a moment to expand on that but Sitain just pursed her lips and looked at the ground. 'Want me to move on?'

'Maybe it's best I get a new name too,' she said hesitantly. 'Not like I can go home now. Someone in the village told the Charnelers about me and my family didn't put up much of an argument.'

'Your ma from So Han, da's a local?'

She nodded. 'How'd you know?'

'Was the best guess. More likely it'd be a woman who'd want to move far away from that place.'

She nodded and scowled down at her hands. 'What now?'

He cocked his head at her, trying to work out the look on her face, which seemed to combine more emotions than Lynx could manage over the course of a whole day. 'Now? First of all I get these horses heading off down the road.' He reached up and pulled the saddlebag off the one she'd been riding. 'Anything in this yours?'

'No, it's just food and pans.'

'Right. I'll fetch the rest, you clear out anything useful or edible and toss the rest like you were robbing 'em. We'll put valuables we can't safely keep in a bag and toss it somewhere.' He glanced back at Teshen, who was already engaged in a brisk, practised search of the commander's body. 'Can you walk?'

Sitain frowned down at her feet. 'I don't know.'

'I'll get you in the caravan, then. Your horse'll get tied up with the rest, but let's put you out of sight just in case, eh?

Don't go through anyone's stuff when you're there or they'll cut your throat, understand?'

'Yes.'

'Good. We can talk later, work out where you want to go once you're free of the Charnelers.'

'Just like that?'

'Aye, just like that. Unless you got any other plans?'

She shook her head. 'No, it's just you're, well . . .'

'A mercenary?'

Another shake.

Lynx felt a slight chill like a cloud covering the sun. 'Ah, a man from So Han. That I am, but you heard the good commander. That shit's been outlawed a long while now and I ain't a fan of bringing up the past.'

He turned away, suddenly keen to be away from people for a minute or two. 'Rest now. We've got a long day ahead of us.'

Chapter 7

Long-tailed swallows knifed through the evening air, slashes of white against the deep blue sky. The dull arc of the Skyriver loomed across a sky unencumbered by cloud, a pale grey sweep as the last golden light of evening filtered through the trees surrounding the mercenary camp.

Sitain deposited her armful of wood and paused to watch the bustle of figures around her. They were efficient, she had to give the mercenaries that. Under a veneer of squabbling, outright abuse and chaotic milling, the camp was taking shape with surprising speed. Tents popped up, fires lit with pots of food hung over them and watches had been set all within minutes of Commander Anatin calling a halt.

She stretched her back, glad to be out of the wagon and on her own two feet again. Inaction didn't suit her, she was used to working and had been first to set out in search of firewood – anything to be moving, anything for purpose after a long day alone with her thoughts.

A black woman with red-tinted eyes walked over to her, tugging her hair loose while she inspected Sitain. Even in battered mercenary garb she was beautiful, lithe and light in her movements in a way Sitain didn't expect from a woman more than ten years her senior. In her village, a few years of marriage left most women solid and careworn, fatigue sapping what sparkle they had in their eyes.

The woman's riding leathers were plain and battered, but the clothes underneath showed signs of an eye for style. Yellow thread had been used to stitch her trousers, the dark outline of fishes had been embroidered into her close-fitted jacket and a wine-red neckerchief was coiled around her neck. The badge on her chest was rather less elegant – the Madman of Stars, a white, tear-streaked face howling up at the night sky.

'Got any kit?' she said as she reached Sitain.

'Kit?'

The woman shrugged. 'Clothes, whatever.'

'Oh. Yes, they let me pack a bag before they put me on the horse.'

'Fetch it.'

'Why?'

An amused smile appeared on the woman's face. 'You'll share my tent. Unless you'd prefer to be in with Lynx, that is. I'm Kas, by the way. Don't let the badge fool you, I'm the sanest of the lot here.'

Sitain's stomach tightened at the thought of sharing a tent and her mouth went dry. Feeling like an awkward little girl she nodded, eyes downcast, but before her humiliation could be compounded further a greying man scampered up. Darker than Kas and another couple of decades older, his face was twisted in some sort of childish awe as he ran up and grasped her hand. Like Kas he wore battered clothes picked out with small flashes of colour; green braiding edged his jacket and every brass button was polished bright.

'Is it true?' he gasped, as though unable to believe what he was talking about.

'Is what true?' she demanded as she tried and failed to haul her hand back.

'Himbel, leave the poor girl alone.' Kas laughed.

'Absolutely not, Kas, this is too important!' he insisted. 'She holds the key to my future well-being!'

'What the hell are you talking about?' Sitain demanded, having to brace herself on the man's shoulder to yank her hand free. 'What's going on?'

'They say you're a night mage,' Himbel continued. 'So your magic can quieten; bring on sleep and the like.'

Sitain took a wary step back, a familiar sensation crawling on her skin as it always did when her magic was being discussed.

'What of it?'

It wasn't illegal or heretical to possess such abilities, but most magic was dangerous and unpopular, so she wasn't happy to talk about it so openly with anyone, let alone strangers.

Before the man could reply Kas burst out laughing, drawing more attention to them. 'Ulfer's horn, Himbel! Of all the dumbshit uses for magic, that's just . . .' She briefly doubled over in more laughter.

'It's the best argument for magic I ever heard,' he snapped, not taking his eyes off Sitain. 'Is it true?'

'I, ah – yes,' she said, eyes downcast, 'I suppose so.'

'You suppose? Can you or can't you? This is important, girl! Can you put someone to sleep?'

'It really ain't important,' Kas gasped beside him, 'but it'll make you loved by half the company if you can.'

Feeling like she was having a trick played on her, Sitain looked around at staring faces. She saw only confusion on all of them, however, not amusement at her discomfort. As she looked, feeling the heat rise in her cheeks, the round-bellied lump called Lynx pushed his way between two of the onlookers, heading to join them. Unlike most of the mercenaries the man wore no trace of colour whatsoever; only the flecks of yellow in his eyes punctured the dull brown of leather and the shades

97

of grey clothing. Even the ridiculous, obtrusive tattoo on his cheek was composed just of black lines.

'I can,' she said eventually. 'I ain't skilled with it, but I can do some things. Maybe calm a mood or put someone to sleep if I really have to.'

She didn't manage any more as the black man grabbed her in a bearhug and almost swung her around in his delight. 'Salvation!' he crowed into her curls. 'A gift from the gods!' When she finally pushed herself free he calmed a little and took her by the shoulders to look her straight in the eye. 'We're going to be best of friends, you and I,' he assured her. 'Anything you need, just say and it'll be yours.'

'Why?'

He beamed. 'Because if you can shut that scrawny gobshite up with your magic, you're worth your weight in gold.'

'What's going on?' Lynx demanded, eyes narrow and suspicious.

'Himbel's found a way to shut Deern up whenever he wants,' Kas snorted, wiping tears of amusement from her eyes. 'I think he's in love.'

'Leave the poor girl alone,' Lynx said. Himbel gave Sitain one last hug then allowed Kas to drag him away, leaving the big man to stand frowning at her while Sitain tried to make sense of what had happened.

'Who's Deern?' she asked eventually.

'Eh? Oh, one o' the company jesters,' Lynx replied cryptically. 'Don't worry about him. You'll want to shut him up from what I've seen, but his friend Reft is the biggest thing I ever met on two legs so you might want to be a little cautious about it.'

'Are all your company mad?'

That made the frown turn into a half-smile. 'Aye, mebbe. They ain't my company, though. I just joined for this one job, but most of 'em look crazy from what I've seen.'

'You're not really part of the company?'

Lynx shrugged and pointed to the breast of his jacket. 'Only just signed on for this job. No badge, see? I'm getting paid like I'm wearing the Stranger of Tempest, but I doubt I'll stick around long enough to actually sew one onto my jacket.'

She looked around at the other mercenaries. All those who hadn't removed their jackets did indeed have playing card badges sewn on. She'd noticed some wearing them but hadn't realised it was the official mark of the company.

'So you picked a fight with the bloody Knights-Charnel on behalf of a company you're not really a member of?'

'That's about the size of it. I'm starting to think maybe Anatin's not so happy about that.'

'Why did you, then?'

He gave her a puzzled look. 'You wanted to be their prisoner the rest of your life?'

'Of course not! But still, I didn't really expect you to step in. Most people we passed on the road wouldn't even look at me.'

'Seemed the right thing to do,' he said with a shrug. 'Next time I won't bother.'

Sitain paused and mentally backtracked. The man *had* put his life on the line for her, a stranger and a woman to boot. He might be a long way from home, but her mother had told her a few stories of the arrogant, warlike men of So Han and Lynx fitted that picture, at least until he spoke. It had been a desperate gamble to ask for his help, but Sitain knew no one round these parts argued with the Knights-Charnel. While the little she'd heard of So Han wasn't good, it was at least clear their views on both mages and women differed greatly to those prevalent in these parts. Whatever his reasons for doing it, she reminded herself, asking why wasn't the best form of gratitude.

'Thank you,' she said awkwardly.

'Eh?'

'I didn't say it before,' she explained, 'what with the killing and looting of bodies, but thank you. You saved me. Once they'd got me to whichever sanctuary they were taking me to, I'd never have left. You risked your life for me.'

He turned away. 'Aye, well, like I said. Seemed the right thing to do. Best you go and get some food now, we're on first watch.'

'We?' she asked, startled. 'You want me to stand guard?'

'Aye – well, I'm going to,' he added with a smile that crinkled his tattoo, 'and you're under my care so you are too. Suspect we're together on Anatin's shit-list, so get used to first watch. You're likely to see a few of them.'

As the camp took shape around them, Sitain realised she wouldn't have long to fetch her belongings and find Kas's tent. She scampered over to the caravan she'd passed the day in, found the one small canvas sack containing the sum total of her possessions – a blanket, two changes of clothes and a carved wooden flute given to her by her grandfather. She had been unable to grab anything more and suddenly she found herself squatting on the floor of the large caravan, eyes screwed up against the tide of despair rolling over her.

Memories of her family filled her mind; her mother's wary face, which always seemed surprised at every kind word or gesture that came from Sitain's father. Her father himself – a slight man and shorter than his tall Hanese wife, but able to labour every hour of daylight and return home to his family's enthusiastic chatter with strength remaining. Felit, her brother, larger than his father by the time he was fourteen and with more than a little of Lynx about him. As quick to anger as any young man, Felit was always quiet and careful around their mother, while little Sutai with her round, guileless face and boundless joy made noise enough for all three of them.

Sitain knew then that she would never see them again – or at least not for a long time – and she would never be able to return properly. Her happy little family, shattered by some grasping informer and the unmatched power of the Knights-Charnel. She knew night mages were rare. Just how rare was anyone's guess, and no one back home had known anything more than rumour about magic. Rare enough that the Charnelers wouldn't let her go easily, though, she guessed that much. Her family would be watched or at least informed on, so there was no return there – no life of farming and family ahead of her, just danger for them all if she so much as visited.

How long she stayed in the gloom of the caravan Sitain couldn't tell, but in a mercenary company there was little time for sentiment. Soon she found herself jostled by the men and women fetching their own belongings, barely noticing the young woman curled at their feet. At last she sensed someone watching her and looked up to discover a slight, middle-aged man with blue eyes and a stern expression staring at her.

'Hop it,' he said once he had her attention. Not unkindly, but Sitain sensed unkindness could be forthcoming. 'You're the mage girl, right?'

Sitain stood up and nodded, wiping the last traces of damp-ness from her cheeks. 'That's right, Sitain.'

'Foren,' he said with a formal little nod. 'Company steward, of sorts anyway. Little advice for you, girly. This caravan's Anatin's bedroom and office come evening. Anything you want out of it, you move quickly 'cos once I turn it down it's off limits.'

'Turn it down?'

He pointed towards the rear of the caravan and edged past her. With shelves and cupboards lining the wooden walls for most of the length, there wasn't much room to pass towards the back, where a high bed-sized shelf went across the rear. With practised movements, Foren jerked the shelf towards him. He slid it off its runners and manoeuvred it around so he could stand it on end and drag it out of the caravan.

At the door two mercenaries were waiting to take it and Sitain guessed it would double as a table to eat at. As though to confirm the idea, Foren retrieved a folded leg frame from the roof of the caravan and passed that out next. In the space underneath was bedding all ready for use, while beside it a cupboard opened out to reveal a desk with a bank of drawers behind. Opposite that Sitain noticed a tiny iron stove was built into an alcove of glazed tiles, red, yellow and blue.

'Out now,' Foren urged, giving her a prod in the shoulder, 'You keep clear of Anatin's stuff or you'll not make it to the next town, understand?'

His tone of voice had hardened and Sitain realised the steward took his duties very seriously. She gathered up her bag and backed down the steps, quickly searching out Kas. The woman was in the process of erecting her tent and Sitain lingered for a few minutes, following instructions until it was done and she could abandon her bag there to find Lynx again.

She found him hovering at the side of one fire, a white-haired woman in a blue shawl warming a pan of fried leeks and potatoes over it. The tantalising aroma of fat was rising up in the air as dusk began to descend, and soon Sitain and Lynx had a stick of bread filled with the mixture to carry to their assigned flank of the camp.

Guarding the opposite side she saw the officer called Teshen along with a young recruit. Clearly Teshen's status wasn't enough to keep him off their commander's shit-list. Sitain ate her half of the bread as fast as she could, watching Anatin stamp up the steps of his caravan until Lynx gave her a nudge and pointed out to the darkening landscape beyond.

My commander now? she wondered as she finished up and handed the other half of the makeshift meal to Lynx. *If only for a few weeks? Do mercenaries let you leave when you want? Or am I just some camp follower and it's only the soldiers they care about? Gods, they don't expect me to fight, do they? Kill people?*

Her thoughts were broken by Kas sauntering over, jacket unbuttoned to a scandalous level. As both Sitain and Lynx blinked at her, Kas grinned and offered a sheathed dagger the length of her forearm to Sitain.

'For you, courtesy of your friends the Charnelers.'

'Why?'

'You're on guard duty, girl. Best you have some sort of a weapon and we're not giving you a loaded bloody mage-gun to wave around while we sleep!'

Sitain blushed, feeling stupid for even having asked, and buckled the knife-belt around her waist. Lynx finished his food and pulled his mage-gun out of the long leather sheath across his back. He thumbed the breech open, slipped a bolt inside and closed it up again, settling himself into some sort of long-practised pose, his arms almost folded and the gun resting on top.

'Thanks,' said Sitain as Kas made to return.

Kas waved it off. 'If I were you, I'd ask for some of the plunder too. Bastards stole you, after all, least you can do is steal something back.'

An image of demanding money from the dead-eyed Teshen appeared in her mind and her guts went cold. 'No, it's fine,' Sitain muttered.

'As you like.' Kas laughed. 'Enjoy guard duty, you two. I'm for a sleep.'

Still chuckling, she headed back into the camp and was soon swallowed by the hubbub of the mercenaries as they finished eating and some sort of card game was announced. Lynx and Sitain kept outside the perimeter of tents, not straying far into the gloom but staying well clear of the fire lights and lanterns which had been hung from brackets on the wagons.

Sitain couldn't help but look at the gun in Lynx's hands as the man gazed off into the dark. It was an unassuming shape, without decoration, and the barrel was almost as thick as her little sister's wrist. The wood of its stock was stained and scratched, the grey metal scored in several places. She tried to imagine the battles it had seen until he caught her looking and shifted the gun's position.

'So tell me about the magic, then,' Lynx said abruptly.

She blinked at him. 'Why?'

''Cos I'm curious. Don't know anything about your lot. Night mages, I mean. Certainly never met one.'

She scowled. 'It's not like anyone's taught me about it, I've only barely worked out what I'm doing at all.'

'Okay, let's try an easy one,' he said, unconcerned by her snappishness. 'What can you do? Put folk to sleep, like Himbel said?'

'Pretty much. Mebbe calm thoughts to help you sleep, or put you down if I've got the burst ready to hit you.'

'Burst?'

She shifted uncomfortably. 'That's what I call it, anyway. The magic comes from somewhere inside me, I need to drag it all together to use it in a burst like that. Like, ah, it's like drawing a deep breath, sort of – your body just knows how to do it because it was made that way. But here I'm drawing from every part of my body. I get a tingle under the skin and in the bones that I never noticed before I started to draw on it.'

'Sleep, eh?' Lynx mused. 'Calming thoughts. That could be useful to Himbel in more ways than he realises.'

'Why?'

'Company surgeon. If you can calm a man's thoughts to the point of him blacking out, that'd be useful to a doctor trying to treat the wounded. Pain'll kill some before you can do anything for 'em.'

Sitain shook her head. 'I don't have that much control over it. I wouldn't dare.'

'Maybe you need more practice first,' he said with a shrug. 'Though for some, anything'd be a mercy once they're wounded. You practising ain't going to cause any more pain. Always takes me a while to go to sleep if I've taken the first watch. Someone who could put me straight out and get me a half-hour more sleep might be a useful friend.'

She gaped at him. 'Are you mad? You'd happily let me practise something like that on you?'

He paused. 'Good point. We'll try it on Deern first, just in case something goes wrong. What about cartridges?'

'What about them?' The lurch in subject matter threw her completely and Sitain had to remind herself not to snap at him. She knew this stranger was the best friend she had now, her patron inside the mercenary company and her best chance to remain free from the Charnelers, so she had to put up with him.

'Can you make 'em? Night-bolts – bullets that mebbe put a man out rather than kill him? A gunsmith told me once that it was the magic that killed; they use porcelain balls 'cos they shatter into dust straight away and help carry the magic at speed. That means a night-bolt might knock 'em down without killing.'

'Well, perhaps,' she hazarded, 'so long as you have someone to teach me and the materials to manufacture the cartridges. Oh, and of course a fragment of some god's shattered mortal form to focus my magic and store it in the charge-glass!'

He nodded. 'Good point, I forgot about the god-fragments part. Ah well, it was a nice idea, I guess.'

Lynx nodded with his head towards the tall silver birch that marked the southern tip of their small camp. In the dull glow of the Skyriver the tree's bark shone like a ghost, where it wasn't shaded. Following his lead Sitain walked with him in that direction, the slow amble of people with no real destination. The moon had not yet risen so the Skyriver was still the brightest thing in the sky. Graduating strata of silvery-grey cut across the southern half of the sky, gauzy and insubstantial for the main but studded with small discs that made it easy to follow the slow spin of the Skyriver around the world.

'Which is yours?' Lynx asked, pointing up. 'Don't they say that's where the magic comes from? Mother Skyriver's blessing?'

'So they say,' Sitain said, squinting. 'But if that's true, there's more types of magic out there than anyone knows about.'

Currently visible on the Skyriver were about a dozen small discs, each much smaller than the nail on Sitain's little finger when her arm was outstretched. Drifting like flotsam, the shade and course of each was unique and students of the heavens could easily identify them all. Sitain only knew the five largest, which were named after the shattered gods, and the relatively small one that trailed the path of Insar the Cold. Insar's priests named it as their god's consort, or child of Ulfer, rather than its true name of Atul, for the magic of night balanced both cold and calm order.

'It's not risen yet,' she said after searching the sky. She pointed at a yellow-tinted dot halfway to the Skyriver's zenith. 'Look, there's the Fire Lord. Mine follows Insar on the Skyriver, so she'll never share the sky with Veraimin.'

'I see it.' He cocked his head at her. 'You believe it?'

'That magic comes from rocks in the sky?' She laughed. 'As good an answer as any, I guess. Magic's got to come from somewhere, right? I've seen how the Militant Orders treat mages. Guess it wouldn't surprise me if there's more forms than the world's heard of, hidden away in some secret prison.'

She saw Lynx scowl and nod as he turned away, but before the man could say anything more he tensed and brought his gun up ready.

'What is it?'

He didn't answer so Sitain tried to follow the direction in which he was staring. The dark had stolen in quickly while they'd been talking and now they were surrounded by the tangled shadows of undergrowth, a spiderweb of contrast that seemed to pulse as her mind formed shapes around it. There was no movement that she could detect, nor sound, but something had prickled the instincts of the bulky mercenary and she had no intention of breaking the silence again. One gift her magic did bestow was night vision beyond excellent, but still she could see nothing. The only sound she could make out was the distant cough of an elk.

They stood still a long while, ignoring the dull chatter from the campfires behind, and Sitain felt her fingers begin to tingle. As she flexed her fingers the sensation only grew. A faint itch of warmth began to pervade them, something familiar, but it took a while to remember what it was. When she did, Sitain gave a tiny gasp that made Lynx tighten his grip on his mage-gun.

'Where?' he breathed.

'No,' she replied, 'it's not a danger.'

He didn't lower the weapon, but did turn to squint at her. 'No?'

Sitain shook her head. 'I've felt this before.'

'Felt what?'

'This, ah . . .' For a moment she was at a loss for how to describe it and just gestured for him to lower his gun. Once Lynx complied she beckoned him forward.

Ignoring his look of annoyance, Sitain picked her way forward over the clear ground beyond their camp. When the bushes started to thicken she paused and motioned for Lynx to crouch down beside her.

'What is it?' He glanced back, adding, 'We're too far from the camp.'

'Don't worry, there's no danger out here.'

'Sure? What *is* out here?' Lynx hissed.

'Something that would vanish if any Charnelers were sneaking up on us.' She gave him a smile, for the first time in a while feeling a burst of genuine happiness inside her. 'An elemental.'

Lynx swore and brought his gun up again, but she held her ground and put her hand on the top of the barrel. While Lynx was far stronger than she was, the act itself was enough to check him.

'What are you doing, woman?'

'It's not dangerous!'

Lynx scowled. 'Tell that to every single person who's reported seeing one and lived. Bloody things are wild and mad, they'll tear a man apart in a heartbeat.'

'This one won't.'

He looked at her as though she was insane. 'Why?'

The smile returned to her face. 'Because it's here to see me. It's a night elemental.' She put her fingers to her lips and turned her back on him, cutting off any further questions with a raised hand. There they waited, a dozen heartbeats, then a dozen more. She could sense the mounting frustration in Lynx, but she refused to pay him any attention. Her body felt as if it was coming alive, a sparkle of life filling her veins and lungs as the elemental came closer. Around them the darkness seemed to brighten and deepen at the same time, the magic singing through her body, unveiling a whole new spectrum of shadow to her.

She had only seen one twice before, just enough to treasure the memories and know what she was looking for. A flicker of movement caught her eye, darkness edged in a sliver of the Skyriver's light. It slipped forward through the trees, so black it was near-invisible but for the movement of its shard-like form.

The elemental was the height of a man but utterly different in every other way – without limbs or a body, just sharp lines and concealing shadows that were a deeper hue of black than the darkest night. It drifted on the breeze rather than walked – a multi-faceted and irregular jewel that seemed to sparkle with deepest amethyst and rich dark sapphire. Surrounded by a haze of shadow, what body it had consisted of flat shards of jet, open like petals but flittering and twitching like a butterfly's wings and never at rest, never quite of the world they existed in. The shadows seemed to blur with each movement, leaving echoes of each passing hanging faint in the air.

Behind her she heard Lynx gasp as he finally saw the elemental, past her shoulder, but Sitain could not tear her eyes away as it slipped closer, ignoring everything but her. She gently reached her hand out, feeling the magic in her body awaken and surge forward to meet it. The elemental came within touching distance and hung there for a while, glimmering and shining with the opposite of light, rather than merely its absence.

It made a jerky, flickering motion towards her and Sitain found her hand suddenly surrounded by the sharp lines of the night elemental. Under the gentle embrace of obsidian teeth magic began to mingle like the waters of an estuary, an embrace of kindred spirits as she let the elemental's power run through her body. It tasted cool and rich, a luxuriant oiliness flooding over her skin while she did the same and felt some part of her flutter through its shadowy shards.

How long the contact lasted she couldn't say. At some point she blinked and the elemental fled, winking away in staccato fashion, five yards away, ten, then gone entirely. The strange, crisp shades of darkness faded from the air and softer shades of night returned. Shouts and laughter cut through the air from the camp behind, but Sitain and Lynx found themselves transfixed still, basking in the unreal echo of the night elemental's presence.

'Now that was a thing worth seeing,' Lynx breathed behind her finally, putting a hand on her shoulder to let her know it was time to return.

Sitain nodded, glad tears beading at the corners of her eyes. She heard him move off at a stealthy creep and waited a few moments more, breathing deeply while she composed herself and wrapped this latest encounter in the cloth of her mind. Satisfied, she followed him back and they passed the rest of the watch in silence, content in what they had shared.

Interlude 3
(now)

The darkness erupted into thunder and flame. Lynx's head spun as the night was torn apart. His horse screamed as bursts of white arrowed past them. He was almost thrown from the saddle as the close-packed horses slammed into each other, barging with the force of hammers as they fought to escape. Light and movement whirled before his eyes, too fast to fathom, then Lynx was half-falling into the rider beside him.

Something struck his head as he was rocked sideways, then the world tipped and he was tumbling backwards. He caught himself on the rump of the other horse, his own crumpling beneath him, and would have dropped beneath its hooves had the other rider not hauled him roughly forwards.

A dragon's cough of flame washed over one side of his vision, searing orange and yellow as it burst into raging flames. Shouts came from all directions, then cries of terror. The group of horses came to a faltering stop, the lead horse crashing down dead ahead of them. Some swept on past, breaking away from the fallen, others reined in and fired off to the side. The rider to Lynx's left had stopped alongside him; Kas, cursing and scrambling clear from the corpse of her horse as it folded with a strange, quiet dignity beneath her.

Lynx looked at his own mount. It seemed to have sat down, rear legs neatly parked while its front pair scrambled frantically at the cobbled street. Blood was splashed all up his leg, a black flood erupting from the gut of Kas's horse while the edges of a ragged wound bore the white trace of frost.

Finally it made sense. An icer had punched through the heart of her horse, killing it before it knew what was happening, then gone on through into the rear of his own. A sudden sense of skin exposed to a freezing wind made him look down at his calf. His boot had been split down the back, leather parted but just a pink streak of frost-burn on the exposed skin where the icer had missed him.

'Just had 'em fixed,' Lynx mumbled drunkenly. 'Bastards.'

A great detonation came from above his head, beating his senses back into place. He looked up and saw the huge pale face of Reft, hairless features contorted like a gargoyle's as he raced to reload under fire.

Lynx snatched up his own gun and let his body take over. A flick of the fingers snapped the catch open, a twist of the wrist flipped up the lid of his cartridge box. The white painted cap of an icer winked in the moonlight as it slid home then vanished as he snapped it closed. He raised the mage-gun and paused a moment, just long enough to feel shock at the conflagration enveloping one side of the street. Fire spilled down the flank of a corner building, the ground windows blown in by the force of the burner shot. Inside it was already aflame and snakes of fire surged up the outer walls, seeking the inhabitants above.

There were bodies near the corner, one writhing and flailing at the flames dancing on their clothes. Beyond them he saw the startled white faces of Charnelers – their livery bright in the half-light. Lynx sighted on one and pulled the gun tight to his shoulder, leaning into the kick as he pulled the trigger. A slender path of white opened up in front of him as the gun roared, its fury briefly eclipsing all sound around him. The Charneler was still staring, frozen in the act of loading, when it struck him in the chest and he was hurled off his feet. A pale cloud of vapour was all that remained in the air.

'Regroup!' a loud voice yelled.

Lynx glanced over, reloading by feel. It was Olut, pale hair flying wildly as she fought to control her horse and aim a mage-gun at the same time. Toil was sprawled on the ground not far from Olut, hers having been the first horse to die. She was moving, but looked groggy and uncoordinated.

Anatin clattered back around after Olut, having more success controlling his horse than she was. He fired from horseback while in his wake came Safir and Teshen with their long guns booming. Kas sighted her bow as Lynx loaded. Out of the corner of his eye he saw one of the remaining ambushers stagger back towards the burning building, fletching protruding from his gut. The last two didn't wait to help him; they abandoned their guns and fled. No one wasted any more ammunition so Teshen tossed his spent gun to Safir and ghosted forward towards the wounded Charneler. A long knife appeared in his hands and he lunged forward mid-stride, piercing the man's heart in one neat movement. The Charneler gave a gasp of pain, then the blade was withdrawn and his strength seemed to flow out of him with his blood. He flopped forward and Lynx heard the crack of the arrow shaft as he fell on it, but by then Teshen had already forgotten the man and turned away.

'Injuries?' Anatin called after a moment of calm, pistol raised in case there were other attackers.

Reft went to Toil's side and eased her up in his huge hands. He bent low over her face then nodded to Anatin.

The mercenary commander slipped from his horse. 'Bad?' he asked Reft.

'Fuck the lot o' you,' Toil slurred from beneath the big man, hands flapping ineffectually at him. 'Am fine.'

For a moment she struggled to pull herself up then found the effort defeated her and sagged back. 'Mebbe I juss sleep here bit.'

'Four horses down,' Safir supplied, reloading and moving past Lynx to watch the way they'd come. 'That squad behind us won't be too long.'

'Lynx, can you walk?'

He frowned down at his leg and gingerly tested it. It was a little numb but he stamped some life into it and the limb seemed to be willing to take his weight. 'Better'n her,' he confirmed.

'That fire's going to bring every patrol in the city towards us,' Anatin said. 'Reft, put Toil on your horse. Tie her on if you have to. The rest of you, we run with the horses we've got left. You feel yourself slipping behind, call out and ride until you got your breath. Questions?'

'Ammo?' Teshan asked quietly.

Anatin snorted and gestured to the burning street. 'Oh sure, now let's be careful about setting the gods-cursed city alight!'

'You really want a firestorm on your soul?' Lynx interjected.

Anatin turned on him with a snarl and levelled his mage-pistol. 'The state o' my soul ain't your fucking concern! You got a problem with my command, tough shit. We need to get to the city gate and all we've got is firepower to do the job. It ain't high summer; folk'll just have to take their chances.'

Lynx didn't reply. Pointedly he reached into his cartridge case and pulled a sparker free. Before either of them could speak, Olut cursed and there was a shout from behind them. She raised her gun, horse now under control, and Lynx turned round to face the new threat. A pale face with a young man's beard and Assayer livery gaped at them from the corner of a building, weapon still pointed at the ground.

Olut's mage-gun roared and the man was hurled backwards amid a small cloud. Lynx dropped his gun and ran with his sword drawn to the alley mouth where the man lay dying. He checked at the corner, the falchion's broad curved blade pulled back across his body. The moment he saw a muzzle peek out from behind the corner he kicked forward at it. The weapon clattered from the man's hands and Lynx chopped down at the one who'd been holding it. He barrelled forward, using his bulk to barge through a lanky, greying man and lunge at the last of the Assayer patrol.

The sword caught her in the gut, a quilted tunic no protection against the steel point, and he felt flesh slice as she fell back. Lynx didn't pause, the hammer of his heartbeat pounding in his ears. There was a familiar jolt in his belly, that frantic roar of fear and rage that came in battle. He slashed wildly at the lanky man, driving him back as he took the blow on his gun stock. Teeth bared, Lynx put his shoulder into the man and slammed him off balance, punching at his balls before stabbing him in the neck.

The man fell, blood pouring from his throat, and Lynx paused, looking back at the woman he'd stabbed. She was lying face up on the ground, yellow hood fallen back to reveal a once-beautiful face now contorted in shock and pain. Her breath was coming in short, pained huffs, the stain of blood on her belly telling its own story. Lynx felt a cold sensation in his stomach but he forced himself to turn away, driving the sight from his mind. Maybe she'd live, maybe not. He wasn't going to finish her off. Only the crazed ignored a wound like that to continue the fight; she'd lie still and pray to Insar someone found her in time.

'You finished, butcher boy?' Olut called.

Lynx took a slow breath to let the fire in his blood cool. 'Shove it,' he growled. He wiped the blade of his sword on his sleeve then snatched up his gun again and slung it over his shoulder. 'We can't outrun mage-shot.'

Anatin gave a snort. 'Would've put an earther through the building myself, but however you like to get the job done, I guess. You Hanese do know how to kill, I'll give you that. We clear back there?'

'We're clear,' Lynx said with a nod. 'Save your earther for the city gate.'

'Aye. Come on then.'

Chapter 8
(then)

As the day's light faded around the turnpike inn on the last stretch of road towards Grasiel, the company pitched camp for the night. The mercenaries had been slow to settle, their spirits raised by the inn's provisions of beer and the new livery that Payl and Foren, the company quartermaster, had distributed. It was one many of them had worn before, kept packed away for instances such as this, where they didn't want to advertise their true identity.

As of that afternoon they had become the Steel Crows and patches bearing a black crow's head image had been roughly stitched over everything bearing a playing card. As ruses went it was modest, but in a city of merchants there would be a great number of travellers and little might be remembered beyond the name and insignia. Given what they planned to do in Grasiel, a city of competing factions in constant flux, it was likely this would be unnecessary. But things might not go as planned and Anatin had no wish to burn any bridges that might lead to future employment.

At one of the fires, there was only one mercenary left – a woman, smoking and staring into the flames. Braqe was so caught up that she failed to notice when she was joined by another and it was only when the newcomer pushed a twig into the fire to light his own cigarette that she jerked back into wakefulness.

'Deern,' she said, blinking slowly at him, white eyes bright against her dark skin and the gloom of dusk. 'Where'd you come from?'

'Thought you could use somethin' stronger,' the small mercenary replied. He pulled a slim bottle from his pocket and offered it over. 'Given the boss seems to have forgotten his loyal troops recently.'

'What're you talking about?' Her voice was slow and measured, but not slurred, the Wisp Dust she'd taken earlier meaning she could see swirls of shifting colours bleeding through the air around Deern's head.

'That fat one, Lynx, and the girl,' Deern said with a scowl. 'Shitty thing for the boss to do, if you ask me. You were at the Hand Valleys, no?'

She nodded ponderously.

'The girl?' Braqe asked after a long moment of thinking.

'You've not seen it?' His voice dropped low and conspiratorial. 'Bitch is from So Han too, half-caste anyway but with that lot it's all the same. It's in the blood with them, ain't it?'

'The girl's Hanese?' That made her sit up a bit straighter. 'I didn't know. Fuck.'

She took the bottle and flipped the top open to sniff the contents. Moonshine of some sort, but not the gut rot that was normally sold to mercenaries.

'Aye, heard her myself, but you go have a look at her face, beneath all that hair she's Hanese all right.'

Braqe took a swig of the moonshine and closed her eyes to savour the fiery liquid as it slipped down her throat. 'Good stuff,' she said eventually. 'Where'd you get it?'

'Made nice with one o' the bar girls.' Deern grinned. 'Uppity cow wouldn't lift her skirts for me, but she sold me some of this at a good price instead.'

Braqe nodded and was lost in the flames for a long while again, letting the flow of her thoughts drift with the colours that danced above the fire. 'So, two Hanese in the company. That's bad.'

'You fought them, didn't you?'

'If you can call it fighting. Bastards tore us apart.'

The colours seemed to fade as her memory took her back to the war, the rain-sodden nights and short, frantic days of fighting retreats that had been all she'd seen of the fighting. 'They strung up all those they caught, hung 'em from trees, opened their guts and let the birds feast while they were still alive.'

Her hand tightened as though she held a gun rather than the bottle of moonshine. 'I had to cut my own brother's throat,' she said, voice choked with the memory. 'What they'd done to him, it was a mercy to finish him off, but . . .'

'But that weren't war, it was a slaughter,' Deern finished. 'I'm just sayin', I got your back if you want to do something about it.'

'Kill Lynx?'

'Risky, man was a commando. Just the sort who killed your brother, most likely.'

She turned to squint at the weasel-faced man. 'What, then? Boss clearly wants him around, Teshen too.'

'Must be something we can do. Sell him out to the Charnelers, mebbe? Grasiel's got lots of Militant Order types, probably Charnelers among 'em.'

She shook her head. 'Won't bring that shit down on my comrades, no chance.'

'Course not,' Deern said, 'but the right word in the right ear, mebbe? Could be we make some money off selling both of 'em out.' There was an eagerness to his voice now, a hunger that sounded almost sexual to Braqe's ears as the slow fizz of Wisp Dust caressed her mind.

'And say what?'

He shrugged. 'We passed 'em on the road, close enough to the truth. Might be Lynx slipped off at night, came back with a full purse and some half-caste girl in tow. He's some sort of exile, easy enough to believe he's kept the old ways alive and reckons she's his property, couldn't stand to see anyone else take her as a slave. You mention she's a mage and they'll be keen enough to get her back.'

'And you'd back me up? Thought you didn't like my kind?'

Deern looked outraged at the suggestion. 'You're solid, been with the company a long while. You proved your worth to us all and I've got no beef with you. That bastard Himbel I hate, sure, but it ain't for the colour of his skin. Miserable shite's always had it out for me, and Kas opens her legs for half the goatherds she passes on the road. I got no respect for either, but I don't hold it against the rest o' you.'

Braqe nodded and took another swig before handing the bottle back. 'Kas is all right.'

'The woman can fight,' Deern conceded, 'and that's what's most important, that you can trust who's beside you – who's giving you orders. Don't mean I have to like her personally to trust her scouting.' He took a big mouthful of moonshine, grimacing slightly at the kick, which made Braqe smile.

'True,' she agreed. 'Anatin knows I ain't the only one who fought 'em. Mebbe I should do something about it.'

'And if we get a small reward in the process,' Deern added, eyes watering slightly, 'that's all the better, and less than So Han owes you.'

'I'll think about it.'

Deern bobbed his head in understanding. 'The call's yours, just thought you deserved to know who might be watching your back one o' these days. I heard Lynx tell the girl she should cosy up to Himbel, get him to teach her healing and bone-setting. Doesn't sound like she'll be moving on so fast if she becomes his apprentice.'

As the moonshine warmed her belly, the Wisp Dust seemed to wax stronger and the air was filled with light drifting on the slight breeze. Soon she was lost in her private pleasures again and never even noticed Deern slip away. The fire burned and the drug carried her up on the warm air, far away from the knot of anger in her belly, until she eased herself back and sank down on the bed of grass behind her, eyes slowly closing as the Skyriver burned overhead.

*

'Have you been to a city before?' Lynx asked.

He spoke only just loud enough for Sitain to hear over the sound of a recruit arguing with Deern over the rat content of bread. A few others were chipping in with helpful comments to ensure the argument continued, gleefully stoking the fires of irritation. The day was much like the last; dull cloud and yet more road ahead of them, but finally they were nearing their destination and spirits were high at the prospect. The faint trace of smoke and muck had been on the breeze all day, a sure sign they were nearing civilisation.

'No, why?'

Lynx ignored the defensive note to her voice. He'd been expecting it. A farm girl like Sitain would've hardly seen a town of note, but no one liked to have their inexperience pointed out.

'Can be a shock is all,' he said calmly. 'I was scared by the size of it the first time I saw one – and I was attacking it at the time.'

'During the war?' Sitain asked in a quiet voice.

'Yup. Guess you heard more'n your fair share about that, did you?'

She shook her head. 'My ma wouldn't have talk o' So Han. She got out well before the war, was married to Da long enough that few got in her face about all the rumours.'

Lynx grunted. 'Good. None of it was her fault, but that doesn't stop most.'

'What was it like?'

121

'Brutal.' Lynx surprised himself by how quickly he replied. It wasn't his favourite subject, the war, but it was behind him now at least. What followed was a rawer memory and one he wouldn't discuss freely, but in recent years he'd found himself able to separate out the two.

'Not much of a war, either, more a conquest. We were just gobbling up principalities for fun it seemed, faced by untrained and poorly equipped troops most of the time. The Militant Orders were tougher, but they weren't ready to bring the fight to us once we were dug in like ticks.'

'And then it all fell apart.'

Lynx nodded. 'Tribes weren't so united as our glorious leader had thought. Nor were his sons, come to think of it. Man thought they were loyal to the death, but once they were out of his shadow and lords of the new lands, they changed their tune quick enough. Were having too much fun for obedience to be the order of the day.'

'So you left? Deserted?'

'I left,' Lynx said curtly. 'Had seen through it all by then and wanted none of that life. Been on the road ever since.'

Sitain sighed and ran her fingers through her hair, an affectation she'd acquired since Kas had cut her hair as short as a boy's, only down to her ears rather than the long curls she'd once sported. They had nothing to dye it with, but in Grasiel there would be a variety of choices and until they found something, in the city itself she'd wear a scarf over her hair. She already had a knife bandolier over her clothes to make her look more like a part of the company.

'And the road brings you to Grasiel,' she said in a strange, wistful way.

'The road brings you all places, if you want it to,' he replied. 'Today it's Grasiel, just a place like any other. It's the people in those places that matter.'

'Grasiel's like no other place I've seen,' she reminded him. 'Have you been there?'

'Once. It's big and messy, so far as I remember. Easy to get lost so stick to the outer districts. I don't know if the Knights-Charnel have any way of sniffing you out, but best you don't find yourself getting questioned by the guards of some merchant palace or chapterhouse for not knowing where you're walking, eh?'

'I'm not stupid and you're not my da,' Sitain snapped.

He bit down his irritation. 'I ain't trying to be,' Lynx said, 'but surprise makes a fool of us all if we let it.'

She made an irritated sound and broke into a little trot, just enough to make a gap and put her close to Teshen at the head of the group of Tempests. There was little in the way of column order with the Cards so that caused no interest from the rest, but Lynx still found himself swearing under his breath at her. The first time he'd been in a city as anything other than part of the army sacking it, he couldn't stop tripping over his feet as the press of humanity ebbed and flowed around him.

But she's right, she ain't my daughter, Lynx told himself. *So if she wants to do something stupid and get herself taken, or worse, it's not on me. There's the job at hand and that's all – not Sitain and not Kas either, come to think of it.*

He looked up and saw a grey haze in the distance, the marks that only something as large as a city could leave on the sky.

So mebbe a day or two rest there? Anatin resupplies the wagons, hits up his contacts in case there's word of more work going while Payl and Teshen scout the job. Doubt this lot will be happy unless they get a couple of nights gambling under their belts either, which means they'll be in no state to do anything useful afterwards.

He brightened. Cities meant bookshops and a merchant city like Grasiel would have a few printing presses, which would mean several shops. Books were heavy when you walked most

123

places and he could only justify the weight of one in his pack. His current had lasted him three months and he was keen to trade it in for something new. With his share of plunder from Commander Ntois he could more easily afford that. In the lean years he'd not been so lucky.

From up ahead came a shout, the order to halt being relayed back to the rear of the group so by fits and starts the mercenaries stopped. Lynx saw Anatin swing up into the saddle of his horse and ride down the line until he was near the middle. There he stopped, his force of forty-odd small enough to address all together. He gave one final check up and down the road but the only travellers within sight were a family with a wagon of vegetables up ahead.

'Right – you all remember what company you're in? The Steel Crows, right? And is anyone unclear about whether we're here to work or fucking play?'

There was a bark to his voice there and even Lynx, new to the company, could tell the man was deadly serious. Best to get in and out as fast as they could, before too much bad luck could follow them up the road. If other Knights or a Charneler patrol discovered the bodies, they might well hurry along to either catch the murderers or inform the Knights-Charnel chapterhouse in Grasiel.

'Good,' Anatin continued after a glare round at his troops that ended on Lynx. 'We'll be taking lodgings and you'll all fucking stay there tonight, hear me? There'll be drink, whores and a game but it stays at the inn. No running into old comrades in the city's pubs, Varain; no picking fights with watchmen, Safir; no getting caught up in a criminal underworld blood feud, Teshen; and certainly no dragging Reft to any sort of bloody pit-fighting arena, you hear me, Deern? We're on a job and no one mentions the company's name or gets themselves noticed until we're clear.'

A grumble of assent rolled around the company like far-distant thunder, but it seemed to satisfy Anatin and he waved the column on again. Lynx paused, half-expecting to be called over by the commander and chewed out a little more, but Anatin simply bestowed one final baleful look on him and reined around to retake his place at the fore of the company.

The afternoon was well under way by the time they reached the city wall – or what passed for a city wall anyway. Grasiel was a merchant city, ruled by men and women of trade and one of many that had seen the folly in impressive defences. Instead they had only a nominal wall and relied on their importance to the region to be their shield, with mostly consortium guards keeping order on the streets.

The outskirts bled into the fields beyond, most of which were occupied by mismatched villages of tents and wagons. Within the chaos it was possible to identify the various flags, symbols and liveries that defined fiefdoms of the merchant princes who controlled each district and made up the Council of the Assayed – judged by their peers to be rich enough to decide the city's laws.

From the highway they were travelling on, Lynx could see much of what characterised the city. A drover clan controlled their left flank, red and blue fetishes in the wild sandy hair of its blue-eyed guards, while on the right was a mining family's domain, expansive hoods shading the pale faces and black eyes of its custodians. Grasiel was dominated by two tribes, the Asann and the Surei, who controlled the major trades and tried to ignore the existence of each other. So while there were no great walls to the city, many districts were made up of enclosed compounds which, at times of tensions, folk like Lynx would be hired to protect.

The streets running off the highway soon evolved into a tight urban sprawl of mud brick, their only impediment to entry being a pair of yellow-caped Assayers, officials of the Council of the Assayed. They were a pair of tall Surei women in quilted jackets with holstered mage-pistols, the hoods of their capes raised to display the symbols of the city. Their interest was more in service of trade than anything else in these lesser parts of the city. Upon discovering the Steel Crows were only passing through the city, they lost interest and waved them towards a large copper-roofed building on the Asann side.

Lynx had expected that much. The Asann controlled most of the things mercenaries were interested in after a long march and he was far from unhappy about that. The city's forges would be Surei-owned, and anywhere metal was being shaped you'd find Knights keeping a discreet eye on things.

It took a long bout of haggling to secure space for the entire company, both Anatin and the innkeeper seemingly unaware that they were effectively blocking the street until the Assayers stepped in. At that point the two immediately agreed on a compromise price and the Steel Crows started to clatter through the wagon-sized archway, calling for beer.

The faces of the inn's other guests told a rather less welcoming story, but the sight of Payl bellowing her troops into order seemed to alleviate matters. With the count at forty-four in the company they easily outnumbered the other patrons and unit discipline would be the only thing preventing trouble. The main part of the inn was a three-storey building on their right, abutted by a wooden bunkhouse, while ochre bricks peeked out through breaks in a curtain of viper rose around the perimeter until it reached the stables on the far side. The wagons were backed up beside that under a battered slate roof, then the horses taken off to be cared for.

As the tables along the inn's side of the courtyard quickly filled with thirsty mercenaries, Lynx followed Teshen and several of his fellow Tempests – no, not currently, right now they were Shrikes – towards the bunkhouse where a shirtless and grinning young lad waved them forward with exaggerated gestures.

'You watch the bunkhouse?' Teshen demanded of the youth. No more than twelve years old, he was so tanned it seemed unlikely he'd ever worn anything more than his ragged trousers, which made his brilliant blue eyes all the more startling.

'I do, sir – come, take your beds. Clean blankets, no lice, and the snakes eat all the rats!'

Lynx almost laughed before he realised the youth was offering his hand forward. Curled around his arm was a dusty-brown snake, tongue questing out towards the mercenaries.

Teshen gave the youth a level look. 'Make sure my blanket's cleaner than everyone else's,' he said, 'and you keep a good watch on our kit. Every one of us has their cartridge count in their head.' As though by magic he produced a blade. Lynx barely saw his hands move; one moment they were by his side, the next Teshen had a knife blade touched to the back of the snake's head. 'Or you'll find out I really am faster'n a snake.'

The youth's eyes widened at that, his air of confidence shaken enough that he just swallowed and bobbed his head.

'Good,' Teshen said, a little more gently. 'What's your name, boy?'

'Calil, sir,' he said with downcast eyes, touching protective fingers to the unharmed snake.

'I'm the Hammer of the Steel Crows,' Teshen said. 'Any o' these fucks mess with you, you just let me know, right? I set a high value on anyone who brings me clean blankets.'

The youth nodded and scuttled inside. Teshen gave his subordinates a cold grin and followed. Soon they each had assigned bunks – nothing in the way of privacy, but at the back of Lynx's mind was a hope that he'd not be sleeping there anyway. Through the open shutters of the window came a gust of wind and the sweet flavours of onion, garlic and pork, frying somewhere in the inn. As Lynx turned to breathe it all in his stomach rumbled loud enough for Braqe to look up from where she was and snort.

'No one better get between fat boy and his dinner,' she muttered.

Lynx looked at the wary faces that turned his way, anticipating trouble, and gave his ample belly a slap. 'Can't argue there, I'm a man of appetites.'

Before she could reply he tossed his tricorn on to his bunk and theatrically pushed his sleeves up, declaring, 'Now all o' you get out my way! There's beer somewhere out there needs hunting down.'

He swept out, noting the smothered smiles as he went but mostly just keen to leave the argument behind. The courtyard was bathed in sunlight as he emerged and he slowed, blinking around at the milling mercenaries, before he spotted a broad woman with a tray full of battered tankards. He headed over, noticing a slate with tally marks by the door that indicated they'd gone through a dozen tankards already.

So this is on Anatin, Lynx thought as he pushed his way forward and grabbed a beer. *Until pay day that is, I bet. Never known a merc captain who wasn't tight-fisted and sneaky and I doubt I've met one now.*

As he got comfortable on one of the benches, he spotted Sitain lurking away from the rest of the mercenaries. The young woman had her arms wrapped tight around herself as she watched the unruly crowd, then glanced at the open gate. Lynx sighed inwardly as he realised she was debating with herself if she wouldn't be better off alone, but before she came to a decision he caught her eye.

Sitain froze like a rabbit in an eagle's shadow, a flush of guilt in her cheeks before she could help herself, but Lynx only raised his tankard and pointed to it, beckoning her over. There was a moment of agonised indecision writ large across her face, then her shoulders sagged and she walked forward. Lynx got up, scooping up an unclaimed beer and heading round to meet her.

'Stay for one night,' he said, holding the beer out. 'If you want out, fine – I'll even help.'

Her resignation turned into astonishment. 'Don't you understand? I don't want your help. I don't know you. You're not responsible for me!' Her voice softened a touch. 'I owe you for those Charnelers, I know that, but I'm responsible for me. I got sold out to them by someone in my own village, someone I must've known my whole life, and that'll happen again and again if I rely on anyone but myself.'

Lynx raised his hands and backed off a step. 'Fine. That's how you want it, I'm done. A man can only offer his help so many times. Not my fault if you're dumb enough to throw it back in my face, so bollocks to you.'

'Dumb?' she said hotly. 'Dumb to trust some stranger and the honour of his mercenary friends?'

'Dumb enough to think you'll do better by yourself,' Lynx snapped, 'in a city you don't know, with no friends and no money.'

'Fucking So Han types,' said a woman loudly behind him, 'can't help themselves but fight, even if it's with their own bastard kind.'

Lynx turned sharply, fists tightening. 'Get to fuck, Braqe, this is nothing to do with you.'

The mercenary gave him a scornful look. 'Except you're disturbing my drinking, fat boy.'

'Still not your business. If you want to take a swing at me, stop standing there with your thumb up your arse and get on with it. I've only been with the company a few days and I'm already bored to shit with your miserable face.'

'Hey!' Anatin called from across the courtyard. 'The pair of you, stow it.'

'You know she won't,' Lynx said, keeping his eyes on Braqe. 'Better we get it all out, right here.'

'Sure, that'll work well. One of you gets knocked down and we're all friends again. Happens all the time, I find. You'll discover a wellspring o' respect for each other and fight side by side for all the years of your life.'

Anatin stepped between them and pressed his fingers into the cheek of each until they turned away. Just in case there was any confusion over what would happen if they turned on him, the silent giant, Reft, eased into the commander's lee.

'The pair of you – don't speak or even fucking look at each other until we're out of this city and our job's done. The first one who starts something gets shot in the head, understand?'

'I've given years to this company!' the woman protested. 'And suddenly this tattooed scum swans in like some blessed son? He giving the orders round here? You too scared of this murdering shite to kick him out?'

'He ain't some blessed son,' Anatin said in a low, angry voice. 'He's far from that, but he's on the roster and I've got bigger things to care about than him. He stays until I say otherwise, and you know why?'

Braqe looked him straight in the eye and shook her head.

'It's because of you, Braqe – all down to you. I'd half-thought to tell him to get fucked and make his own way in the city, beat a separate path to us, but you've been whining for days and it's really pissed me off.' Anatin jabbed a finger into her chest. 'You don't give the orders round here. You don't get to decide who goes and who stays. I'm in command here and so long as you need reminding of that, the man stays. Now, walk away. Go inside and have a drink, eat some food and get ready to lose all your money once we start a game.'

Not wanting to give her time to reply in anger, Teshen appeared and slipped an arm over Braqe's shoulders to walk her inside. Braqe had the sense to accept his urging rather than shrug him off and Lynx watched them all the way into the main building before finally relaxing.

'Now keep your head down,' Anatin growled at him as the conversations at the tables slowly started up again. 'She fought in the Hand Valleys; she's got a right to hold a grudge against So Han—'

'Doesn't make it my fault,' Lynx replied, careful to keep his voice quiet and calm, 'and if that's what her grudge is about, you know she'll come at me again. You're the commander, I know that, but a man might observe that someone taking her gun away from her while we're in close confines could be safer for everyone nearby.'

Anatin paused. 'The observation's noted,' he said frostily, 'it'll be mentioned to Teshen.'

Lynx nodded, realising he'd be pushing his luck by suggesting anything more there. 'Curfew lasting beyond the morning?'

'There's work to do in the morning.'

'Any for me?'

'You'll do what your sergeant orders.'

'Aye, sir, sure there'll be something that can keep me out of the way.'

'Count on it.' Anatin stamped off towards the main building, but paused before he reached the door and caught the elbow of the waitress. 'That one pays for his own drinks,' Anatin said, jabbing a thumb back at Lynx.

She nodded and gave Lynx a level look. For want of anything to say he shrugged and raised his current beer in toast to her.

A small smile appeared on the woman's face as she started to gather up empty tankards and Lynx turned to Sitain.

'Now, where were we? Stupid and friendless, right?'

She gave a snort and shook her head. 'Oh shut up and give me that beer.'

Chapter 9

Sitain floated in the dimness of near-waking, adrift in sleep but tethered by some small thread of the world beyond. Her thoughts were clouds in a pre-dawn sky; dark, drifting formless shapes, while the glow of faint awareness edged the horizon. Elusive glimpses of shadow shards danced at the edge of her thoughts, the memory of the night elemental.

Her eyes jerked open. At first she could see nothing, then a grey outline of the bunkroom unfolded. There was a figure beside her bed, unmoving, the thin gleam of a blade in its hand. Sitain gasped, in shock, in fear, and the figure flinched. It took a step back and the weak light showed enough to outline a woman's face, broad build, dark skin – Braqe.

Braqe's mouth opened, but whatever she intended to say went silent. Sitain felt a tingle rise from deep inside her, an involuntary welling up that swiftly built and seemed to take hold of her body like a sneeze. She felt it run out to her fingers, sparkling motes of blackness distorting the air around her fingers. Braqe's eyes widened, a white gleam of fear echoed in the shine of her blade as she instinctively raised it.

Sitain threw herself against the wall behind her, scrabbling to be out of the knife's reach. As she slammed her shoulders into the wood the magic in her fingers spat out like venom. Fractured shadows swallowed Braqe and the woman reeled – fell back a step then folded and crashed to the ground.

Curses and shouts rang out all around the bunkroom. A figure jumped down from her right and for a moment the air before Sitain went black as a haze of magic burst out. When she could see again there was a man staggering drunkenly, she couldn't see who. Before he could fall someone else scrambled out of their bunk and grabbed him, ducking under the reeling man's shoulder.

Faces started appearing all around the room, shock and fear made grotesque in the gloom. Panic started bubbling up from inside her then the tingle of magic again. Sitain tried to back away but all she could do was wedge herself into a corner of the bunk's wooden frame. More and more mercenaries got up, growling curses, demanding to know what was going on, some just pointing accusingly at her.

'I . . . I didn't, I just . . .'

Words failed her in the face of mounting anger and fear, but before anyone could move or the magic demanded a release, Lynx shoved his way forward. The man wore only his small things, his pale belly rounded like an egg, hair wild and plastered across his face until he swept it back. The tattoo on his cheek was as black as midnight in the dark; it seemed to hover just above his skin as though it was some fragment of night magic that he wore as a charm. With one hand Lynx hauled back the mercenary nearest to Sitain, showing the power inside his bulky frame as he almost pulled the man off his feet.

'All o' you step back,' he growled.

The angry faces turned his way as he placed himself between the mob and Sitain.

'Are you fucking mad?' demanded one. 'Look at what she did to Braqe!'

'I saw it all right. I saw Braqe had a knife in her hand – she was standing over Sitain with it. I thought for a moment she was going to stick her, was reaching for my gun when Sitain woke.'

Lynx turned side on to point down at the discarded blade and his back caught what little of the Skyriver's light crept through the window shutters. Sitain gasped, not at the weapon but at the mass of lines and ridges that marked Lynx's back. There was barely a scrap of skin that was smooth flesh. From shoulder to buttock there was just a haphazard mess of scarring. A landscape of brutal and repeated punishment. Sitain had never seen anything like it but her hands trembled as she imagined the pain it depicted.

He heard her gasp and glanced at Sitain, his face tightening as he realised what she was looking at, but he didn't pause.

'She's a night mage,' Lynx continued. 'Someone check Braqe, my money's on her just being out for the count. She'll wake up with a sore head and that's all.'

There was a long pause before Himbel stepped forward. The company surgeon knelt at Braqe's side and put his fingers to her jugular.

'Alive,' the scowling, dishevelled man pronounced. 'Pulse is steady.' He straightened up then crouched back down and with two stubby fingers grabbed Braqe's upper lip, giving it a hard twist. The woman didn't move and Himbel was grinning when he stood again. 'She's not waking any time soon. You'll be useful when we get injuries, girl!'

'I don't give a shit about injuries,' another mercenary muttered, looking at Sitain uneasily, 'you keep your cursed magic away from me, hear?'

Sitain bobbed her head, still curled up on her bunk and too startled to speak, but Himbel shuffled forward before the woman could say anything more about Sitain's magic.

'You'll feel different after a battle,' the ageing doctor pronounced, 'whatever superstitions your head's filled with.'

'Sitain,' Lynx said, 'maybe best you get out of here for the rest of the night. Go find Kas and Estal, they took a room. Better'n this one waking up right in front of you anyway.'

135

'I'll stay up with Braqe,' Himbel said. He glanced over at the dazed man who was sat on the edge of a bunk, lolling with both hands wrapped around a support to keep him upright. 'Darm too. Guess I need to make some observations if this magic's going to be useful.'

Sitain didn't move. She found she couldn't tear her eyes off the woman she'd felled.

'Sitain,' Lynx prompted.

She flinched and stared up at the big man's face with incomprehension for a moment until her wits returned. 'Oh. Yes, okay.'

She had just a shift on because of the warmth in the bunkroom and suddenly felt vulnerable, but with her blanket wrapped around her shoulders like a cloak, Sitain managed to get out of bed and pick her way around Braqe before scampering to the door.

'Darm,' she said suddenly, surprising even herself. A few of the nearer mercenaries actually drew back at the sound before they realised she wasn't talking to them. The groggy man looked up, frowning as he struggled to focus on her.

'Sorry,' she said, at first just managing a whisper before she repeated herself. 'Sorry. She'd frightened me, then you surprised me. I didn't mean . . . well, I'm sorry.'

Darm, a red-haired white man with a spider-pattern tattoo on his chest, blinked at her as though he couldn't understand what she was saying, but eventually it filtered through to his confused mind. He gave a grunt and nodded, head sagging as though the effort to look and think was too much for his night-struck mind.

'You'll sleep if off,' she added, 'I did it to my brother once. Give it a few hours and you'll be fine.'

'Go on now, Sitain,' Lynx said. 'Everyone get some rest.'

*

Lynx failed to sleep. He watched Braqe's chest rise and fall, her limbs never moving throughout those hours of magical sleep. As the dawn light appeared and sounds of activity came from outside he sighed and slipped off his bunk. He would get no more rest, better he be dressed and ready for the day once Anatin found out what had happened.

He pulled on his clothes, draped his jacket over one arm and paused with his hand hovering over his mage-gun.

'Leave it,' Himbel yawned from his vigil beside Braqe. 'No shooting before breakfast.'

'So that's the rule,' Lynx said, 'I'd been meaning to ask.'

'Not where you're from, mebbe. You commandos did all your best work at dawn, no?'

Lynx felt his face fall. 'Yeah, we left the shitty bits for later.'

'She won't come after you with a gun,' Himbel advised. 'She won't come after you at all, not once Teshen hears about it I reckon, but she ain't one to shoot a man in the back.'

'Even me?'

'You ain't that special.'

'Tell that to my ma.'

Himbel chuckled. 'So that's why you left home. Mine was the same, bless her. If she'd had her way I'd have been too fat to leave town and too swamped by children to find time to try.' He stood and stretched his back, tilting his head to one side then the other and grimacing at the pops and cracks that came from his joints. 'Braqe's a different sort o' woman, but she ain't the type to murder you. She'll pick a fight mebbe, but you'll see her coming that's for damn sure.'

'What about earlier? Fucking looked like she was—'

Himbel cut him off with an angry hiss. 'Woman's a skilled soldier. If she wanted Sitain dead, she had more'n enough chance. That was all about herself and her memories. She fought in the Hand Valleys, never forgave your lot for that, but she had it under control or we'd be waking to Sitain's open throat.'

'I never forgave my lot for it either,' Lynx commented bitterly, 'seems no one gives a shit about that, though.'

'Funny, you'd think they'd be full of sympathy for a slightly different commando to the ones who butchered their friends and family.'

Lynx gave a snort and headed for the door. 'Want me to bring you anything?'

'I'm good, you go find your girl and sit on her 'til Teshen or Anatin feel the need to scream at someone.'

'Teshen screams?'

Himbel cocked his head to one side. 'If he ever does, you fucking run,' he said slowly. 'Leave the women and children behind and run for your life.'

Outside, Lynx discovered the soft light of dawn had lent a yellow warmth to the now tidy courtyard and he felt a moment of peace settle on his shoulders. He stopped in the middle of the courtyard and took in a few deep breaths, trying to shake off the nagging cloud of fatigue.

'Coffee?'

He turned in surprise to find the waitress from last night leaning out of a window, clearly in the middle of her morning chores.

'Coffee sounds good,' Lynx agreed.

'Sit out there and I'll bring you a mug. I'm mopping in here so you keep your boots out.'

Lynx hesitated a moment then realised if Sitain was coming down, she'd be passing this way most likely anyway. *Or she ran in the night and is long gone now. Either way, coffee will make the world a shade better.*

'Gladly,' he said with a smile. 'Got anything to eat too?'

'The baker's boy'll be along soon.'

'Guess I'll make myself comfortable, then.'

Lynx settled in and listened to the sounds of the inn and its patrons waking around him. With a tall ceramic pot of coffee and an end of bread, he was content to let the hubbub of the inn and the city beyond flow over him, exchanging grunted greetings to mercenaries as they passed or joined him at the table. Before Sitain arrived, however, the rather more formidable sight of Payl appeared in front of him. She didn't say anything at first, content to let him squint up at her and savour the sinking feeling in his gut.

'Is every day going to be trouble when you're around?' she said eventually.

'To be fair, there's been at least two that haven't,' Lynx replied. From Payl's expression, his levity wasn't helping. 'Hey, I don't always get to choose when trouble seeks me out and what Braqe does ain't my fault.'

'Doesn't mean you're worth keeping around.'

'Does that come from Anatin?'

She paused. 'He's determined you'll be useful for this job. If I were you, I'd think on that detail a while. He's never been one for giving much of a shit about anyone he doesn't know well.'

'Yeah, I hear you.' Lynx sighed. 'Orders?'

'For you? Keeping clear of everyone else may be the most useful thing you could do, but I ain't sending you on company errands with that girl in tow and I don't want her left alone much.'

'You could put her in Himbel's care, I think he wants to see what she can do.'

Payl frowned. 'So the pair of them can start knocking folk out to see what happens? Himbel's a good man, but he's not burdened with much of a conscience.'

'Is that how he ended up with a bunch of card-happy mercs?'

'Nah,' she said with a shake of the head, 'more a case of fucking every woman in sight for more'n a decade.' Payl gave him a brief grin. 'Oh yes, our Himbel was once a real charmer, handsome too.'

'Until?'

She shrugged. 'You screw around like you're running out of time, life'll catch up with you at some point and kick you in the fork. He's better this way, trust me.'

'Okay,' Lynx said. 'Well I doubt either Himbel or Sitain are in too much of a rush. Sure they can wait until someone starts a fight and needs patching up.'

'Don't even think about it.'

Lynx laughed. 'Didn't mean me, but point taken I guess. I could do with time in the city though, errands of my own to run.'

'Like?'

'Selling a book, getting my boots fixed. All quiet stuff, nothing that'll get me in trouble.'

'Will Sitain stay here, out of sight, while you're out?'

'I don't know her so well, but would you? This is her first visit to the city, any city.'

The Knight of Sun nodded at that. 'Take her with you, then. Keep a tight rein on her if she's going to stick with us. If not, tell her to go far and fast.'

'Understood.'

'And if you've got any company insignias – Card or Crow – lose them before you go out. We never heard of you if you end up getting arrested for picking a fight with some Charnelers.'

Lynx nodded and stood. 'I best go find Sitain then.'

'Get back before evening. Anatin's meeting his contact in the city, we won't pull the job tonight but we'll be starting on details.'

'Who's we?'

'The team. You, me and the other Knights of the company – Teshen, Reft, Safir and Olut—'

'Who?'

'Olut. Big woman, face like a mother bear whose cubs just got killed.'

Lynx paused, but the face appeared in his mind easily enough. A northerner with wild hair and heavy muscles that added to the ursine impression. 'Ah yes, gotcha.'

Payl raised a hand. 'As for the rest, Varain, Tyn and Kas. Nine in all. Shame your girl Sitain hasn't combat experience, her being a mage o' dark and all.'

'Night mage,' Lynx corrected. 'Dark mages are the ones they tell little mages about to make 'em behave, remember?'

'It's all fucking magic to me,' she said dismissively.

'Not if you meet a mage of dark, not if half the stories are true.'

'Fine, she's a night mage. Point is, she'd be useful, but we can't take the risk this time round.' She nodded towards the inn. 'Go and fetch her and the pair of you get scarce, enjoy the city – just leave your gun. That cleaver on your hip's fine, but don't wear a gun openly here.'

'Aye, sir. See you this evening.'

*

Lynx banged on the door of the room Kas and Estal had taken. He called Sitain's name and waited. When it was jerked open, it was the enticing smile of Kas that greeted him – her hair swept down over one shoulder and tunic half-unbuttoned in a way made Lynx think she'd been up and waiting a while to tease him.

'Morning.'

'No flowers?' Kas pouted, mostly succeeding in not laughing at the look on Lynx's face. 'Courtship in So Han must be a dull business.'

'Never, ever, go to So Han,' Lynx said gravely. 'They ain't ready for a woman like you.'

'Lucky for me So Han has come to my door then.'

'If I was here for you, sure.'

She tossed the door open and flounced away as though she was born to the stage. 'Spurned! Men, they're all the bloody same.'

In the narrow attic room behind her Estal sat on one of the two beds, pulling on her boots, while Sitain was hunched on a chair looking anxious with dark rings around her eyes.

'Didn't get much sleep either?' Lynx said with a smile. His warm and fatherly manner yet again failed to register with Sitain. She just looked up at him warily and chewed her knuckle.

'Come on,' he said, 'get your jacket on. We're heading out into the city.'

'He whisks her away, Estal,' Kas grumbled loudly from her bed, 'her just a mere slip of a girl and him old enough to be her father, while we just sit here and mourn our lost prime.'

'Oh shut up,' Estal moaned, bending over with her head in her hands so her white hair cascaded forward. 'It's too early and I'm too hungover to hear you playing with your newest toy, woman.'

Kas cackled at that, prompting another groan from her comrade, and turned away to gather her hair up and tie it back.

'The city?' Sitain asked suspiciously. 'I thought I was to stay at the inn?'

'Last night changed that. Payl wants us out for a few hours, give Braqe time to wake up and tempers to cool. So you're coming with me on a few errands.'

He cast a quick look at Kas who, very theatrically, pretended not to notice. Her grandiose game was a long way from anything he was used to, but there'd be no time for anything over the next few days and playing that up might be for the best anyway.

'Might as well show you the city's sights at the same time; eat at the hanging gardens, that sort of thing. All the sights a man might want to show a young woman.'

'I need the rest of my clothes,' she said, pointing at the blanket that still covered her shift.

He nodded. 'I'll fetch 'em. Best we get out of here before Anatin finds us.'

When he returned, Sitain was upright and more composed. Kas and Estal had left in search of breakfast so Lynx awkwardly handed the young woman her clothes and a bowl of porridge before retreating behind the door. He buckled on his sword and settled in to wait, unconsciously turning the silver ring around his finger until he caught himself.

It was a plain band as battered and unassuming as most worn by soldiers, but still it drew his eye. The three diamond shapes of the Vagrim seemed to stare back up at him, an unwelcome reminder of years past but one he had learned to live with. The ring had been given to him by an ageing soldier called Lorfen, along with the slim book that nestled in his jacket's concealed pocket.

He remembered that first meeting as though it was burned into his mind. Lynx had been at his lowest ebb, close to breaking point and as dangerous as a starved wolf. They all had been, the inmates of To Lort prison. Miles from anywhere, they had barely heard news of the army's collapse by the time foreign troops arrived at the gate and Lorfen was installed as governor.

All they'd known was the privations of the prison and hardship of the mine below it. The lack of food and water had become chronic in those last few weeks, the savagery of the inmates worsening with every passing day.

'I've been reviewing the files of every prisoner,' Lorfen had said as Lynx shuffled into the man's office, stinking and trembling at what was about to happen. 'Yours is an interesting case. A point of honour?'

Lynx hadn't replied. He'd not known what to say, but beyond that he'd had a fear of speaking to guards beaten into him. He'd stayed silent, looking at the floor.

'*You may speak.*'

Lorfen's voice had been gentle despite coming from the grizzled face of a veteran soldier. It had startled Lynx, unsettled and frightened him. He'd been there long enough that he'd forgotten kindness, had forgotten everything bar fear and violence.

Lorfen had commanded the guards to unshackle Lynx and leave them alone. He'd offered food and clean water, and the luxury of both had brought tears to Lynx's eyes.

'*A point of honour,*' Lorfen had continued at last. '*Your commander ordered the massacre of a village and you refused, perhaps? Ah, no, that doesn't fit what is noted here. You must have done something like call him a coward; had you simply refused an order you would be dead.*'

Still wary, his mouth crammed full, Lynx had briefly nodded.

'*So he challenged you to a duel, his honour impugned, and you killed him. Your superiors were undecided as to what to do with you, but killing a superior officer was a precedent they disliked so you were flogged and dumped here.*'

A shuffle of papers, the scent of dust and old leather still strong in Lynx's memory.

'*What reports there are of your time here support the idea that you're a man of honour. You killed a man trying to rape a fellow inmate, you stopped the murder of a new guard.*' Lorfen had sighed and put the papers aside at that point, looking at Lynx long and hard enough to make the once-stout soldier tense, ready for a beating.

'*The laws of So Han do not apply any longer, and the myriad offenders in this prison are now mine to dispense with as I see fit. I am going to release you – you've done nothing wrong, to my mind, and you can leave as you see fit. But first . . .*' He had paused a long while before seeming to win an argument with himself. *'But first, let me tell you about a man called Vagrim.'*

Lynx's reverie was interrupted by a prodding finger and the suspicious face of Sitain. 'So are we going or what?' the young woman demanded.

He sighed and pushed off the wall he'd been leaning against, leaving his memories lingering behind him. 'Yeah. Come on.'

Chapter 10

It was still early when Lynx and Sitain set out into the city. They made good time ahead of the day's crowds as the cool of autumn sparkled under a low sun. The main road continued a further half-mile into the city, where it ended in an enormous square with huge white archways dominating each side.

Lynx beckoned Sitain forward to a monument that dominated the centre of the square, a slender obelisk rising out of a stepped platform. She followed him up to within touching distance of the obelisk itself, its pale marble flanks inscribed with the names of the city's notable dead, lost during a war fought a generation ago.

'Good place to get a first proper view of Grasiel,' Lynx said, pointing out through the north and west arches.

Sitain turned and gasped. They were only about ten feet above the floor of the square, but the grandest parts of the city seemed to have unfolded in the morning light. She could scarcely decide which way to look first to drink in the sights and found herself turning left and right, mouth hanging open as she felt the vastness of the city all around her. She'd known her village was in a small and unimportant corner of the region, but to be presented with street after street, choked with people by the standards of her home, was like a punch to the gut. She had to rest a palm against the chill obelisk as a wave of dizziness broke over her, and the morning sun seemed somehow more dazzling.

'The Law Forums,' Lynx supplied, pointing to a blockish set of buildings sheathed in verdigris copper to the west. 'Above them, those white domes are the Maze Markets, where the big merchant houses trade.' He turned north to where the view was dominated by a spray of needle spires rising from several dozen palaces and lesser mansions, all built from a yellow sandstone that had turned golden in the morning sun.

'The island of the Assayed, and past it is the temple quarter. That white wall behind the pyramids of Insar, that's all sovereign ground of the Militant Orders, where we'll be keeping as far from as possible. There's no sanctuary in this city, no great presence of any Order so far as I'm aware, but I'm not pushing our luck.'

'Where are we going?' Sitain breathed, cowed by all she saw. The tangle of streets blurred into the distance and she had already passed ten times the number of people contained in her home village.

'Riverside, down that way,' he said, pointing to the western arch. 'Takes us to the printers' district, between the Forums and the markets.'

'You want a printer?'

'Bookseller.' Lynx hefted the bag he was carrying. 'Time to sell the one I've got and find something new.'

'You can read?'

'Surprised?'

'I, ah. Well, yes. I doubt most mercenaries can.'

'None of us were born soldiers. My da was a shopkeeper, taught me his trade and then some. Wanted me to be a merchant until the war came and changed everything.'

Sitain hesitated, unsure of whether she should enquire further, but Lynx caught the look on her face and nodded, though his face darkened slightly as though the shadow of memory had crossed it.

'Aye, the stripes on my back. Weren't fool enough to go home again. If I did, my da mightn't have turned me away, but that'd be a mistake. I'd not last long back there and I'd bring him nothing but harm.'

Lynx turned slightly away as he tailed off and Sitain realised that was as much as he was willing to say.

'Looks like neither of us can go home again,' she said in a small voice.

'Looks like it, aye.' He straightened and slung his bag over his shoulder. 'There's a whole world away from home, though. Some of it's worth seeing, too.'

*

Lynx left his boots at a cobbler they passed, put on a battered pair of Greensea moccasins and led the way to the printers' district. There they investigated the booksellers until they found one who served the poorer end of the market. None of the works on its shelves were new, some were in a very poor state indeed, but that only meant that Lynx found it simple to sell his and pass a while browsing for its replacement.

It didn't take Sitain long to get fidgety as she had little interest in the books herself, so Lynx took the opportunity to make use of the owner's local knowledge. He was a small man with thinning hair scraped over his head and round brass-framed spectacles perched on his nose that gave him a disapproving air.

'You know the city well?'

The man peered at him suspiciously then at the book Sitain held, in case the conversation was some sort of ruse. 'I do, sir,' he conceded. 'I've lived here my entire life.'

Lynx nodded in a manner he hoped was amiable. 'I heard a friend of mine settled here, man I knew from years back.

Opened an inn – called the Diamond Chequerboard or something strange like that. Ever heard of it?'

'I do not frequent inns,' the bookseller replied gravely. 'The name is not familiar to me, but the city is a large one.'

Lynx shrugged. It was perfectly likely there was no such place; he'd just mingled the names of two taverns he'd seen elsewhere. Both had been owned by Vagrim, the three diamond symbols subtly worked into their signs as a welcome to those who knew to look for it.

'Perhaps my boy knows of it,' the bookseller said, adding 'eleven silver arcs,' as Lynx pulled out a blockish history of the eastern bank wars.

'Eleven?' Lynx mused, having no intention of buying it at any price. 'Hmm. Is your boy around?'

'Suler!' the man called over his shoulder to the back room. A grunt came in reply, but then a similarly rounded face poked around the door jamb.

'Yes, Father?'

'This gentleman wondered if I knew of an inn called the Diamond Chequerboard.'

'Chequerboard?' replied the youth. He entered and blinked at Lynx, giving the sword on his hip a long and careful look. 'Not round here.'

'Maybe in a less distinguished area of the city?' Lynx hazarded.

'There's a wine shop called the Chequerboard up near the lesser river. Old men go there to play Stones.'

'The lesser river? Around the Island of the Assayed?'

'Aye, the common side. Never been myself, but a girl I know, Ifrain, her father plays there most afternoons. They take it real serious – small bets only, but you'll see the Assayed there even, so Ifrain tells. Only the best players bother trying their hand, those old Stones give no mercy.'

Stones was a game of tactics played on a black and white chequerboard with pebbles that represented the icers, burners, earthers and sparkers that made up the bulk of mage-gun ammunition. It was popular across the continent and one of the few ways a pauper could sit as equals with a duke, mastery of the game bringing respect from all quarters.

Lynx thanked them, leaving the book to one side, and briskly headed out with Sitain in his wake. She kept quiet for a dozen paces then tugged at his sleeve as his pace didn't falter.

'What's wrong?' she asked.

'Nothing. I just walk faster with somewhere to go.'

'Where's that?'

He sighed and slowed a touch. 'Might be they gave me the name of someone we can trust.'

'Trust with what?'

'With a certain person's secret,' he said with a level look at her. 'You'll not come in with me, I ain't stupid, but if they are who I think they are, they might be a good source for information.'

'Like what? You want to palm me off on some stranger?'

'Nope. I want to ask a stranger if they know of a network or refuge for certain folk, well away from prying Knights. It's a long shot, but a mercenary company ain't the safest place for you 'less you plan on learning how to fight. Might be we can find you an alternative and if not' – he shrugged – 'we were told to make ourselves scarce. Unless you want to look through shelves of books all day, we've got time to spare.'

The crowds had picked up a little by the time they found the large, elegant building that housed the Chequerboard. Like the rest of the street and the palaces across the diverted stretch of river serving as a barrier around them, it was built of yellow sandstone with large diamond-pattern windows that declared the wealth of the establishment.

Lynx was impressed. The chequerboard sign hanging outside it did contain diamonds of black, grey and white at the corners. Most likely a Vagrim owned the place, or at least once had. Given that most of his nebulous, unsociable brotherhood were poor wanderers like Lynx himself, it was unusual to come across one with actual wealth. The Vagrim inns he'd encountered before were clean and honest places, but that's as much as you could say.

'Best you hold back.' He nodded towards a stall in an alley where a tall polished samovar promised pale tea and honey-cakes to the servants of the area. 'Perch yourself there, have a second breakfast.'

Clearly unwilling to argue in the street with him, Sitain scowled and did as he suggested, leaving Lynx free to cautiously open the wine shop's double door and step inside. There were only a handful of patrons; two white-haired men bent over a Stones board and a trio of elegantly dressed women, three generations of a family Lynx guessed, breakfasting and smoking slender cigarettes at a corner table.

A sleepy-eyed Asann lounged at the bar, half-engrossed in a ledger but sharp enough to take in everything about Lynx in one look. He eased himself upright and nodded to Lynx, gesturing to the seat beside him.

'Drink, sir?'

Lynx took the seat and looked the owner up and down. One eye was milky-white, the skin around it marked by a sparker burn, but the rest of him was as neat and tailored as his rich customers. He was a native of the city, Lynx guessed – blue-eyed with blond hair running mostly to grey. The only suggestion of the Vagrim about him was a single stud earring in his left ear, a black diamond shape.

'Got something to wake the day?' Lynx replied, never having been a fan of beer in the morning, unlike many mercenaries.

'Of course.' The man waved a hand at the wine bottles stacked behind the bar. 'Even in the evenings, some of my patrons want a clear mind as they play. There's tea brewed.' He paused fractionally and his eyes turned towards the silver ring on Lynx's finger. 'On the house.'

Lynx smiled and placed a copper piece on the bartop anyway. 'Appreciated, but a man should pay his way when he can.'

The patron grunted in acknowledgement. The brotherhood had no rules beyond honour, but there were small traditions most followed to keep interactions simple and respectful. Wearing his ring in here meant Lynx would be offered a drink for free, but to reassure his host it wasn't just jewellery meant he would pay all the same. If he didn't have any money, he'd work for the kindness instead – after which, charity towards a brother might still be forthcoming, given that was the main purpose of the Vagrim.

'My name's Sujennet,' the owner said as he rounded the bar to fetch Lynx a clay cup. 'Just arrived in Grasiel?'

'I have.'

'Looking for work?'

Lynx shook his head. 'That I've got, but I've a problem too.'

'Broken some law?' Sujennet said, a touch more quietly. Lynx saw he pointedly didn't comment on Lynx not giving his name, but his eyes grew wary.

'None of this city's,' Lynx said dismissively. 'I've found myself responsible for another, one who's done no wrong but others wouldn't care about that.'

Sujennet nodded and handed Lynx a steaming cup of tea. The bulky mercenary accepted it gratefully and sipped tentatively at the pale liquid.

'Life's done me a few favours,' the older man said, spreading his hands to indicate the wide, sunlit barroom they were sat in. 'Might be I'm in a position to help someone in need.'

Lynx hesitated. The man was Vagrim, he had no doubt about that, but he didn't know him still. It was hard to just blurt Sitain's secret out to a stranger, but he didn't see much alternative if he did want help.

'My friend's got an unusual ability,' he began. 'Some might pay good information to track him down.' *Best I pretend it's a man, in case anyone sees us in the street later.*

Sujennet nodded, understanding. 'To make sure he says his prayers every day? I know the type.'

'It occurred to me there might be a few sympathetic citizens in Grasiel, those who thought his right to live free and practise his art might be worth taking an interest in. Maybe as a native who hears the gossip, you might know of some.'

Sujennet gave him a long, hard look. 'How about some pastries?'

Without waiting for Lynx to reply, the man stood and fetched a large bowl from behind the bar, carrying it across the room to the furthest table. Lynx followed, a little confused, as Sujennet sprawled in a large armchair and made every sign of settling in. Once Lynx did the same, Sujennet offered over the bowl and Lynx accepted a twisted strip of pastry covered in tiny white seeds.

'It's funny you ask that,' the older man said at last.

'It is?'

'Aye. Mind if I ask a few more questions?'

Lynx shook his head.

'I remember a tale I was first told almost thirty years back, about a man and a turtle he found on a beach. You heard it?'

Lynx nodded. 'I have,' he said, realising Sujennet was testing him. 'Fishermen got angry with him for returning it to the water. They'd planned on cooking it.'

'That's the one.' Sujennet gave him a long look. He didn't bother finishing the story, it was a minor tale in the history of the first Vagrim, but it at least proved Lynx had read the book hidden inside his jacket. 'I ask because, though I'm not active among them, I've heard of the citizens you mention. Surei in the main, working through a temple of Banesh.'

Lynx had a sinking feeling. 'And?'

'And they've been awfully quiet in recent months. Almost like the recent increase in Knights-Charnel has had an impact on them. Might be they're just lying low, but one or two used to play here on a regular basis and they've been absent a month or more.'

'Doesn't sound encouraging – for anyone.'

'Nope. But you're not here 'cos of the Charnelers?'

'First I've heard of it.' Lynx leaned forward. 'There trouble coming?'

'Allegiances within the Assayed are never fixed; all it takes is one grasping or pious bastard to upset the balance. But that's always the case and it might be the Charnelers are up to something entirely different. There's a Charneler sanctuary maybe three weeks ride to the south, a Brethren of the Shards fort on the shores of Lake Udrel – coldest dark, there's more'n a dozen explanations if you start to think. All I know is there's a lot more Knights-Charnel around these days.'

Lynx nodded glumly. The underground mage networks were a better-known myth than the Vagrim. While Lynx had never come across one, a place of industry like Grasiel would have been a likely place to find it. He doubted there really were secret mage guilds, as some of the more fanciful tales suggested, but any alternative would be better than a Charneler sanctuary. Unfortunately, the Charnelers knew the myths too and if they were actively hunting mages again, those networks would be targets. Lynx had no idea of the truth to any of it, but it didn't really matter. Whatever was really happening in Grasiel – and

Sujennet was right, it could mean anything or nothing – the option was closed to Sitain.

*

'Hey, you.'

The man in the black and white livery of the Knights-Charnel of the Long Dusk turned slowly. The heel of his palm pressed on the brass butt of his mage-pistol. He gave Deern a long hard look then checked around him in case he was being distracted. Deern grinned at him and slipped his boots off the other chair at his table, nodding towards it before swallowing another large mouthful of beer.

The Knight slowly walked over. Unusually for the Militant Orders whose origins were more northern, he was a dark-haired Surei; tall and lithe, with high, pretty cheekbones and a flawless complexion.

'You want something?' he said with distaste.

'Buy me a drink,' Deern suggested. 'It'll be worth your while.'

'I doubt that.' He made to turn away but Deern reached out and caught him by the arm. 'There's one o' me and five o' you,' he said rather more gravely, nodding to the group the Charneler had been returning to. 'Think I'd piss you around when I'm outnumbered?'

The young Knight looked down at Deern's hand. The mercenary waited a moment longer then opened his fingers to let the arm slide free. 'Tell me what you want,' he advised, 'and I'll decide if it merits a drink or a beating.'

'Fair enough.' Deern forced the smile to stay on his face. 'In the meantime, take a seat.'

The cocky young shit looked and sounded like some sort of nobility, of whatever sort they had in this merchant city. It was unlikely he'd ever been in a proper fight before. If it wasn't for his friends back there he'd either have checked the attitude or been facing a beating of his own. Deern was easily the smaller of the two, but a confined barroom was home territory for him. Reft kept him out of trouble often enough it was true, but few appreciated that trouble could just as easily be fighting a little too dirty for the local law to tolerate.

The young Charneler gave the chair a brush with his hand and eased himself down, keeping his mage-pistol within easy reach, but Deern only chuckled and poured him a beer from the pitcher on the table.

'I'm here to proposition you.'

The Surei scowled. His tribe were the more conservative and religious half of the city, but at least he had the sense not to be riled. 'Start talking.'

'You're a ranked man, right?'

The Knight tilted his head towards his shoulder where two gold studs lay, signalling a lieutenant of the Order. His collar was red too, which was why Deern had picked him. Not a regular officer, but a man of the Torquen.

'Right, so you can find me someone important to speak to.' That didn't amuse the Charneler and Deern had to restrain a laugh at the young man's stony expression. 'No need to pout, but you'll be wanting to find a paladin or captain once you hear what I've got to say.'

'And what's that?'

'I know of a rogue mage in the city.'

The Charneler blinked. 'Rogue?'

'Yeah, might be she killed some of your lot too. She was under escort by some, then later she weren't.'

'Where was this?'

'Road towards Janagrai. We passed 'em during the day, four Knights-Charnel, mebbe five. I didn't think to count.'

'And later?'

Deern gave him a cold smile and leaned forward. 'And later is what I tell someone who'll be able to pay me for the information, understand?'

'You can lead us to her?'

'And the man who I figure must've killed some of yours when he helped her escape.' Deern shrugged. 'In case you're interested.'

'Your price?'

'Ten gold rings – and a promise. The rest of us weren't involved, but the Orders ain't much known for restrained retribution. You take one or both how I say, so none o' the rest o' us get dead, plus half the neighbourhood given how some of my lot always keep a burner ready. For preference they'll be on their own so no dumb bastard even considers putting up a fight.'

The young man was quiet a moment then he nodded. 'I will put your terms to Exalted Uvrel, but if one is a mage and the other a murderer, I believe they will be accepted.'

'I'm a reasonable feller,' Deern declared, reaching for another drink. 'But I do like a drink, so tell the Exalted to hurry up. And not to forget his purse.'

*

A trough-like platter of food was placed on the table between Lynx and Sitain and her stomach voiced the growl of hunger that she'd felt building half the morning. There were a dozen twisted dumpling parcels with steam pouring out of them, flanked by lettuce leaves filled with a red, pungent mince, neat piles of cured meats and pale nuggets of cheese singed golden at the edges. The legs of some small game birds were arranged in a crown on a striated bed of grilled leeks and peppers, crisped wedges of pork belly and fat fingers of bread stacked all around the platter.

'Gods,' Sitain breathed, 'I see how you keep your figure.'

She sat cross-legged at one corner of a U-frame bench, Lynx opposite her with his elbows resting heavily on the table. Panes of stained glass in the windows above them cast spots of yellow, green and blue across the eatery floor, colours echoed in the worn cushions and the drapes that covered every wall bar the windows.

Lynx glanced down at his belly and shrugged. 'You spend too long on the road, you need a few things to look forward to.'

'And those things brought all their friends and family!' She laughed. 'Anyone joining us for lunch?'

'It's just us,' he confirmed. 'Some mercs spend all their money on games and whores when they make a city like this. I just got different appetites.'

'This's on you, right?'

'Aye.'

She'd popped a dumpling in her mouth almost before he'd finished saying the word and could only mumble her thanks, but his attention was elsewhere by then. It was only when the eatery's owner brought a glazed jug of beer that either of them took a breath. Even then they only paused long enough to agree the cook was better than the decor suggested. The eatery sat at the mouth of a dead-end street, but given most of the tables were full the cook's reputation clearly counterbalanced the owner's parsimony.

Once they had demolished half the platter, Sitain determinedly keeping up with Lynx for as long as she could manage, their pace lessened off. The view from the windows behind her eventually called for Sitain's attention and she manoeuvred herself around so she could rest one elbow on the sill and still reach the platter. Lynx raised an eyebrow until he saw what she was doing, then gave a non-committal grunt and continued sucking the meat off one of the last legs.

Sitain could only imagine what the view was like from the buildings she saw, but the chief marvel of Grasiel lay beneath them. A steep-sided hill rose above the houses opposite and atop it stood the Maze Markets, a complex of buildings topped by four huge and four lesser domes. There the merchant princes of the city administrated deals that affected the entire region, well away from the actual goods involved or common people.

As magnificent as the Maze Markets were, it was the hill itself that caught the attention. Somewhere in Grasiel's past there had been stone mages, skilled ones working in unison. The eastern half of the hill had been carved open; a smooth and seamless archway more than a hundred feet high and a hundred wide, through which now ran the river's tributary as it circled the Island of the Assayed. Great stepped paths ran over that, all mage-cut, down to the palaces where the merchants lived, while up one side ran a funicular powered by the water running underneath.

'Aye, that's a sad lesson for the world, ain't it?'

'What do you mean?'

Lynx pointed at the hill. 'All that work, all that skill. We could do great things if we put our mind to it.'

'What's so sad about that?'

A grim smile twisted his cheek. ''Cos we don't. The world ain't run by those with the skill to make it better. Power lies in the hands of those able to destroy all that's wonderful. Everything else is reduced to dust by their passing. In this life those best at winning succeed, not those who've done most for the world. It don't matter how skilled a mage is, an icer will punch right through his, or her, body just as easy. Build the finest monuments you like; write the fairest laws and love your neighbour with all your might – the world belongs to whichever fucker can tear it all down.'

'The Orders.'

'Are the latest sort of bastard,' he said with a wave of the hand. 'They weren't the first, nor was So Han, whatever our beloved Shonrin might've claimed.'

Sitain flinched. 'Mother wouldn't let that name be spoken,' she said in a subdued voice. That a monster's name could be spoken so easily was unthinkable in her home. The warm flame of her family rose in her heart – no longer her home, now just a place she could never return to.

'The Shonrin?' Lynx nodded. 'Can see why, must've seemed a devil to her.'

'Why did he do it? I've never known. No one ever understood what happened.'

'Why we went to war? Shattered gods, so you're asking the easy ones today?'

His face darkened as though a cloud had crossed the sun, but just as he stared off into nothing he seemed to surprise himself by continuing. 'Why? 'Cos people are bastards – narrow-minded, greedy or just plain stupid. The Shonrin wasn't the only one to blame, not by a long shot, but he was the hero we all wanted. The proof we were better'n the rest and shouldn't be ashamed of that.

'We were so wrapped up in our self-appointed reputation as the greatest warriors on the continent, we had to prove it. The clan leaders wanted us to fight. They controlled the industry, they controlled the mages, and the monster they'd created needed to consume, so it was our neighbours or each other. It all gathered like stones of an avalanche and before long, you couldn't look back or slow – there was only the crash forward.'

Lynx shook his head sadly. 'But you know what? Was the same fact that saved these parts. If we'd been the united people we'd been told, the oaths would've been honoured and the pillaging wouldn't have happened. No army stopped us; we turned on each other and tore ourselves apart. Supplies got diverted, clans kept warriors back and settled old scores. Mages were bribed or killed – some regiments ran out of ammunition just as they were ready to push forward.

'The whole thing stalled not long after the second front opened up, just as the Shonrin ordered a new offensive. He couldn't keep it under control and couldn't get home to impose order. It gave the central states time to regroup and counter-attack, to build an accord with the Militant Orders who, some say, had also been ready to join So Han and roll up the continent.'

Sitain listened in disbelief. If the So Han armies had reached her home, her whole family would have been killed or sent to a punishment camp. With a shaky hand she raised her cup. 'Here's to people being bastards, then,' she said in a choked voice.

'Aye, I'll drink to that,' Lynx replied with enough feeling that she immediately remembered the scars on his back.

They lapsed into silence for a while. Sitain watched the distant look on Lynx's face as he chewed the food without tasting, barely swallowing before the next morsel was in his mouth.

He'll have been starved, she realised as she watched him cram more into his mouth, the earlier look of pleasure gone from his face. *Wherever he was, he'll have been worked every hour of daylight and been given slops to eat.*

An unexpected belch rumbled up out of his gut, apparently surprising Lynx as much as Sitain. It was enough to make him pause and frown down at the food, jaw tightening for a moment before he dropped what was in his fingers and leaned back.

'So what's it like?' Lynx asked, making a visible effort to dispel the memories haunting him.

'What? This cheese?'

Lynx snorted. 'Nope, your darkness.'

She paused. 'Oh, that. Gods above – and you said I wasn't asking the easy questions!'

'Was just curious. Not my business if you don't want to talk about it.'

She felt a pang of guilt at his haunted look and shook her head. 'No, it's fine. Though I don't know where to start.'

'When did you start?'

Sitain shrugged. 'I could sense it all my life, that tingle in my bones, but it came on when I was about twelve. The ability to draw on that tingle, to make the darkness glitter. It was a game, nothing more, until my brother caught me and we both blacked out. We didn't know what had happened, but a week later I put the fire out as supper was cooking. Just went black and cold, like I'd drawn the life from it, and my dad guessed what it was.'

'And after that?'

'They told me to stop, that it was dangerous. I tried, I really did, but it's a part of me. It happened when I didn't mean it to; when a boy was fighting with my brother and I got scared, when a horse panicked in the street. And once others knew, I suppose it was only a matter of time before the whole village did.' She stopped and gave a small laugh. 'It sounds silly, but the best I can describe it is like when you're being sick. This thing wells up inside you, a movement you've no control over. But it comes from your bones, not your stomach, from deep inside every part of you.'

Lynx was quiet a long while, staring hard at her. 'So we really don't want you frightened in the street, then?'

'I've more control than I did,' she said, realising as she spoke just how defensive that sounded, 'but no – we don't want that. Someone'll notice.'

'Right.' He picked up a blackened strip of red pepper and brandished it. 'Let's finish this off and head back. Suddenly I reckon I want to be around mercenaries again.'

Chapter 11

'I am Exalted Uvrel.'

Deern groaned with the effort of moving his head. A tall white woman in an immaculate Knights-Charnel uniform stood a few yards away. Neither Surei nor Asann, she had the small, neat features of the far north-east, the powerbase of the kings of old and now heartland of the Militant Orders.

Different names, same sort o' kiddie-fiddling hypocrites.

Her hair was cut short and what remained was tucked under a black hat with a jutting prow of a brim, edged with silver thread. The shield on her chest was embossed with silver and her collar was studded with battle honours. Behind her, almost as an after-thought, were two hard-faced privates wearing dragoon uniforms – troops of the elite Torquen branch of the Knights-Charnel.

'You're a woman,' Deern said, blinking stupidly at her.

'Is that a problem?'

The look on her face made it clear whose problem it would be, but still it was a moment before Deern's brain woke up.

Four pairs of gold studs ran down her left shoulder, the double line signalling high station. Exalted commanded a small personal fiefdom of dragoon squads, so far as Deern could remember, but they held equivalent rank to colonels. The one aspect about her that was less than immaculate was her knee-length boots – no amount of polish was able to hide the scored leather or steel toecaps.

'Nope, just, ah, wasn't – never mind.' He shook his head to clear his thoughts a little then waved in the direction of a spare chair. 'Lovely to meet ya. Take a load off.'

She ignored the offered chair. 'You'll be coming with me.'

'I don't reckon so.' Deern laughed. 'Can see why you'd expect that, but I don't have all the info you need. Thought it'd be safer that way, in case I got carried out of here for being drunk and helped all the way into one of your cells. My partner's waiting for me and some cash before anything more happens.'

She leaned forward. 'Except for things that happen to you.'

'Sure,' he said with the disregard of a man well into his cups, 'but I've kissed death on the lips more'n a few times. He don't scare me no more.' Deern cocked his head and glanced down at the mage-pistol in a sheath on his hip. 'Also, I got a burner in the pipe so I'll take the rest o' you down with me. Look me in the eye and tell me I ain't drunk and stupid enough to do it without thinking first.'

She didn't speak immediately, but he could see in her face she believed him. There wasn't fear, though, just acknowledge-ment. *No surprise there*, Deern thought to himself. *Exalted are fanatics, their elite. She probably don't understand folk who'd think twice about burning the world down.*

The warm buzz of alcohol started to fade from his brain, the Exalted's gaze as sobering as a kick in the balls, but then she abruptly sat.

'Your price is ten gold rings.'

'That's what I told your boy.'

'What sort of a mage?'

He grinned at the tacit acceptance. 'Does it matter?'

'When we take them into custody it will.'

'Fair point. I ain't witnessed anything myself, but the talk is she's a night mage.'

It was barely perceptible, but Deern was sure the woman stiffened as he said it. 'You are certain?'

He shrugged. 'Folk who told me were. That good or bad for you?'

'I heard intelligence that spoke of a night mage, and apparently it was correct. Commander Ntois was dispatched to extend our protection.'

'Protection, right. I only caught half a look as they rode past, but sure, he could have been a commander. Whiskery bloke, silver spoon stuck up his arse.'

'And one of yours killed him?'

Deern slipped his feet off a chair and sat forward. 'A recent recruit, not one of us, get me?'

'I understand. You do not wish to have your friends tarnished by this recruit's actions.'

'They're a pretty tarnished bunch all by themselves, but I don't want 'em wiped out 'cos of some So Han fucker. They don't deserve that.'

'Tell me the name of who is to blame.'

Deern scowled, but he knew he was committed now. 'Goes by Lynx. Don't know his real name but he's easy to spot. A heavy So Han veteran with a tattoo on his face. Moves well enough, you don't want to underestimate him, but you'll spot him easy enough round here.'

Uvrel pursed her lips. 'This man from So Han ambushed a squad of Knights-Charnel under the command of an experienced commander, killed them all and made off with the mage they were escorting?'

He shrugged. 'He slipped off in the night and came back at dawn with her. The rest's guesswork, but we didn't get burners up our arses the next day so I'm guessing that's how it went. She said something to him as they passed. I heard it was his own language, that she's a mongrel or something.

Might be that's what swayed it for him, who knows with those mad bastards?'

She was quiet a while then reached into a pocket. 'Two rings now, the rest when we get sight of the quarry.'

'Five.'

The Exalted shook her head. 'Five is too great a lure. You could be making all this up. Two gold rings is a lot, but not enough to risk scamming the Knights-Charnel, given what I will do to you if this is a lie.'

'A stern talking-to, eh? Mebbe a spanking if I'm lucky.' Deern chuckled at the dark look that appeared on her face. 'This mage, she's got you interested I reckon. I'll take your two, but the balance is fifteen then.'

Uvrel opened her mouth to curse at him then caught herself. 'Do you really think you're in a position to demand more?'

'As good a time as any. The information's good so I ain't worried about you cutting my toes off one by one for screwing you over.'

'I wouldn't start with your toes,' she said darkly, but Deern only grinned.

'Oh stop it, you're making me hard with talk like that.'

'Good, you'll lose more blood that way.'

Deern raised an eyebrow. 'We gettin' a room or makin' a deal?'

She opened her hand and showed him two gold rings before flipping them around so they were trapped beneath her palm, flat on the table. Putting the tip of a finger inside the hole of each, she slid the pair across the table but didn't release them.

'You'll be followed back to your lodgings by Tovil here,' she said, tilting her head to one side to indicate one of her dragoons. 'Hand the money off to your friend and get the information you need, then return here. These two are a gesture of good faith. We take the murder of our own very seriously – as we do being played for fools by people stupid enough to try and steal from us. I will have agents verify your information then you'll be released, assuming you've not drunk so much you can't walk.'

'Done,' he said with a nod and swept up the rings when she released them. 'I'll be going, then,' Deern announced, draining his drink.

'Pay your tab first,' Uvrel advised him with a stony expression. 'My generosity is at an end.'

Deern didn't argue. In fact, he realised he'd have been suspicious if she'd have let him stick her for it. He tossed a coin on to the bar and sauntered out, the smaller of the two guards pulling on a plain cloak over his uniform and following him out.

*

Once he was gone Uvrel beckoned over her remaining soldier. 'The rider is already gone, Harril?'

'Yes, Exalted. I sent a scout off towards Janagrai as soon as Lieutenant Eshan brought word.'

'Good. Only a fool or a madman would attempt such a lie, but that man is crazed enough that it's not beyond the realms of possibility.' She stood. 'We must go carefully, however. The Princip would not appreciate a pitched battle on the streets, especially now. Stay here and wait for Tovil. I'll return to the cloister and get the troop ready then inform Lord-Commander Ifiran. If Ntois is dead he will want to know.'

*

Back at the tavern, Lynx and Sitain found the courtyard full of mercenaries. They had made it barely three steps before Payl appeared in front of them, barking orders.

'Weapons check!'

'Sir?' Lynx gestured to the falchion on his hip, but she shook her head.

'Your gun, fetch it. Company fine for anyone not looking after their kit.'

'And just a day after the company was paying for drinks. Fancy that,' he said drily.

'Just get it.'

Lynx did as he was told, noting a few glum faces at the tables. Some scrubbed with oiled cloths at their mage-guns, others forced thick steel needles through the leather of tattered cartridge cases. He suppressed a smile, but knew perfectly well his own weapon was in perfect condition. Even after a decade those lessons remained and the boredom of a life on the road ensured he kept it up.

In the bunkroom his mage-gun lay on his bed, just where he'd left it. He glanced at the beds on the far side of the room, realising Braqe's now lay empty and experiencing a moment of anxiety, but when he drew his gun it still looked in good condition. To be sure he opened the breech and unpinned the barrel so he could tilt and peer down the length. It was clear, light from the window gleaming in the traces of oil on the rifling.

Satisfied, he gathered up his cartridge box and carried both outside. Payl was waiting for him and jerked the gun out of his hands to peer down it too. She grunted and produced a white cloth to wipe around the breech, but it came away almost spotless.

'Good. Now the case.'

He opened it up and presented it to her. The cartridge case was a solid affair, hard-wearing leather stiffened by a steel plate. Some saw the steel as excessive, but Lynx had seen men hit in their cartridge cases; sometimes the entire squad was killed. A hand span and a half long, it contained three rows of cushioned divisions, enough to fit forty individual cartridges.

'The count's two burners, nine sparkers, twenty-eight icers,' he announced, though she hadn't bothered asking.

Payl glanced down at the paint-smeared clay caps and nodded. Red for burners and the sun emblem of the god Veraimin, blue for sparkers and the jagged slash of Banesh, white for icers and the three stars of Insar. Earthers were left brown, naturally, and engraved with two curved tusks representing Ulfer, but Lynx rarely bothered with them. The other forms of magic – Light, Stone, Wind and a handful of other even rarer types – didn't lend themselves to weaponry well and weren't bothered with, or were so exotic only the rich could afford them.

'No one likes a show-off,' Kas called from the table, oiling her bow. Being the company's lead scout she didn't carry a mage-gun, but apparently wasn't exempt from the snap inspection.

'Some of us have standards,' he said with mock primness.

'Damn right.' She laughed. 'Just as well for you, others of us ain't so picky!'

'Keep rubbing at that wood, Kas,' he advised her with a wink, 'one day you'll get good at it too.' Lynx snapped his gun closed again and swiftly changed the subject while he was ahead. 'Braqe's up, then?'

'Just about,' Payl said, nodding towards Sitain. 'Useful skill you've got there, girl.'

'One day, maybe,' she said with a scowl.

'But she's no worse for it?' Lynx asked.

'Nah, just her pride hurt. Otherwise, she could just be hungover and no one'd notice the difference.'

Lynx nodded. That was encouraging, both for patients of Himbel's and Anatin's mood towards his So Han recruits. 'So I heard the city's lousy with Charnelers,' he said brightly.

'You're shitting me?'

'Afraid not.'

'You know why?'

'Nope, but if it's true, life just got more complicated.'

Payl snapped her fingers to attract Kas's attention back from her weapon and nodded towards the inn. 'You two, come with me.'

They went inside to the common room, which was mostly empty at that point in the afternoon, and headed through to the smaller annex where guests of slightly higher quality would eat, if any turned up. The three of them sat around the furthest table and Payl fixed Lynx with a stern look.

'You saw Charnelers? Have a run-in?'

'Nothing like that. I just made friends with a wine shop owner who mentioned it in passing. Doesn't sound like it's any great secret, which may or may not mean anything. Could be some religious thing for all I know, or some conclave of their Order.'

'Anatin's out meeting his contact for the job right now. If the city's busier than usual, I should mebbe march the company out today.'

'You?'

She shrugged. 'Anatin says he's leading the mission. Think he wants a last bit of excitement before he gets too old. Been saying for a few months now he'll sell his stake in the company one day soon.'

'We can only start scouting the place out once Anatin gets back,' Kas pointed out, all business now. 'Only act tomorrow night at the earliest. Cut the rest loose tonight, tell 'em to be back for a midday muster and march 'em out then. You get at least half a day jump on our group.'

'And if Anatin pushes the job a day, it gives you time to keep on down the road and find somewhere good to camp,' Lynx added. 'In case things go wrong.'

'With a city full of Charnelers and the least trustworthy parts of the company let loose on the city, what could possibly go wrong?'

'No chance you'll tie them down another night?'

Payl gave a snort. 'Amazed they did what they were told last night. This ain't the So Han army, Lynx. Those boys and girls will be hitting the gaming houses by nightfall then screwing anything that moves until dawn or they pass out. If we only get one arrested or killed tonight, we'll be doing well. Company's had little chance to cut loose these past few weeks and some folks been itching to find trouble as fast as they can.'

'Sounds like you've got a job on your hands tomorrow morning.'

'Didn't you know? Trawling whorehouses and the alleys behind pubs is my idea of fun,' Payl said with a grimace. 'Fortunately, all the Knights have to do the trawl and most o' the troops are scared shitless of Reft, plus Anatin's free with the fines for those we can't find.'

'Guess that means it's a quiet night in for us select few,' Lynx commented.

'Sure, once you've done a first sweep of the target streets it'll be all silver cutlery and brandy. O' course, after that Anatin'll take all your money at this very table.' She grinned. 'He, ah, gets all hot and competitive the night before action.'

'More competitive than normal?'

'Almost shot Kas here once for winning.'

Kas nodded. 'Never could work out if I got lucky he was so drunk that night. He *did* shoot Himbel once, but the man was being a real misery so no one was surprised there.'

'Sure I'll be fine,' Lynx said as he stood. 'Not like the man's one drink away from shooting me anyway.'

*

True to Payl's prediction, the strike company ate together in the private room of the inn while the rest were unleashed on the city. Anatin had returned late and immediately shut himself away with his lieutenant, so Lynx was well on the way down his second drink before he saw the commander.

Lynx and Sitain sat almost in silence, watching the senior officers pile into a whole shoulder of pork surrounded by a wall of spice-tinted potatoes. Payl and Anatin had ducked their heads in briefly as the food arrived, but it was Safir and Olut who presided over the table as, by fits and starts, they jointly told a tale of an implausible night of drinking. The Knights of Stars and Snow were as close to opposites as Lynx could imagine, yet the pair seemed even closer allies than myth suggested the gods of their suits had been.

Safir wore a fine embroidered coat of green and yellow over a grey and green kilt that reached his calves, his hair and moustache neatly oiled, his gestures deft and restrained while he spoke. There was a white silk scarf around his throat and polished silver cutlery in his hands, poised over his plate for when Olut next broke in.

Olut was taller and heavier than the lithe nobleman, her sandy hair tangled and greasy, her sallow northern skin blotchy after some past illness. She wore a much-repaired leather jerkin which had already been stained before her careless eating habits added to the toll. Lynx couldn't imagine her in a dress or skirt, while the sight of Safir in his kilt no longer looked odd at all to him.

Obviously the rest of the table had heard the story several times before, given the interruptions and catcalls that came from Kas and Tyn. Even Reft snorted his derision at the overblown description of jumping between rooftops, but Lynx noticed Sitain drinking it all in with a broad grin on her face. He realised it didn't matter how true the story was, it was a fantasy of the life everyone hoped they might lead and the books he read were no different, aside from the pieces of gristle that were spat out as Olut took up the mantle once more.

Just as the pair of adventurers tumbled, half-naked but still armed, through a roof hatch and into a merchant prince's private orgy, the dining room door banged open and Anatin marched in.

'And Safir got sold as a eunuch 'cos they couldn't see his balls, what with it being so cold out,' Anatin broke in loudly, 'while Olut charmed her way to freedom by way of a combination o' erotic dancing and a sea shanty so filthy the whores anointed her their goddess.'

Olut gave a roar of good-natured rage and hurled a bone in Anatin's general direction, but the commander ignored her as he sat at the head of the table.

'You all sober?'

There was a variety of grunts, outraged denials and laughter from the various parties, which Anatin took as a yes as he helped himself to a plate of food.

'Glad to hear it. We've got some scouting to do in the morning.'

'It's tomorrow?' Teshan asked, his quiet voice cutting through the general murmurs.

Anatin shook his head. 'Following night. With all the Charnelers in the city, Payl's gonna take the rest o' the company out tomorrow – get some miles between them and the city before any shit goes down.'

'And find an ambush point?' Lynx asked.

'You prefer to split off and go cross country?'

'Toward Shadows Deep?' Lynx scowled. 'Hoping that's a last resort.'

'Damn right it is. Girly, you – Sitain. You stick close to Payl and make yerself useful. If you stay with the company you pull your weight, understand? We're a fighting troop and it's all business until I say otherwise, so you work and you work harder'n the rest unless you learn to shoot. Braqe will leave you alone, just don't get in her face.'

'Just like that?'

Anatin paused over his food. 'Yeah, just like that. The woman's a soldier, not a fool or fanatic. She knows an order when she gets one and she knows the rules, so she'll steer clear.'

Teshen nodded. 'And I told her I'd cut her face off if she killed you.'

'Aye, there's that too,' Anatin said. 'Sound leadership tactic.'

'If she kills me?' Sitain echoed in disbelief. 'That's hardly reassuring.'

'We can't stop her hating you, just doing anything about it. You got a problem with that, the door's over there.'

Sitain matched his gaze for a moment, then realised she was picking a pointless fight and ducked her head in acknowledgement. Anatin maintained his level stare a while longer then grunted.

'Good. My contact gave us everything we need so we walk it through tomorrow while the rest are leaving. Muster mid-morning, dunk 'em one by one in the horse trough. With luck you'll be ready to move early afternoon, Payl. Send the troops separate to the carts, different gates if you can. A couple of guards without badges is all they'll need and we don't want any association made 'til it's too late, just in case.'

'You expecting trouble?' Lynx asked.

Anatin's lip curled. 'With you around? Damn fucking right, seems like you attract it. I didn't live so long in this game without being careful.'

'True,' Tyn agreed loyally, 'all those times you told us to run away, the rest of the army got royally screwed.'

The permanent smirk of her scarred cheek seemed to betray her studied expression, but before Anatin could turn on her Safir raised his glass in toast. 'Don't forget those times we were paid to change sides – double the money and we ended up on the winning side.'

'The captain of the Sulian honour guard,' Kas added, 'I didn't hear exactly what he shouted after us as we marched away, but I'm pretty sure it was congratulating our tactical nous.'

'It was hard to ask him afterwards,' Safir agreed. 'A little crispy for conversation.'

'Oh, I got one,' Olut cried, but a spice-stained potato hit her in the face before she could speak.

'Sure, keep it up,' Anatin said with a nasty gleam in his eye. 'Next time there's a one-sided fight I'll leave you to it and fuck off with your share of the pay. It'll buy me a few new sergeants I reckon, 'specially when my strongbox holds most o' your money.'

Teshen leaned back in his seat and patted the huge arm of Reft, who was sat on his left. 'Yeah, reckon you're right, Reft, we should just kill and rob him once we're out of the city.'

A slow, horrible grin spread across the hairless giant's face, revealing neat rows of white teeth with the left-hand canines replaced with gold points. Even Anatin faltered in the face of that disconcerting reveal. It was the most expressive Lynx had ever seen Reft and gave a sudden insight into what the man might be like in a fight. Around the company he was as calm and serene as a priest. Lynx knew men who cast such a long shadow were rarely part of the banter, but in that moment he glimpsed a little more.

Maybe Deern and he ain't so strange a pairing, Lynx reflected. *Whatever sort of pairing that is. There's a flash o' nastiness in that smile, for all it looks like he's joining in on the joke; nastiness with a stone elemental's body. That's one scary combination.*

'Piss on the lot o' you,' the Prince of Sun muttered. 'Fuck's sake, Reft, what've I told you about smiling? Gives me the willies.'

That only widened the grin and Lynx glanced around the table. Aside from Teshen, everyone seemed to share their commander's disquiet. The cold-eyed scout raised his mug of beer and chinked it gently against his neighbour's.

'Who's for a game then?'

*

Hours later and a good few coins poorer, Lynx pushed himself unsteadily to his feet to give Sitain space to walk behind his seat. The table seemed to move under his hands as he leaned on it and he groaned as felt the full force of brandy hit him.

'Dark and long,' he muttered, 'turns out I'm drunk.'

'No five mo' here,' Sitain said as she slid past, shoulder resting against the plain whitewashed wall. 'Got spoon, see?'

'Eh?'

'She's fuckered,' Kas explained, giving Lynx a thump in the thigh. 'More drunk'n you even.'

Lynx turned himself to watch Sitain leave. She wasn't paying attention to the rest of them, so focused was she on making her way around to the door. Her tongue was pressed against the inside of her cheek with the pantomime effort of thinking, a slight sheen of sweat on her skin.

'Heh, gods, she really is too.'

'Go tuck her in, Kas,' Tyn called, 'girl's been makin' eyes at ya all evening.'

'Only after she got too drunk to see straight,' Anatin said. 'Was probably aiming at me an' just missed. Who's still in?'

Hands were raised, Lynx didn't see who, but he caught the flash of cards darting out across the table.

'Nope, too drunk for this game.'

'Too drunk for any game!' Kas said, looking up at him as she took another swallow of beer. The alcohol had given her dark cheeks a deeply attractive pink flush, Lynx noticed, and the cat-like lick of the lips that followed it made him shake his head violently.

'Some games're worth sobering for.'

'Oh really?'

'Aye.'

'I ain't sharing a room with that snoring lump,' Payl warned, sparking a great roll of laughter from Olut, who'd been outpacing Lynx all night.

'I'll have him, I'm drunk enough,' she announced with a slap of her palm on the table, hard enough to spill Safir's wine.

Lynx blinked and focused on the bear-like northerner as best he could. 'Gods, not sure I am. Might break me in half, woman!'

Kas leaned back in her seat and took a firm grip of Lynx's buttock. He swayed but managed not to fall over. 'Not drunk, eh? Go get yourself some fresh air; I've got money to win back first.'

Lynx took that as encouraging and made a heroic effort to hide the grin that appeared on his face. He nodded, following Sitain's lead and guiding himself around the room to the door. A low comment and more laughter followed him, but he was determined to exit gracefully and almost managed it until he tripped on the step up into the bar. Fortunately there was only a tall stool in his way, handily placed for a steadying hand, and he headed on through the near-deserted common room.

The barman watched him with the steady, distrustful look of a man who'd seen too many drunks, but he gave a nod in response to Lynx's greeting. Lynx hauled open the inn's main door and a gust of cool air flooded in. Outside, there was just one lamp above the door. It did little to dispel the darkness of a cloudy night when even the Skyriver was hidden from view, but Lynx could at least make out Sitain standing with her back to him, all alone in the middle of the courtyard.

He looked up to the shadowed sky and took a few long breaths. The breeze swept down as though answering his call, bringing the damp promise of rain. The clouds above were mostly invisible in the black, only the hint of shape and movement but enough to tell him they were speeding past. Faint flashes of light shone out from behind the clouds, illuminating little but enough to spark Lynx's memory all the same.

Elementals, he thought, straining to make out more, but the brief occasional glimmers were all he could see. *Lightning elementals, wonder what they look like?*

The memory of the night elemental was fixed in his memory, those twisting and shimmering facets of darkness a wonder like nothing he'd witnessed before. To get so close to an elemental was a once in a lifetime opportunity for most.

Huh, more likely end of a lifetime, he corrected himself. There were stories of travellers seeing such things from afar, the raging storm of firedrakes or inexorable bulk of stone trolls, but this was as close as most got – watching the dance of the thunderbird, hidden by cloud. Those who got closer never lived to tell the tale. Lynx hadn't sensed any such threat from the night elemental, but whether that had been its nature or Sitain's presence, he couldn't tell.

A little steadier he looked back at Sitain and cocked his head, squinting to look at the young woman.

Gods, I must be drunk.

The air seemed to twist around her; near-invisible eddies and fractures forming from the gloom of night. Sitain wasn't moving, just swaying as though listening to a rhythm in her head, but as Lynx found his eyes watering he realised what it was.

'Oi,' he called across the courtyard. He glanced up at the windows of the rooms above, but few were not taken by the company anyway and most of the shutters were closed against the autumn chill.

The darkness seemed to snap back into place as Sitain flinched and swung around, eyes wide with surprise.

'Enough o' that,' Lynx said, taking a hesitant step forward even though the glimmers of night incarnate had vanished as soon as he'd spoken.

'Wha'?' Sitain peered at him, face screwed up like a child in thought, before finally recognising Lynx and giving him a vacant smile. 'Lynx. Hello.'

'You're pissed. Get yer bunk,' he said, jabbing a thumb in the direction of the bunkroom.

'Tha's where'm going.'

'You weren't going nowhere.'

'Just enjoyin' all this,' she announced, spreading her arms out wide.

Lynx looked around at the empty courtyard. 'Space?' he hazarded. 'Smell o' horse shit? Quiet?'

She shook her head and began to pluck at the empty air around her. 'Nah, all this.' Whatever she thought she was touching, Sitain's face seemed to fall into a state of calm as she teased and pulled at the darkness around her as though working a loom. Lynx couldn't see anything happen as a result but something shouted a warning at the back of his mind all the same.

'Stop foolin' around,' he said urgently, 'you're seein' things.'

'Wha' about all this?'

'Moonshine-whispers,' he said dismissively, just about sober enough to say whatever it took to get her inside.

'Thought I were drinkin' brandy?'

'Shows how pissed you are.' He flapped his arms in the direction of the bunkhouse. 'Go and sleep before you fall down. I've got some soberin' up to do.'

'Why?'

'Guess.'

179

Her face twisted in thought then distaste as she realised what he meant and with just a dismissive wave of the hand she staggered off to the bunkhouse, banging on the door until a sleepy-eyed boy opened it and helped her inside.

'Good,' Lynx said with a satisfied nod. 'Now me.'

He took another step forward and swayed as the ground lurched under him. Shaking his head he tried a few more, attempting to cross the courtyard, but as he neared the spot where Sitain had been standing the dizziness only grew, the fog in his head making his limbs feel weaker than ever.

Without warning he staggered backwards and fell hard on his backside, blinking in surprise at the empty courtyard. Suddenly everything seemed an enormous effort and he groaned at the idea of standing up again.

'Ah fuck it,' Lynx muttered, casting on mournful look back at the closed inn door. He rolled sideways and got himself onto his hands and knees. Standing up didn't seem to be an option, but the bunkroom was a short crawl away. He set off, the vision of his bed displacing every other thought from his mind.

Interlude 4
(now)

Up ahead the darkness winked and writhed. Lynx blinked, his head pounding from the fall and the exertion of jogging through dark city streets. They only had a handful of horses left and only two of the group were riding – Anatin leading the way and the beautiful madwoman, Toil, who lolled uncertainly in the saddle and would have fallen without Reft's support.

'Girly, where are you?' Anatin called out, somehow contriving to whisper as loudly as he could. They were in a small square, just an opened-out section of street with a humped shrine to the god Veraimin on one corner. A pair of oval glass lanterns shone there like eyes, the intricate cut-glass casting lines over the cobbled ground and illuminating a mural of the sun across the shrine's back.

For a moment there was no movement then the darkness ahead shimmered and Sitain stepped forward from the overhang she'd been lurking beneath, fear etched clear on her face.

'Was she just doing—' Kas exclaimed until Lynx broke in.

'Later!' he barked. 'Let's get clear.'

'That ain't a surprise to you?' she said, turning to give Lynx a strange look as Sitain scampered forward.

'Not really.'

Kas shook her head in disbelief. 'Oh, shitting marvellous.'

'Shut up all of you,' Anatin said. 'We need horses, not complaints.'

'Coming right up,' Teshen said as he ghosted over to a closed set of gates and yanked one open. Above a nearby door was a sign that in daylight could be read as Threegates Livery Stable.

The whinny of horses came from inside, then the scramble of feet on straw. Lynx pressed a stubby finger to his temple and tried to massage the ache from his brain while he watched an emaciated stablehand with a tangled mass of black hair lead a pair of saddled horses out to them. Teshen followed with a pair more and passed the reins on to Safir before heading back in.

Soon they all had a mount and half had a spare tied to their saddle. Anatin tossed a small purse of coins to the stablehand, who opened it and nodded briefly. Before the order to move out could be given, Toil lurched to one side and vomited noisily.

'Someone get me out of this bastard city,' she growled, wincing up at the Skyriver as she swept her hair back. 'Had enough o' this place.'

'Can you ride?' Anatin demanded.

'Yeah. Don't ask me to jump walls or nothing, but I can follow someone through streets.'

She briefly looked around at the saddle of her horse, flapping briefly behind her back before giving up. 'Guess I'd not be much of a shot anyway,' she added, as much to herself as anyone. Her hand came to rest on the short-swords that hung from her belt, but she didn't try to draw one, just took comfort from their presence.

'Come on,' Anatin said after a glance around his small command. 'City gate's just down this street, we're going in hard. Reft, you blow the Poorgate, everyone else spark up the walls. If they drop the cage we'll never make it out.'

The Prince of Sun slammed his spurs into his horse's flanks and the beast leaped forward through an archway. Behind him went Olut, Reft and Teshen, with Safir, Toil, Varain and Kas following close behind. With his mage-gun shouldered, Lynx followed with Sitain riding close to his side.

'Where's Tyn?' the young woman asked just as they crossed through the arch into a narrow street. Up ahead loomed the imposing blockish shape of Threegates, through which some of the company had left the city.

'Didn't make it.'

'She's dead?' Sitain gasped.

'Lot of people dead in our wake,' Lynx snapped. 'Now shut up and watch the horse in front.'

They rode out into an empty marketplace. Abandoned rows of stalls spread left and right, the majority clustered around a public well away to the right. Lynx couldn't see anyone at first and breathed a sigh of relief. A large part of him was expecting a rank of Knights-Charnel, a sudden volley of icers or a shouted ultimatum.

'State your business!' roared a great bear of a man from the gantry above the Poorgate, the smallest of the three city gates there.

His yellow-hooded livery and dark Surei skin were obvious by the light of a torch he carried – certainly no Charneler, this one, but Anatin didn't bother replying. Quick as a snake he raised his mage-pistol and fired on the man. The sparker caught him full-on and lightning exploded around the small gantry he was stood on. Screams came from further back, but Lynx didn't see who was there. As Olut put another sparker into the guard-room window, Reft nudged his horse around Anatin's and fired on the gate itself.

The deep crash of his earther boomed against the stone walls and made the stalls around them shudder, leaving Lynx's already-pounding head ringing. Dark spots burst before his eyes and though he heard the great crack and splinter of the earther striking, it took him a moment to make out the damage it had done.

Up ahead the Poorgate lurched with a tortured creak. The uppermost of its massive iron hinges had been torn right through and a chunk of stone chewed out of the wall beside it. Somehow the gate held up but Varain was already pushing his horse forward with a calculating look on his face. The second shot burst right through the reinforced wood just as a yell came from the lower guardhouse and Teshen fired at its barred window. Sparks exploded all around it and screams came from within, but suddenly that wasn't the only sound hammering at Lynx's ears.

He turned left, hearing the drum of feet, and saw a horseman clatter around a corner towards them, the Skyriver palely illuminating a Charneler uniform. He raised his gun on instinct but the Charneler wheeled as soon as he saw the mercenaries, sawing hard at the reins and yelling at the top of his voice. Safir turned and fired in one smooth spin, but was defeated by the sudden movement and Lynx saw the white blur of an icer dart wide.

In the next moment the man was gone again, away round the corner, and they had no time to pursue. Anatin jammed his pistol into a sheath and darted forward, Reft and Varain close on his heels. Lynx roared for Sitain to go and the young woman crouched low over the neck of her horse and jabbed her heels into its flanks. The group tore towards the gate, Lynx taking up the rear with his gun ready, but other than a flash of white he saw nothing before he entered the short covered section that led beyond the city.

He couldn't help but look up as he went, the dark points of the cage just a suggestion in the blackness overhead, but a creeping sense on his neck seemed to feel their presence all too clearly. The cage was principally there to present an obstacle to attackers, to mangle and deform under the impact of an earth-bolt that could break down any wall, but Lynx knew what that heavy rattling framework of spikes could do to men.

And then the blackness vanished and cool welcoming air washed over him. There were more shouts from the city, the clatter of boots and hooves, but he felt a moment of elation all the same as the starlit ground opened up around them. The main highway stretched out ahead, a dulled grey sliver of packed earth punctured by star-speckled puddles from the earlier rain. There was no cover here, no houses or trees within a hundred yards of this stretch of wall, only a set of fenced livestock pens that deliberately narrowed the road for traffic entering the city. They were forced to move at a canter, one behind the other to avoid the nervous horses jostling each other as detonations echoed through the short tunnel behind. Lynx turned to see the white trails of ice-bolts linger a moment longer in the air.

It was enough to drain his elation. The memory of open walkways up to the wall became very clear in his mind, the clatter of boots on stone echoing through the hushed night as though Charnelers were racing up them to take firing positions on the unprotected mercenaries.

'An— Boss!' he shouted forward, realising only just in time that they didn't want their leader's name heard by any pursuers. He might not have been a famous mercenary commander, but he'd led his own company for years now and wouldn't require much identifying.

'What?'

'Coming up behind!'

Anatin urged his horse forward past the final pen and wheeled to one side to allow Reft out. 'Keep going!' he ordered, waving them past.

There were more shouts from the street behind and Lynx turned as far as he could in the saddle. He caught a flash of movement and pulled the trigger without aiming. The sparker raced forward and was swallowed by the darkness of the tunnel.

For a moment he thought it had failed, fizzled out to nothing instead of exploding, but then a great jagged flower of lightning blossomed in the confined space.

Two figures were caught in agonised tableau, impaled by crooked claws, before disaster happened. A shudder of movement, some wrench of the world that Lynx's straining eyes couldn't make out, then the cartridgecase of one Charneler blew up. A pale cloud filled the tunnel and an ear-splitting sound louder than an earther slapped forward against Lynx's ears.

He flinched away, automatically hunched up against the blast, and felt the sting of fragments – ice, stone or flesh, he didn't want to know – smack into his back. Some survival instinct kept him riding straight and once his vision cleared he saw Sitain's horse a few yards away, pushing forward into a gallop. Nearby, Anatin had his pistol out, levelled and pointing at the walls behind.

Lynx fumbled at the breech of his own gun, flicking away the spent casing, but Anatin just cackled and slapped the flank of Lynx's horse, shouting, 'Ride!'

A sixth sense made Lynx look away, off towards the inky night where Sitain was labouring forward, but still the brightness seared into the back of his brain when Anatin pulled the trigger. His horse stumbled, terrified by the flare of light and unguided by its half-blinded owner, while Anatin only laughed the harder.

Lynx growled and blinked furiously as a great hiss tore through the night behind him, then Anatin was at his side and riding past, roaring with laughter all the while. Lynx glanced towards the city walls through blurred eyes but stopped before he could look straight at them. A great beacon of searing white burned somewhere on the wall, but he couldn't see where or put anything into focus.

Shattered gods, a light-bolt?

He didn't bother looking back again. Even out of the corner of his eye it hurt to see the white blur raging on the wall, the whole of Threegates lit up like day. He forced himself to head on after Anatin through the blur of darkness – trusting to the gods or fate or something that he would find his way.

*

The Exalted was almost at the top when the light-bolt struck. She threw herself away from the searing light, barging the troops who followed her and almost knocking one from the steps. But a tidal wave of heat and pain never broke over her, just an intense brightness that she could see through her eyelids. That single moment of fear and anticipation stretched out, two heartbeats, three, four. Then the light began to recede and primal panic fled before the steel edge of her will.

Not a burner.

Uvrel hauled herself upright, treading on her dragoons as she staggered to the top of the wall. She blinked and cursed as trails of light swam across her vision. The sharpshooters she'd sent up first howled with pain, all three on their knees with their hands clamped over their eyes. Their mage-guns were abandoned at their feet so the Exalted snatched one up and tried to level it.

It was no use. She could barely keep her balance, the sway of her body was enough to ruin any shot and she couldn't even see anything to shoot at. Beyond the wall was just a darkened blur, her night vision ruined and her best soldiers half-blinded by the light-bolt. In disgust she dropped the gun again and grabbed the stone crenellations for support while she fumbled at the nearest man. Her fingers closed around long greasy hair.

'Hagan? Is that you?'

The man whimpered until she shook him. 'Exalted? Veraimin's rage, I can't see!'

'It'll pass,' she shouted to the three of them, praying she was right. 'Stay still, I'll send for help.'

She lurched drunkenly back the way she'd come, grabbing a soldier coming the other way who gratefully took hold of whatever he could for support. She ignored where his hands had fallen and tried to focus on his face.

'Tovil?'

'Sir! What was that?'

She pushed him back against a wooden post and stood straighter, though she could still only half see. 'Where's Harril?' Uvrel demanded, realising Tovil was as useless as her.

'Here, sir!' called a voice from somewhere further down.

'You can see?'

'Yes, sir.'

'Good – rouse the rest of my dragoons, all of them! And any scouts you can find, we need guns and trackers. The rest of their company might be waiting. If we walk into an ambush I mean to outnumber our Steel Crows.'

She turned to Tovil. 'Get the men on the wall looked at. If they can't see anything when we're ready to move, leave them with the doctors – otherwise tie them to horses if need be. Lieutenant Sauren?'

'Sir.'

'Run to the Lord-Commander, ask to commandeer as many troops as I may, get whatever you can and lead them out after us.'

'Yes, sir!'

As Tovil slipped past her to the men on the wall, Uvrel sank down to sit on the top step. She closed her eyes and forced herself to take a long breath. She'd only glimpsed the fleeing riders, but one thing had jumped out at her, other than the pale giant and the portly Hanese soldier, Lynx. A woman with long red hair streaming in the wind – strikingly beautiful, a face to remember. A face she'd seen before, out on the street last night when she'd laid in wait for the mercenaries and they'd failed to come.

The courtesan. She must be a foreign spy in need of an exit.

Despite her aching eyes Uvrel stood and turned to face her troops. 'The rest of you, get to your horses and be ready to move out. Insar has granted me a lesson in my blindness – I underestimated these mercenaries and let them slip through our fingers. We will not fail our god a second time!'

Chapter 12
(then)

Lynx opened his eyes and immediately regretted it. Daylight streamed in through the high window, scraping like tiny claws at the back of his eyes. Motes of dust glittered amid the fug of unwashed bodies, a miasma of alcohol-saturated sweat filling the air. He moaned and rolled over, tugging his blanket up to try and escape the light. His limbs were sluggish and heavy, his crotch warm and damp.

Damp?

Lynx did his best to ease his eyes open again. Trying to focus made them hurt even more, with little result. A blur that seemed to be his hand untangled from the blanket and worked its way down. The throb in his skull continued to build, a colony of mine-spirits hammering away inside.

Eventually he managed to fumble at his crotch. Everything was wet – not just damp but completely sodden. His trousers from waist to knee were soaked through, and the mattress beneath too.

Coldest dark, I pissed myself in the night? Was I that drunk?

Brief flashes of his stagger back to his bunk appeared in his mind. Of ending up on his arse as he tried to yank his boots off, of a few verses of the Wisp and the Whore while he pissed into a pot.

Mebbe. Was that bit a dream, or not really a pot? And why in buggery do I still need a piss so bad?

A creeping sense of shame crept down his neck. Nose wrinkled in anticipation, Lynx couldn't resist bringing his fingers back up to his nose to sniff them.

Beer?

There was a long moment of relief, one interrupted by a renewed burst of insistence from his bladder. He scrabbled the blanket off and tried again to focus on the mattress below him. A dark stain covered the middle portion, a warm, pungent hoppy smell overlaying the bunkroom's stink of sweat, feet and flatulence.

'Which prick brought a beer to bed?' whined someone from a nearby bunk. It took Lynx a while to identify Himbel's voice. The company doctor sounded in as much pain as Lynx and as bad-tempered as ever.

'Ah, 'parently me,' Lynx said, having to put all his strength into sitting upright. Too late he remembered there was a bunk above his and he cracked his aching head against the wooden frame. He fell back into the damp patch, fighting the urge to whimper.

'Got any left?' Himbel replied with a pathetic note of hope.

'Fuckin' shitsticks,' Lynx moaned, cradling his stinging forehead.

'Eh?'

He blinked and again pushed himself upright. 'I, er. Nah. Spilled it, I reckon.'

'Oh gods!' broke in a third voice.

By the time Lynx had worked out who it was, Sitain was leaning over the edge of her bunk and vomiting onto the floor below.

'Get the fuck out!' growled a few voices as others retched at the sour stink filling the room. 'Bastard recruits,' added someone else.

Sitain didn't reply. Lynx watched her roll off the edge of her bunk, her face green, and struggle to avoid the puddle of puke.

'That way,' he called, pointing towards the door.

She wavered and barely managed to keep on her feet, but by will alone Sitain stumbled towards the door, heading for the outhouse beyond it. On the way she had the sense to grab an empty chamber pot, some sense of self-preservation deciding the courtyard would be a better place to be sick than a stinking outhouse.

Quiet returned to the bunkroom, but there was a restless shifting of limbs as the mercenaries reluctantly surfaced from sleep – the voices and sharp smell of puke enough to drag all but the most comatose to wakefulness.

Lynx stared at his boots for a while, trying to fathom how he'd get his feet into them, before noticing a pair of shoes nearby. Too small and caked in dirt, they still looked like an easier prospect so he wedged his feet in and hauled himself upright. A few shuffling steps across the room gave him confidence he could make it, but just as his bladder started making insistent noises he saw a dark hand point towards him.

'Filthy shitbag Hanese,' Braqe said, squinting forward in the unwelcome light. 'One pukes, other pisses hisself.'

'It's beer,' Lynx replied, feeling a hot flush of embarrassment all the same.

'Sure.'

'You wanna get your face down here and smell it?'

Someone laughed from a bunk behind. 'Kas went to sleep alone, eh?'

'Eh?' Lynx turned and searched for a face, but couldn't tell which of the occupied bunks it was.

'Comp'ny tradition,' said the mystery comrade. 'You piss beer on our plans fer a screw, you get beer pissed on you.'

Lynx stared at the bunks for a while. Eventually he shrugged. He wasn't happy about it, that was for sure, but with a pressing need and a certain trouble thinking, he found he didn't much care. Instead he followed Sitain out and found her at a table outside, illuminated by crisp morning sunshine as she retched and heaved over her chamber pot. He left her to it and went to relieve himself at the adjoining outhouse, the filthiest verses of last night's serenade running through his head.

Back out in the fresh air, he finally had the chance to appreciate the morning sun peeking over the rooftops and eased himself down on a warm bench to let his body recover a while longer. At some point he knew he'd need to go back inside and try to peel off his wet trousers, but the thought of such effort confounded him at present.

'Better?' he called after a few deep breaths.

Sitain looked up through a bedraggled curtain of hair. 'Uh.'

'Glad I ain't the only one then.'

'I blame you.'

Lynx smiled at that and rubbed a greasy palm over his face. 'Aye, me too. There's blood sausage for breakfast if you want.'

He chuckled to himself as Sitain went through another round of puking, idly looking up at the thin darts of cloud that drifted slowly through the sky. The black dots of birds danced and wheeled across the dull grey arc of the Skyriver, their faint cries just detectable over the muted sounds of the city beyond. Lynx closed his eyes and felt the warmth on his eyelids, revelled in the sensation he'd once thought he would never feel again.

A door banged open past the hunched, spitting form of Sitain and a gust of welcome smells escaped to greet him; frying meat and brewing coffee. He squinted up at the tall man who'd exited, pock-cheeked Llaith carrying a fat ceramic pot of coffee and a handful of brown squat cups.

Sparing a brief, sympathetic look at Sitain, Llaith deposited the coffee and cups in front of Lynx and sat on one of the other benches. 'Needs a few minutes,' he said, nodding at the coffee.

'I could kiss you,' Lynx said as he stared at the coffee, almost fantasising about the hot bitter taste of it.

'It's a fine morning,' Llaith said with a shrug. 'Deserves coffee and a smoke.' With a deft flourish he filled a wisp of paper with tobacco, rolled and twisted up in a matter of seconds. He paused in the process of depositing it in one of the empty cups, seeing Lynx's attention fixed on it. 'You want?'

'Like you said, it's a fine morning.'

Llaith smiled, the pattern of his scarred cheeks folding away. He held up the clay coal pot he carried at his waist. 'Make yerself useful then. I forgot this.'

Lynx took the pot and headed inside to where the fire had already been revived. He ushered a few ash-coated lumps of coal into the pot before closing it up again, but before he could head out he found himself face to face with Kas. Even in the gloom of inside, Lynx could tell the dark-skinned woman was less than her usual sunny self.

'Morning,' he said feebly.

'It is,' Kas acknowledged, glancing down at his damp trousers. 'Looks like you had an accident.'

Lynx nodded. 'Folk say that happens sometimes, when you get too far in your cups.'

'Probably your age.'

'Aye, I reckon so.' He scratched the ghost of a beard on his cheek. 'Might be brandy don't agree with me.'

'You need a head for it, true enough.'

'I'm guessing you have one, then.'

'What makes you say that?'

He attempted an endearing grin. 'You're smaller'n me and hit it just as hard, but here I am feeling like shit warmed up an' there you is, beautiful as ever.'

The frown didn't leave her face, but her eyes seemed to sparkle just for a moment. 'Right answer. Maybe you've got more've a head for it than I thought.'

Lynx snorted. 'Just don't ask me hard stuff like what my name is, not 'til I've got over-familiar with some coffee.'

'You eaten?'

He shook his head.

'I'll get 'em to bring something out. Some of Tempest take a while to round up.'

Lynx nodded, feeling unconcerned. 'Won't take long. I already seen Braqe and Llaith.'

'Go on then.'

'Yes, Mistress Kasorennel.'

That seemed to earn him another slight softening of expression as Kas turned away, telling him he'd pronounced it well enough. Lynx headed back out to discover a small bundle of smokes in the cup before Llaith and the ageing mercenary in the process of pouring himself a coffee. Before too long, wisps of smoke were being dragged away by the breeze as the pair slurped at their steaming cups. Sitain watched them balefully from the neighbouring table, one arm still wrapped around her chamber pot as the colour gradually returned to her cheeks.

'Morning, old man,' Kas called as she arrived to join them, settling in beside Llaith.

'Kas, ain't you a lovely sight for a lazy morning?'

'Lovely sight for any morning,' she corrected.

'Ah, but most days a man can't stop an' appreciate it.'

She smiled and inclined her head, not intending to contradict the man when it was spoken in friendship. 'Looks like I owe Teshen some money. I was sure you'd still be face deep in some courtesan at dawn.'

Lynx almost choked on his coffee at the image while Llaith laughed filthily.

'Weren't for the lack o' trying,' the older man said, 'but a good fisherman knows when he ain't getting a bite.'

'Courtesans?' Lynx hadn't been to these parts for a while, but courtesans were to whores what Reft was to the average army private. They had the education and manners of the highest echelons of society – and cost enough no one else would be able to afford them. In a merchant city full of jockeying factions and businessmen looking to broker deals, they would be an influential force and know their own worth exactly.

'Something of a speciality of our friend here,' Kas said. 'Talks his way into those gatherings they host and charms 'em somehow. We never worked out how, but Safir went with him once. Swears Llaith didn't slip anything in their drinks or pay a scrap o' coin. Reckon Safir was left troubled by what he saw, truth be told.'

Llaith gave some fashion of bow to Lynx's incredulous face. 'What can I say? I scrub up well and overflow with charm.'

'Oh gods,' Lynx said eventually, the fog of hangover in his brain not permitting much else.

'Aye, that's what they all say.'

More mercenaries began to filter outside, most half-dressed with blankets wrapped round their shoulders and bleary-eyed. Several sported bruises, one a poorly wrapped gash on his arm that Himbel was half-heartedly trying to attend to. The mercenary, a lean man covered in scars and mismatched tattoos, was clearly no stranger to injury and interested only in the coffee. Eventually Himbel gave up and eased himself down beside Lynx, Llaith handing the scowling doctor a smoke without it even being asked for.

A young man pushed his way out of the main door to feeble cheers from mercenaries, half of whom were still drunk by Lynx's fuzzy estimation. The youth carried a platter of fried bread and fat slices of blood sausage, piled so high he could barely carry it, while a girl who could have been his sister followed him out with a stack of wooden plates and a large bowl of boiled eggs.

Their breakfast was interrupted when one of the still-drunk mercenaries grabbed a handful of the girl's backside and some of the female members started swinging, but just at that moment Anatin arrived outside and the violence evaporated as quickly as the puffs of smoke drifting up to meet the breeze.

'One happy little family, eh?' Anatin commented as he used his boot to gently nudge a woman out of her seat and settle opposite Lynx.

The Prince of Sun had bloodshot eyes with great grey rings around them, but he walked more easily than Lynx had.

Lynx grunted. 'Aye, something like that.' He picked up a slice of blood sausage, the surface fried to a dark crisp, and tossed it to Sitain. 'Here you go, time to eat!'

She held the slice up and took a tentative bite before going pale again.

'Oh gods.'

*

Sauren stifled a yawn and rolled her shoulders to try and work some of the stiffness from them. She looked up at the sky and saw the sun creeping over the rooftop ahead. Checking around her quickly she found she was alone and briefly dropped to her knees, left hand on her heart, to speak the salute to day.

'Veraimin we honour your warmth. Light of life we greet you and charge you with our care.'

She spoke under her breath, head bowed but eyes staring forward all the while. The gate to the inn's yard didn't move an inch while she prayed, as it hadn't for hours. Sauren hauled herself upright again and edged back into the dark nook she'd colonised the previous evening. It was an unobtrusive corner of shadow from which she could watch the inn's entrance without being visible to a casual observer. She wasn't quite dressed as a vagrant, but her muddied and torn greatcoat certainly ensured few people would spare her more than a glance, should they notice her at all.

'I had forgotten you were a Quorist,' said a voice away to her left. Sauren jumped in surprise as Exalted Uvrel stepped around a corner and cocked her head at Sauren. 'Give Veraimin my regards, won't you?'

Sauren ducked her head once more, touching her fingers to her forehead. This time she did take her eyes off the entrance.

'Exalted, good morning,' she said, just about able to keep her voice level. A Quorist was a member of the Militant Orders who prayed to all of the gods, not just the one their order was dedicated to. It was not a shunned practice, but she knew many of the more radical elements disapproved. Sauren was new to Uvrel's service and had yet to get a read on the woman, to know where she sat in that particular debate.

'I offer the salute to the gods,' she added, unable to hold back from explaining herself under Uvrel's steely gaze. 'I pray only to Insar, I assure you.'

'Don't worry,' Uvrel replied, 'I've no issue with your devotion; you'd not be here otherwise. A healthy respect for the gods shows a practical turn of mind and that's something I've use for.'

The Exalted walked forward until she was almost opposite Sauren – hidden from the inn's entrance by the wall she leaned against, close enough to the corner that Sauren could talk without turning her head. As she did so, Sauren properly took in what the woman was wearing and had to fight the urge to goggle at her. She'd never once seen the Exalted out of uniform before, but now Uvrel wore a long skirt and fitted tunic that buttoned right up to her throat, over which she wore a matching coat with brass buttons and brocade. Not only civilian garb but elegant and flattering too, cut to fit and clearly not brand new.

'Yes – I own clothes,' Uvrel said levelly.

'Sorry.' Sauren's gaze dropped and it was almost with relief that she saw Uvrel still had her tall boots on. The skirt mostly hid them, but in the place of pointed toes and heels were her usual blackened steel caps and soles made for marching. Delicate heels or some sort of silk slipper might have been a shock too many this early in the morning.

'Report?'

Sauren shook her head. 'Little at all. A handful staggered back after I took over the watch, in twos or threes mostly. No one's left yet. No sign of Lynx or the girl.'

'The informant insists they're in there,' Uvrel mused, 'and he returned to us willingly enough. I'm still half-convinced he's mad, though.'

'No sign of the scout yet?'

'Not yet, but it's too early. Even riding hard and with our friend's directions, he'll be a while searching. This afternoon, I hope.'

'And if I see the girl before then?'

'Do nothing. One of them has been underestimated once, it will not happen again.'

She bowed her head. 'I understand, Exalted.'

Uvrel nodded in the direction of the inn. 'Have you seen enough to gain any sense of these Steel Crows?'

'No, Exalted. Some returned only as dawn was breaking, others had to be carried by their comrades. No doubt more never made it back, but I would expect nothing less from mercenaries. There was no fighting or disruption here, or city patrols arriving in pursuit, but I doubt much conclusion could be drawn.'

'But their commander and sergeants never left all evening.'

She nodded. 'I sent Lubest in to check before he returned to barracks. He's a local, no one will have looked twice at him. He said the commander had them in a back room, drinking and playing cards. The company's taken most of the tavern so there were only a few others drinking last night. He didn't stay long, heard female voices in the room but only saw a black woman while he was there.'

'But you don't keep your sergeants back unless you need them. Otherwise you send them out with the troops to maintain some sort of control. So are they planning something? Waiting for a contact?'

Sauren frowned. 'One of the factions?'

'Perhaps.' Uvrel shrugged. 'Perhaps this commander is simply smarter than the rest and heard of the Order's build-up. He plants his flag and sees what sort of commissions come his way.'

'He just happened to be passing?'

'Never rule out bad luck. But our friend said they numbered under fifty, so nothing for us to worry about. At best they'd be able to escort a few council members and their wealth out to safety. I've tasked a unit to see if there are other mercenary companies lurking in the city. A handful of sell-swords is one thing, but these companies have arrangements to merge for large contracts. A few hundred to support the Assayers might complicate matters.'

'Our friend knows nothing about that?'

'Would you trust him with such information?' Uvrel said scornfully. 'I've avoided asking directly – perhaps the time will come later, but at present he's happy to be our guest. I don't want that to change. He insists . . .'

She tailed off as Sauren held up a hand. 'His contact,' the woman muttered, eyes turned towards the inn. 'Black woman with a red scarf.'

Uvrel nodded, reaching one hand round to the back of her tunic, no doubt checking her mage-pistol was still concealed under her long coat, but then she paused. 'You've been here since before dawn, right?'

Sauren nodded.

'Go and stretch your legs then. I'll watch for a while.'

Sauren scrambled up with a sense of relief and looked across the street to where the contact had turned into an alley. The black woman, *Braqe*, Sauren recalled, caught the movement and gave her a guilty look before gesturing back round behind the inn. Sauren inclined her head and left the Exalted to squat down in the nook as she headed out into the main street. It was still early and only a handful of people were out yet, this being Vigilday which followed the more raucous Feastday. She jammed her hands into her pockets and headed over the dew-damp cobbles across the face of the inn's gate.

Out of the corner of her eye she could make out a number of figures in the courtyard moving past the gate, but it was only half-open and she only glimpsed movement before she was past. At the end of the block she crossed the street and cut in behind the buildings, circling back behind the inn. At the corner of one alley, Braqe stood waiting. The woman was stiff and nervous, fighting the urge to look around all the time. She didn't carry a gun, of course, but there was a battered sword-bayonet hanging on her belt that her hands twitched towards when she spotted Sauren.

'You've got news?' Sauren said softly as she reached her.

'You're one of . . .'

'Yes.'

Braqe swallowed, her expression a fascinating mixture of anger and concern, Sauren realised now she was closer. *Perhaps not as comfortable with betraying her own as the madman is.*

'We're moving out early,' Braqe said. 'This afternoon. They've changed plans, didn't say why.'

'The whole company?'

She shook her head. 'Don't think so, looks like the boss is staying with a few. I heard mention of another inn, a better type for his sergeants.'

'Why?' Sauren fixed her with a level look. 'What's being planned? Don't give me any shit about not knowing anything. We've heard enough of that from your friend.'

'To the deepest black with all o' you!' Braqe snapped, recovering herself momentarily. She took a half-step forward but Sauren was ready for her and had a hand inside her coat, half-drawing her mage-pistol. Braqe saw the weapon and stopped, lips tight with anger.

'Tell me or we're done.'

'I don't know, that's the truth. Commander's got some sort of job, but it ain't a usual merc one. He don't need the company, just a handful 'cos he never does anything alone. Something about a woman running away from home or some such shit.' She scowled. 'I don't get told stuff that I ain't involved in, and I don't care much for stuff I'm not being paid for.'

'It's personal?'

'Fuck knows, mebbe, but with all your friends here he's not taking chances.'

'My friends?'

'Knights-Charnel, who else? Word is there's a thousand of you and that's not good news for the city. If there's to be a coup, it ain't our problem unless we're being paid to get involved, but your lot ain't exactly subtle or much for leaving loose ends. No merc company wants to be in a city when you're taking control of it in case we get dealt with. Understand?'

Sauren nodded, realising the Lord-Exalted would no doubt have planned for as much if they were readying for an armed coup.

'So if some of you're moving out, where's our quarry going to be?'

'Lynx is with the commander. My guess is if things go wrong, a So Han veteran's a useful scapegoat to have tucked under your arm. Sitain's with the main group, commander wants her out of sight for as long as possible.'

'Why has your commander let her stay around for so long?'

Braqe spat on the ground. 'Like I said, your lot ain't subtle. We don't fancy being asked questions about who did what when they're asked at knife point. If he turns her out in the city, she could raise a scene easy enough with Lynx around. Man's not subtle himself and as stubborn as a lame mule. And murder brings its own attention.'

'So you get her out of the city, nice and quietly, and deal with the matter in private – whichever way your commander wants to take it.'

'One problem at a time,' Braqe agreed.

Sauren cocked her head in thought before a smile crossed her face. 'It looks like we'll have to force your hand then.'

'Eh?'

'I'll have the gate guards search everything leaving the city. We've just had word there's a fugitive mage on the loose – wanted for murder too. Either we take her at the gate or we force her to stay in the city and buy ourselves time to arrange a safe arrest.'

'Safe? Commander's keeping back some o' his best fighters.'

'Best *soldiers*, I'm guessing,' Sauren pointed out. 'Not crazed, trigger-happy mercs, but soldiers who can see when they're outnumbered and won't make rash decisions. We'd have taken you already if it wasn't for that. All we need's some damn fool with a sparker or burner in the pipe and we'll be lucky if we're only explaining fifty bodies after the ensuing battle.'

The woman's expression tightened, but she wasn't an idiot. No doubt she'd seen a gun battle inside a city before and knew what her comrades would do to fight their way out of a corner.

'I get it,' she admitted. 'What about the rest of our money?'

Sauren sighed inwardly. *Bloody mercenaries.* 'We're still waiting for our rider to bring confirmation. Once we have that, we'll give the money to Deern and he can catch the main company up on the road. The price includes making our job to take them easier – meaning more bloodless – if they somehow catch up to you on the road.'

'Don't screw us on this,' Braqe warned. 'That wasn't part of the deal.'

'*We* are not mercenaries,' Sauren spat, feeling a spark of anger. 'Do not mistake us for your kind. We don't care about the money, but keeping to a bargain is a cornerstone of faith. If you think you know stubborn, you'll learn a lesson if you test my Order's resolve on a point of principle.'

The look she received was withering. 'Aye, you lot and your damn faith. I've seen the results of your moral high ground an' devotion to the gods.'

Without waiting for a reply Braqe turned on her heel and headed back the way she'd come. Sauren watched her disappear round the corner, a bitter taste in her mouth, before she did the same and hurried back to Exalted Uvrel.

Chapter 13

Sitain dumped the sack of potatoes at the top of the caravan steps and puffed out her cheeks. Strangely, it was good to be doing some proper work for a change. Life on a farm had been hard despite their prosperity. Certainly the hauling and digging involved had never been enjoyable for her – not in the way her brother had seemed to relish it. And yet this loading of supplies was a reminder of something real and her body was glad of the exertion.

She looked around at the mercenaries in the yard. Half of them were still barely able to stand, most were in no great shape to be doing anything useful, so it was Sitain and a handful of others doing the work. She'd never before realised how sedentary the life of a mercenary was, how the inaction piled on day after day when soldiers would be drilling or set to work. Her head pounded and her muscles trembled after the previous night's drinking, but she refused to submit to it.

'Tired, girly?' asked Foren, the quartermaster. He was a small man with lines around his eyes and hair going mostly to grey, but he hefted each sack with ease and loaded the shelves as quickly as his four helpers could bring goods.

'Not even close. Most of your mercenaries wouldn't last a day on our farm.'

Foren chuckled and nodded. 'Most'd only stay long enough to finish the booze. First few weeks of a campaign is hard on 'em. Anatin gets Payl to sweat the fat out and that hurts, let me tell you. Second rule of the mercenary life, don't be the slowest troops in the army.'

'Second?'

'Aye, first is to make sure you get paid.'

Another woman arrived with a second sack, one of the younger mercenaries called Ashis who'd only been with the company a few months. Just a year or two older than Sitain, the woman wore a permanent scowl and seemed to live within a bubble of resentment that Sitain had already decided to avoid.

She went to fetch more from a pile of goods stacked by the inn door. Her portly protector, Lynx, was not one of those helping, and she watched him carefully pack a shoulder bag of food. The care and attention he put into arranging the various pouches reminded her of the meal they'd shared and she almost laughed at the man's obsession with food.

Guess you got to have something to care about, she reflected, a pang of sadness welling up through the nagging hangover. *No home, no family, he takes his pleasure in food. What about me?*

She blinked back the tears and grabbed the heaviest box she could reach, jerking it up hard as though to punish herself. *I've got nothing too, nothing but this cursed magic the Charnelers seem to want. How to take pleasure in that without risking them catching me again?*

Lynx had taken her aside once she'd stopped puking, earlier that morning. In that infuriatingly helpful, fake-fatherly way of his the man had told her what he'd seen as he staggered to bed. Sitain's hands tightened as she hauled the box over to Foren and she didn't even notice the man hesitate at the black look on her face. She was lost in that conversation; in her sudden, intense urge to hit Lynx right in the face her mother would have feared so much.

She hadn't. For all that she'd wanted to curse him, to spit in his face and call him a liar, a drunk, she hadn't. Her dreams had been of magic and a nagging sense of guilt had flowered at his words. She wanted to disbelieve him, but she didn't, and that meant she'd done something so incredibly stupid and dangerous it took her breath away.

Abandoning the load, she headed inside, pushing past a mercenary without caring who it was and seeking out the darkest corner she could find. Her heart was pounding, beating a tattoo of grief and fear that filled her ears and threatened to crack her chest open. She buried her face in her shaking hands as the images of her parents and siblings forced themselves into her mind – smiles and sounds that seemed to cut so deep her stomach was a hollow, raw wound.

The day they'd come to take her away had been like any other. The patter of rain had accompanied their breakfast, just another unremarkable morning. Sitain had barely started her chores when a knock came on the door. It had startled her mother and father both. No one knocked in the village; it had to be a stranger. Their neighbours would have called out before they reached the house or simply walked straight in.

Sitain had stared dumbfounded at the woman's face behind the door when her father had opened it. They'd all just watched, frozen with fear, as that hard-faced soldier had pushed her way in and stepped aside for her commander. Commander Ntois, he'd introduced himself as – all stiff formality and noble arrogance, but not rude or threatening. That had surprised her as much as anything. He had almost verged on apologetic, though Sitain had been so terrified he'd needed to make no threats.

Only when one of his men had escorted her to fetch a bag of clothes had the spell been broken. They had all wept then, parents and children alike. Her mother had grabbed her arm and tried to pull her close, but the female Charneler had caught her wrist. The outpouring of emotion had seemed to irritate Ntois. His tone had grown colder and more reserved, as though such a display was not fitting around strangers, but he had remained polite and coldly certain. Sitain would be going with them, for her own protection.

She would be kept safe from the wilder elements who might try to exploit her ability, Ntois had proclaimed – trained in the arts and instructed in the ways of Insar, god of stillness and the dark night. She would be a valued ward of the Knights-Charnel, guided along the godly path of using magic only in the name of the gods and kept safe from the corrupting effects of unfettered magery.

They had tried to fight, but the Knights had been so quick and efficient – as though they knew already when her father was going to reach for his daughter, when her brother was about to reach for a kitchen knife. Only one mage-gun had been drawn and Sitain's own numbing shock had made her stand docilely as her hands were bound.

In her quiet corner of the inn, Sitain found herself biting down on a knuckle so hard she tasted coppery blood. That brought her back to her senses and then she realised she wasn't alone. The fear vanished from her mind, ousted by anger once more – anger at herself for being so foolish the previous night, anger at being so obedient that last day at home.

'You okay?'

'Just leave me alone,' she muttered, fighting a sudden urge to laugh in Lynx's face.

'Sure?'

'Yes, I'm bloody sure. You can't fix this, you can't undo it. You can't do shit to help, so just leave me alone!'

Lynx didn't reply then. His rounded face took on a vexed look, but then his expression hardened. He shook his head and turned away. Sitain opened her mouth to call out and apologise, but the words died unspoken and a moment later the door banged shut behind him. She watched the door a while longer, feeling foolish and angry and embarrassed all at the same time.

Did the man really not know he was intruding? Gods in shards, I've lost everything – my whole life – and the bastard's always there watching over me. Like I owe him something. Like he's just waiting to step in and be my father. I can't ever go home. My family are as good as dead to me – or I'm dead to them. Doesn't he understand how much that hurts?

She lowered her face and felt the tears splash on her palms. *Cold eye of Insar, he's all I've got. Maybe he knows that much.*

*

Sitain's black mood continued as the mercenary company slowly came to its senses and sobriety hit them all. A thick stew was the final spark that woke them up and once they'd eaten, final preparations were made to move out. The last of the baggage was packed and the entire company shambled out into the inn's courtyard with weapons and packs at their feet for the muster.

There was only one man missing, which seemed to cheer Anatin up – not least because it was the rat-faced Deern, who'd be missed by no one except his long-time companion Reft. Even the pale giant didn't seem surprised by Deern's absence, Sitain heard several mercenaries laugh about the scrapes Deern had got himself into. The discussion swiftly devolved into taking bets on whether he was alive or what charge Deern was being held on. Before money could change hands, however, Reft clipped a man round the head hard enough to knock him down and the talk ended.

Sitain paused at Anatin's caravan. She was to travel out of sight until they were clear of the city, just in case there were agents watching the gates, but a pang of conscience made her hesitate. She looked back at Lynx, sat alone at a table with his gun in a long leather sheath across his lap. He was watching the company at large, but it didn't take him long to notice her gaze and match it.

Ah hells.

She walked over, feeling her resolve drain with every step so once she'd reached him, Sitain just stood there dumbly. Lynx cocked his head but said nothing, which made her feel even more foolish and tongue-tied. She gritted her teeth and took a slow breath.

'Look, I'm sorry, okay?'

Lynx snorted. 'Damn, woman, you're worse at this than me.'

'I . . .' She sagged a little. 'Sorry, yes. You're right. That was . . .'

'A decent start,' Lynx said, his face softening. 'Most folk can't swallow their pride enough for that, so you're not doing too bad.'

Sitain managed a hesitant smile. 'You've done a lot for me, I'm grateful – I really am. I just – when I realise that, I end up remembering what I'm grateful for.'

'I know. Your life got turned upside down and your family got cut away in a way that don't feel quite real yet.' Now it was Lynx's turn to pause. 'Let's just say I've seen something like that myself. Last thing I wanted was anyone's help, but I got it all the same.'

'Did you do as well as me?'

Lynx looked away. 'Let's just say it was a bad time for me. You're doing okay.'

'Well then,' Sitain said awkwardly. 'Sorry. Did I say that bit?'

'You did.'

'I'll just walk away now maybe.'

'See you on the other side, Sitain.'

She nodded and fled back to the caravan, still feeling foolish but her heart was a little lighter. Lynx hadn't been telling her what to do, not really. For all it wasn't his business, only a fool kept slapping away helping hands. There was a yawning pit of loss in her stomach, one that made her want to curl up and howl, but for all that she didn't want anyone interfering, part of her knew facing that pit alone would be worse.

*

'Ah, come in. Sit. Are you hungry?'

Lynx didn't respond, though he couldn't take his eyes off the food and his stomach growled long and loud. A handful of apples sat in a bowl alongside half a loaf of bread and a hunk of creamy white cheese. He felt a tremble in his bones as he imagined the sweet sticky juice of an apple on his tongue, the rich salty tang of the cheese. He had no need to imagine the fresh-baked bread. Its aroma had already fogged his mind.

'You're looking better,' the old man said, the scars on his cheeks twisted by a smile. *'Less like the ghost I first met.'*

This was the third time he had been called to Governor Lorfen's office and each time he had been so frightened he could barely think. Just two weeks had passed since the brutal regime had ended, and the prisoners had still to adjust. They were quiet and wary, glad of the increased rations and reduced work hours, but still they struggled to accept it. Most had never fought in the army, but they had all grown up with the recruiters and the criers loudly proclaiming the superiority of So Han. To then discover it was untrue, that their conquest had failed and the Shonrin's regime had imploded, was a remaking of the world around them.

It had to be a lie that the Shonrin had not even given battle at the end and fled to a mountain fastness, but the defeat was undeniable. How else could two dozen soldiers and this old man be so assured inside So Han territory?

Lynx hovered by the table, unsure what to do with himself while the governor rounded his desk and sat at the table where the food was. The man had green eyes, pale and cold. Lynx had never seen such a thing before and he found he distrusted them – it was all too foreign and strange to accept.

'*Come, sit with me.*'

Lynx obeyed, hands folded in his lap, shoulders hunched. Lorfen nudged the bread closer to him, but Lynx wouldn't move. There was a knife on the board with it and Lynx had seen that trick before. One man had been beaten half to death by the guards for something similar, touching a knife left deliberately out. He'd died a few days later Lynx had heard, through starvation or another prisoner's actions he didn't know. Either was possible. An injury meant weakness in the eyes of the rest, and that was as dangerous as not being able to work.

With a sigh Lorfen cut two thick slabs of bread and put the knife to one side.

'*I'm not here to trick you,*' he said in a gentle voice. '*I just want to talk.*'

Lynx lowered his eyes and hesitantly reached out a hand for a piece of bread. Expecting a blow at any time, none came and he snatched it back with a flood of relief. The soldiers under Lorfen's command were less than gentle with the prisoners, for all that it was a vast improvement on their lot before. They remained soldiers who remembered what it was like to fight against So Han's armies.

'*Will you tell me of the duel you fought?*'

Lynx froze. The duel was of another time. Another man had fought it, not him. A man with a family and a home, a man with a name. The prisoner had none of those things. His family was just a dream he had woken from. His home was a place full of people who had done this to him, faces and voices filled with cruelty. His name was Lynx now. He had seen one on a work detail to cut wood, far in the distance – living lone and free. Grey fur spotted with brown, outlined just for a moment against the sky before it moved on. The image haunted him still, had buried itself deep in his heart and become the small spark of hope that remained there.

'*Called him a coward*,' Lynx said in a voice made hoarse by lack of use. '*What he did to those people was wrong. He liked it, though, the killing and the rest. Laughed as he watched it. Ordered us to rape and cripple the women, cut the hands and feet off the men and boys.*'

'*So you called him a coward and he challenged you to a duel to preserve his honour. And you killed him.*'

Lynx nodded. '*Nobles duel with pistols, but I only had a sword so we used those. Cut his arm off and he wouldn't stop screaming, not until I cut his throat. Then they sent me here.*'

Lorfen sighed and was quiet a long while. Eventually he sat a little more upright and steepled his fingers. '*My homeland is a long way from here, almost across the continent,*' Lorfen said. '*I know little of your people, I admit, but what I do know tells me that was a tremendously courageous act. The soldiers of So Han are taught to love bloodshed, to show no mercy towards their enemies, to obey their rulers without question. That makes you fearsome warriors for certain, but what does it rob you of, I wonder?*'

Lynx frowned and looked down, unable to really understand what he was being asked. It wasn't a prisoner's place to offer opinion but even if he could, he had been robbed of nothing. There was nothing to take beyond the dim and distant dream of the other man.

'*This prison is an abomination,*' Lorfen continued. '*We have slaves in my homeland. It is an ancient practice – one I take no great steps to defend – but I know the slaves there would be appalled by what I have seen here.*'

Lynx said nothing. What was there to say? A world beyond the prison was also part of the dream of the other man, one it hurt to imagine.

'I suppose what I want to ask is what you will do, once you are released. Where will you go? I cannot do it yet, for the weather will turn before you reach the nearest town, and they would likely arrest you as soon as they saw that mark on your face.'

Lynx touched the tattoo on his right cheek. He hardly thought of it, every prisoner had an identical mark and here it meant little. But outside these walls he would always be marked by it.

'If I'm released,' Lynx said hesitantly, not yet believing such a thing would ever happen, *'I'd go east, leave So Han for ever.'*

'They will not welcome you there. It might be they would kill you for being Hanese. South would be better, safer.'

Lynx said nothing, but a sudden urge to go east filled his heart. To follow the wild cat he had seen, disappear over the horizon and away from this man and his questions, his orders.

'Would you do it again?'

'What?'

'Call your commanding officer a coward. Refuse the orders of a coward, a murderer.'

'No.'

'No?' The word seemed to disappoint Lorfen and he sat back, lips pursed. *'You would follow his orders so you could avoid this place?'*

'I'll never take orders again,' Lynx replied. *'No man gives an order like that, only a monster. They were civilians, unarmed. I'll kill any monster I see, wherever they're from. Kill them before they can murder anyone else.'*

'Even if it means being sent to a place like this?'

Lynx cringed, but his hands tightened into fists. *'I'll never come back, if you let me out. I'll die before I come back.'*

'So you would still choose to do what's right even if it means your death?'

'I've seen right, I've seen wrong – I've seen life, I've seen death – but I only hate one o' those. Death's just another day here. It don't frighten me. I won't be like him, or any of the monsters in here. Life's not worth that.'

'I believe you,' Lorfen said after a pause. 'And I admire you.'

'Not trying to be admired,' Lynx said, shaking his head. 'Just all I am now. All I got left.'

'There's more to you than that, I think.'

'You don't know me. You read one file and you think you know everything?'

'I think we're not so dissimilar, when all's said and done. And I think that when I needed it most, there was someone to help me – as I am helping you. You're not the only man in this prison I'll be releasing, but you are the only one who reminds me of me.'

'I never asked for your help,' Lynx snapped. 'I never asked for anything. I don't owe you anything.'

'Indeed you don't,' Lorfen said. 'But I owe the world. My life is not blameless and I owe it to myself to help those who deserve it.'

'You don't know me,' Lynx repeated. 'How do you know what I deserve?'

'Simple. There will always be monsters in this world, so there should also be those who refuse to fear them.'

*

Sitain was glad to hide herself away in Anatin's caravan, closing the door behind her as the order to move out was given. As it jerked into motion she sat down on what little space remained, the cloak of gloom settling about her again. Out of the courtyard and a lurch to the left, then the slow lumber down the rutted road in to the city before they turned right on to the wide avenue that took traffic around the narrower streets of the centre.

It was then that she saw it. A small shape at the base of a low cupboard door – the very centre of the bed platform where Anatin slept out on the road. A nondescript leather purse hung by a piece of string from the wooden peg handle of the cupboard. Sitain frowned. From what she'd seen of the man, Foren was meticulous in everything he did and certainly took his duties as supply master most seriously. To leave anything out was strange. Sitain checked around the rest of the caravan. Everything was put away or tied down, absolutely everything, while as the caravan rumbled on the purse swung freely with the obvious clink of coins inside.

Sitain checked the door in a fit of paranoia, but it remained shut. She gently slid the bolt shut, just in case, and went to investigate the purse. It was dark inside the caravan with the shutters on the window also closed, but enough light crept through the cracks to reveal a handful of silver coins once she emptied the purse out. All currency local to Grasiel, a dozen silver pieces in total.

'That's no mistake,' Sitain said to herself, again glancing nervously at the door. 'Foren's too tidy and Anatin's too miserly to forget his purse.'

She spent a long while looking at the coins before she tipped them back into the purse and cinched it tight again. There was only one explanation that came to mind for her and she was struggling to decide if it was a welcome one or not.

'So someone doesn't want me here, Anatin most likely. And this is what? A bribe? Twelve silver coins must be enough to give me a head start, but not enough for a man to hold much of a grudge against someone taking it. Certainly not a girl he doesn't want around much. Even if he can't bring himself to kick me out, he'll not lose sleep if I slip off and take the danger I bring with me.'

Or he's just looking for an excuse to kill me and be done with the problem?

She sat in silence a while longer, as she contemplated the second scenario. Was it cowardly not to take the offer? Would she in effect be committing herself to the company?

Gods above, what do I even want? If Anatin would prefer me gone, should I even be thinking about this? What is keeping me with them? Is it really just Lynx?

Or am I too frightened to go it alone? Where would I go? Far away from here, far from the Militant Orders, but that's a long way. Their reach stretches for hundreds of miles. And where would I even go? The Mage Isles? Five hundred miles or more through lands which more often than not have armies roaming them. The Eastern Seas, where I'd stand out like a sore thumb?

Or do I stick with the devils I know? It's not like these mercenaries are a devout lot. Only one who objects to me does so 'cos of where my ma escaped from before I was born. Maybe I can stay and learn some healing – put all this to some use and be a burden to no one. If they want me to stay, if I really become part of them, it'll take a small army to make the Cards hand me over.

The thought seemed to lessen the weight on her heart a touch, but just then the caravan jolted to a halt and sent her sprawling. When she'd recovered from the surprise, Sitain hopped up and went cautiously to the window, pushing it open as best she could to try and peer out at what was going on.

Before she could make anything out the door suddenly rattled violently. Sitain jumped, panic filling her mind as a hand banged on the wood.

'Sitain, dammit girl, open the bastard door!'

She gasped in relief, it was Foren. She scrambled forward and unbolted the door, pushing it open and almost knocking him over in the process.

'Hells! Careful, girly.'

'Sorry,' she whispered, scanning the street behind as she spoke. 'What's going on?'

'Traffic's backed up,' he said with a frown. 'Don't know why but I don't like it. Looks like they're searching carts leaving the city.'

'What? Why?'

Foren shook his head. 'Don't know,' he said, 'but I ain't much keen for them to find you here.'

As he spoke a figure rounded the corner of the cart and almost collided with Foren. It was Payl. She had remained in charge of the wagons, where the strongbox and supplies were, while the troops had gone on ahead.

'Time to move,' Payl announced. 'Sorry, but you're getting off early.'

'Are they looking for me?'

'Who cares? You're hiding in a caravan while the rest of us walk, they'll take an interest and there are Knights-Charnel liveries up there. We're not getting you out of the city today.'

'I'm trapped?' Sitain gasped, snatching up her small bag of belongings.

'It's a big city. That's a problem for another day.' Payl waved her forward. 'Come on, move yourself before the queue starts moving.'

'Wait,' Foren said, holding up a hand to stop Sitain heading down the steps. 'There's a purse in there, hanging off a cupboard at the back. Funds, in case you need them. I'm sure you didn't notice it earlier.'

She met his gaze for a moment and a flicker of a smile crossed Foren's face. Sitain ducked her head and headed back inside, scooping up the purse and returning a few moments later.

'You remember where the others were moving to?'

Sitain nodded. The strike group would be leaving the inn and heading to another closer to the centre of the city, closer to their target. If there were complications, Anatin hoped the change would make it harder to link them to the rest of the company.

She got down from the caravan and tucked the purse into a pocket of her jacket. Behind them the street was starting to build up with people, drifting warily forward as they tried to get a sight of what was happening at the gate. Sitain peered around the caravan but could only see a tangle of people and carts ahead. There were plenty of black and white liveries on view, though, more than enough to rekindle the spark of fear inside her.

'What is it?'

She shook her head. 'I don't know. Just thinking someone else could be watching, see who leaves before they get to the gate.'

'You've a nasty suspicious mind there, Sitain,' Payl said, adding, 'it's what I'd do.'

Payl looked around. There were winding side streets leading off in most directions. This part of the city was an old and evolving mix of tall warehouses and tenements punctuating low clusters of houses. 'That way,' she said, nodding towards an alley. 'I think that leads off along the city wall towards the temple of Veraimin over there.'

As Sitain followed the woman's directions she saw there was a bulbous dome peeking over the rooftops, a distinctive Surei construction of devotional elegance amid the functional homes of the city.

'Midday prayers must be about now,' Foren agreed. 'There's no way to cut you off before you reach it and with luck a crowd to lose yourself in around the temple. Nothing like Veraimin's worshippers for some usefully noisy chaos.'

'And if I'm followed?'

'Once you're out of sight of the gate, run,' Payl said. 'If anyone's following, I'll get in their way.'

'Are you sure?'

Payl smiled. 'Reckon Ashis and I can manage that, the girl can pick a fight with a wall. I'll just get in the way as I pull her off anyone who might be trying to follow.'

Sitain forced herself to return the smile. *Gratitude, Sitain,* she reminded herself, *some of these mercenaries are good people. Even the ones that ain't are keeping your secret.*

'Thanks.'

'Hop it.'

She jumped to obey, walking as fast as she dared towards the alley mouth Payl had indicated. No one obviously moved to follow, but she kept her eyes forward, hands jammed in her pockets and clutching the purse. As she passed the tavern that protruded from the corner, the sun broke through the clouds and seemed to cast a golden path down the mostly empty street ahead. She took it as a sign and broke into a sprint, not daring to look back.

Chapter 14

After half an hour of trying to keep to the largest and busiest streets, Sitain finally found herself somewhere she recognised. The great square Lynx had taken her to was also a major junction, seeing a steady flow of traffic beneath each of its four tall white arches.

The sight of something familiar felt like a cooling salve but as the panic waned, Sitain realised her hands were still shaking. She ducked into an eatery and spent a little of Anatin's money on a small stack of pork-stuffed buns and a steaming cup of tea. She found herself a stool in the darkest corner and wedged herself in with her back to the wall behind, watching the square from the security of the shadows.

Did I lose them? She blinked and forced herself to eat, taking long, slow breaths. *Was there even anyone following? Coldest dark, am I just frightening myself now?*

She slurped at the scalding tea, glad of the sharp and very real sting on her tongue. *Don't be a fool*, she reminded herself. *You've always got something real to be frightened of, never forget that. You can't be too wary, not when you're out on the streets alone.*

'So where now?' she muttered.

The man nearest her gave a start. 'Eh?'

'Sorry, talking to myself,' Sitain gabbled, feeling a fresh burst of panic.

'Ah. Not to worry.' The man paused and squinted at her. 'You okay, miss?'

'Fine.'

'Sure? Looks like ya got an elemental on your tail, if ya don't mind me saying.'

Instinctively, Sitain looked down at her clothes, then pulled her dishevelled hair back into some semblance of order. Whether he was right or not, she didn't need to be looking like she'd been running away from anything.

'Bad morning is all,' she said eventually.

He cocked his head and Sitain took a proper look at the man. A light-skinned Asann with grey eyes and a scrappy beard that failed to hide his gaunt face; under a grubby coat he wore the clothes of an itinerant priest, a Jaian. A brown cassock with bone toggles on one side from waist to shoulder, a belt of five cords like a flat hand and a simple iron pendant of Ulfer's tusks around his neck.

'No stranger to the odd bad morning misself,' the priest said gently. 'But in my case it's the drink, more often than not.'

Sitain frowned at the memory of her morning. 'Mebbe that too, come to think of it.'

The priest laughed and slapped a palm down on to the counter-top. 'Hah! In that case, the only answer's more drink. Come, join me.'

'No, thanks,' she said, shaking her head. 'Couldn't stomach more, just need a moment to catch my breath and think.'

'In trouble?'

'Just a man, thinks he owns what he don't,' Sitain replied.

'A story old as time,' the priest said with a sage nod. 'I'd like to say we mostly grow out of it, but most fools grow into old fools.'

She scowled. 'Aye, well some don't take no for an answer.'

'Then keep clear o' that one.' He cackled. 'An' keep a knife handy. You cut his balls off an' I'll teach him a new path.'

Sitain didn't join the old man's mirth. You couldn't geld an entire Militant Order, just like you couldn't reason with them. Controlling mages kept them rich and powerful so they didn't care for the right or wrong of it. Few did when they had the gods on their side.

'Think I'll just keep clear,' Sitain said between mouthfuls, suddenly anxious to be away again. 'Go where he can't find me.'

'May Lord Ulfer guide your path,' the priest said, lifting his pendant to kiss it as he spoke.

Sitain grunted, biting back her first response. 'If he could tell me how to reach the Threegates without running into any red-headed bastards, that'd help.'

The priest eased himself off his seat. 'Well now, guess I'm Ulfer's appointed servant hereabouts and I recognise a holy charge when I see one.'

'No, I didn't—'

'My god commands, I hear his voice clear as day,' he said, waving away her protests. The priest winked and plucked one of the remaining two small buns from her plate. 'But this small tithe wouldn't go far wrong all the same.'

Sitain found herself smiling at that. 'Fair enough.'

'Excellent, ah, delicious.' He shrugged his coat off to fully reveal his priestly robes and handed it to Sitain. 'Carry yer own and keep the hood up. More'n a few priests trail acolytes in their wake, nobody'll look twice.'

'Thank you.' She pulled the coat on and bundled her own up with her meagre bag of belongings.

He shrugged. 'A small act o' devotion. Name's Kurobeil, by the way.'

'Payl,' she said.

'Heading back home? I'm guessing ya came to the big city following this boy?'

'Can't go home,' she said sadly, 'but a friend works up that way. He'll put me up a night or two 'til I work out where to go.'

'Fancy life as a wandering priest's acolyte?'

'Think I'd prefer to join a mercenary company, if I'm honest.'

Kurobeil laughed. 'Life's taking a strange turn if they're your only options.'

He headed outside, leaving his own pack on the floor before Sitain. She looked at it and sighed, pulled her hood up to hide her face and heaved the pack up.

*

It didn't take them long to cross the city and reach the district around Threegates. As they walked Kurobeil maintained a near-constant drone of plainchant prayers while Sitain kept her head low, hoping it was a case of hiding in plain sight. She kept having to remind herself that the Charnelers shouldn't know what she looked like, that her face wasn't going to betray her, but the threat they posed remained like a cloud over the city.

They might ask difficult questions of any young woman trying to leave the city alone or have some way of hunting mages, but although they were out in force on the streets she was just one face among hundreds.

At a fork in the road they stopped, one street leading towards Threegates itself while the other headed away towards the Island of the Assayed. In the distance Sitain could see the spires of mage-built mansions and the funicular track marking the hill-side behind. It remained a wondrous sight, but her attention was instead grabbed by the road to the gates and the crowd waiting at it. Noticing where her attention lay, Kurobeil broke off from his prayer and cocked his head at her.

'That's not for you, is it?'

She shook her head, trying to hide her panic. 'I don't know what that's for.'

Sitain glimpsed a sceptical look on his face but turned away from him, heading towards a side street where a covered bridge connected two buildings. Beyond it, the street opened up into a small courtyard where painted wooden signs for a saddlery and inn hung from the bridge. Brenn's Saddlery meant nothing to her but the Yellow Hood Inn was what she'd been looking for.

'Glad to hear it,' Kurobeil called after her. 'So, where now?'

'I find my friend.'

As though to make a point to the itinerant priest, she slipped his pack off her shoulders and pushed her hood back. After a look around at the bustling street she took the coat off and returned it to him. Sitain headed into the shadows of the covered bridge and, stepping to one side to make room for a horse being led around the square, found herself at the door of the inn.

'There really is a friend?' He raised a hand as Sitain opened her mouth to speak. 'Ain't casting no stones here. We're all allowed our reasons to go where we like. A man like me lives that way, not suited to much else. Just wonderin' if an old man can't be of any more service to a girl in need?'

'You've done enough,' Sitain said sharply before catching herself. 'Damn, that came out wrong. I just mean, I think I'll find my friend here. You've done me a good turn, thank you, but I can go from here.'

Kurobeil gave her a long look before shrugging. 'Like I said, we go where we like, so I pray Ulfer will walk with you.' He nodded in the direction the gate lay in. 'For me, I reckon Ulfer wants me out there on the city road. Mebbe I'll set up at the roadside a few days, give a few blessings to travellers and—'

He didn't get any further as the door to the inn opened and there was a startled noise.

'Shit, damn and dark places,' growled a voice. Before either of them could move a hand emerged from the gloom within and hauled Sitain bodily inside.

Kurobeil yelped and raced to follow as Sitain was roughly dragged through a short corridor. She struggled a moment, trying to reach for the knife at her belt, but had her hand slapped away by a stinging blow. Panic bloomed as she was pulled into a warm smoky room beyond, sensing a flurry of movement as Kurobeil barrelled after her, protesting loudly. Before he could finish, he was also grabbed and slammed against a wall.

Sitain blinked and looked into the cold dead eyes of Teshen. The Knight of Tempest grunted and released her.

'Afternoon, princess.'

Behind Teshen, Kurobeil whimpered and startled her back to her senses. She dodged around the Knight and threw herself forward, grabbing Kas's arm to pull it back so the woman's blade wasn't pressed against Kurobeil's cheek.

'Wait!' she gasped. 'He's with me.'

'With you?' Kas's eyes flashed a moment then she lessened her grip on the priest's throat. 'How's that, then?'

'He ah . . . well, guided me here.'

'Explain,' Teshen advised, 'or I'm cutting his throat.'

Kas sheathed her knife and stepped back to allow a shaky Kurobeil to steady himself on a nearby chair.

'So these're your friends, eh?' Kurobeil croaked. 'Friendly bunch, ain't they?'

'We're the nice ones,' Kas said nastily.

At that moment a door opened and Reft loomed through, having to duck to get his head under the lintel.

'Him, on the other hand,' Kas continued, 'I'd definitely worry about, if I was you.'

Kurobeil looked the huge muscular man up and down and his face went as pale as Reft's. 'Ulfer preserve me.'

Reft offered that wide, humourless smile that showed his gold teeth. Kurobeil shrank back at the sight as Kas chuckled.

'So, girl,' Teshen said, 'what're you doing here? Who's this priest? An' most importantly, do you know how pissed off our Crow-Lord's going to be?'

Sitain blinked at the man for a moment before she worked out who he was talking about. Crow-Lord was the title Anatin had adopted in the city, given they were masquerading as a company called the Steel Crows.

'Um, lots I'm guessing, but there wasn't much I could do.'

'What with her having all those man problems,' Kurobeil said, fixing Sitain with a look. 'Reckon it's time I was going.'

Kas stepped between Kurobeil and the door. 'Yeah, not so much.'

'You reckon I'll run to those Knights-Charnel out there? Wrong god. Don't tar us all with that brush.'

'Who said anything about Charnelers?'

Kurobeil forced a smile. 'Hope you ain't a card player, you can't bluff worth a damn.'

Teshen snorted at that, but before anyone could reply another figure joined them through the rear door. Cigar wedged in the corner of his mouth, Anatin sauntered across to rest one elbow on Kas's shoulder and blew a cloud of smoke across Kurobeil's face.

'She ain't much of a player, it's true,' the commander of the Mercenary Deck agreed. 'But she can put a half-dozen arrows through yer eye faster'n I can load my gun so best you don't piss her off.' Anatin grinned and drew on his cigar again. 'You're a card player then, Jaian whatever-your-name-is?'

'It's Kurobeil – Jaian Kurobeil. And I've played a few hands on my travels, aye.'

The grin grew wider. 'Excellent! Let's have ourselves a friendly hand o' Tashot while we wait, Jaian Kurobeil.'

'Wait? For what?'

Anatin shrugged and draped an arm around the priest's shoulders. 'Sufficient reason not to crack you over the head and dump you in the cellar. C'mon, Ulfer will provide, I'm sure.'

'I'm a Jaian priest,' Kurobeil said, indicating his robe. 'Do I look like I've money for cards?'

'Pot game it is!' Anatin replied. 'I'll spot you a silver, pay me back if you win. Teshen, search our friend here then break out the cards and the copper pieces. Kas, go relieve your latest toy from his post. Tell the bugger to get back here fast as he can.'

Kas nodded and vanished out of the door. Teshen spent an efficient and somewhat intrusive while frisking Kurobeil before he ushered him and Sitain towards a table. One more joined them, the woman with the flame burn on her face, Tyn, and they all sat at a narrow table. A cup was found and silver coins tossed inside, Anatin raising an eyebrow at Sitain until she did the same.

Tashot wasn't a game she enjoyed, but Sitain had realised she was going to have to learn to put up with it around the mercenaries. By the time she'd settled into her seat a pair of cards had appeared in front of her and Anatin started to announce the table cards as though some of them were blind.

'So why're you still here, girly?' the Prince of Sun added, not even glancing up at Sitain.

She blinked at him. 'Is now the best time?'

'Aye.'

She looked at Kurobiel, the startled priest yet to even investigate the cards in front of him. 'I couldn't go,' Sitain said at last, trying to be as vague as possible. 'Got a bit complicated.'

'They're checking wagons leaving the city,' Kurobiel added. 'Knights-Charnel of the Long Dusk, not Assayers, which seems odd.'

'Where'd you meet this one?'

'At a tea stall. He was already there, eating. We got to talking and he escorted me up here in case anyone was searching for a lone woman.'

'Because of all the man problems she was telling me about,' Kurobeil said pointedly. 'That man being a Knight-Charnel, I'm guessing?'

'Guess what you like,' Anatin said. 'Sure he weren't following you?'

'Yes. Someone maybe, I wasn't sure, but not him unless he's the luckiest bastard in the Riven Kingdom.'

'You know they're looking for you?'

'Didn't hang around long enough to find out. Might be it's something different entirely.'

'But more likely we got some bad luck in our wake and a highway patrol reached the city,' Anatin concluded. 'Unless our missing friend got arrested and offered you up as a deal.'

There was a deep growl in Reft's throat and Anatin raised a hand to acknowledge the objection. 'Yeah, I know, but all sorts o' things are possible. I know our friend ain't scared of dying quick, but give any man long enough to stare at the noose he's made for himself, he'll think twice.' Anatin nodded at the table. 'Let's find how lucky you are, Sitain, I raise it one.'

Teshen turned over a fourth table card; the Four of Stars.

'Piss on you, Insar,' Anatin said to the card, 'no bastard use to anyone you are.'

Sitain frowned and looked down at her cards. She had a Four of Blood to match the Four of Stars and a Thirteen of Snow that matched one of the Tempest cards on the table. Insar's suit of Stars was help enough to her whatever Anatin said so she raised the bet. With a hard look at Anatin, Kurobeil matched it and so did the mercenary. The other cards did Sitain no favours, but with only one raise coming before the end, she doubted they helped anyone else much.

At the reveal, Kurobeil had a pair of fives and Anatin a solitary Prince of Snow.

'Looks like your luck's holding, girly,' Anatin commented as Teshen turned over Banesh's card, the one left face down on the table. The Prince of Tempest – help only to Anatin but nothing that could beat Sitain's two pairs, fours and thirteens.

'What? So you believe me because of the turn of some cards?' she said in disbelief.

'Nope,' Kurobeil replied before the mercenary could. 'He cleverly curses Insar an' watches my reaction. Apparently that passes fer subtlety round here.'

'You can't tell a man's soul from one hand,' Anatin said dismissively, 'that'll take me all night and we ain't got that long. But I've seen a few practised liars in my time. Might be you're so good you can fool me, but if that were true, why're you sitting here some penniless Jaian?'

'Maybe I ain't one.'

'Aye, but if you were that good and an agent o' some sort, you'd not be wasted on some little job like her. And if you're just some pious shite who'd sell her out, you'd not be a gambler – nor mostly ignore me cursing any god. Could be you're some scam artist who thought she was a mark, but you'd be carrying a weapon.'

Kurobeil pursed his lips. 'Guess I ain't one to argue yer logic, not if the alternative's being hit over the head.'

'Good plan.'

'So now what?' Sitain demanded.

'Well, I ain't in a trusting mood and we've got a job to do.' Anatin scratched his cheek and indicated for Teshen to deal the next hand. 'Guess we entertain our guest for a while an' I think how to change the plan, just in case I'm wrong about him. Unless you're seeing the benefits of becoming our new company chaplain, Jaian Kurobeil?'

The Jaian shrugged. 'I'm a wandering priest – wandered alongside mercenaries more'n a few times. Can't say any o' them wanted a man o' prayer around for long. Apparently it takes the fun outta sinning.'

'How about for a week?'

'The alternative bein' hit over the head?'

'Somethin' like that. Teshen's real good at it, pretty likely he won't crack your skull.'

'Reckon I'll take the hospitality.'

Anatin smiled nastily. 'Thought you might. Teshen, you an' him take a walk out beyond the walls. Take my pistols and kill him if he does anything you don't like. No offence, Jaian, but best we don't take any chances. Teshen here's more than capable of killing you and escaping from under the noses of a bunch of soldiers.'

'I'll take your word for it.'

'Good.' Anatin looked at the cards he'd been dealt and brightened. 'Looks like this is your last hand, Jaian – everyone's all in, right?'

*

'Good news, Master Deern.'

Exalted Uvrel walked around behind the unpleasant little man sat at the mess table.

'It's done?'

'No, there are complications, but those aren't your concern.'

'Eh?'

She paused at the window and looked out over the view of the Knights-Charnel compound. A high wall surrounded everything, whitewashed like all of their buildings to serve as a point of brightness amid the darkness of heretics. The inner face of the wall was painted with black letters, the script of Uvrel's homeland.

231

'We have made a deal with your comrade. You will be released now.'

'Rider arrived?'

'Indeed. Funeral arrangements are being made.'

'But you've not taken Lynx yet?'

Uvrel didn't answer immediately as she watched the Lord-Exalted himself hurry down the steps of the compound temple, a grey stone pyramid with a doorway-sized section cut into one wall. Her commander looked harassed, no doubt dealing with the latest squabble between the Princip's fractious coalition.

'Did you notice the words on our wall?' she asked.

'Words? Sure.'

'It is a continuous prayer, an invocation of Insar's favour. The words are written in such a way that the end could run seamlessly into the start should you read it aloud.'

'So?'

'So it serves as a reminder that the gods are eternal.'

'Thought they were broken?'

Uvrel pursed her lips. 'Their physical forms are shattered, but their souls guide us still. The Knights-Charnel of the Long Dusk is an ancient order and we have learned the value of patience. It appears your commander remains set on his plans, despite sending his company out of the city, which means this is important to him – or to someone, at least. Your comrade gave my agent the impression this mission is personal, but I prefer to be sure.'

'Why?'

'Because there is a delicate balance in the city right now. Several games are being played out. I would quietly see where this one leads if I can. The Knights-Charnel making a very public show of force would make some parties rather nervous. We are not the authority here, now is not the time to test the Council of the Assayed's tolerance.'

There was a moment of quiet behind her. 'Lost the girl, eh?'

'There is that too,' Uvrel admitted, cursing the man's amused tone in her mind. 'But I doubt it will be for long. We have Lynx under surveillance and she is alone in the city. Either she is lost thanks to the hastiness of my agent or she'll return to Lynx. Insar will provide us with an opportunity to remedy matters or let it serve as a lesson in vigilance.'

'In the meantime, you're waiting for the boss to make his move?'

'I am considering his assignment, whether it impacts on the wider city or not. Mage hunting is not my principal job.' She shook her head and turned to face Deern as he stood and grabbed his belongings. 'Should either of our fugitives escape the city and rejoin your company, I will expect your assistance when we catch up.'

'Just like that, eh?'

'Just like that.'

Deern shrugged, a half-smile on his face, but didn't argue. 'Just one more thing to do, then.'

'Which is?'

'If I got arrested, I'll have picked up a shiner at the very least.' He turned his head slightly, presenting Uvrel with his cheek like a relative asking to be kissed goodbye. 'Only other explanation'd be I found myself a woman. So unless ya fancy helping me smell o' sex and sweat, you get a free shot. Enjoy it.'

Her hand tightened into a fist. 'Gladly.'

*

Deern winced up at the drizzle falling on the city and jerked his duffel bag into a more comfortable position. An autumn chill accompanied the rain and he was feeling dizzy after crossing the city to fetch his belongings, then retracing his steps. He shoved his hand in a pocket and felt a flush of warmth as his fingers closed around the cloth bundle where his gold rings were.

He stumbled on a protruding stone and a sharp jolt of pain raced up the side of his face, the skin feeling hot and throbbing.

Bitch broke my cheek, Deern thought with a mounting sense of rage. *She don't know how close she came to getting shot.*

He blinked and hissed at the added discomfort that brought, but forced himself to keep trudging on. An extra five gold rings in his other pocket – maybe the price of that broken cheek, but all his.

Braqe ain't getting a share o' that now, not with my face hurting like a bastard. He chuckled inwardly. *Not that she'd have got it anyway.*

He walked on, Threegates now in sight, and joined the queue of foot travellers at the smallest of the three. When it came to his turn he was waved through with only a cursory glance. He'd expected nothing else. They were hunting Sitain, after all.

Once he was out of the city he walked another few hundred yards then felt another bout of dizziness. He stopped at a tavern that served the rough streets of houses clustered within sight of Threegates and bought a cup of brandy. The liquor was harsh and bitter, but it warmed his belly and sent a flush of warmth up into his aching face. Finishing the cup he was about to order a second when he spotted a familiar face heading up the road.

It took Deern a while to be sure he was seeing right. Exalted Urvel's punch had packed a lot more weight than he'd expected and he felt like his brains had been scrambled, but as the figure came closer he realised it wasn't just his imagination.

'Teshen!' he called.

The man didn't notice him at first so Deern put his fingers to his mouth and gave a piercing whistle that had half the street looking his way. He waved and the burly man hurried over, a stranger in his wake. Both were scowling as they ducked under the tavern's awning, but Deern just nodded to the barman to refill his cup and raised it in greeting.

'What you doing out this way?' he said as he took another swallow.

'Could ask you the same question,' Teshen growled. 'What happened?'

'Don't rightly know. One moment I was expressing my opinion all civilised like, the next someone cold-cocks me right there in the street.' He touched his fingers to his cheek. 'Never saw it coming but I reckon they used a pistol butt. Next thing I know I'm in some district lockup.'

'What did you say?' Teshen asked wearily.

'Fucked if I can remember now, I'd had a few. Don't think I was even trying to be rude, they just had a bodyguard who took a dislike to me. Think it was something to do with worshipping the gods all in one go.'

'Were they Surei?' the other man asked, a grey-eyed old Jaian by the look of him.

'Aye, fuck's it to you? Who are you, anyway?'

'Most Surei are deeply against Quorism, that'd be enough to offend 'em.' The man cocked his head at Deern. 'Even without yer friendly, welcoming tone.'

'Piss off. Teshen, who's this preaching shite?'

The Knight of Tempest flashed him a brief, humourless grin. 'Name's Kurobeil, and he's your problem now.'

'Mine?'

'Take him and catch up with the wagons. They're only a couple of hours ahead of you. He's to be Payl's guest for a day or two, after that he can travel with us or not, as he likes.'

'But before that, I can shoot him in the face if he annoys me?'

'Nah, just cut his nuts off. If he tries to run or talk to a Charneler on the other hand, use your imagination.'

Deern eased himself off his seat and finished his second cup. 'I can live with that.'

'Will I?' asked Kurobeil.

'Depends. Fancy carrying my pack?'

'Not really.'

'Try again, my friend,' Deern said, patting the sword-bayonet that hung from his belt.

'Still no.'

Teshen laughed and turned to leave. 'You two'll get on okay. See you in a few days, Deern.'

'Heading back?'

'Aye. Boss is feeling paranoid, in case our luck's as messed up as your face. The girl found her way to our base, but ain't sure if she was followed so we're switching taverns all sneaky like, in case we're being watched. All that searching at the gates makes it look like bad news followed us up the road somehow.'

'Reckon someone caught sight o' her little trick with Braqe?'

'Either that or they got folk sensitive to that sort o' thing. Who knows, right? But we're not going tonight so we've got time to spare and one bed's as good as another. Taking too many precautions never hurt anyone.'

Deern nodded. 'Luck to you.' He patted the rounded butt of his mage-pistol and gestured for Kurobeil to start walking. 'Come on sunshine, my mood ain't getting any prettier and nor's the day, so let's catch the rest before sundown.'

*

Lieutenant Sauren caught sight of the Exalted heading down the street and turned into an alley. The sun had just fallen and the ground gleamed wetly under the faint shine of the Skyriver. She had been about to say the greeting to night but bit the words back. Though the god Insar was patron to the Knights-Charnel of the Long Dusk, she didn't want to be pegged as overly pious by her commanding officer.

Sauren had seen enough of that in her career to be careful. The most devoted were never trusted by the hierarchy – never opposed overtly either, to do so would be foolish in a religious order, but dogma and morals impeded power. Well before she'd left the seminary-militant, Sauren had observed the perils of doing that.

She inclined her head when the Exalted joined her. Neither was in uniform, but she could sense Uvrel's ire and thought the extra measure was necessary.

'Report.'

Sauren sighed inwardly. 'Nothing, sir. I've not seen any of them in the last few hours, nor can I work out why they were here.'

Uvrel didn't reply, just turned to look out of the alley over the street beyond. There was little enough to see, beyond shops and workshops of the upper-scale variety and houses belonging to merchants and clerks. A horse and trap clattered past and they watched it go, a fleshy, bald driver hunched over the reins. Behind him sat a strikingly beautiful woman with deep red hair pinned up with jewels and a wine-dark stole wrapped around her shoulders. A courtesan, most likely, returning home to prepare for her latest gathering.

'Not those?' Uvrel asked, nodding after the trap. 'The jewels in her hair?'

'This isn't a district known for them, according to Lubest. The most influential take houses on the lesser river, merchants too, so the ones here won't be wealthy or be visited by anyone particularly important. Those jewels will mostly be paste, I suspect. There are no jewellers hereabouts or anything requiring eight or nine armed soldiers. It's a good neighbourhood but quiet and unimportant. If there's anything our Steel Crows are interested in here, it must be criminal in nature unless the answer's more complex than we can reasonably guess.'

'And they just walked this road, up and down – one pair after another?'

'Yes, Exalted. They stopped nowhere and paid no obvious attention to any one building, coming so far as that tall house, but not lingering.'

'So we will have to take them to learn more?'

'I believe so. Should I start making preparations?'

Uvrel's face tightened. 'We've lost them. Somehow they must have realised they were being watched and slipped away without Harril's squad seeing.'

'That doesn't bode well,' Sauren muttered.

'Which means this street is all we have,' Uvrel continued, as though she'd not heard Sauren. 'Harril's in place a hundred yards further down, two more squads of dragoons are on their way to take up positions around us. They have orders not to move unless something happens or they see the Hanese and the mage together.'

'Looks like we've a long night ahead of us.'

Uvrel nodded and returned her attention to the darkening street beyond, her jaw tight. Sauren watched her out of the corner of her eye. Within the structure of the Knights-Charnel they were part of the Torquen – a highly competitive sub-sect charged with preserving the integrity of the Order and its protectorate principalities. The Exalted were the Torquen's elite and each was given significant autonomy, but any failure could prove costly. Sauren knew the ramifications of losing the mage would be on Uvrel's mind – but allowing something to disrupt their plans in Grasiel too? *That* might lead to her entire detachment being assigned some sort of dead man's posting.

And the others will know that too. I just hope in their eagerness they don't start a gun battle in the street. The last thing I need is death and destruction making anyone ask who screwed up first. I pray to the four noble gods and Banesh too that we catch these mercenaries before they achieve whatever mischief they're here to do.

Chapter 15
(now)

The mercenaries rode away from Grasiel in silence, pushing their horses as hard as they could in the dark. The Skyriver brushed their road with a dull silver sheen, picking out the stones that were lying in wait and painting puddles as hollows of deepest black. They paused only once; the shriek of Safir's horse pierced the night as it stumbled and there was a snap of bone. The easterner pitched himself sideways as his mount lurched, hit the ground heavily and rolled as the horse fell.

The troop reined in hard, Lynx hauling his horse wide to avoid the fallen man. Safir's horse continued to scream, its piercing cry echoing off the buildings that flanked the road. Just a village, in truth, dark and silent. No watchmen came to investigate the sound before Reft silenced it.

Sitain watched the man turn his horse back towards the floundering creature and lean slightly in his saddle as he reached towards it. The horse didn't seem to see the axe swinging and didn't flinch away as he chopped right through its gullet, stopping the cries instantly. It fell back, legs kicking so furiously no one could get close enough to safely finish it off without an even-louder gunshot. Sitain felt a jolt in her stomach at the piteous sight and, unbidden, the tingle in her bones welled up, but before she could do anything the horse jerked one final time and fell still.

A sudden sense of grief washed over Sitain. Caught unawares, she gasped in surprise and felt tears spill from her eyes before she could roughly swipe her sleeve over her face and hide them. On the ground ahead Safir rolled over and groaned, clutching at his shoulder. Kas jumped down and helped the man up, her efforts prompting a hiss of pain.

'Is it broken?' Anatin called from behind Sitain. 'Can you ride?'

Safir gave a pained cough and fought his way to his feet. He cradled his left arm in a way Sitain had seen before, face drawn. 'I don't much fancy staying where I am.'

'You could hide, let them chase on after us,' Kas said.

'Yeah, sure the locals wouldn't sell me out in the morning,' Safir spat. 'Tie this up and get me on a horse, Kas.'

The effort of talking made Safir pant, but Kas didn't wait to let him catch his breath. She yanked a silk sash from around Safir's waist and wrapped it around his wrist, deftly slipping that around his neck and under the other arm to bring around and pin the injured one. By the time it was tied Safir's teeth were bared in a grimace of pain but Kas had been as gentle as the pursuit permitted.

'Some help, Reft?' Safir asked in a rough voice.

As Teshen retrieved the man's belongings from the dead horse, Reft grabbed Safir by his belt and the scruff of his neck, hoisting him bodily up to dump him in the saddle.

'Right fucking mess we are,' the newcomer, Toil, said, grinning drunkenly as she leaned low over the saddle.

'Who in deepest black are you, even?' Sitain found herself saying, the moment of rest finally allowing her to catch up. 'Weren't you lot supposed to be rescuing some innocent little girl?'

'Hey,' Toil replied, 'no need to go pointing out a woman's age. It's rude.' She winked. 'And anyway, innocence is overrated. Most men get bored of it quick enough, trust me.'

'What?'

'Starting to think my wit's wasted on you lot.' Toil nudged Lynx. 'She simple or something?'

'She ain't a merc,' he said. 'Doesn't expect to be lied to so much as the rest of us.'

'So who are you?' Sitain persisted.

'Just a woman with a young girl's heart,' Toil said, fluttering her eyelashes at Lynx, 'hoping to be rescued by some dashing hero.'

'Yeah? Where do you keep it then? Your pocket?'

Toil's eyes narrowed. 'Aye, mouthy bitch got uppity so I took a memento. Got more pockets if you push me, girl.'

'Sitain, fucking shut up,' Anatin snapped. 'You too, Toil. We ain't got time for this.'

'Keep the help in line then,' Toil said, 'or I will. Doesn't look like she'll be a whole lot of use if those Charnelers catch us up.'

'She might help us stay ahead, though.' Anatin gestured towards Safir. 'Safir can barely stay in his saddle. Time to earn your keep, Sitain.'

'What? You can't be serious!'

'Bloody am. Despite that ridiculous moustache and tendency to fire earthers past my nose, he's a friend o' mine. Don't want him falling or falling behind.'

Sitain gaped, on instinct glancing back down the road as though expecting a company of Knights-Charnel to storm up through the dark that very moment.

'What? She a night mage or something?' Toil demanded, unexpectedly cackling with laughter when no one answered. 'Shit. Well, that I didn't see coming, I take it all back. You'll be useful right enough.'

'I don't have the control to do that,' Sitain said, ignoring Toil. 'I could put him out entirely!'

'Don't hit him with the full force of it, then,' Anatin said. 'Hold back as much as you can, anything that takes the edge off means he's got more of a chance to stay in the saddle.'

Sitain glanced around at her companions. Most of them just stared blankly back at her. Lynx only gave Sitain a small nod, while Kas didn't wait for her to make a decision. She grabbed the reins of her horse and pulled it forward until Sitain was right beside the grimacing Safir.

'Do it, girl,' he said, teeth gritted against the pain. 'That lot still fight wars in the east, remember? They don't like my colour much. Not keen to find out how politely they'll ask me questions if they find me.'

She just stared at him, mind blank. She'd practised of course, in secret, but never on a person. It wasn't a gift she could just ignore, but the danger it had posed coupled with the disapproval of the temples had limited that. A drawing of shadows together to try and hide herself at night, a stilling of the odd chicken when she'd been sent to wring its neck. Nothing complicated, nothing that required her to really know what she was doing.

'Hey,' Kas called, slapping a hand against Sitain's leg. 'No time to think, boss gave you an order.'

'But I—'

'Need to try,' Kas finished for her, 'and try now before any pursuit turns up.'

Sitain opened her mouth to argue then closed it again, feeling the eyes of the whole group boring into her. She nodded and reached out as gently as she could. She placed her hands on Safir's shoulder and tried to clear her thoughts, to let the tingle in her bones rise.

Like that first night with them, Sitain reminded herself. *When the elemental came. Just let it come free a little, don't push.*

She closed her eyes and concentrated on the feel of her magic inside her, the image of a flower opening in her mind. The sensation was always there but dormant inside her, quiescent as she went about her day. It took a moment to look inwardly and coax the magic forward, but once she'd started it was no different to breathing or raising an arm – the action was just another part of her. The magic surged forward, eager for release, and Sitain found herself leaning back as she tried to restrain the flow.

Finally she found an equilibrium within herself. The shadowy gleam of magic that danced behind her eyes slowed its restless movement and began to follow her breathing, in and out, in and out. She let it settle into that rhythm for a few breaths then slid her hand gently down Safir's injured arm as she exhaled. The man gasped and flinched, causing her control to waver, but as she let him go the balance returned. Again breathing out, she just brushed his arm with her fingertips before settling her hand very gently over the point of his shoulder. Safir hissed but didn't move and Sitain let her other hand rest against his collar-bone. Again the magic drifted forward with her breathing and on the third breath she felt the tension lessen in Safir's body.

She withdrew and opened her eyes. The man still looked uncomfortable but he gave Sitain a wan smile. 'Still hurts,' he croaked. 'What sort of crapshit wizard are you?'

'Ready to move?' Toil called.

Safir nodded. 'Better than I was, anyway.' He winced as he spoke, but it was clear from the way he sat more upright that the shoulder was improved.

'Let's go then, kiddies,' Anatin said, pointing up the road ahead. 'Another hour, then we'll stop to rest.'

The mercenaries set out, but Lynx held back. As Sitain trotted forward he inclined his head towards her. 'Good work,' the big Hanese said. 'Not the easiest way to test your limits.'

'Thanks.' She ducked her head, trying to hide the fatigue that was filling her body even after that small effort. She continued on ahead, out of the corner of her eye seeing Lynx grin widely at Anatin.

'Not such a shit idea now, eh?'

'What?'

'Saving her. Already showing her value, ain't she?'

Anatin growled. 'Aye, she's showing she could be of use. You, however, you smug overfed bastard – you're still the one who first got the Charnelers after us, so you ain't forgiven yet. We survive a day, it'll be a fucking miracle. You get no thanks from me, Lynx.'

There was a pause and in the dark Sitain was probably the only one who saw Lynx's jaw tense. It only lasted a moment and then Lynx shrugged it off.

'No pleasing some people,' he said carelessly. 'Did the other kids pick on you, when you were young?'

To Sitain's surprise, the Prince of Sun laughed out loud. 'Not twice they didn't. Now shift yourself, afore that poor horse collapses under the strain.'

'Aye, sir.'

*

A whistle from the rear of the column made Exalted Uvrel turn and squint behind them. Dawn was just a pale smear over the eastern horizon, trees looming like ghosts in the mist. She could make out little in the grainy gloom, but it was enough to catch the waving arm of the last rider. She called a halt and turned her horse, trotting back to join the young sergeant who'd signalled.

'What is it?'

'Riders, sir.'

He pointed back down the road. For a moment she could see nothing, but then the twitch of movement in the mist caught her eye. One, then two – moving fast to catch them.

'Dismount,' Uvrel barked at her troops, 'let the horses breathe.'

The troopers gratefully slid from their saddles. They'd been riding through the back half of the night without a break, maintaining a hard pace all the while to try and eat into the mercenaries' lead. She cast her eye over them; seventeen in total, most wearing the black and white livery of their order with the red collars of the dragoons. Two more ranged ahead, a pair of Surei locals with proven loyalties to the Order. The scouts were endeavouring to keep track of the mercenaries, to gauge their lead and ensure they didn't disappear into the darkness.

Uvrel dropped from her horse and tottered a moment as her numb legs wavered. She had been riding for half her life but had never really enjoyed it; never found that rhythm in the saddle that some did. The beasts were a tool, nothing more – to be cared for properly as all tools were, but not to be loved or gloried in as though riding was some mystical experience.

The pursuing riders put on a final burst of speed to catch them and Uvrel could see the foam at both horses' mouths before the knights reined in. It was Lieutenant Sauren and a young trooper with a broken nose she didn't know, presumably just the best rider among those she'd found. The lieutenant half-fell out of the saddle in her haste to report, but remembered to yank her uniform straight before she offered the Exalted a crisp salute.

An effort to make amends, Uvrel noted. *At least she has the brains to try.*

'Lieutenant Sauren,' she said, returning the salute. 'Not the reinforcements I had quite hoped for.'

Sauren's eyes widened a fraction before she realised Uvrel was offering acknowledgement of her effort. An officer would not normally ride ahead of troops she commanded. 'More follow, Exalted.'

'How many?'

'Two companies of mounted, sir, under Commander Quentes, and the rest of your dragoons. The Lord-Commander has also dispatched a squad each of grenadiers and light infantry.'

Uvrel was silent a moment as she finished counting heads. 'So about six score. Good. They'll be foolish to make a fight of it if they're outnumbered three to one.'

'There is more, sir,' Sauren said hesitantly. 'News from the city.'

'What's happened?'

'The man who was murdered. Word reached the Lord-Commander just as I did – I did not wait for confirmation, but it seemed a trusted source. The Princip of the Council of the Assayed.'

'What? He's dead?' Uvrel felt a cold sensation in her gut. 'And I failed to stop them,' she said slowly.

'The Lord-Commander instructs—'

Uvrel held up a hand. 'I don't give a damn what the Lord-Commander instructs. The Lord-Exalted will have my skin for a wall-hanging if I don't return with the assassin, at the very least. If there's no one left to put to question, it would be best if I didn't return to Grasiel at all – compared to that a murderer and a rogue mage are almost unimportant, so far as the Order is concerned.'

Sauren ducked her head in agreement. Her face told enough of a tale there. No officer would be advised to return and report such a failure, not when there were likely to be such disastrous consequences of the Princip's death.

'The Lord-Commander is taking steps to secure our position.'

'Will he take the city?'

Sauren shook her head. 'That did not seem to be the direction of his plans. The caches were to be opened and a regiment sent to monitor each of the deep armouries, but not assault them.'

Uvrel nodded in understanding. The deep armouries were storerooms deep underground, each one topped by a small keep where most of the city's Assayers were quartered. The Princip had provided them with details of all three deep armouries in Grasiel, enough to take control of them if necessary. They were where the siege weapons were kept – the ammunition for the great catapults that defended the city.

While mage-guns could wreak terrible destruction, beyond a certain size of cartridge they tended to explode inside the gun upon firing. Instead, clay balls clad in iron were made with glass cores that ranged from the size of an apple to a man's torso – the former hurled by grenadiers, the latter by huge catapults, and all charged with magic that would be unleashed upon impact.

They were monstrously destructive, but volatile too. Legend spoke of the city called Uttaranash to the south that more than a hundred years ago had been struck by a powerful earthquake. There had been four deep armouries beneath the city. Now there was only a crater.

'Mount up!' Uvrel roared, startling her dragoons into movement. 'Those mercenaries murdered an ally of the Knights-Charnel, and they have killed soldiers of our own Order! We will have their heads and drag the assassin back for questioning or we'll die trying.'

She swung herself up into her saddle, a surge of strength filling her limbs as her mission took on a deadly clarity. 'Do not spare the horses. We must catch them before they reach their comrades. Our Lord Insar, Wielder of Silent Justice, demands this insult to his will be met with righteous punishment! Will you fail your god?'

'No, Exalted!' the dragoons roared back.

Uvrel slammed her heels into her horse's flanks and it surged forward to the head of the column, her troops soon racing to keep up.

*

It was well into the morning before Lynx saw the red and blue of the mercenary company's wagons up ahead. Despite being far from safe he still felt a sudden upwelling of relief at the sight. The faces of the others told a similar story. In the daylight they were a bedraggled lot, exhausted and soaked by the persistent bouts of rain that had fallen throughout the dawn hours. Safir was flagging badly, head bowed and body swaying with his horse's movement, while the strain was clear on the faces of Sitain and Toil in particular.

'We making a stand?' Lynx asked as they urged their horses into a final burst.

All of them were labouring hard. Lynx could feel his current mount's lungs working like bellows beneath him. Just ahead of him Reft's horse looked half-dead, despite the man changing mount every hour. The pale giant's bulk was simply too great for any animal to carry at speed for long. Lynx guessed the man was easily double Sitain's weight and they were all pushing their horses harder than the livery stable's owner would want, but they weren't returning to Grasiel any time soon.

'Don't be a fool,' Toil replied before Anatin could. 'Didn't you see their uniforms at the gate? The red collars? Those weren't normal Knights-Charnel, they were Torquen dragoons.'

'Torquen?' Sitain asked.

'Aye, the Charnelers' elite. Spymasters and assassins one day, saboteurs and assault troops the next – squads filled with men pulled from the regular ranks by whichever Exalted commands them. Defenders of the Torquen Temple's Exalted Servants, so they call themselves. The Torquen Inquisition to you and me.'

Toil rubbed her face as she spoke, prodding at the bruise on her cheek and the split skin at her hairline. Fatigue and that blow to the head had lessened her fierce manner, it seemed.

'I thought they weren't troops o' the line, the Torquen,' Lynx said.

She shrugged. 'Like I said, elites. If the Charnelers go to war, the dragoons will go with them. But also, they're a powerful wing of the Knights-Charnel, able to suborn whole companies when they need to.'

'We don't need to win a fight,' Anatin pointed out. 'Just hold them off. We've got the greater supplies, give them a day or two and they'll be recalled to the city.'

'Or a battalion catches them up in a few days and we're screwed.'

'Don't they have a city to overthrow?'

'Not now,' Toil said. 'Not without the Princip. Otherwise, there'd have been no bloody point me killing the man. They could maybe take it, but they'd never hold it and they know it. Council of the Assayed wouldn't fall in line.'

'So no reason for all their troops to stay in the city.'

Lynx shook his head. 'And every reason to catch you and start cutting pieces off until they find out who sent you.'

Toil flashed him a grim smile. 'Chances are they'll be able to guess, but I reckon they'll still have some questions.'

'Also you just embarrassed one o' the most prideful bunches of armed fanatics in the whole Riven Kingdom.'

Silence descended over the small group at that as they drew closer to the now-halted caravans. Grey clouds scudded overhead, the Skyriver mostly obscured behind them. Shrill calls of birds rang out from the hedgerows and stubby trees lining the road while the soft buzz of cicadas seemed to rise from the grassy plains beyond. Lynx saw the knife-wing shapes of hunting lizards swooping and darting over the plain, while in the distance a herd of what he guessed were antelope steered away from the mercenaries. The rain had muted the scents of the open country, but Lynx was glad to have the city's stink washed away at last.

As they neared the wagons, Lynx saw the remaining members of the company scattered around the road, watching them.

None seemed to be setting up any sort of barricade, though. This wasn't a force getting ready to defend their position.

'Ah, good work, Payl,' Anatin said aloud.

Lynx frowned, not seeing what his commander was talking about, but as they closed he realised the ground on their right opened up and the path forked. The chatter of a river became audible and as the distinctive figure of Payl started walking towards them, the flattened ground of a ford was unveiled behind the trees.

'She's had the same thought as me,' Toil pointed out. 'We're not outrunning anyone with those wagons. Either we set an ambush or we leave the road.'

'Ambush, then,' muttered Kas, looking round at the cover they had. 'Cross the river and dig in, tear 'em up as they try to follow. Leave a Suit behind to hit 'em with earthers and burners from behind.'

'That Suit's as good as dead if they outnumber us. Heading cross-country levels the playing field – improves our chances, even.'

'We can't get the wagons out that way,' Anatin snapped. 'And on that west plain their cavalry will run us down.'

Toil snorted. 'Sure, but the ford leads east, not west.'

'Go east? You're bloody mad.' Anatin shook his head and stood up in his saddle. 'Payl, good to see you! Himbel, where are you?'

A dark face pushed forward out of a knot of mercenaries as the strike group closed the last few yards.

'Got injured?'

'Safir's broken something,' Anatin said, glancing back. 'He's done, been riding all night.'

'I'm fine.'

'You're not, you'll faint clean off that thing if you have to ride an hour more.'

Two men wearing Snow badges came forward to help their Knight off his horse. Safir grumbled and hissed, but was too weak to put up much resistance and eventually he let them half-carry him over to Himbel. The rest of the mercenaries gratefully eased themselves off their horses and the quartermaster, Foren, directed the young recruits to start handing out bread and watered wine. More than a few gave Toil suspicious looks but the woman ignored them all and stalked over to where Anatin was talking to Payl.

'We need to leave the road,' Toil repeated, stepping between the two. 'All their advance group needs to do is pin us and slow us down.'

'Sounds like your plan was flawed from the start, woman,' Teshen said, joining the group. 'They were always going to pursue us and we ain't dumb enough to delay them while you ride on ahead.'

'Do I look dumb?' she snapped. 'Course I know that. I just didn't count on hiring a bunch of cowards.'

Teshen's eyes narrowed. 'Best you choose your words more carefully.'

Toil's scornful look made more than one mercenary twitch their fingers towards mage-pistols, but before anyone drew she said, 'Sounds like you drew attention down on yourselves and killed my first plan. We could've ridden on by easily enough if they were just after a small party.'

Toil sighed and shook her hair out to retie it properly. 'Mercenaries on the road ain't such an unusual sight,' she continued. 'More importantly, *mercenaries staying in the bloody city while a completely separate group of assassins escape* ain't likely to draw note. But you lot wanted to have your guns outside the city in case it got nasty, and now you're all frightened to go east and take the best chance at losing our pursuit.'

'East isn't exactly safe,' Anatin said slowly, as though he was speaking to a child. 'East is bloody dangerous, in fact.

There's a few reasons why we'd have a good chance of losing the Charnelers there, but firedrakes and trolls are near the top o' the list. But even if we don't see any elementals at all, we're only twenty miles from bloody Shadows Deep and once you're there things get really nasty!'

'Huh. You'd think professional soldiers would have some stones to share among themselves.'

'It's a Duegar city-ruin! You really are bloody mad. You even see one of those hell-holes?'

'Better'n you,' Toil snapped. 'I've gone over, under, through and round half a dozen Duegar ruins. You think I'd suggest an escape route like this if I hadn't?'

'How should I know? I've only just met you and like I said, you're pissing mad!'

'I've walked the deepest dark,' Toil said, prodding Anatin in the chest for emphasis. 'I've broken bread with the Whisper clans and I've looked out from the highest tower of Skyreach. I can get you through Shadows Deep and it'll be a whole lot safer than picking a fight with a regiment of Torquen dragoons.'

'And we're just supposed to trust you?' Olut broke in. 'We don't know you and you ain't paying enough to take those risks.'

Toil flashed the big woman a smile. 'No different to any battlefield – and those risks just got smaller.' She pointed a finger at Sitain. 'We've got a mage. Skilled or not, the Falesh will sense her magic and be drawn to her.'

'Falesh? You mean night elementals? That supposed to be a good thing?'

Toil nodded. 'They're not dangerous 'less you piss 'em off. So long as she smells nice to the Falesh and doesn't do something stupid, there's no problem and other elementals are likely to steer clear.'

'What? Some shadow can frighten off a firedrake?'

'No, but they'll avoid other elementals by choice so if night elementals are close, the rest aren't likely to be.'

'Who in coldest dark says I'm going anywhere?' Sitain yelled, her voice suddenly shrill with alarm.

'I do,' Toil said with a fierce grin. 'You'll be damn useful there.'

'Good luck with that. I'm not signed on with this company.'

'Sitain, you're coming,' Anatin said firmly. 'She's right, the wilds are full of elementals and a mage is a real advantage. We can call it forced conscription if you like, but you're in now. Full pay and rights from here on, but you're coming with us.'

'Bloody aren't.'

Anatin drew a mage-pistol. 'If I am, you are.'

'Hold up there,' Lynx said, stepping forward. 'Threats now?'

'Aye, there's no time for discussion. If I'm going, she is too and you're following my orders. You don't like it I'll leave your bodies on the road, give the Charnelers the impression we killed the Princip's murderer and left the body for 'em. Anyone can leave the company after the job's done, you can walk with your pay intact, but not now – not when there's lives at risk.'

Lynx took a long breath, realising Teshen was edging towards him, but before anyone else drew a weapon Sitain put a hand on his arm. 'Don't, it's not worth it.' She turned to Anatin. 'You'll let me leave?'

'If that's what you want. You want to stay and work with Himbel, that's also good. Showed potential with Safir, you'll be worth the pay.'

'Sitain,' Lynx began, 'you don't know—'

She held up a hand to stop him, a thoughtful look on her face. 'I start as a noble card,' she said eventually. 'I've got skills none of this lot do, fighters are ten a penny.'

Anatin gaped at her then burst out laughing. 'A card, eh? Piss and wind, yer a girl after my own heart! Aye, you got skills. It's a deal. What card's spare?'

Payl cocked her head in thought. 'Girl after your own heart,' she repeated, 'looks like we just found a new Jester of Sun.'

Sitain ducked her head in acknowledgement, her expression wooden. 'So long as it's not anything under Stars. I'm done with Insar. I'll wear any god's card but his so long as the Charnelers are after me.'

'You think any card'll be worth going into a Duegar ruin?' Lynx warned.

'What other choice is there?'

'There's always a choice.'

'What? Walk away now? Take this road on foot and hope they don't see me for what I am? Those bastards want to make a slave of me, want to take everything I've got and make weapons out of it.' The anger burned in her eyes now and Lynx realised she wasn't to be swayed. More than ever before she looked Hanese then, and he made himself step back and bite down the instinctive snarl welling up inside him.

Anatin watched him a moment then nodded and looked around at the company. 'Jester o' Sun,' he said slowly. 'Sounds fitting to me. Estal, you agree?'

'All the current Jesters are trouble,' the company seer replied. 'Reckon she belongs there, aye. We'll tell her what happened to the last one another day.'

'It's settled then. You're in and you do what I say. Now, about your pay . . .'

Lynx left Sitain to it, seeing she would hammer out a good deal for herself and wanting a little space for the sparker in his blood to subside. He turned away from the knot of mercenaries and pushed his way through the onlookers. Back down the road he could just about see a pair of riders watching them. He reached for his mage-gun then checked himself. They weren't advancing, but keeping as far away as possible.

'Riders behind,' he called. 'Scouts maybe.'

255

Anatin pushed his way over while Toil grabbed the nearest horse and mounted to get a better view.

'No one else?' Anatin asked her.

'Got a spyglass?'

Payl handed one over and Toil spent a long moment scanning the open road and what she could of the surrounding fields. 'Looks like scouts, yes,' she said eventually. 'Just keeping us in sight while the rest follow. One horse each. Probably killed a few spares to catch us up. Time for you to make a decision, Anatin.'

The Prince of Sun scowled and glanced back at Payl. The taciturn woman nodded back at the wagons.

'Supplies all ready if you need, food and ammunition.'

'You serious?' Teshen asked quietly. 'Shadows Deep looks like a good option?'

'Can you see another?'

'Kas and me double back, take their scouts. Maybe ask one how many troops they have.'

'They might not even know, and what if it's more than we can handle? We lose hours of our lead.'

'Have you been through a Duegar ruin?'

Anatin exhaled loudly and slowly as though reluctant to admit it. 'Skirted one, never went deep.'

'Me neither – and there's a good reason for that,' Teshen said. 'Stonecarver nests and Tanglethorns are dangerous enough, let alone the elementals that're drawn to the wilds. You travel the darkest deep and you'll find maspid packs, even if you steer clear of all the traps left there by the Duegar.'

'I know all that,' Anatin snapped. 'You think I don't?'

Again Toil physically interjected herself in the conversation. 'Stonecarver beetles you can burn out, Tanglethorns are easy to avoid if you know what you're looking for. We don't go into the dark unless we need to, of course, but I've done it a dozen times. Maspids are quick and nasty, but that's what we've got guns for. Traps I can steer us around or fool. I've done it before. Remember, I'll be the one at the front out there. I'll get eaten first if I screw it up.'

'That's not as reassuring as you might think.' Anatin sighed. 'Coldest dark, we don't have a choice, do we? They'll catch us on the road; we've got to leave it.'

He turned and waved for the quartermaster. 'Foren, get those supplies loaded on to our horses, we're going east. Payl, you're taking the rest round to Chines same as before, but make it quick or they might send for reinforcements to chase you down.'

A mutter ran around the mercenaries, even those who weren't braving the horrors of Shadows Deep.

'Short rations,' Toil added loudly. 'By my guess, we'll be no more than a day in the saddle. No roads into a Duegar ruin, not on the surface anyway. We'll have to lose the horses and keep going on foot.'

'You're a man short,' called someone from the throng of mercenaries, faces turning to reveal the bruised face of Deern. 'Safir ain't goin' nowhere.'

'Where the buggery did you appear from?' Anatin said. 'Thought you were dead!' he sniffed as he looked the smaller man up and down. 'Looks like you've had one o' the kickings you so richly deserve.'

Deern smirked. 'Missed you too. Got let out two mornings back. Turns out I'd been rude to some stuck-up cow and she had her guards jump me.'

'Well that's a shock right up there with daytime being easier to see in.' Anatin shook his head. 'One man down, you're right. Don't want those scouts to see we're light on numbers, might think Toil's stuck with the company. You volunteering, Deern?'

The wiry man stood a little straighter, a sly smile on his face. He looked around the small troop, looking Lynx straight in the eye with his mouth slightly open, poised to speak. But nothing came but a small laugh as he made to take a pace forward then veered away instead.

'Did you hear me volunteer?' Deern said, a mocking smile on his face. 'Buggered if I'm going with you, I don't need bonus money that bad. Reft's big enough to look after himself I reckon, don't need me to hold his hand. I'll see you all on the other side, but I can't see any good reason to go through Shadows Deep myself.'

'Suppose not. Well, anyone? A Knight's bonus pay for whoever takes Safir's place.'

There was a general looking around at their comrades.

'No one? Llaith? You're a fine woodsman.'

The pock-cheeked man nodded slowly, cigarette smoke curling up across his face as he considered the idea. 'Terrain around a Duegar ruin ain't the same as elsewhere,' he said eventually, 'and I ain't getting any younger. Not sure a trek like that's for me.'

'Dor? Estal? Ashis? None of you up for the challenge?'

The white-haired Seer shook her head, no apprehension on her face but Lynx had been told she wasn't the fighter she'd once been, not since her injury. He didn't know who Dor was and didn't see a reaction from them, but before it could drag out any longer a sour-faced young woman stepped forward.

'Always wanted to see a real Duegar ruin,' Ashis declared. 'Now's as good a time as any, I guess.'

Anatin nodded at the woman and turned to the rest of his elite team. 'Time's a-wasting, then. Best we get away fast and give them a harder choice between us and the rest of the company.'

Lynx felt weariness bubble up from his boots as he took the pack a mercenary offered him. He glanced at Sitain then Toil. The young woman was standing wide-eyed, apparently astonished that she had just agreed to accompany them, while Toil just rubbed a hand over her face, rolled her shoulders and went back to work.

I knew joining this lot would be a mistake, Lynx thought to himself, but his eyes lingered on Toil for long enough that he realised it wasn't just orders or some sense of responsibility towards Sitain taking him east. There was a fascination, too, with this wild agent of some city-state he didn't even know yet. Willing to march time and again into the jaws of danger, clearly driven by something deeper than greed, there was more to Toil than Lynx knew. He realised now that he craved answers to that puzzle. Toil was as darkly alluring as Shadows Deep, beauty and danger moving as one, and Lynx knew he wasn't a man to always desire what was good for him.

'Someone give Sitain a gun,' he called. 'Can't ask anyone to go there unarmed.'

Payl nodded and handed over a mage-pistol and cartridge pouch which Sitain awkwardly belted around her waist.

'Shadows Deep?' she asked in a hoarse voice. 'What have I just agreed to?'

Lynx forced a smile. 'Sure it's not as bad as it sounds. You know how mercenaries like to whine.'

Chapter 16

Uvrel refused to simply stop and wait for Sauren's promised re-inforcements to catch up. She reluctantly lessened the dragoons' pace to at least give them a chance, and save the horses they'd brought, but they still moved quickly and rested infrequently. As the sun brushed the outer edge of the Skyriver she raised her hand to bring her small column to a halt, Sauren waiting just a moment before ordering the dragoons to dismount.

'Sir?' the lieutenant asked quietly. 'Shall I order rations?'

'How far ahead do you think they are?' Uvrel asked, staring off down the road.

They had glimpsed one of their scouts half an hour earlier, the man returning just far enough to give a signal before retracing his steps. Other than that, they'd had precious little trace of their prey, just one exhausted horse tied up by the road and a second that had been put out of its misery.

'Not far at all. Their pace must be slowing by now, surely?'

'Let us hope. Once they reach those caravans they'll see they can't all escape us. Mercenaries won't sacrifice themselves.'

'Will they fight?'

Uvrel scratched her armpit irritably. 'There's no way to tell. With reinforcements we can flank them, they'll see our numbers and then surrender, I'd say. Probably put an icer in the brain of their captain themselves. If we catch them as we are, they'll believe they have a chance.'

'We could be walking into an ambush.'

'If they have the guts for it,' Uvrel said dismissively. 'No reason they got a good look at our numbers before they fled the city.'

'But if it's their only chance?'

'They still have to wait for a good ambush point and we've passed none since dawn.'

'Should I ride ahead? It'll make any ambush all the harder. They might not even try it if they lose the advantage of surprise.'

'Surrender instead? A small hope, Lieutenant, but the idea is a good one. Do it. Keep well within sight though.'

'Exalted!'

Uvrel turned at the voice from the rear of the column, but no explanation was necessary as a rider was coming up hard behind. Not a dragoon, but wearing the black and white of the Knights-Charnel all the same. His cloak flapped free behind him as he tore towards them, mage-gun visible in a white saddle holster. He jumped down from his horse and abandoned it as he stumbled towards Uvrel and offered a sloppy salute.

'Exalted Uvrel.' He was an evil-looking man with sandy hair and blotchy, uneven cheeks that made him look like a brawler or a drinker, most likely both.

'Yes, Trooper? You're ahead of my reinforcements?'

'Yes, sir. Commander Quentes sends his compliments. They're about an hour behind, if you hold here.'

'That I will not, Trooper, we've still got the numbers to deal with them so Quentes will have to catch us. Dragoons, make ready to move on!' Uvrel shouted to the rest. 'Time to earn your pay!'

'Shall I wait for my commander, sir?' the trooper asked, more out of hope than anything else.

It was clear he'd be keen for the rest, having pushed on to catch them and only earning a regular man's wage, but Uvrel wanted all the numbers she could muster if an ambush was imminent.

'You too, Trooper. Lieutenant Sauren, go up ahead and keep within sight. Drop back if you spot an ambush site or anything else unusual.'

The column continued on in the same manner as before, a quick pace for travelling but a curtailed pursuit. As the afternoon warmed and the sweat built under her tunic, Uvrel felt her frustration wax with every passing mile. She watched Sauren keep as far ahead as possible on the long, straight road, dropping back a shade when there were other travellers, but this was a path many avoided. It verged too close to the wild of Shadows Deep for most tastes, the majority of traders taking the north road from Grasiel instead.

To her intense frustration they did pass an escorted caravan train from the coastal towns of the inland sea, Parthain, where the mercenaries were likely heading. From one of those they could hire a ship and set out across that great inland sea to any of the three city-states that might be behind this murder.

There was a sizeable escort to the caravan, all wearing a green uniform flashed with red that marked them as Knights of the Sacred Mountain – a warlike Militant Order dedicated to Ulfer. While the two orders were not exactly allied, scripture and regional politics meant the Mountain Knights would likely have joined any battle as Uvrel's allies, had they come across the mercenaries at the same time.

As it was, the captain commanding the escort was happy to stop and answer Uvrel's questions. They had indeed passed a mercenary company a few hours earlier and a smaller group no more than half an hour after that. The two would have met up by now given the pace set by the second party, their numbers and insignias conforming to what Uvrel already knew.

They parted quickly after that, the captain offering Ulfer's blessing on their mission and regretting that he was already commissioned to a duty. Exalted Uvrel was brief in her thanks, not wanting Ulfer's blessing when it didn't come with additional guns, and pressed on. There was a renewed eagerness in her troops, however, having heard solid news of their prey, and in less than an hour Uvrel found herself standing at a bend in the road with both local scouts, hooded against the sun, and Lieutenant Sauren, glowering at a river ford.

'You're sure they parted company?'

'Someone did, sir,' the scout replied. 'Saw nine riders break off and their tracks lead out of the ford, heading into the wilds. The rest of the company carried on down the road.'

'And where is our assassin? Where is the mage?' she wondered, looking past the ford at the grassy plain beyond.

'If I might, Exalted?' the scout continued, hesitantly. He was a middle-aged man with white stubble on his chin, eyes looking black in the shadow of his hood.

'Go on.'

'I've gone a way into the wilds here before. It's no more'n two days of plains before you reach hills and ravines, easy to track horses over that. If they know what they're about, no decoy would try to lead you off that way.'

'Surely they could buy enough time for the rest?' Sauren argued.

'If they were Knights-Charnel, fine. We'll obey orders and run off round the wilds, but mercenaries? Not a chance they'll risk their hides like that.'

'What if they're not in fact mercenaries?'

'Then they're damn loyal troops, doing that for the others. They ain't getting out of the wilds easy. We can track and encircle 'em on the plain, they're pinned by the river on this flank and Shadows Deep beyond.'

'And they can't get back around us, not if they're returning to the road. They must expect us to have some form of reinforcements following.'

'Exactly, sir. They're running for Shadows Deep is my guess. Mercs often sign up with adventurers to serve as added muscle; maybe they've been there before and know a path.'

'And they're banking on us not, or following the main company who can just stop and deny everything. If they don't put up a fight and there's none of the faces we've seen, what evidence do we have to offer the Lord-Exalted? The best we can hope for is names and descriptions to put a bounty on.'

'It's still not a move you make lightly,' Sauren said, doing a fair job of keeping the apprehension from her voice.

'When the Knights-Charnel are your pursuers, there are no easy choices,' Uvrel replied. 'Sauren, hold here and direct the rest after us into the wild. Have a company hold position at this ford to watch our backs in case the rest of the mercenaries try to double back. You had grenadiers and light infantry following you, Sauren, correct?'

'Yes, Exalted.'

'Good. We'll want the light infantry to follow them in the wild.' A tight smile appeared on Uvrel's face. 'And grenadiers are mad enough to enjoy the many delights of Shadows Deep.'

'Let's hope it doesn't come to that.'

'Indeed. Dragoons! Ride as hard as you can! A Duegar ruin awaits us if we fail!'

*

The mercenaries rode in silence for an hour. The plain had a steady, gentle slope for the main and they made good time, but in the distance a dark shape lurked. Lynx felt it preying on his mind and as the ground beneath them climbed, the presence of Shadows Deep loomed larger.

'What exactly are we riding into?' he called to Toil, unable to hold out any longer.

'Don't you know?'

'A Duegar ruin, I get that much, but I've never seen one. It was a city? There are streets and buildings?'

'Ah – not like you've ever seen. Well, there are, but mostly underground. They didn't build on one level but followed the course of the ground and the minerals they mined. Folk call it Shadows Deep after the rifts, two of them. One's open to the air, the second is deeper but you'll only find it underground.'

'There are bridges?'

'Dozens!' She laughed. 'But it's been a while since there were Duegar stone mages to maintain them. Lots will have fallen, many more you wouldn't want to cross.'

'So we have a plan here?'

Toil glanced back at him. 'Getting anxious there, Lynx?'

'Course not, what's there to be worried about? Walking into the unknown where most folk are too sensible to go? Where the nicest bits are the wilds where elementals rule?'

'Oh, take me home,' Toil sang out, 'where the elementals roam!'

'That knock to your head worse than we thought, Toil?'

'Pah, you people all fear the wilds and you've never really seen them. Duegar ruins are sights to beat any human city. Sure there's danger, but there's beauty too and you've got to realise the rules you live by don't mean so much in there. Fear this place and it'll eat you alive, embrace it and it'll live inside you all your years to come.'

There was a pause.

'Like some sort of grub?' Anatin asked finally. 'Flies laying eggs in a wound?'

'You just wait,' was all Toil would say in response, refusing to rise to the bait.

After their first rest the ground started to break up more. Great boulders the size of houses, then palaces, jutting up out of the landscape, sharp gullies where streams flowed and the horses could barely negotiate their way. The sound of birds and cicadas grew more distant, though eagles circled high above and Lynx saw beetles gleaming red and blue as they buzzed through the air or scrambled through the grass around the horses' hooves.

The haze on the horizon remained, however – a bank of grey that could have been cloud but for its jagged profile. To the south of that, three mismatched peaks too slender to be mountains, too large to be any sort of towers Lynx had ever seen. It was the underground that Lynx feared, though, the thought of scrambling through narrow cracks in the rock and the horrors that might lurk in the deepest black beyond.

I do know one thing about Shadows Deep, Lynx reminded himself. *Those great rifts and the lowest mines of the Duegar. Didn't I meet a man in some town who'd been an adventurer? A relic hunter? One leg and seven fingers left, that bit stuck in my memory – that and the fact his mind was cracked.*

He had a maspid tooth on a cord round his neck, a trophy of the one that'd almost got him. Didn't mind telling that story, did he, but then he got to the great rift. Someone asked how deep it went, what you could see there, and he went from laughing to crazed drunk in a heartbeat. Whatever he saw in that fissure, it broke his mind.

A hiss from Toil brought him back from his reverie and at a gesture the company slowed. She raised a hand to ward off the inevitable questions and the mercenaries readied their guns. For a while there was nothing, but then Lynx heard a tremble run through the ground. It came and went, slowly growing in intensity, before the rise ahead of them began to shudder and distort.

'Everyone stay calm,' Toil said without looking back. 'No need for guns, so put them away again.'

No one obeyed until she turned, the anger clear on her face, whereupon Reft slung his gun back over his shoulder and the rest followed suit.

'Good. Guns wouldn't be a clever idea.' She nodded towards Kas. 'That bow, on the other hand, might be useful.'

The rumbling from the rise continued and as Kas nocked an arrow, not really knowing what she was going to be aiming at, the rise itself distended and a stretch of earth heaved up. Almost as one, the horses shied away and it took a while to get the startled beasts under control. As they fought with the reins of their own mounts and spares, a pair of grouse flew up from the undergrowth in a flash of white and red and the musky scent of earth filled the air. The earth continued to shudder from some great pressure rising deep under the ground and Lynx's horse stumbled, the party grinding to a halt as the shaking became too great to safely walk through.

In the next moment brown streaks flashed away off to the south, three then four rabbits fleeing their burrows and risking the open ground. As the shaking subsided Kas let fly but missed and they were gone, then more followed. Kas fired again at a second pair just before they reached the cover of bushes. She hit the larger of the two and the arrow slammed it backwards, feet hammering frantically for another few moments before falling still.

'Earth elemental,' Toil said in a low voice. 'Don't think it'll break the surface. I've never seen one.'

The knots of long grass on the rise waved and shook as though a strong wind was moving slowly over the length of it.

The earth rose again then fell back and split open as a crater appeared in one flank of the rise. Then it moved on towards a copse of trees that had grown up just downwind and Lynx heard the creak and snap of wood as they writhed amid its passage. One tree seemed to snag the monster and the roots were ripped out from under it as the entire tree lurched and almost fell. The ground gave another shudder of movement then all was still again, the distant shaking Lynx could feel through his horse swiftly falling away to nothing.

The tang of cold, damp earth was all that lingered and soon Toil motioned for them to move on. Lynx found himself wanting to ask her questions, but his eyes were drawn to the wrecked tree that had been almost entirely uprooted without much apparent effort. The sight alone was enough to keep him quiet for a while longer and when they next rested, Anatin took Toil aside to converse quietly.

Lynx dropped down on a hump of ground and cut himself a few slices of cured sausage while he gave his aching thighs a chance to rest. Before long Kas arrived beside him and squatted down on the ground, nodding towards the meat.

'Cut me a piece?'

Lynx did so and handed over a finger-joint-sized chunk, the meat stained red and speckled with fat. They chewed in thoughtful silence, the dried meat slowly succumbing and releasing such a rich flavour that Lynx found his aches and worries fading away for one brief, wonderful moment.

'What do you think of her?' Kas asked, nudging his boot to bring Lynx back to reality.

'Who? Toil?'

'Aye.'

Lynx shrugged. 'Don't know yet.'

Kas smiled. 'No thoughts at all?'

'Sounds like you have.'

'No more'n the rest of us. She's beautiful an' she knows it.'

'Don't you?'

Kas made a dismissive sound. 'That woman wields beauty like a weapon. My guess is, there's a sharp edge there too. I suggest you be careful.'

'Me?'

'All o' you men. Ain't hard to see the effect she's had. I'm not telling you anything specific, just saying to be careful.'

'Nothing specific?' Lynx frowned at her. 'You sure about that?'

'Pfft. I don't share men – I don't own 'em, neither. That detail's all your concern, but she's not a Card; she's some prince-elect's agent. And just like a Charneler, she's got a mission she believes in.'

He nodded. 'Whatever gets the job done? Believe it or not, I've met the type before.'

'Did you make puppy eyes at those others too?' Kas said with a smile. 'Ah, I'm only messing, don't look so hurt. You're a big boy, if I thought she was going to lead you by the nose all the way across Shadows Deep, I'd not be risking my own oh-so-perfect hide.'

She looked around at the rest of the group. 'It's still worth saying, mind. Anatin's a suspicious old sod who's misused his own charm more often than he can count, I'd guess. Teshen's got no soul and Reft ain't interested. Out o' the rest of us, she'll likely not waste her efforts on the girls so that leaves just you an' Varain.'

She winked at Lynx. 'Him, you're prettier than,' she said, nodding towards the battered and drink-scarred veteran currently shaking a stone from his boot then sniffing at it. 'But mebbe that's just me.'

'Prettier than Varain,' Lynx mused. 'Guess that's something.'

'Hey, you're happier'n Himbel too.'

'Whoa, any more and you might turn my head.'

Kas grinned and rose, leaving Lynx alone with his thoughts. He watched the rest of the group for a while, but most were tired and just sat without talking, so after a while he groaned and stood, searching around for the Charneler scouts who'd been following them. There was still no sign of them, he was glad to see, but the party's trail was obvious, straight through the russet grasses that reached past Lynx's knee. There was simply no way of hiding the passage of almost a score of horses.

So Shadows Deep really is our best chance, he thought glumly. *Let's hope Toil knows what she's doing.*

He watched her talking to Anatin, outlining their route, he guessed from their gestures. From where Lynx was there was no clear break in the hills to the east, no obvious destination for them. He suspected they didn't have one, Toil couldn't know the ground as well as that. More likely they were just making for difficult ground. The Charneler horses were likely to be better stock than most of theirs, able to travel faster for longer. But on foot and in less open terrain, the Charnelers would be unused to hard travel, wary of the new dangers and cautious. Close terrain meant bunching and ambush opportunities; the mercenaries had enough burners to wipe out a force far greater than their own should the right ground present itself.

He looked up at the sky. Cloud covered the Skyriver, a dull curtain of white through which the sun could only be guessed at. A dark speck turned far above, something large searching for prey. As he watched it, the bird seemed to edge closer, descend and move more directly over them. For a moment it seemed a reminder from the wilds they were in. Despite their mage-guns and blades, out here they weren't the hunters. Not even the pursuing Charnelers were. This was a place that couldn't be tamed. A place apart from civilisation, a place where humans – for all their weapons – couldn't live quietly or safely.

And she knows this, he reminded himself, looking at Toil once more. *But still she comes here. She knew this would be possible, so did her cause drive her out here, or something else?*

*

Lieutenant Sauren watched the double column of Knights-Charnel appear on the road and put on an added burst of speed to reach her. She stood by her horse with just one other, the trooper named Gullin who'd ridden ahead with her. The cavalry led the way, Commander Quentes ahead of his two companies, each one with thirty-two troopers and NCOs riding two abreast. Behind them came the Exalted's remaining two ten-man dragoon squads, then the sharpshooters of the light infantry looking rather less comfortable on horseback.

The cavalry wore tall polished boots and bore a lance device in one corner of their standard, black and white quartered uniform. The dragoons' uniform was differentiated by their red collars and the Torquen's pyramid temple device, while the light infantry wore green and black. A little way behind, as was standard order, came the grenadiers – a sloppy and evil-looking bunch whose uniforms were dirty and incomplete, a mish-mash of stolen property most likely, though they all were careful to sport the fractured disc symbol of their designation.

Grenadiers were close-assault troops and their eccentricities tolerated for the damage they could do. They and the dragoons were the only troops of the line permitted burners or sparkers and each grenadier also had a pair of small bags strapped to their hips, where their grenades were stored. Just one of those exploding amid the squad could kill the lot and most likely set off all the others too, hence the distance between them and the rest.

'Commander, Exalted Uvrel presents her compliments.'

The commander was a whiskered man with near-black hair

and a bull neck. 'Does she now? Doesn't sound like her. Orders?'

There was a heavy air of resignation about Quentes. *Career soldier*, Sauren guessed. He'd not like Torquen officers, who'd steal away his best men. *But he's no fool and he's under the Exalted's command.*

'One company is to hold this ford, dig in and be ready for any possible assault. There's a mercenary company of thirty-odd heading up the road, that way. We doubt they'll double back or that our quarry can evade us on the plain, but we will take no chances.'

'They've run for Shadows Deep?'

'They have.'

Quentes nodded, a sour look on his face. 'Lieutenant Mohrim.'

A young Surei officer rode smartly up. 'Yes, sir.'

'You're to hold the ford. The second company will go with me.'

'Yes, sir.'

Quentes gestured towards the ford. 'Lieutant Sauren, please do lead the way.'

Chapter 17

The sun broke through the clouds some hours into the afternoon. Lynx felt warmth on shoulders made damp by sweat and rain, shaking him loose from his thoughts, which had been lost in the past. He looked around and saw the gentle slope of the plain was giving way to hillocks and streams, studded with low hawthorn trees and vast solitary oaks. A sweetly resinous musk seemed to be awoken from the gorse-like shrubs that studded this higher ground. It wasn't enough to hide the taste of ice and ashes that carried on the breeze from Shadows Deep, though.

As they crested a rise Lynx saw the ground up ahead was patchy and bare, great beds of rock protruding slightly from the undulating terrain. A sheer cliff of rock stretched away to their right, as though a hill had been ripped open and its guts exposed. Small pines skirted the jagged rock face, but they seemed insignificant beside the great cave opening that lay behind it.

'Shadows Deep,' Toil called, pointing towards the cave. 'Or a tunnel to it, at least.'

'We going down?'

'Can't take the horses down, best we get as many miles out of their legs as we can.'

There were no cut stones visible, but Lynx realised it was also too regular to be natural. This hadn't been built but mage-carved, the very rock manipulated into shape. He tried to see inside, but there was a veil of darkness hiding the interior and he couldn't even tell how deep it went. If it was an entrance to Shadows Deep it might lead a mile down or just a few dozen yards, he supposed.

'Those of you who carry earthers, time to load 'em,' Toil added.

Anatin looked around. 'Why?'

She gestured to the stretches of bare rock. 'Troll country. Icers won't do much against a stone elemental, 'cept piss it off.'

Lynx glanced down at his cartridge case. Even with the additional ammo Payl had supplied, he didn't have any earth-bolts. 'How about burners?'

Toil shot him a sceptical look. 'Better than harsh language I guess.'

Behind them the scouts were back, trailing far enough behind to dissuade Teshen and Kas from lying in wait, but keeping an eye on the group still. Occasionally, Lynx had thought he'd glimpsed a larger party as they crested some patch of high ground, but the broken terrain and tree cover made it impossible to be sure of numbers. It wasn't a large force – there would be more signs – but not so small that Anatin would want to throw away what lead they had and attempt an ambush.

A sudden creak of stone echoed out from somewhere ahead. Lynx felt his hand tighten instinctively, but then astonishment seemed to drain the strength from his arms and he could do nothing but watch open-mouthed.

'Hold fire,' Toil warned instinctively, but Lynx saw no one even remember to raise their guns as they watched.

A massive shape rose up from the rock beds fifty yards off, amorphous and bulky, the rock peeling away in great chunks that tilted and turned towards the sky. Then limbs became visible, perhaps an arm span in width and four in length. A blockish body connected them, its shape dictated by strata more than anything natural, but there was no head or face visible – only pale streaks of stone running across the top.

The great grey elemental eased itself up, rising with ponderous grace until it was poised on four limbs, the fore-limbs almost twice the size of the hindlimbs – assuming it was facing them, Lynx realised. As with the night elemental, the troll had nothing of the natural about it and the body and limbs seemed misshapen and haphazardly constructed.

'It's like a spirit,' he breathed in a moment of realisation. 'It just moves through the rock, using whatever stone's at hand for a body.'

Toil gave him a curious look. 'Well done,' she said after a moment. 'You're right, so if it turns on us, don't no one run for the tunnel entrance. It's all rock down there.'

'Are we in danger?' Anatin asked in a tight voice.

'Not so long as we don't disturb it. We don't mean anything to it.'

The troll lifted one great limb and seemed to turn their way, bringing the stub of stone down in an earth-shaking crash. Uncertain what was happening, the horses all whinnied and circled as the riders kept a tight rein.

The angled slab of body twisted left and right with the jud-dering grind of stone, but made no further move towards them and turned around to start moving across a thin strip of earth.

'It can sense Sitain.' Toil laughed suddenly. 'The magic inside her.'

'And it doesn't mind?' Kas asked in a muted voice.

'Why should it? Like a horse scenting a cow, it knows broadly what she is and doesn't give a damn. They don't prey on each other or protect their territory. They're elemental forces, not animals.'

A distinctive crack echoed in the distance and the mercen-aries ducked almost as one. They looked around then a white streak cut through the afternoon air, followed by a second crack rolling out in its wake.

'Oh screaming hells,' Toil gasped, turning in her saddle.

Lynx blinked. 'What—'

In the next moment he realised what; the streaks of white were not directed at them, but the troll. The elemental paused and tilted itself more upright as though catching a scent on the wind. Lynx looked back and saw the Charneler scouts had ridden closer, near the edge of icer range, but they weren't trying to hit a man-sized target now. A third shot dropped short, but just as the report came a fourth plinked against the stone hide of the troll. A low rumble seemed to echo out from the stone elemental.

Lynx looked around for an escape route. That wasn't a roar of pain from the troll – the scouts were shooting from the best part of a thousand yards – but he had a sense of anger from it that was increased when he saw the panic on Sitain's face.

'Fall back,' Toil shouted. 'Split up!'

They didn't need encouraging as the troll hunched down and another icy trail darted past. The horses were only too happy to oblige, but before anyone could run far the rumbling suddenly increased in power. The elemental reared up as far as it could on its hind legs then smashed back down into the ground. Great chunks of stone and earth exploded up as the troll hammered its body down so hard it seemed to shatter itself against the ground.

It's an elemental spirit, Lynx reminded himself as the split shards of stone tore the earth and broken boulders thumped against each other as they tumbled apart. He hauled his horse back and turned it, fighting with the reins until he had it under control again. A grind and shudder came from underfoot but it moved away faster than a horse could sprint, and his eyes were drawn inexorably towards the faint blur of the two pursuing scouts.

'What's happening?' Sitain wailed, struggling with her own horse until Reft caught the reins of her spare mount and pulled it off her.

'Think they just made a big mistake,' Lynx breathed, unable to take his eyes off the scouts further down the plain.

He sensed Toil nudge her horse up beside his to get a better view, the woman now silent as she joined his vigil. For a while nothing happened. The scouts stopped firing with the troll gone from view and were in the process of collecting their horses when those suddenly spooked. Lynx could all too easily imagine their confusion and panic as the ground began to shake, but all he witnessed was a sudden burst of grey come up from the ground in front of the scouts. It was over in a flash, a rise and fall of movement that left a churned scar on the landscape. Beyond that, nothing remained – neither of the scouts nor their horses. The mercenaries seemed frozen to the spot at the sudden perfunctory eruption, the sound dulled by distance, and then equally sudden quiet.

'Guess they won't be following no more,' Teshen commented after a long pause. The grey-eyed man shrugged and swept his hair back out of his face. 'Two down, more to go.'

He didn't wait for an order, just set back out on the trail. By fits and starts the rest followed until it was only Toil and Lynx left, staring back at the empty ground behind them.

'Could've been us,' Lynx said at last.

'Nearly was,' Toil agreed. She cocked her head at him. 'Regretting this?'

'Regretting a lot o' things.'

'Hah, don't we all?'

'How about you?' Lynx said, meeting her gaze. 'You regretting being out here in the wilds?'

Toil gave him a secretive smile. 'Oh, I'm a city girl; don't like to be too far from my little pleasures.'

'But the wilds don't scare you.'

'Scare me? Can't say much does.'

'That's a bold claim.'

She paused, her smile wavering. 'My dad was a famous mercenary. I got taught to fight by some of the most vicious fighters around. I thought I was scared of nothing until I signed up with a relic hunter.'

'And then?'

'Then I found I was scared of plenty. Never was afraid of the dark until I met the dark on its own ground – saw it as a hungry, living thing.'

'Night elemental? I saw one of those, was too surprised to be scared.'

She shook her head. 'Not any sort of elemental, just the perfect pitch black you get deep underground. So dark you can't see your hand in front of you, don't know if you're in a tunnel or a huge chamber, if there's stone under your next footstep or nothing at all. That dark's a living thing all by itself.' She gave a small laugh. 'Of course, it's not only the dark that'll kill you. Plenty lives inside it that'll take a damn good swing.'

Lynx fought the urge to shiver, memories of his own time underground never too far from his thoughts. 'You're scared of the dark and you want us to go to Shadows Deep?' he asked, realising he sounded more fearful and less incredulous than intended.

'No. I *was* scared of the dark,' she said with a small smile. 'That deep dark. But I faced it and I lived. Since then, I don't get scared of much. I find it works better the other way around.'

She turned her horses and set out after the others. Lynx watched her go a while longer then shook his head and followed along in silence.

*

The mercenaries rode into dusk until it was unsafe to continue, then went on foot for another hour to try and preserve what remained of their lead. Once the last of the light faded from the sky and the moon and Skyriver probed at a veil of cloud, they finally made camp, unable to see the path ahead and sapped by the hours of travelling. A heavy dew descended with the chill of evening, but they all knew they couldn't risk a fire. Instead they huddled together in a hollow beneath the branches of a fat old oak, eating strips of spiced, dried beef and the few ends of bread they had remaining.

The exhausted horses were given a last meal and hobbled, one more day of travel required from them. They would be turned loose by the end of the following day, once the terrain became impassable for horses – the Knights-Charnel would probably catch and keep those worth feeding. Professional cavalry wouldn't abandon their own horses so easily. No doubt a few would be detailed to drive them back to the relative safety of the road.

With Varain taking the first watch, the mercenaries settled down to sleep like a pack of wolves; in the dry shelter of the oak, bundled up tight against the chill and pressed up close to each other to preserve heat. Sleep was elusive at first, however, despite the fatigue they all felt. Sitain found herself staring up at the dark suggestions of boughs above her instead of succumbing to rest, her mind racing with thoughts of the stone elemental and what horrors the dawn might bring.

'Sitain?' Anatin said softly from further up the pile.

'Yes?'

'Can you weave a shadow round us? If we got maspid packs roaming the hills I'd like any cover we could get.'

'They won't be,' Toil broke in, slightly muffled from the hollow she'd made for herself between Reft and Lynx. 'They don't go far overground and there's no cave mouth near here.'

'Still, any sort of cover'd help me sleep.'

'I'll try,' Sitain said with a renewed sense of weariness. Just the idea of trying to work magic made her tired but Anatin was right, it might keep them a fraction safer while they slept. She looked briefly around to get her bearings and realised every pair of eyes was watching her. Even Varain, perched on a hump of fallen branch, had turned her way. His mage-gun was cradled loose in his arms, a pale sliver of moonlight running the length of its scratched steel barrel.

Sitain took a long breath and closed her eyes. She'd had little chance to practise control over her magic, but every night since escaping the Charnelers she'd tried something small. Just a modest drawing out of the tingle from her bones, no larger working than that, but with every day had come a greater familiarity.

The dark flicker at the corner of her eyes that was a part of her – *had* been a part of her for four or five years now – intensified. It was less effort to tease the magic out now and Sitain coaxed it gently forward with just a thought.

In moments she sensed a faint darkening around her and knew that if she looked up those watching eyes would now be dimmed. There was mutter from someone, Ashis or Kas, sounding uncomfortable at what they were seeing, but there was no word of complaint and Sitain took a moment to let the shadows settle in the air above them. It would be all too easy to let the darkness drop like a blanket over them, but that might prove disastrous and send them all to sleep past dawn.

Just as she thought she had the shadows settled a great roar split the sky, rolling like thunder across the quiet night. Sitain flinched and lost her grip on the magic. It seemed to dart away from her grasp like smoke on the wind.

'Gods, what was that?' Anatin muttered, sitting up.

'Nothing good,' replied Toil, already reaching for her gun.

The others followed suit and Sitain felt a moment of panic until she remembered where she'd put her pistol. She flapped around in the dark until she found the holster wrapped in its own belt and yanked it free. A straight blockish steel tube set in a wooden stock, there was nothing elegant about the weapon. Jutting out the back, just above the grip, was the breech housing. With cold fingers Sitain lifted the catch lever and worked the breech open. It was an old gun and not as quick to load as some of the others, but she'd been promised it was reliable. She pulled a cartridge, checked its symbol, and slid that into the breech. Slipping the breech and catch closed in one movement, she thumbed the hammer back until it clicked into place then froze, waiting for whatever came next.

The moment stretched out, a dozen heartbeats or more, before a second roar cut the night. Deep and bestial, she felt the force of it in her gut and knew this was no lion or bear hunting in the wilds. It was something far larger and as a flash of light burst out from behind a line of trees, she realised her fears were correct.

'What's that?' Ashis hissed, trying to keep the fear from her voice as she searched around in the darkness.

'Where?' asked Teshen, who'd been looking the other way.

'Over there,' Toil said, still calm. 'A light past those trees, mebbe a hundred yards.'

'I don't see—' The words died in his throat as a second, brighter, burst of light flared through the crooked limbs of the trees. This time there was a sound with it, a great rush and crackle that sounded like a forest fire bursting to life. 'Shattered gods, a firedrake?'

'Yup.' Toil reached over and attracted Sitain's attention. 'Hey, you; finger off the trigger. In fact, maybe holster that for now.'

Sitain stared back at the woman for a moment in astonishment, then realised how foolish she'd been. She carefully unpeeled her finger from around the steel trigger and placed it down the side of the stock as Lynx had been at pains to show her.

'All of you, hold fire. Last thing we want to do is tell it we're here.'

'Ah, Sitain – you call that thing here? Attract its attention with your magic?' Lynx asked, staring off towards the trees still. It was all dark there again but the crackle of flames and the sound of something large moving were still audible.

'How should I bloody know?' she whispered back angrily. 'Wasn't my idea now, was it?'

'Still, best you stop whatever you're doing.'

'I'm doing nothing.'

More bellows rang out, deep cries that rose in intensity and volume until the shudder of them echoed inside Sitain's gut and turned it cold with fear. Then the light returned, red and orange flames that burst up from nothing. It moved abruptly, heading north, and the trees screening it caught alight. Leaves that were starting to wither under autumn's touch ignited in a heartbeat. Soon the whole line of trees were alight, fire consuming the branches and spitting sparks at the undergrowth as a dirty yellow light was cast over the whole scene.

'Guess that's why I could smell ashes on the wind today,' Lynx commented.

'It's coming for us,' Anatin said, struggling up, 'we need to move.'

'Stay there!' Toil insisted. 'Just wait.'

'You mad, woman?'

She stared up at him for a moment. 'Fine, fucking run then,' Toil said angrily. 'Just not back the way we came. If it follows you, I don't want to get in the way and I'm staying right bloody here.'

That was enough to make Anatin hesitate. 'What if it's coming this way?'

'Then we're fucked anyway, firedrakes are a whole lot faster'n us. Even on horseback, assuming we could see well enough to gallop.'

Another, even louder, roar came from the far side of the trees and the whole group instinctively ducked low. Then it was answered by a second, further away, and the sound seemed to antagonise the first. The night sky shuddered under the force of its bellow and the light intensified – then Sitain saw a shape moving against the blackness. For a moment she couldn't make out what it was, just a great ball of yellow flame, but then a long curve of fire extended out above it before sweeping down and turning the nearest trees to ash.

The fire elemental left a dancing trail of red as it surged forward, heading away from the mercenaries. Great sheets of fire beat at the wind while a spear of light reached forward from the massive body, just the suggestion of a blade-like head visible before it disappeared from view. More roars followed, the ground trembling distantly with heavy impacts while the crackle and flash of fire hung in the sky above.

'They fighting?'

'Who knows?' Toil shrugged. 'Hard to know much about firedrakes. Anyone who gets close gets crispy soon after so taking notes proves tricky. Gives us a new problem, though.'

'Another?' Lynx growled.

The man had been subdued since they'd entered the wild and Sitain didn't think it was just the lack of cuisine. There was a harder look in his eyes now, an edge to his manner he'd been careful to keep in check back in Grasiel. He looked more like the sort of man her mother had feared, the sort many in these parts would fear.

'Might be a lair up there,' Toil said. 'Hard to tell until daylight. But we don't want to cross one, we'll have to skirt around.'

'And give the Charnelers time to catch up?' Anatin snapped.

'Not a lot of choice there, 'less you want to fight a firedrake?'

'Thought you said they'd leave us alone?'

'It'll not seek us out. We cross its lair carrying magic-charged weapons, that's a whole different matter.'

'So what, then?'

She sat up and pointed south-east. 'The ridge that we saw running that way. Most likely there's a road below it, from that tunnel entrance we passed. Oftentimes they cleared the rock by shoving it upwards, the Duegar mages. We follow that, we'll find an entrance or a path around the firedrake. Leave the Charnelers to walk into that mess instead.'

'Assuming they don't catch us up.'

'Aye, but at least they don't have those scouts no more.' Toil settled back against Reft's hip. 'We'll start out at first light, see if we can get a jump on 'em. Until then, catch whatever sleep you can. Tomorrow's going to be a hard one.'

Sitain forced herself to lie back and settled into the comforting warmth of Kas. The image of a Jester card appeared in her mind – the short cape and bell-festooned mask that were characteristic of the Jester in every deck. In the Mercenary Deck, however, the Jester carried a stiletto in one hand, a wine bottle in the other. She looked down at the short-sword she'd been given on her first night. It was hardly a stiletto and right now she'd have gladly traded it for some wine.

'Just a Jester,' she muttered sourly. 'I should've asked for more.'

'Me too,' was Anatin's muffled reply.

*

Exalted Uvrel stood at the edge of the Knights-Charnel camp, facing away from the small fire they'd lit. It would warm too few bodies to serve the entire force, but normally she'd not have permitted anything at all. The troops were weary, though, she could see it in their eyes and knew she couldn't trust regular troops to endure too long. Not in the wilds where humans rarely ventured and rumour was all most of them knew. One campaign mug of bitter black tea, or whatever else they had to hand so long as it was hot, had revived spirits.

She cradled her own in her hands, the tapered mug almost empty and the warmth spreading through her body. Uvrel was used to hard riding, she had done enough of that in her time, and the discomfort was only minor after two days. She had pushed them hard, done her best to erode the assassins' lead, and her troops had obeyed, but still it hadn't proved enough. Every turning on the road had provided a delay; every minute trying to recover her vision after that light-bolt had let them slip further away.

The dragoons were picked soldiers, well aware that the price of their elevated position was hardship, while the cavalry knew this routine well enough. The light infantry and grenadiers were suffering, however. She could hear the muted griping in the background and once they reached Shadows Deep the going would be harder and on foot.

She smelled tobacco on the wind and nodded to herself. A few small luxuries, that was all they had time for, but it was easier to ask a soldier to risk their life after such moments. Uvrel had risen through the ranks of light cavalry then the dragoons; she knew exactly how far troops could be pushed.

Someone joined her, wreathed in pipe smoke. Out of the corner of her eye Uvrel saw the magnificently whiskered profile of the sergeant in charge of the grenadiers, an old campaigner by the name of Oudagan. Unusually for the Knights-Charnel he was from the south, dark-skinned and squat-bodied.

The Order had fought dozens of campaigns there, gathering up the abandoned boys and girls not of fighting age. Many became servants of fighting units, camp followers in the employ of officers, before coming of age and earning a uniform of their own. Taken far from their home, such recruits had nothing beyond the Order and fought accordingly.

'Sergeant,' she acknowledged.

'Exalted,' he replied in a thick homeland accent, clearly having learned the language from the roughest of northern troops.

'Problem?'

'No, sir. My lads reckon this is why we joined up.'

'To see the sights?'

Oudagan chuckled nastily. 'Aye, see the sights then blow the shit out of 'em.' He patted one of the bulky boxes on his hip where he carried his grenades. 'Any idea how far we're behind?'

'Perhaps five miles? Our scouts can't have been further than that and they'd have kept a good distance from the Crows for fear of ambush.'

''Cept that didn't work for 'em.'

'No mercenary did that,' Uvrel said with a shake of the head, remembering the mess they'd found earlier which, they'd had to assume, was the remains of their vanished scouts.

'Could've been a grenade. An ice-bomb leaves something similar once it's melted back.'

'For a pair of scouts? I doubt it. They won't have grenades to waste on just two men.'

'Bad luck for them, then.' Oudagan grinned. 'We've got fifty-odd to play with.'

'Save them for the wildlife. I want the assassin alive if I can. You'll find enough to kill elsewhere.'

'That I don't doubt, sir. How about, ah, the locals, sir?'

'Locals?'

The man's grin widened, teeth bright in the gloom. 'Wisps, sir. The way I hear it, those Wisp hunters can be troublesome.'

'We have a mission here, Sergeant,' Uvrel said sternly. 'Whatever games you want to play with Wisps, they happen only after we take these murderers. Any of your men thinks otherwise and I'll shoot them myself.'

'Yes, sir.'

Uvrel took another mouthful, grimaced at the cooled tea and spat it out on the grass. She tossed the rest away. In the distance a dulled orange light shone out and the pair stood in silence and watched the brief flares past the treetops.

'Good few miles off,' Oudagan commented. 'Whatever it is. Firedrake, mebbe?'

'Or our mercenaries using fire-bolts on the wildlife.'

'Let's hope the locals've done our job for us.'

'Do you want to be the one who tells the Lord-Exalted we have no one to interrogate or execute?'

'No, sir.'

'Nor do I.' She looked back at the camp. Her dragoons had claimed control of the fireside, four squads of handpicked men and women. On one flank they had the ragamuffin woodsmen of the light infantry, on the other the neat uniforms of Commander Quentes's cavalry. The grenadiers had again kept their distance, an understanding both sides seemed to take as a sign of superiority. Almost a hundred soldiers now they'd left the other cavalry company at the ford – odds of ten to one in a straight fight. But it meant they moved slower too. It was a natural law of soldiering.

'Have your men ready to leave at five minutes' notice. As soon as it's light enough to ride, I intend to move out. The last man ready runs the risk of getting shot.'

'Aye, sir. You'll never find grenadiers disorganised, that I promise.'

Uvrel nodded. She'd never erase the memory of the first time she saw a fire-bomb hit a company of men. With destruction like that in their hands, grenadiers were meticulous about their kit. The ones that lived beyond the first few days, anyway.

Chapter 18

A boot in the side woke Lynx. For a moment he flailed, reaching for a weapon. His hand tightened on the first thing he grabbed and Sitain howled as his fingers dug into her arm. The woman tried in vain to haul herself free before the panic cleared and Lynx released her.

'Someone's fun in the mornings,' Teshen commented, standing over him.

'What do you expect if you kick me?' Lynx growled, frowning as he blinked the sleep away.

'Next time slap his arse instead,' suggested Kas. 'Gets him going a treat.'

Anatin raised an eyebrow as Varain snorted and reached over to pantomime doing just that. Lynx flinched at the touch, still jittery after a poor night's sleep.

'Thunder's teeth,' Sitain hissed, rubbing at her arm. 'Careful, Lynx.'

'Sorry,' he muttered.

Teshen squatted down in front of him. 'Bad dreams, eh?'

'Why d'you say that?'

'You were all elbows there, think I got a bruise for every time I moved.'

'Yeah well, normally I . . . ah.' Lynx sighed and ground to a halt. 'Nope, I got nothing.'

'Bit early for wit?' Teshen straightened and scooped up his pack. 'For the rest of us too.'

Lynx sat up and looked around. There was a morning mist lurking around the trees, while the sun hadn't yet risen above the tree-line. Everything was washed in a grey, ghostly gloom – one that had seeped into his limbs, given the chill numbness he felt as he moved.

He stood and felt a black knot tighten behind his eyes. The presence of bodies on either side of him as he slept, as welcome as their warmth had been, meant he'd only dozed fitfully across the night. Now that was coming back to haunt him.

'Get your shit together, Lynx,' Teshen added after a few moments of watching the former commando totter like a man searching for another beer.

'I'm getting there.'

'Do it faster,' the cold-eyed Knight snapped. Teshen pulled his hair back from his face and fixed Lynx with a look as he tied it back.

'Aye.'

Lynx stretched up as far as he could then started to shake his arms and legs out, trying to restore some warmth and movement into them. That done, he swallowed a mouthful of water and slipped his long gun sheath on to his back, having slept in his coat. His tricorn hat he found battered on the ground, where they'd all slept, but he worked it back into shape and rammed it on his head anyway.

'We head for the ridge over that way,' Toil announced, returning to the camp with her mage-gun resting on one shoulder. 'There should be a way around the firedrake lair. If we're spotted, we run and duck down the first hole we find.'

'Since when were you giving orders round here?'

'Since I'm both paying your wages and the best chance you got in these parts. You don't like it, fine. I'll just head into Shadows Deep first chance I get and leave you to your chain of command. You're welcome to tag along if you don't slow me down, but I'll make it through alone if I have to. The rest o' you, I'd not give good odds on you crossing the wilds by yourselves, let alone the deepest dark. The Charnelers'll find it harder to follow us underground, though, I promise you that much. We'd have to be more than unlucky to find the Exalted on our tail as one of their relic hunters.'

'Why? Why harder to follow?'

Toil patted her pack. 'I'm a girl who likes to be prepared. Half of this is rope, a grapple and a lantern.'

'They could have all that.'

'Doubt it, not like mine.' She pulled a compass from her pocket and checked it briefly before nodding to herself. 'You all ready? Good, let's not waste time.'

It was still firmly twilight so they walked their horses for the first half-hour, packs on their backs in case they needed to abandon their steeds. The mercenaries finally mounted only once the ridge was back in sight again, skirted by a ghostly veil of mist as the morning sun caressed the peak. It was an uneven line of ground that Lynx wouldn't have much noticed at any other time. An obstacle, little more, but the idea that there would be a road beneath it almost eclipsed his apprehension at walking that path.

It was still hard to imagine a city under the ground. His mind constantly returned to the cramped, airless mine tunnels where he'd worked ten-hour shifts at To Lort prison. Just remembering that time, digging at the rock with shackles weighing him down, seemed to tighten a collar around his throat and choke his breathing. The smell of greasy skin, mud and coal rose like a cobra in his memory.

They made good time once they were in the saddle, riding parallel to the ridge and pausing only on the edge of a shallow escarpment where the view opened out. A small valley, perhaps a mile or two long, stretched out beyond – blasted lifeless and grey by the presence of the firedrake. In the distance Lynx could make out a spot of white – nothing more than that, but a shape that moved over the dark and dead landscape. Then he realised there was more than one, smaller than he'd expected for either, but so bright he could make out no detail.

'They get bigger,' Toil said as Reft pointed. 'When they're roused, they're bigger.'

Reft grunted in response. Though Lynx couldn't read anything in the big man's expression he saw Kas nod and smirk.

'Coldest black!' Teshen hissed. 'Time to go.'

All faces turned behind them to see where he was looking. Riders coming up fast – still a way off, but closer than anyone would have liked. The mass of black and white uniforms was clear enough and as they watched a cavalry troop with plumed hats broke from the pack to stream forward.

'Lancers!' Toil yelled, slamming her heels into the horse's flank.

They leaped forward almost as one, charging across the top of the escarpment until trees narrowed their path and they were forced to slow. It was still a fast pace to maintain and Lynx just had to hold on and follow, heart juddering in his chest as the horse laboured beneath him.

'We can't outrun lancers!' Anatin yelled over the drum of hooves. 'We'll have to turn when they catch us!'

'Fuck that!' Toil replied. 'Look, there.'

She pointed up ahead. Lynx couldn't make out much other than a high outcrop of stone abutting the ridge, a lone tree at its peak. The hump of grey rock was draped in strips of scrappy grass, which made Lynx think of a flayed skull, but the others charged straight for it. He glanced back. The lancers were covering the ground fast and he realised he couldn't hesitate any longer. He spurred the horse forward and leaned low in the saddle as he raced to keep up. Toil was out in the lead, guiding her horse over the uneven terrain with as much skill as Teshen close behind her. The rest followed at a remove, Reft and Sitain at the rear as they struggled to match the pace.

By the time they reached the outcrop Lynx could see Toil was right. The brow of the skull was a low overhang with a twenty-foot void beneath, as though the face had been shot clean through. As Lynx reined in, Toil was already on foot and scouting around the entrance.

'What're you doing?' Anatin asked as he unhitched his saddlebag and slung it over his shoulder.

'Looking for spoor,' she called back, not looking up. 'No good if this is something's nest these days.' She continued on into the dark space until Lynx could barely see her, before giving a small yelp. In the next moment he'd slipped from his saddle and brought his gun up, advancing on the cave. He stopped abruptly as Toil reappeared, relief on her face.

'Looks clear, think we got lucky.'

He glanced back at the path where the lancers would be following very soon. 'How's that, then?'

'This is Wisp forage ground,' she said, pulling her mage-gun from the scabbard on her horse and her pack onto her back. 'Follow me and watch for the tripwires.'

With a slap on the rump of her horse she sent it back the way they'd come and headed on inside. The other mercenaries looked at each other dubiously. Lynx doubted any of the others would have met a Wisp either and there was enough fanciful rumour about the underground-dwelling race that he doubted anyone knew anything real about them. When the alternative was waiting for the Knights-Charnel, however, lingering would do no good.

'Come on,' Teshen said finally, heading after Toil. 'No lancer's following on foot without orders, but we don't want to get pinned down.'

'I see in the dark better'n most folk anyway,' Sitain muttered as she followed with the rest. Soon it was only Lynx again, standing dry-mouthed with a crawling sensation on his neck. He drew his gun and held it so tight his knuckles went white, but the feel of the wooden stock under his fingers only reminded him of the pickaxes he'd once wielded.

He couldn't say how long he was stood there. It was probably only moments until Toil headed back out again.

'What's the hold-up?'

'Caves,' Lynx croaked.

'Scared o' the dark?' she asked, a brief laugh dying when Lynx's expression tightened further.

She edged forward, mage-gun slung over one shoulder. 'We don't have time for this.'

'I know,' Lynx croaked, throat so tight he could barely breathe. Some part of his mind was raging away at the back of his head, screaming for him to move and get to safety, but that part was locked behind walls of stone and bars of iron.

Toil slowly reached out and put her hand on Lynx's arm. He flinched but managed not to smash the butt of the gun into her head the way every instinct screamed for him to do. His body was so rigid with the conflict of emotion that Lynx couldn't even speak, but Toil drew herself closer with the care of horse trainer.

'We need to move,' she whispered as softly as a lover. 'Do you hear me, Lynx?'

Toil moved closer still, one hand on his arm and the other rising slowly to touch him on the cheek. Her skin rasped against the dark stubble, strong fingers resting tenderly along the line of his jaw.

Somehow he found the strength to suck in a breath and nod. Toil brought herself right up to him, close enough to kiss, and suddenly the musky scent of her skin filled his mind. The spice of her sweat on the air overlaid the cold stink of mud and stone. It felt like a flame moving close to his face – thawing the icy hold fear had on his body.

'Come with me,' she whispered.

Lynx nodded and she turned away, one hand slipping down to his and tugging him along behind her. Lynx stumbled forward a few steps then the spell was broken. He gasped for air and found strength in his body once more, blinking at the gloom behind him until the jagged shapes of fallen stone suddenly resolved themselves.

He almost barged Toil over as she stopped in front of him and her free hand slammed against his chest.

'Tripwire,' she said, pointing down. A white length of cord was strung between two great lumps of rock, spanning three feet of space. 'You good?'

'I'll manage,' he croaked.

Toil nodded and released her grip on him, picking her way over the tripwire. Lynx followed as closely as he could, able to make out little in the weak light that crept inside, but a second tripwire was obvious enough too and once they headed up a shallow slope of grooved stone he found the rest of the mercenaries on a broad shelf. There Toil stopped and pulled her lantern from her bag. It had a long loop of rope attached to the top and she slipped her head and one arm through so it hung at her hip.

Through the jangle of his thoughts Lynx remembered that he'd seen it hanging from her horse the previous day. The wall of blackness behind the others seemed to be a yawning maw waiting for him and he closed his eyes against it, fixing on the strange lantern to distract himself. It was a cylinder about a foot long and half that across – a solid case of brass with some strange fretwork cut into the outside. Inside that was some dark shiny substance like tinted glass or jet, so he'd not realised it was a lantern.

'Not lighting it yet?' Anatin demanded, pointing past the shelf to the darkness beyond. 'We can't see a damn thing past here.'

Toil gave him a look Lynx couldn't make out and grasped each end of the lantern. She gave it a small twist and . . . And nothing happened.

'Seven fiery hells, we're all gonna die,' groaned Ashis, her head sagging.

'Stow that,' Anatin snapped, drawing his guns. 'We're not— Hey, where are you going?'

Toil had headed straight past him, lantern at her waist and gun held loose in her hands. She turned and faced them all. Lynx realised there was a now strange tint to the air, her skin taking on a very faint glow as she smiled at them. Beside her the huge pale face of Reft seemed to loom like a phantom above his dark clothes.

'Like I said, the Charnelers won't have a lantern like this. But if you want to stay and fight, go for it.'

She headed off and Sitain hurried along behind, the mercenaries frowning at each other in the darkness but wasting little time in following. There was a faint light, Lynx realised, but he couldn't tell where it was coming from at first. The lantern was emitting nothing, it remained barely an outline in the dark, but a pale glow now seemed to trace the curves of the rock as they walked. He glanced back and saw the darkness had returned to where they'd been standing, while just beyond he could see a sliver of light from the cave entrance.

It was a tunnel, he realised as the outline ahead tilted right. Wide enough for them to walk three abreast, it continued for a dozen yards before dropping away in stepped sections of grooved slope that spiralled gently down into the belly of the earth. With a heavy feeling Lynx pulled his tricorn from his head and flattened it again, shoving it in the side of his pack.

'This some sort o' lichen?' Olut asked from up ahead.

'Something like that,' Toil replied. 'The lantern's good for a few days underground, but we'll get up in the daylight before it runs out anyway.'

'The lantern's working?'

'Of course!' spluttered Sitain. 'Can't you see it is?'

'They're not night mages.' Toil laughed, looking askance at Sitain who was walking alongside her. 'They can't see like you do in the dark.'

'You all can't see this?'

Toil shook her head. 'Not so well as you, nothing like it I'd guess. We can only see an outline of the walls.'

'Gods,' Sitain breathed. 'I knew I was better than others at seeing in the dark, that only makes sense, doesn't it? But this . . . It's beautiful, every line of rock is shining. I could read your book, Lynx, if you wanted me to.'

'No one likes a show-off,' Kas called.

'If our new Jester of Sun can lead us through all this, I'm inclined to forgive a little showing off,' Anatin muttered.

'Aye, fair point,' Kas said, relenting. 'Show off as much as you like, Jester, so long as you keep an eye out for maspids as well.'

The spiral stair descended for two full turns, so far as Lynx could estimate. He was finding it hard enough to focus on putting one foot in front of the other, his whole body trembling at the descent, but when the rock abruptly opened out around them even his fear faded into the background.

He heard someone gasp beside him as the mercenaries stumbled to a halt, looking up and around in wonder. Only Toil thought to have a gun ready, but after a brief sweep of the great tunnel they found themselves in she lowered it again and waited for the others. The air was cool, but lacking the crispness of dawn they had just left. Above their heads the tunnel reached up to a remarkable height, Toil's lantern only just managing to grasp the rough lines of a curved roof that seemed to undulate in echo of some organic form a good fifty feet above their heads.

Their view was aided by veins of the pale blue rock exposed on the tunnel walls, glowing in a way that seemed bright after the dim stair. These strata lit the way in both directions, revealing a long empty tunnel twenty feet from wall to wall, while opposite them stood a rounded opening in the rock that revealed some sort of room beyond. Some quirk in the rock had permitted a strange overhang to form above that, a loop through which someone or something had threaded a steel bar that held a rudimentary grille. The builders – *Wisps?* Lynx wondered with a faint thrill – had dug down into the powdery earth underfoot too, creating a trench in which the grille fitted neatly.

'What's this?' Anatin asked, taking a few steps forward until Toil caught his arm.

'Wisps,' she replied. 'Keeping out the wildlife.'

'Out of what?'

'Let's find out.'

'What about the Charnelers?'

'They won't follow.'

'You're betting our lives on that?'

Toil grinned wolfishly at him. 'If they do, this tunnel's long and straight. They don't need to do a lot of catching up before they shoot us down.'

'That's supposed to reassure me?'

'Nope, but we'll see them coming if they do have torches; time enough to stand back and fire burners from a safe distance. They'd be mad to follow us underground; they'll make better time following the ridge to the main ruin on horseback and run fewer risks. You want to stand guard, that's fine. I'm going this way, introduce myself to the natives.'

'*Introduce* yourself?' Anatin said, raising an eyebrow and nodding at the gun she carried.

Toil sighed. 'Oh for . . . Don't you think we've got enough people trying to kill us?'

'The thought did occur.'

'Damn right. The Wisps live here – we start just running round these halls, stirring up nasties and blowing the shit out of their tunnels, they might have something to say about it. If we announce ourselves it'll help if they're deciding between friend or foe – and maybe we can borrow their knowledge of the tunnels too.'

She headed for the heavy steel grille and knelt, releasing some sort of catch at the bottom and trying to haul it up. The weight was considerable and in the end it took three of them to raise it to above head height, but once it was up, Reft supported it alone while the others passed under. Closing it up behind them Toil was careful to replace the catches that held it shut. Her lantern illuminated a broad circular room with a single sloped pillar in the centre. Aside from the pillar it was empty; a second archway and a half-dozen alcoves in the rock walls were the only features.

Before going any further Toil pulled a small wooden pot from her pocket and carefully unscrewed the lid. Inside was a whitish substance that glowed in the arcane light of her lantern. She dipped one finger in and covered the whole tip before replacing the lid.

'What's that?' Kas asked.

'Old relic hunter's trick,' she said. 'Well, the ones who don't just kill everything in sight, anyway.'

'Ain't that more your style?'

'Just folk who deserve it or get in my way,' she said point-edly. 'You can trust Wisps more'n people, though, and this is their home ground, which could be the advantage we need.'

With the pot tucked safely away she shouldered her gun and gestured for the others to do the same. That done they headed through the room and into a small tunnel, low enough to make Reft duck his head but short enough for Lynx to cross without rekindling the fear in his belly. Beyond that appeared to be some sort of shrine room. A complex array of interlocking stone arches running from floor to ceiling occupied most of the centre of the room. At the heart of it on a broad pedestal was a massive crystal geode that glittered with remarkable light as Toil picked her way through the arches.

While the others marvelled at the light – Sitain enraptured – Toil merely sniffed and passed by without a second glance, heading for a wider doorway on the far side. As Lynx neared it he began to detect a warm, organic scent that seemed to have no place underground and he realised there was faint light coming from beyond. Down another spiral slope, this one glittering with crystals, the light grew and Lynx started to be able to make out colours in the rock. As the tunnel opened out on to a large room he saw green and red lichens on the walls and floor with a trodden path running down the centre. Scents filled his nose as he walked, nothing he recognised, while the sound of trickling water came from all around. Sweet and earthy organic odours, a faintly acrid smell of smoke and musky scents he couldn't guess at all mingled in the air, but as his eyes adjusted Lynx immediately forgot about them as he gasped at the sight ahead.

They stood on a high ridge of rock that led down to a great dark lake two hundred yards in length. It was studded with small islands that surrounded each of several dozen natural columns which supported the undulating ceiling. Strata of shining rocks shone down over it all, whether crystal or not Lynx couldn't tell, but somehow a strange sort of garden had grown up across the cavern.

It was made up of moss-like plants in the main, but larger shrubs rose up from the bigger islands and twisting sprays of blue spotted the edges of most formations. Oval leaves with a white star-shaped flower at each end floated alone or in clumps on the water, while trailing curtains of brilliant green clung to columns and outer walls. Insects darted through the air, some dark and others perfectly white, while V-shapes in the water betrayed the movement of something just below the surface.

Toil walked to the top of the grooved slope leading down to the first of the columns, but instead of descending she knelt and bowed her head. The mercenaries stared at her in surprise but after a moment she glanced back and gestured for them to do the same. One by one they did, Sitain the last to do so, being too occupied by the dark shadows on the walls until Varain grabbed her arm and dragged her to her knees.

There was a long moment of quiet, but then the Wisps stepped forward into the light.

*

'Looks like our quarry's gone to ground,' Sergeant Oudagan commented. The man was stood beside the empty cave mouth that Exalted Uvrel was glaring at. 'Want me to flush 'em out?'

The man was idly tossing a grenade up and down in his hand, an evil smirk on his face.

'I can see that grenade's not primed, Sergeant,' Uvrel said, not bothering to look directly at him, 'but you're making the cavalry nervous.'

Oudagan's grin widened. He tilted his head to look around her at the main troop of Knights-Charnel. 'Why'd you think I'm doing it?'

'Enough.' Uvrel went back to staring at the cave in silence.

The last thing she wanted to do was pursue them underground, for tactical reasons as much as the skittishness of her command. The dragoons and grenadiers would be no problem, but the rest would likely drag their feet or even refuse. The fear of Duegar ruins was ingrained for many and taking a soldier out of their comfort zone was asking for trouble. Lines from the creed of Insar's worshippers appeared in her mind – *to embrace the dark, the holy stillness of night* – but she doubted their daily prayers would be in the minds of most.

'Sauren, how are we for torches?'

The lieutenant hurried forward. 'Some, not many. Not enough to cross the entire city-ruin.'

'Mebbe there's light down there,' Oudagan suggested. 'Duegar can't have used torches all the time. Burn all the air bad.'

'They lived there,' Uvrel pointed out. 'I doubt they needed to see as we do. Anything that may once have been down there will likely be long since looted by relic hunters anyway.' She shook her head and turned away. 'We can't risk the ambush either. It's too confined, just takes one burner to hit a grenadier and we're all dead.'

'Grenades'll spread fire a lot further down any tunnel.'

'Grenades can't be thrown too far if the ceiling's low and unless you can see in the dark, you don't know where you're throwing. No – we follow the ridgeline. That runs all the way to the city proper. If we can get ahead of them we can set an ambush of our own.'

Uvrel twisted in her saddle to call behind her. 'Commander Quentes, gather the mercenaries' horses and bring them with us. Set a few troopers to watch the cave, in case they try to double back. They'd be fools to attempt it on foot when the ford is under guard, but let's not overestimate the intelligence of these mercenaries. They *have* chosen to enter Shadows Deep, after all.'

Chapter 19

Lynx heard his comrades gasp or breathe soft curses at the sight, but his astonishment was so complete he couldn't even move. There were four Wisps up on the ridge with the mercenaries, but he caught sight of more moving on the nearer shore of the lake. The Wisps were tall, about Reft's height and similarly pale but slender where he was muscular. Their narrow hairless heads sported four large cat-slit eyes – an upper pair set slightly wider and higher than a human's, and a lower pair where a jaw hinge should be. The mouths were almost invisible, just a narrow opening below a short flare of a nose.

They wore complex wrapped lengths of cloth around their torsos that bore intricate swirling patterns, while their arms and legs seemed to be covered in something more like leather – textured with ridges or scales and all segmented to allow for a double set of joints in each limb. Three carried hooked axes on their belts but none had the weapons drawn – instead they all four had their hands outstretched towards the mercenaries. In the palm of each was a flicker of movement. Flames danced over the skin of two while a trio of pebbles spun slowly in another's hand and a coil of darkness in the last one's – four mages all standing guard together, as many as Lynx had actually spoken to in his entire life.

The stand-off continued for half a dozen heartbeats, then the Wisp holding the darkness make a gesture with its free hand. One of the fire-holders closed their long fingers and extinguished the flame before moving to kneel before Toil to echo her pose. As it did so Lynx saw two of its fingers glow with a similar dull light to the rocks in the tunnel. Toil raised her hand and made some gesture which the Wisp returned in one fluid sweep.

Toil continued to move her whitened fingertip through the air, hesitantly at first but then with a greater fluency. The mage, the largest of its kind, with a grey darkened brow, watched her intently, fingers folded inward to partially obscure the light.

'What's going on?' Ashis asked, her voice startlingly loud in the hush. 'We dead yet?'

'They're talking,' Lynx whispered back.

'Eh? I don't hear 'em.'

'Talking with their hands. Look.'

Ashis blinked. 'Oh. That's fucking weird.'

'Someone shut her up,' Toil called back, pausing in her gestures.

'You heard the woman,' Anatin snapped. 'Let her work.'

It didn't take long. A minute or two more, just as Lynx's knees were starting to ache, Toil gave a grunt and stood up as the Wisp stepped away.

'All good?' Anatin asked.

She nodded. 'Aye.'

'Just like that?'

Toil shrugged. 'They don't give much of a shit about humans, one of the reasons why I like 'em. So long as we don't cause trouble for their kind or their light-gardens, we're fine. They appreciated a warning about the Charnelers; they'll pack their things and head home to pass on the word. The Orders don't have the best history with Wisps, you won't be surprised to hear.'

'Light-gardens?'

She gestured to the lake. 'Places like this, where they grow most o' their food.'

'What about us?'

'We're going with them.' Toil smiled. 'Bit of escort duty, you lot should be good at it by now. Better, anyway.'

'Escorting what?'

'The thirds, down there, and whatever's been harvested.'

'Thirds?'

She rolled her eyes. 'Watching dark, don't you know anything about Wisps?'

That produced a scowl from Anatin and a general round of non-committal grunts from the rest. Lynx kept quiet. He'd been surprised they even wore proper clothes, of a fashion – from what little he'd heard Lynx had been expecting animal skins and warpaint.

Toil nodded towards the stone mage. 'He's male,' she said, 'the other three warriors are female.'

'So what are thirds?'

'What I call the others, not like there's a word I can speak for it. The thirds look different to the males and females.'

'Slaves?'

'Nah – a third sex. They're the ones that carry the children, all three make 'em though.'

'All three?' asked several of the mercenaries at once in varying tones of disgust and wonder. Kas cackled loudly, startling the Wisps.

'All three,' Toil confirmed. 'Don't ask how it works, I never got that close to proceedings.'

As she spoke, more Wisps came up the slope from the lakeside, each of them wearing tall reed baskets on their backs, mostly containing plants Lynx couldn't identify. The last basket held small fish, some still wriggling fresh from the water amid the coils of what he assumed was some sort of eel. Several of the Wisps themselves were noticeably shorter and thicker in the torso than the others, the thirds Lynx assumed, but others were clearly male or female. They all filed past the mercenaries, sparing them only what seemed curious glances, while two of the warriors led the way out.

'Come on,' Toil said, hefting her mage-gun again. 'We've got a long walk ahead of us.'

As Lynx went through into the first chamber he saw the Wisp warriors moving with an eerie silent grace as they stalked towards the grille, magic ready. It didn't take them long to be satisfied that the great tunnel was empty and the whole group started off along the level road towards Shadows Deep. Lynx saw that the Wisps had no lanterns of their own, just the faint glow from their fingertips when they conversed, which illuminated nothing.

He shivered at the thought, a crawling sensation on his skin as he imagined a life underground all too easily. The memories slithered back into his mind; cramped half-lit tunnels, the stink of bodies and headaches from the poor air. His heart began to judder, his chest tightening as he felt the prickle of sweat on his skin. With an effort Lynx fought his memories back, forced himself to look up at the high ceiling above and send his thoughts away from fears of the dark.

He looked around him and saw Sitain nearby, one hand perched nervously on the butt of her mage-pistol. Suddenly he was desperate to talk, to hear a normal voice pierce the cloying dark that surrounded them and seemed to seep inside him with every breath.

'Sitain,' he whispered, sidling over to the young woman. 'How far can you see?'

'Down the tunnel?'

'Aye. Further than the light o' the lantern?'

She squinted forward. 'I guess. The rough shape of the tunnel anyway, no detail. Why?'

'Just trying to work out what advantages we've got down here. What if you let a little magic out to play?'

Sitain shrugged and didn't reply, but from the little Lynx could see she seemed to be focusing on doing what he'd asked. Before she could say anything the nearest of the Wisps gave a start and turned its narrow face her way. It was one of the thirds, a half-full basket on its back and a long robe down to its lower set of knees. It blinked its lower eyes twice in quick succession then rubbed its hands together with a papery rasp. One of the others made a long fluid gesture with its glowing finger and others joined in the rasping of palms.

'What're they saying, Toil?' Sitain said, alarmed.

'Don't worry, it wasn't very rude,' Toil replied with a small laugh. 'No malice in it, just friendly mocking, like you might a child.'

'Aye well, they don't get strung up or sold off for magery.' Sitain scowled. 'Sure they've had more time to practise.' She looked at Lynx. 'I can see better now, further. Wouldn't be able to hold it for too long, but at a pinch, sure.'

'Hey, Reft,' called Varain from behind them. 'You sure these ain't your people? You half Wisp or something?'

'Ulfer's horn, there's a thought!' Anatin said. 'Would explain a few things. What you say, Reft?'

The big man shook his head but before they could press him Toil spoke up again. 'Keep it down back there. Sound travels well underground. Best we keep it to a minimum less we attract something nasty.'

Lynx bit back a reply, pursed his lips and kept his eyes on Toil up ahead instead. The anxiety settled back around him again like a cold blanket tightening, but he ignored it as best he could, trying to focus elsewhere. There was little distraction to be had, though. The darkness was a veil he wanted to ignore and no sound reached him beyond the crunch of dirt beneath human feet and the soft pad of the Wisps.

The dry and still air carried only the faint musky sweat of his comrades and an earthy, bitter smell he guessed was the Wisps, so he contented himself with watching the sway of Toil's hips instead. The memory of her naked was an easy one to conjure up, it was burned into his mind, and once more he cursed himself for just standing there like some gormless little boy.

He half-stumbled as the memory filled his thoughts. Grunting, Lynx glanced around to see Sitain watching him and he straightened, hoping she couldn't see the guilty flush that coloured his cheeks.

'You glazed over a bit there,' she whispered.

'Ain't a fan of underground,' he said in a gruff voice. 'Trying to think of something else.'

'So I saw.'

A sharp glance over her shoulder from Toil hushed the pair of them, but Lynx could sense the knowing grin on Sitain's lips even as they trudged on in silence. He felt his hand tighten at the thought, but knew perfectly how his anger smouldered at such times. A dozen long, slow breaths were enough to dispel the urge to lash out. When he was composed again he kept his head up and focused on the miles ahead of them instead.

The tunnel floor was not far off a highway in terms of being level and free of debris. The lack of light meant occasionally there would be an unseen stone underfoot, but for the main part they could keep to a swift pace which would somewhat lessen the Charneler advantage of horseback. They pressed on, the longer-limbed Wisps pushing the mercenaries as fast as they could walk, and by Lynx's estimation they covered the ground quickly.

An hour passed, then another. The Wisps showed no sign of pausing for a rest despite some of their number being burdened by the baskets. There were thirteen of them in all, nine labourers and four warriors as escort. Occasionally one

308

of the warriors would lope on ahead, breaking into a lazy jog that nevertheless meant they disappeared into the darkness only moments later. They didn't go far from what Lynx could tell, just enough to scout the ground ahead where an obstacle or bend in the tunnel must have obscured their view. Once or twice it took a few hundred yards of walking before the scout was caught up, but Lynx couldn't tell if they had gone further or just continued at a distance and the pace was such he didn't bother to ask.

An old rockfall slowed them briefly, the Wisp warriors silently creeping up over a great uneven pile of stone where the tunnel had collapsed and been dug open long ago. The mercenaries waited well back with the labourers while the warriors investigated for threats. Lynx took the time to inspect his comrades in turn, determined to distract himself from the gnawing anxiety of being underground.

Reft stood tall and still, a statue of a man undisturbed by everything going on around him, while Teshen prowled like a restless panther – not nervous, but brimming with energy. Anatin and Olut leaned close, talking in whispers, while Toil retreated back down the tunnel to watch their rear.

She almost vanished from the meagre reach of the strange lantern, having left it with a jittery Sitain, and still Toil looked unruffled, as though the dark was her true home. The idea disquieted Lynx. Just imagining it made him breathless. But before the panic could mount Kas plonked herself down beside him, her face a picture of calm as though they were in a quiet tavern rather than some monster-haunted mine.

'Take a load off,' she whispered to him. 'Keep me company.'

Lynx complied with a forced smile and sat down beside her, a long-familiar saying of his homeland's army appearing in his thoughts. '*The body can be trained as easily as a dog – a warrior must make his body obedient to his every command.*' It was something Governor Lorfen had quoted to him, just before releasing Lynx into the So Han countryside.

'*I've seen slaves and prisons, more than I care to remember,*' Lorfen had said. '*They break minds and some damage cannot be undone, but you So Han warriors understand mastery over the body better than most others. Regain that mastery, choose to be the one in command, or you will be a slave to the broken parts inside you. Force yourself to smile, to stand tall and face the sun rather than the shadows of your fears. Wear it as armour against the fears and the body will learn such habits again. It won't heal the breaks, but it'll ease their pain. Sometimes having that armour to hide behind is enough.*'

'Reckon we're getting through this alive?' Kas said, nudging him from his reverie.

'This ruin?' Lynx shrugged. 'Getting friendly with the natives can't hurt. Toil seems to know what she's about.'

She nodded and took a swig of water from her canteen. 'Aye, guess so. Still can't get over that bit. Never seen one in the flesh and now look at us.' Kas gestured around at the pale, inhuman faces clustered in two groups. Several pairs of hands were moving rapidly, the glow of fingertips leaving a faint trail in the air.

'Looks like they can't believe it either.'

'Or they're debating how to eat us,' Kas said with a small shiver. 'Those eyes creep me out.'

Lynx couldn't argue there. The lower pair was set slightly further apart than the upper pair and he could see the pale slit irises swivelling as they conversed, keeping a wary watch in all directions. The thirds were the most garrulous, in so far as Lynx could guess from the gestures, and were at the heart of both discussions, but nothing he saw bore out Kas's worries.

A flash of movement made him raise his gun, almost firing on the lithe figure descending the uneven pile of rocks until he recognised it. The largest of the warriors bounded down past him, fingers pulsing bright until it reached the tunnel floor. It looked around for Toil then saw her away down in the tunnel and made a quick gesture. She sprinted back without saying a word, kicking up dust and stirring the mercenaries to shrug off their packs ready for a fight.

'Something's coming,' she hissed. 'Don't fire unless you have to.'

Lynx felt a jolt in the gut at her words. There were few Duegar ruins in So Han but they'd still heard the stories of maspids – a monster to scare children and adults alike. Toil raced past him and hopped up the smaller fallen rocks so the mercenaries followed, Anatin waving Olut back to watch their rear.

'Burner in the pipe,' he hissed as he went and Olut nodded, patting the closed breech of her gun to indicate she already had a fire-bolt loaded.

Lynx laboured up the easiest path he could find, struggling his way to the top where the warriors, Toil and Teshen waited. Beyond the barrier he could see only a solid wall of darkness, but as Anatin joined him the leading Wisp warrior hurled a fistful of fire down the tunnel ahead.

The magic made no sound, just the hiss of flame over stone as it struck thirty yards away, but it was enough to cast some small light over a stretch of ground. Lynx flinched as he saw jagged shapes dart away from the light – angular shadows writ large on the rough tunnel walls.

'Fuck me, this ain't good,' growled Varain, tracking a dark body with his gun until it melted into the darkness a moment later.

'No guns unless they charge,' Toil muttered as a zip of air was followed by a whip-crack of stone on stone up ahead.

A series of rapid clicks emerged from the darkened tunnel, darting back and forth like orders being shouted, before falling briefly silent. Lynx glanced over and saw the stone mage silhouetted against the fire circling its kin's hand. As he watched, a walnut-sized chunk of stone darted out into the dark along with a second stream of fire. This time something alive was struck, the brief wash of flames illuminating a bulky body.

It reeled and flipped over and away from the fire, a chatter of furious clicks emanating from it. Larger than a man but hunched, a pale belly and darker limbs, that glimpse alone enough to remind Lynx of the stories he'd heard. Thick, blade-like limbs and a great maw of teeth – blind, but able to sense their prey and move with deadly speed.

Again the creatures disappeared into the darkness, but the Wisps seemed to know where they were still and one flash of movement drew an arrow from Kas as the warriors continued their barrage of fire and stone. Then, just as suddenly as it had begun, it was over and all went still. Lynx blinked at the darkness and noticed how sweaty his hand was against the stock of his gun, wiping it on his coat before scanning the tunnel ahead for movement.

'They're gone,' Toil announced as the warriors straightened and one padded back down to where the labourers waited.

'Sure?' Lynx asked, his mouth dry.

'They are,' she said with a nod at the Wisps. 'Good enough for me, they're the experts.'

'Will they come back?'

'Doubt it. Think there were only a few and we winged some.'

'How can you tell?' Kas asked, relaxing the tension on her bow.

'The sound. They make a crackling sound when you pierce their carapace.'

'I didn't hear that.'

Toil shrugged and started back down the rubble to fetch her pack. 'Was your first time, you'll miss a lot.'

'Those were maspids?' Kas pressed.

'Aye, but just a few of 'em and they weren't expecting us. If they're the ones doing the ambushing, they're a whole lot nastier.'

'Anything we need to know for next time?'

Toil stopped. 'They're quick,' she said after a moment's thought. 'Quick and tough, but they die like everything else. If they charge, shoot 'em. If you miss, get the fuck out the way.'

'What about the noises?' Lynx pressed. 'That clicking sound? They were talking, right?'

Toil snorted. 'Oh aye, they're smarter'n wolves and a whole lot nastier. Don't expect a conversation out of 'em, but they're good pack hunters and they know how to use the dark. That wasn't an ambush; we'd not spot that until it was too late. They're clever enough not to hunt Wisps unless they find 'em alone, but humans are another matter. Wisps reckon they can smell fear, gets 'em all hungry and worked up.'

'Why didn't you tell us that before?' he snapped.

'Easy,' she called over her shoulder, dropping down on to the tunnel floor. 'You might not've come.'

Chapter 20

Lynx wasn't sure how long they walked. An hour, half a day, he couldn't tell. Just like when he'd been in prison, his time underground seemed unreal and dislocating. A permanent night that left daylight a mere memory. They rested after a period of time, probably more for the labourers than the mercenaries but still Lynx and his comrades sank gratefully down against the rough stone walls. Varain sang a low, mournful folksong as they settled, but after a minute or so tailed off without finishing, and then they sat in silence.

The scraps of sleep they'd managed in the past few days were starting to count against them. Sitain was struggling the most. Though she was strong and young she had no experience of forced marching and the light-stepping Wisps set a hard pace. As for the others, they could maintain the march for a while longer but there was a dulling of their edge, each passing hour adding weight to their weapons and packs.

They made no fire, resting only for an hour before setting off again, and Lynx found himself staring at the faint traces of light that veined the stone walls. Whether they came from some lichen or strange mineral he couldn't tell, but Toil's curious lamp magnified the bare gleam that came from them. Without it the tunnel might not be perfectly black, but would be as near it as would make no difference to human eyes. The Wisps clearly could see better and carried no lamps themselves, nor much of anything at all.

He realised they had very little equipment with them, which told a tale of how close they must be to their settlement. A few weapons and small packs on the backs of the warriors, tools and baskets of food for the labourers. This was not an expedition of several days but a regular trip to tend their strange gardens. Lynx tried to hold on to that thought, the idea of some sort of underground village a point of reference in his mind.

The darkness remained oppressive, but the scale of the tunnel and the light-garden had diminished the squall of panic at the back of his mind. It remained, but the tall tunnel was a far cry from the cramped and winding paths he'd been used to. It was broader than any road he'd walked on, with the prospect of some sort of ruined city at the end. None of it was ideal, but at the same time it wasn't the panic-inducing disaster he'd feared.

'Anyone else missing the Skyriver?' Varain muttered, looking around at those beside him.

Kas grunted and nodded as she massaged her foot a few yards away, having jarred it on a stone a while back.

'Hard to,' Sitain said, looking up, 'with all this on show.'

'All what?'

'You can't see any o' this?'

Varain squinted up. 'I see the lines of rock, bluish veins glowing very faint.'

'Ah. I, ah, well, it's better for me.'

'How much better?'

Lynx saw Sitain's face twitch and guessed she was grinning. 'Like every sapphire in the world got set into the stone above me, forming a map of every road, river and stream on the continent.'

'Huh. So better'n a bluish glow then?'

'A bit, aye.'

'Still wouldn't mind seeing the Skyriver again,' Lynx said.

'We'll get there,' Toil called. 'Maybe a day or two. Can you hold out 'til then?'

'I'm fine,' he growled.

'If you say so.'

'You got a problem?'

Anatin made an angry sound in his throat. 'The pair of you, shut it.'

'I've got no problem,' Toil continued, ignoring the man completely. 'The dark takes some different to others, that's all. Took me a while to get comfortable underground, there's no shame in feeling twitchy.'

'Glad to hear it,' Lynx said, pushing himself to his feet again. 'Now I got your approval, mebbe it's time we kept moving?'

'We move when our friends want to,' Toil said, but as she spoke the warriors seemed to rise as one, apparently prompted by Lynx. She shrugged. 'Or you could have it your way.'

With little to do but hoist their belongings on to their backs, the party soon resumed their long trudge down the tunnel. It was surprisingly level going. Any incline up or down remained shallow and was soon corrected, restoring them to a plane not far below the surface, by Lynx's estimation.

It was a dull and functional tunnel, though, roughly made and lacking anything in the way of detail or variety. Eventually they reached an arched exit that at least bore some sort of deliberate stone-working. The Wisp warriors had checked it for safety before Lynx even reached it and they led the mercenaries into a great high chamber with a small pool just about visible in the centre.

The dimensions were elusive in the darkness, but Lynx guessed some sort of upper level ran around the whole chamber twenty yards above. Only piles of rubble suggested where the way up might once have been. A smooth conical roof bore several black fissures and water dripped steadily through one, running off the upper level and carving a silvery trail across the stone floor to the pool at the centre.

The Wisps paid the whole chamber little regard, marching straight through towards a zigzagging staircase built for longer legs than those of humans. Only Reft could take each step one pace at a time and before he reached the top the big man had given up, preferring the slow method forced on the rest. Great protrusions of fungi lined the walls of the chamber and while those were ignored by the Wisps the soft scurrying behind tumbled stones made several of them look up. They didn't wait to flush out whatever game or scavenger was hiding there, however, but kept up their pace.

Sitain lingered a little longer than the rest, falling behind until Kas dropped back and gave her a nudge. The young woman ducked her head and muttered an apology. 'Caught a glimpse of a night elemental,' she said, nodding towards the upper level. 'Was hoping it'd come closer but I guess with various types of mage here, they're skittish.' She straightened and pushed on to catch up the rest.

'If they're close,' Toil called back, 'that's enough for me. Probably a good sign nothing else is.'

Lynx felt his fingers twitch at that thought, the desire for a weapon in his hand pulsing stronger. He'd seen nothing in the threatening curtain of liquid blackness, but the memory of that night on the road felt less wonderful now he was underground. The magic of the elemental's presence dimmed in his mind, eclipsed by darting angular movements and knife-sharp edges.

Unexpectedly the tunnel branched left and right, the old debris of a rockfall visible on the left-hand branch. The nearer stones were just about visible as they passed and bore strange tapering grooves on them, too regular to be naturally formed but like no tool-working Lynx had ever seen.

317

'Stonecarver beetles,' Toil supplied, seeing a few of the mercenaries look that way. 'Must be a nest down there somewhere.'

'So we're steering clear?'

'You keep clear of their nests, they won't bother you,' she confirmed. 'Easiest way to die down here, just wander down the wrong tunnel. By the time you realise there's a nest nearby, it's too late to back away and they won't ever give up if their queen's threatened.'

The Wisp warriors led them down the other path, one that wound an oblique route for reasons Lynx couldn't fathom, but he did wonder if he could made out regular breaks in the glowing veins of rock above, as though there were ledges or windows near the peak of the tunnel. Rounding one corner the right-hand wall opened up on them and revealed a similar highway to the one they were walking on, a great rounded lump of stone punctuating the join of tunnels as they made for the Duegar ruin.

Without warning a grey blur erupted from a high fissure and smashed into Olut. The woman was knocked sideways, twisted right around as she was thrown to the ground. Lynx threw himself back as something whipped past his face and Sitain screamed. Shouts and movement whirled around them as Olut yelled, battering at some shape around her waist. Then the mercenary howled in pain as she was wrenched right and left. Her gun went off with an ear-splitting roar and orange flames exploded over the tunnel wall.

Lynx abandoned his gun and dived away as the wash of heat and stabbing light surged towards him. Sitain's shrieks grew louder, but in his peripheral vision Lynx saw a haze of night surrounding her, not fire. The tunnel was divided into darkness and light, a blurred boundary reaching up in the air for a second until the fire fell back. Olut continued to cry out, slashing madly with a knife while the Wisp warriors jumped forward and darts of fire and stone hammered into the writhing confusion surrounding her.

The hammer of gunshots followed, white streaks lancing through the dark. Reft roared and jumped forward, slamming the spiked reverse of his hatchet into their attacker. A great blade-like shape whipped through the air towards him, cleaving into the pack on his back and dashing the giant to the ground. Then the deep boom of an earther sounded and the creature was punched in the side by a huge dark fist. It crashed hard into the still-burning rocks behind it. Olut fell, now silent, while the Wisp warriors advanced, firing gouts of flame at the head of the creature while shards of stone cracked its pale underside. It writhed and lashed, twisting itself into a tight ball bigger than a man as it sought to hide from the onslaught, but Lynx could hear and smell its flesh burning.

Before he could retrieve his gun to join in the attack he heard Anatin roar a curse and fire his pistol from beside the Wisps. The jagged line of a sparker tore through the dark and enveloped the creature in crackling energies. It wrenched around under the impact then fell limp, uncoiling in a clatter of armour and claws.

There was a long moment of silence before Teshen and Ashis ran to Olut's side and turned the woman on to her back. Lynx saw her legs twitch, but then she stilled. Even before he saw the blood he knew the big northerner was dead.

'What,' panted Anatin, 'the hairy fuck was that?'

They all turned to Toil but the woman looked as shocked as they did. 'Buggered if I know,' she said hoarsely, reloading her gun and advancing gingerly.

The Wisp warriors looked less wary than the humans, and one drew its axes and hooked one edge of the creature to tilt it back. It was long, twenty feet or more, and as thick as Reft's torso, with curved grey plates of chitin armour and spear-like legs.

'Shattered gods,' Anatin breathed. 'It's a centipede.'

As soon as he spoke the words the image seemed to resolve itself into some sort of sense for Lynx. A centipede, albeit one of monstrous proportions. He could see the half-dozen wounds in its plated underside, most obviously the great hole punched by that earther. He could even see the remains of the legs shattered under the impact, pale fragments embedded in the bloodied mess of the wound.

'Did you not think to warn us about these?' Anatin roared, waving his spent mage-pistol in Toil's face.

Her expression twisted into anger and Toil snatched at the gun, yanking it from his grasp in one deft movement. 'I've never seen one of those things before, so fuck right off!' she snarled. 'You want a full list of all the nasty shit I've seen down here, fine. There wasn't much time before, remember? But even if I'd told you about the horrors down here, the risk'd have been better than the certainty of getting caught up on the surface.'

'Tell that to Olut.' Anatin pointed back at the dead mercenary. Ashis stepped aside so the brutalised mess of her abdomen was clearly visible, but the sight of terrible wounds didn't make Toil hesitate a moment.

'Dead up there or dead down here, you think she gives a shit? You're mercs and this is no different to a battlefield. I can try to help us avoid the fight down here, but folk like us don't get promises that it'll all be okay. You're a gambler at work and play, you choose the hand to go with and let the cards decide your fate. You know the risks.'

'I know what's going to happen on a fucking battlefield! Down here, I got nothing.'

'That's why I'm leading the way,' Toil said, pausing just long enough to swallow her anger. 'It's darker down here, but it's still a game you know. The pictures on the cards may be different, but some bastard big centipede or a burner – both'll kill you and the difference don't really matter in the end.'

'Hey,' shouted Kas behind them, loud enough to startle both.

They turned to see her interposing herself between one of the Wisp warriors and Sitain. The young woman was sat on the ground, wide-eyed with terror at the attack and now scrambling backwards as the strange figure loomed over her. Lynx moved to join her but the Wisp didn't force its way past, merely raised a flat palm towards Sitain. Before it the air twisted briefly, a spiral of turning dark that vanished almost as soon as it had appeared.

'He's saluting you,' Toil explained, casting one last angry look at Anatin. She tossed the man's gun back to him and went to help Sitain up. 'Best you return the gesture.'

'Saluting me?' Sitain asked, looking dazed. 'Why now?'

'He's a night mage, same as you. What you did when that burner went off made it pretty obvious to everyone. Don't worry. They don't like humans much, but mages they've got something in common with at least.'

Shakily Sitain stood up and raised her hand. It took a moment but at last she gathered a few twists of darkness and let them play across her skin. The Wisp made an elegant sweeping gesture with its hand and turned away to rejoin its kin, but as it did so Toil took its place.

'You're cut,' she said, touching her fingers to Sitain's arm.

Sitain hissed and pulled back, seemingly noticing the bloodied tear on her sleeve for the first time. 'What happened?' she whispered, opening the cloth to reveal a short spine protruding from her flesh.

'Oh, that's not good.' Toil gripped Sitain's arm firmly and held her still while she touched the spine. Sitain hissed, but it didn't seem to be barbed and Toil delicately withdrew the needle-like spine from Sitain's arm. Toil glanced back at the

Wisps and attracted the attention of one while the others continued to surround the dead centipede.

'I don't feel well,' Sitain murmured.

Kas eased her back down to the ground while Toil held the spine up to the Wisp's attention. The two had a brief conversation with their hands, the only part of which Lynx could make out being when the Wisp gestured back to its fellows by the centipede.

'There's good news,' Toil called, inclining her head to the Wisp. 'Bit o' bad too, though, I'll admit.'

'It's poisoned?' Sitain asked, her breath coming in tight little huffs.

'Aye,' she confirmed, but there was a hint of a smile on her face. 'But don't worry, only a little bit.'

'A bit?'

She shrugged. 'Some things down here have the most lethal shit you've ever seen. When you're huge with massive fangs, though, it seems like you can afford to skimp on the venom.' Toil nodded back at the Wisps. 'I've had a dose o' this myself once, I think, didn't know it came from a centipede but they're harvesting the venom. If it's what they call a Whiteshadow, you'll live.'

It was too dark to tell if Sitain paled at the news, but when she spoke again it was in a weak voice. 'And the bad news?'

Toil's grin widened. 'You're going to have really messed-up dreams for the next day or so. We'll need a travois of some sort, mebbe the carapace of the centipede will work. You ain't going to manage one foot in front of the other soon, so just lie back and don't fight the spinning. It'll all go dark soon enough.'

'How did you get dosed, then?' Lynx asked. 'You said you'd not seen one o' these before. This like some sort of shaman's mushroom?'

'Something like that, but this isn't the stuff of rituals. The warriors take it; they say they can explore the lower depths with just their minds.'

'Eh?'

'I dunno, they get all spiritual about the darkness, but they're not so stupid as to travel too deep underground. The low places are the hunting grounds of the maspids; the deepest black home to horrors that we don't have names for. The deep mines hold treasures beyond your wildest dreams, but only the crazed go down after them, and none come back.'

'Is that why you took it? To see what you could find down there?'

Toil shook her head. 'I ain't that stupid.' She paused. 'It was because I lost a bet. Anyway – what I saw didn't make a whole lot of sense, but it *was* a whole lot of fun in parts. Now come on, help me with this travois. She's glazing over.'

*

The landscape of the surface changed dramatically as they neared what Exalted Uvrel guessed was the ruin proper. It was difficult to be sure. She had never been so close to one before and the Duegar had been extinct for a few thousand years, but where they rode had the feel of a dead city rather than the life of the wilds.

There was a natural path running a winding route towards the great peaks of the dead city. It was a strange middle ground between a narrow glacial valley and wide streets of another age. Great slabs of stone rose up on either side; sheer rock faces and tall monument-like outcrops defined their path. She occasionally glimpsed lines too regular to be natural and a few weathered devices carved into the stone, all mostly obscured by great trailing creepers and yellowed grass seemingly able to grow in the smallest space.

They were forced to backtrack only once, their path rising suddenly to cross a sharp gorge and narrowing so sharply it would have been madness to try and persuade any horse across. Bottlenecks started to appear on the meandering path, the scouts forced to race back and forth to clear the way of possible ambushes without losing the main group. Uvrel could see the cavalry troopers starting to look increasingly nervous as the looming formations took on a greater variety and size. The hardened dragoons remained wary and professional, while the grenadiers just grew increasingly animated.

The work of centuries had broken some structures and obscured almost everything else, but as they pushed on Uvrel found herself more easily able to imagine the shapes of the civilisation hidden underneath the decay, preserved far better than human structures thanks to the stone magery used. Archways and gently curved roofs became more frequent, and once they passed a colonnade that screened a vast recessed plaza, now an enclosed miniature forest.

Huge half-covered windows opened on to the overgrown interiors of stone buildings the size of palaces, flocks of chattering yellow-capped birds wheeling through the twisting lines of some unfathomable structure. Uvrel watched them swoop like a hunting cloud on the insects that surrounded the pinkish flowers of dense spiked bushes that seemed to themselves be devouring the stone formations they had grown up around.

The day passed in unnerving quiet – the song of birds and hum of insects unable to break the reverential hush that surrounded them. The breeze dwindled early in the day to a feeble whisper through creeper fronds and a dull sun shone down on the sheltered path. When the sun began to fall and kissed the misshapen tower-like peaks ahead, Uvrel gave instructions for a campsite to be found. They had passed several shallow-sloped ramps that led to rooftops or grand terraces according to the scouts and she had hopes of finding something similarly defensive again.

Any high ground with limited access would be useful – there was no shortage of wood now as their biggest impediments were the various low-spreading trees that had colonised much of the open ground. Uvrel's limited knowledge of these ruins did extend to an awareness that darkness hid a multitude of terrors and, despite their firepower, she was concerned about finding a secure camp.

At last they found what she was looking for, a strange half-open rock formation that was certainly not natural, but seemed to be unfinished or unfathomable in its original purpose. A mossy meadow was enclosed on three sides, twenty yards above ground level and almost a hundred across, with the only access being a great stepped slope up the eastern flank. Once Uvrel ordered the camp to be set her soldiers raced to obey, eager for food and rest after the miles they'd covered. Pickets were set on the steps and the horses corralled as the cooking fires were lit.

The sun had dropped behind the ruin's great jutting stones by the time they stopped – the sky was still light but a chill descended and Uvrel could see a long drawn-out dusk was upon them. By fits and starts the sergeants of each squad waved their troops down on one knee and spoke the dusk greeting to Insar then barked a repeat of their orders as soon as they were done.

In short order the scent of food wafted over a regulation line of tents, and the squads slumped down around their assigned fire. Uvrel heard snores escaping the tents before she'd even managed a mouthful of beans and rice, but with the light fading fast she knew the reveille would still come all too soon. While shovelling food into her mouth from a shallow metal bowl, Uvrel forced herself to visit each fire in turn and speak to the officers there. They were all as drained as their men, but she knew both the effect an Exalted's presence had on regular troops and that what she asked of them would need every ounce of strength and resolve they possessed. Careful not to tarry, she soon found her way to the pickets on the slope where a squad of dragoons, bolstered by a pair of sharpshooters and grenadiers each, stood watch under Lieutenant Sauren.

'As you were, Lieutenant,' Uvrel said, acknowledging the woman's salute. 'Damn, you can't see much out here, can you?'

Sauren gestured at the fires behind them. 'You need a few minutes more, sir. It's not great, but the line of sight's clear. We've no issue with friend or foe and there's enough to make out movement. Besides, Jokaim there has got eyes like a cat, I'm assured.'

A slim figure ahead of them touched the upturned brim of their hat as Sauren mentioned their name. The sharpshooter didn't turn and Uvrel couldn't work out if it was a man or a woman, only that Jokaim also possessed that innate stillness of a natural hunter.

'Nothing's been tracking us, Jokaim?' Uvrel asked.

'Mebbe,' the sharpshooter replied, the whisper of his voice sounding younger than Uvrel had expected. 'Can't be certain what I've seen, not out here.'

'But you've seen something?'

'Aye, glimpsed. Just pale shapes is all, though. Folk say there are ghosts and monsters out here. I couldn't tell you which it was I saw. Could be cougars catching scent of the horses, or a chamois with its winter coat.' He shrugged. 'Or my mind playing tricks 'cos of where we are.'

'Best guess?'

'Don't care to guess. If it's maspids, I'll shoot 'em. Not much else will bother us so far's I know and ghosts I can't do nothing about anyway.'

Uvrel grunted in acknowledgement and repeated the man's name in her head. An Exalted was always on the lookout for good troops and Jokaim's unflappable manner was the sort of thing she valued, given the usual missions dragoons were sent on.

The activity of the Knights-Charnel in Grasiel would have been noted by the other Orders as well as other cities, their failure as much as their purpose. Wherever the Lords-Sovereign intended to direct their attention to next, their actions would be opposed by a number of factions and the elite Torquen would be at the forefront of any conflict.

She shook her head as thoughts of political manoeuvring began to encroach on her clarity. *Time enough for that if we survive this cursed ruin*, Uvrel reminded herself. *Keep to the task at hand.*

'Carry on, Sauren,' she said with a nod at the lieutenant. 'Try not to wake the rest of us unless it's important.'

Sauren smiled as she saluted, both knowing perfectly well that a single mage-gun would wake the whole camp. 'As you say, sir.'

Chapter 21

The mercenaries left Olut's body where she fell and Lynx let the others see to her. There was enough to do for Sitain, who had quickly become feverish and dizzy. It was impossible to tell how far they were from the surface, or anywhere else that might serve as a burial site, but clearly the mercenaries had their own more pragmatic traditions. They stripped Olut of her gun and cartridge case then searched her clothing with the swift efficiency of battlefield looters. A few possessions were removed and handed to Anatin, then to Lynx's surprise Ashis helped herself to Olut's boots after comparing their feet.

No one seemed to bat an eyelid at this so Lynx kept his own counsel and accepted Olut's coat when Kas brought it to him. The Wisps had cut four segments of chitin from the centipede with practised efficiency, using some sort of sinews from the body to turn it into a drag cradle. With Olut's coat laid over their neat butchery, Kas and Lynx placed the shivering, chattering Sitain onto the travois before Reft took hold of the sinews and wound them around his left hand.

'I'll take her, she's my responsibility,' Lynx had said to the giant, but Reft had simply regarded him for a short while then started to haul Sitain forward.

'We don't argue with Reft as a rule,' Kas had told him, patting Lynx on the shoulder. ''Specially when it comes to matters of strength.'

Unwilling to lose any more time, they had set off leaving Olut with hands folded across her chest and a single silver coin protruding from her lips. Lynx noticed it wasn't one from Olut's purse, they had been particular about that. Whether her money was to be shared among the rest or not, Anatin had selected a large, relatively shiny piece from his own coin purse and placed it in the Knight of Stars' mouth.

'We'll miss you, sister,' he had said to the corpse, words echoed by each of the rest as they pulled on their packs and started off down the tunnel. Once the party was a short distance away Anatin stopped and turned, levelling a mage-pistol.

'Let the gods see your pyre and gather your spirit to them.'

The mercenaries lingered only a moment longer to watch the burner's flames spread over Olut and start to consume her clothes. The mage-shot would burn hot and fast, and flames still lit the tunnel as the curve of the passage took them out of sight. They left her death behind them and pushed on as fast as the Wisps were willing to accommodate, covering several miles in silence before another rest was called.

That pattern continued for a while; bursts of walking and brief rests in an unreal, eternal night that seemed to just hold exhaustion at bay. Lynx had lost track of time by the attack and after a few more rests he was unsure whether it was night or day on the surface. They had walked well into the night, knowing that their pursuers had horses up on the surface, but where dawn was Lynx couldn't guess at and was too tired to try.

One massive tunnel turned into the next, a great crossroad was passed where smaller tunnels merged to meet theirs. One ran like an aqueduct above their heads as they crossed a huge cavern, faintly lit by unknown constellations of crystal set into the far-off roof. The light there was too feeble to support any life beyond lichens and a few pus-filled fungi, the cavern as quiet as a tomb.

The Wisps were efficient and almost silent as they scouted the path, assured on their home terrain but never complacent about checking each overhang or tunnel. The mercenaries were too tired to offer to help, but Lynx knew one word of alarm would snap them back into battle readiness.

Only their footsteps and tiny whimpers from Sitain broke the hush, the young woman moving from fevered twitches to periods of alarming stillness. After three rests they came to a complex of chambers set off the main tunnel that were also protected by an iron grille over the single entrance. There they managed a few hours' sleep, by Lynx's estimation. Not enough to feel fully refreshed, but that and a few scraps of food restored some life to his limbs at least. He tried to take a turn pulling Sitain but Reft gently ignored him, the giant's strength indefatigable, and Lynx left the man to it after that. Sitain had woken by that point and mumbled some sort of curse at Lynx, enough to fill him with relief. She was too weak to walk by herself, certainly at the pace they were setting, but Toil proclaimed the worst past and said Sitain would be on her feet soon.

They continued on under the direction of the Wisps, veering steadily right – Lynx's head said east but he knew he could have been turned around long ago – and passing other parties of Wisps also out on foraging missions. The greetings were brief and Lynx guessed they knew each other, most of their darting conversations probably taken up by explanations about the humans.

One such silent conversation resulted in a thin youngster being sent at a sprint towards their settlement to herald their arrival, which made Lynx both relieved and apprehensive. Nothing was explained to the mercenaries and Toil just shrugged when Anatin asked her what was said, falling in behind the warriors as they set off once more.

They came to an even larger cavern soon after, at the recessed heart of which was a pool of water and three great columns. The peak of each column shone with weak light, gleaming from cottage-sized chunks of crystal that seemingly passed sunlight down from the surface. It was briefly blinding after their travels underground, but once he became used to it Lynx realised the light was still low and would only barely sustain the strange glowing vegetation that filled the cavern.

To his surprise there were grazing animals of a sort there, half a dozen hairless, six-limbed creatures the size of lambs under the watchful eye of more Wisp youngsters. The warriors didn't stop, only made a brief acknowledgement of the greeting offered and continued on through the curious underground oasis. On the other side the tunnel was even larger and Lynx made out scraps of decoration on the increasingly smooth rock walls, great geometric designs surrounding elegant flowing shapes that could have been Duegar script. Before he could make out much detail in the twilight they had passed on by and through one of a half-dozen peaked archways. Beyond that was the Wisp settlement and there the mercenaries stumbled to a halt, gaping at what they saw.

A long shimmering lake, the water faintly phosphorescent, stretched away in front of them. Nearby stood a complex, multi-tiered building set just back from a narrow strip of what Lynx assumed was beach. The windows and doors were high and wide, but covered with grilles, and a curve of spiked defences skirted it, behind which half a dozen warriors stood. Behind the guardhouse were more buildings of similar size, also carved straight from the rock but without the defensive details. A long path led past them, up and around to where dozens of such houses were located on the shallow slope of a huge arch that ran all the way over the lake itself.

Lynx couldn't see how big the lake was. The far shore looked a long way off and his view was obscured by the great arch supporting the village and narrow boats clustered around large rafts on the water. It was at least half a mile, though, he realised, and by the jagged seams of glowing bluish rock scattered across the roof he guessed at significantly more.

A Wisp in long robes moved forward to meet them, one arm raised, and their escorting warriors stopped. The labourers made their way around and off towards the main part of the settlement, but Lynx could see the mercenaries weren't welcome. The elder – at least that was what Lynx assumed it was, by its slower movements – approached them and Toil was waved forward. She knelt respectfully and waited a long while as the elder and the leader of the warriors conversed.

'What's going on?' Sitain croaked from the travois beside him.

'Looks like we're not so welcome,' he said. 'But no one's shooting, so that's a good start.'

When gestures started to be directed their way, Lynx found his fingers twitching for his gun. He had to force the feelings down, remembering that the warrior had made a specific point of greeting Sitain. Despite the growing rumble of anxiety and fatigue in his gut, Lynx kept very still as the elder turned to gesture towards the warriors behind, waiting for Toil to be invited into the conversation. When that did happen the Wisps were careful to move more slowly for her and Toil spent a long while explaining their intrusion.

By the time she was finished the mercenaries were all sat on the dry gravelly cavern floor, legs splayed and leaning back on their stuffed packs. If it had been a human settlement they waited outside, Lynx knew most of them would have gone to sleep where they were, but the alien scene was at once too unnerving and fascinating despite their fatigue. Weak blue and red lights dotted the edges of the high settlement, white painted lines marking the flanks of boats that plied the lake.

There was a perceptible drift of the water towards them, nothing so large as to make waves, but a regular creep up the narrow beach every five or six heartbeats, so Lynx counted. It never encroached beyond a certain point and receded quickly again, but where any sort of tide was being generated he couldn't fathom.

He jerked back to wakefulness when Toil stood and walked stiffly over to Anatin. None of the mercenaries rose, but they all blinked owlishly at her as they waited for news.

'There's good news and bad,' Toil announced eventually.

'Well? Give us one of 'em first.'

'We're not welcome to stay,' she said with a shrug. 'Was no point lying to them about why we're here, their scouts will find the Charnelers quick enough on their night patrols.'

'So?'

'So lovely to meet us and can we please piss off as soon as we're bloody able to. We're free to sleep a few hours here under their watch, but not in the settlement itself and then they'll expect us to move smartly on. They've got warrior-mages but too few to start a fight with a score of guns and they know enough about humans to know how much the Militant Orders like their kind. This isn't a fight they want anywhere near them.'

'Can't say I blame 'em. Supplies?'

'They've no interest in our coin, but they'll give us some. Even better, they've got a lamp like mine for Sitain. Not something they have much use for given how well they see, but they know humans like 'em. Mages are welcome here, we'd not get the offer if it weren't for Sitain – sounds like they consider human mages halfway to being a Wisp.'

Anatin frowned. 'Given as a gift?'

'Olut's gun and a dozen cartridges should get us the lamp and food. To me it's worth ten times the price,' she added, expecting some sort of argument, 'so unless we really can't spare the gun, hand it over. I'll buy the lamp off the company once we're out of here.'

Anatin shrugged and with a flick of the fingers directed her to the travois. Toil collected the gun from where it lay beside Sitain, offering the young woman a brief smile as she did.

'Can they guide us further?' Teshen asked. 'Get us past the ruins?'

'That's more bad news. They've brought down the few tunnels that might take us around to make the village more secure. They've told me the lie of the land we need to travel, but everything this side of the city gets filtered to the open rift that was the heart of the city.'

'Bottleneck?'

'And a jungle too,' she said with a flashing smile. 'Dense and on a dozen levels, so mebbe we can creep through, mebbe not. That takes us to the inner tunnels which'll be just like every other ruin I've explored, but there's the deep rift beyond that. That's the biggest problem.'

'No way across?'

'Oh several, it sounds like, but . . .' Toil hesitated. 'Well, the rift will lead down to the mines, which are the lowest parts of any Duegar city-ruin. Deep; really bloody deep mines. The rift will be dangerous.'

''Cos if we fall it's a long way down?' Lynx asked, more hopeful than anything else.

'Sorry. Oh, you'll fall a long way, no doubt, but it's what lives down there you don't want to come across.' She paused again and this time there was no humour in her face. 'Or have a gun battle nearby to wake them up. Especially that.'

*

Their hosts were true to their word and while the warriors who'd escorted the mercenaries followed their labourer charges, others came with food and drink. Lynx recognised neither, but hunger overtook fascination and he devoured all he was given without paying much attention to the unfamiliar flavours. The rest seemed more hesitant, prodding at the steaming dough-like but fungus-coloured parcels, but eventually they all ate and even Sitain managed to keep some down. With Teshen happy to stay awake and keep watch, they settled down and slept fitfully for a few more hours.

When Lynx awoke he found himself staring up at a pair of tall, scarred Wisp warriors. He still couldn't tell which was male and which was female, but behind them was the shorter frame of a third and it was that one that Toil went to speak to. The third wasn't dressed as a warrior, instead wearing some sort of flowing white robe that looked almost priestly to Lynx. The conversation was brief and before Lynx had cleared his head Toil was back to report.

'Time we buggered off?' Teshen commented as she arrived.

'Correct. Sitain's welcome to stay if she wants, though,' Toil replied. 'Like I said, they don't mind mages nearly so much.'

'Stay?' Sitain croaked, struggling up. 'Alone?'

'If you can't go on. They'll see you to the other side in a few days. Probably safer than sticking with us.'

Sitain blinked at the woman, clearly alarmed at the prospect. Accepting a hand offered by Reft, she pulled herself up to her feet and wobbled precariously as she tested her strength. 'I . . . I don't want to be left on my own.'

'Sure you're strong enough?'

'I—' She wavered and Reft raised a hand to stop her talking any more, gently urging her back to the ground and pointing at the travois.

'You sure, Reft?'

The big man nodded.

'I'll take a turn too,' Lynx said. 'Give you a rest.'

Reft inclined his head to acknowledge the offer and scooped Sitain up in his hands, placing her as easily as an infant into the travois and setting his mage-gun down beside her.

'Well,' Toil said doubtfully, 'if you're certain, I'll tell them. If you can stand now you should be okay to walk soon, but if we get caught in a fight . . .'

'I'll take my chances,' Sitain said as firmly as she could.

'Fair enough.'

Toil went to report as much to the third Wisp, who made a curling gesture with its hands that Lynx took as acceptance. The third bowed its head slightly and removed a fist-sized metal object that was hung on a cord around its neck. This it held out to Toil while making a complicated gesture with one hand. The muscular woman nodded and brought the lamp over to where Sitain lay propped on the travois. It was much smaller than Toil's lantern but made of the same dark glass-like substance.

While Toil's had a solid brass casing to protect it, this one looked more delicate and was entirely encased in a thin filigree of some dark metal. Toil turned it over in her hands briefly before handing it over. Sitain cradled the lamp reverentially until Toil pointed at the bottom end.

'Looks like you twist in there,' she said, 'but don't turn it on yet. Just in case we need it later. Probably not got much light stored.'

'Okay. Ah, will you thank her, them, for me?'

Toil nodded and raised Olut's mage-gun. She handed that to the third with a similar degree of ceremony as when she'd been given the lamp, then pulled a handful of cartridges from the case she'd taken off Tyn's corpse. There was a short discussion over how many and what type, Lynx guessed, which resulted in Toil adding another handful to the pile. The deal done, Toil returned to the mercenaries as the third walked away with the mage-gun slung over one shoulder.

'These two are to guide us,' she said, jabbing a thumb towards the two warriors who'd stayed behind. 'They'll see us safe to the rift.'

Anatin stretched and grunted as he hauled his pack on to his back. 'Good enough. First things first, though, where can an old man take a piss round here?'

Once their bladders were emptied and waterskins filled, the Wisp warriors led them past the guardhouse that watched the archways and on to the slope leading up to the main settlement. They didn't get far enough to see more of the lake and had to content themselves with a clearer view of the stone mage-built houses surrounded by makeshift huts. Lynx struggled to estimate how large a population the settlement contained, but he guessed it was almost the size of a small town. Going by the lights and elusive columns of smoke, there were also houses on the far shore of the lake itself.

They didn't enter the town, however, a huge double-vaulted archway coming into view around a spur of rock. The warriors ushered them through to a now-familiar sort of huge tunnel – taller and narrower than the one they had arrived by, but still wide enough to walk arm in arm should they choose to. With Toil's lantern illuminating enough of the darkness to walk safely, the pair of Wisps swiftly led them to a bewildering crossroad of tunnels on four separate levels, then up a pair of ramps to take a much smaller one. Lynx lingered for a moment but as the rest walked on he was left with no choice but to follow and with a pounding heart he trudged along behind, gritting his teeth as he prayed for the tunnel to open up again.

It took a hundred yards for the corridor-sized tunnel to oblige, climbing through twists and turns and meeting three other similar ones before it became a road again. Only once did the Wisps halt them, one creeping further forward to scout the path while the other scooped a handful of rock from the wall and left it hovering above one palm as it waited.

'Maspids,' Toil reported once she'd asked. 'Hunting party passing us.'

'After the Charnelers?'

She nodded. 'Fair chance of it. If they've still got their horses they'll smell delicious to maspid foragers, but they know not to tackle a large group of humans without numbers on their side.'

'Just how intelligent are those bastard things?' Anatin growled.

'You don't want to know,' was Toil's dark, humourless reply. 'Let's just hope they do us a favour, eh?'

'From what I heard about maspids, I won't wish that on anyone.'

'That's where we differ, then. If it keeps me alive, I'm all for it.'

'Where's this rift?' Lynx broke in, unwilling to hear how far Toil would to go to save herself.

'Half a day I'd guess. Needing some fresh air back there, are you?'

'Something like that.'

Up ahead the Wisp released his magic and continued on down the tunnel, gesturing for them to follow. Toil gave the mercenaries behind her a nod.

'I'd keep a little more distance from Varain, then. I've not seen him bathe in days.'

*

With the dawn's light, Exalted Uvrel dragged herself from her blankets and stood to survey the camp while she cleared her head. Sleep had been fitful, the near-complete silence of the ruins enough to keep her on edge. Her limbs now felt shaky and weak, her head cold and muzzy. She rubbed her palms roughly over her face to scrub the sensation away, swilling a mouthful of water around her mouth to wash away the sour taste.

All around her, soldiers were doing the same, sergeants kicking the last few awake. Most were already up, having slept as warily as her, and they were already pulling down tents. There was the usual morning hush, murmurs and grumbles all restrained as eyes turned her way. Once Uvrel was sure her troops were standing she gave a short nod and dropped to one knee. Head bowed, she didn't need to see to know the rest would follow her example.

'Insar, Lord of the Still Night,' she intoned in a loud voice, 'we thank you for your gift of rest.'

All around came the susurrus echo of her words from officers, sergeants and more pious troopers, darting around the camp as though carried by the fluttering wings of the dawn chorus.

'Insar, Voice of the Dark Night,' Uvrel continued, 'we thank you for watching over us and seeing us safely to dawn. Great Insar, Breath of the Cold Night, be with your servants this day. Lord Insar, protect us should we enter your blessed dark this day, and guide us to the heretics we seek.'

All around her the soldiers replied with the usual refrain, 'Bless the still night,' and then she stood, saying, 'Insar's blessings upon us all.'

As the camp set about their morning preparations Uvrel caught the eye of a dragoon sergeant and nodded towards the steps. The grey-whiskered man nodded and snatched up his gun, growling for two others to follow, and the four of them headed towards the picket. The guards there were awake and alert still, the cavalry officer in charge a man she didn't know. He snapped a textbook salute as she approached and

Uvrel couldn't help but notice the man's boots looked freshly polished, even out here.

Not one for the recruiting list, she decided. *I can't waste my time breaking soldiers of their parade ground habits.* 'Anything to report?'

'Nothing, sir. A few of the men getting twitchy at shadows, that's all.'

'Right.' She pointed at the sharpshooter and grenadier who'd been assigned to the morning duty. 'You two, with me.'

Without explaining, Uvrel headed down the ancient crumbling steps and on through the scrub beyond. With her gun out she moved as quickly as she could, keen to see what lay ahead. After fifty yards she had seen nothing alive at all, which disquieted her, just the sound of a handful of birds greeting the dawn. The grassy road they were following wound an oblique path ever onward, the mountainous misshaped towers looming close now, until quite suddenly it ended. Or rather, it didn't – it just led somewhere she didn't want to go.

Ahead of them, at the end of a long open stretch of ground skirted by trees, was an ornate pair of pillars fifty feet high, through which some grand domed chamber was visible. Guano stained the stonework and vegetation had crept over and inside, but so enormous was the space that it was perfectly distinct despite the passing of years.

'Damn.'

'Looks dark,' commented her sergeant in as neutral a tone as he could.

'Suspect it'll get darker further in,' Uvrel replied. 'But that's the way the ridge was heading. Time to get underground and see if we can't work out which tunnel our prey will scuttle out of.'

'Let's just hope that's all that scuttles out.'

'Stow that talk, Sergeant,' she snapped, glaring at all the men with her. 'The troopers are already twitchy. I don't need your jokes spooking them further.'

'Aye, sir.'

'Come on.'

Uvrel checked she had a fire-bolt in her gun then led the way towards the entrance. Beyond was a shallow sloping bridge underneath which a small spring ran. She moved cautiously over it, blinking at the gloom, then headed on in with her gun at the ready. Beside her came the grenadier, a pretty young girl who didn't seem to suit the coldly calculating expression most grenadiers wore when they had a grenade in hand, while the others followed.

The chamber was huge, bigger than any single room she'd ever seen before. The keep of Forvern Castle, where she was technically stationed, could have fitted inside. The great dome was worryingly fissured but still whole and stood over the entrance only. There was a larger stretch with a vaulted roof that only reached the base of the dome but ran for a hundred yards, the side walls alternately dotted with fat pillars and small enclosed structures. The vaulted ceiling was smooth, bare stone while the ancient decoration on the dome was largely intact. Great slabs of some dark blue mineral were set into the dome, cut into the shape of constellations and seemingly held in place by metal studs to mark the stars, while an arc of veined marble described the Skyriver.

There was a carpet of dirt underfoot but nothing growing until the far end, where the carpet became topsoil and stunted plants rustled their spiky leaves. The foliage extended through a variety of smaller archways, some leading up and others down. Uvrel took one of the upper ones through which grainy light filtered, picking her way past spindly bushes until she was out in a strange sort of galleried hall – beyond which were miniature jungles enclosed by high stone walls. One was brighter than the rest so she gambled on that path, telling herself she would see what lay beyond that corner before turning back.

Uvrel headed out and looked around the corner on to a clear stone floor that ended in a jagged tear. She barely noticed the ruined mess where a whole section of stone seemed to have been ripped away. Beyond it the world seemed to open up around her and Uvrel's jaw dropped as she surveyed the steep, greenery-choked rift.

The chasm was enormous, running for several miles in either direction, plunging for hundreds of yards to a tree-covered floor below. Fifty yards to her left was a covered stone bridge, wrapped in coils of creeper as though it was being devoured by some great snake.

The far side was a steep, stepped slope at least half a mile high and almost entirely covered in dense foliage, most likely the same sort of overgrown galleries and enclosed gardens as she had seen on this side. The bones of stone outcrops and pillars jutted from the morass to punctuate the regular steps of huge balconies all the way up the cliff side.

Away to her right, one fifty-yard-wide section had been ripped away entirely, as though a giant had smashed its fist down on the cliff. The foliage was reclaiming the shattered section but only slowly, and Uvrel could see the trace of wide doorways and windows all the way to the rubble on the ground.

She had rarely seen a human-made weapon capable of such damage – it would take the largest bombardment spheres to achieve that. Perhaps it had been a shooting star or some agent of the gods, but Uvrel felt a flicker of fear as she imagined it as the work of something that lived amid these ruins.

Uvrel found herself frozen to the spot as she tried to put the thought from her mind and instead work out how they would find the mercenaries across such a great space.

'Damn,' the sharpshooter said quietly from beside her, 'that's a whole lot of cover.'

Uvrel ignored the low whistles of agreement that came from her dragoons and tried to clear her thoughts. She looked left and right, trying to map the path of the ridge they had been following. It was hard to estimate and she had no idea of how many tunnels there were in this city, but the rift was so enormous it was a reasonable assumption most would lead here.

'Decent vantage for us too,' the dragoon sergeant pointed out. 'If we can get across this bridge we can cover both sides.'

'Can you even see the bottom? A small group might walk the length of this without us seeing.' The sharpshooter gestured up and down the rift. There were glimpses of movement everywhere, darting wings and long fronds drifting in the breeze, while a clamour of birdcalls and buzzing insect wings echoed out across the rift.

Uvrel cocked her head and looked at her soldiers. 'The gods favour those who strive,' she said thoughtfully. She went to the very edge of the broken balcony, testing the ground underfoot to ensure it was solid. Looking down at the slope continuing below, she nodded to herself and waved forward the young grenadier. Uvrel plucked the grenade from her hands and inspected it. A sphere the size of her fist, it had a thin outer skin of iron, ridged for grip, while at the top a mushroom-like disc protruded. A band of red paint made it clear this was a fire-bomb while a white line ran perpendicular to that all the way around the sphere. She twisted the detonator so the line on that matched up to the one on the grenade then hurled the grenade out into the rift.

The soldiers ran forward as one to watch it fall. For a moment Uvrel thought it had failed, the dark shape of the grenade disappearing from view before it reached the bottom. Then there was a shudder and a distant crack of noise. A flower of white light blossomed below them before a dome of orange fire hammered out and simply obliterated the foliage around it. The fire raced in all directions, flowing over stone and smashing apart anything alive.

From their high vantage the soldiers stared in fascination. Rarely did they have the luxury of seeing a fire-bomb's effects and the view from almost directly above only increased the sense of wonder. The swift firestorm lashed tendrils of flame out beyond the clearing it had made and a great flock of birds erupted from the branches of nearby trees, wheeling and shrieking.

'Reckon we can spare another,' the grenadier commented. Before Uvrel could say anything the young woman slotted a second grenade into one end of her steel thrower and hurled it off to the right, as far clear of the first explosion as she could manage.

Uvrel felt her breath catch as she waited for the second to explode; again that anxious moment after it had disappeared, but the explosion's roar followed a second later and this time she could see the trees shudder and bend from the impact. The grenade tore another section from the narrow strip of jungle below and soon its snaking flames were spreading and hungrily consuming more. Before long the flames of each grenade met and merged, driven by a steady breeze. The fire raged across the rift floor and between the two epicentres Uvrel could make out the skeletons of trees writhing as the fire consumed them.

'That should serve,' she said after a full awestruck minute of watching the fires rage. They had started to die back now, their ferocity consuming everything in that section so swiftly the fire hardly had time to move too far beyond it.

'It won't take the whole thing,' the grenadier said, 'too damp to burn long or spread too far.'

'I'll not waste all our grenades clearing the rest.' She pointed at the grenadier and sharpshooter. 'You two stay here; keep a lookout for anything we've flushed out. I'll bring the rest of the troops so we can clear that bridge and set up shooting positions to wait for our mercenary friends. They can't have passed this already so we will wait.'

'And if they have?' asked her sergeant.

'They won't have, Sergeant!' she snapped. 'Any damn fool who thinks they could have kept ahead of us on foot, however, is welcome to head straight into those tunnels. Am I clear?'

'Yes, sir.'

'Get your hide moving, then.'

Chapter 22

'So do you trust her?'

Lynx looked sideways at Kas, who'd dropped back to walk alongside him.

'Toil?' he asked, nodding towards the head of their small column. 'I trust she wants to get through this place.'

'That's all?'

'You got a point to make?' Lynx growled, slowing slightly to give them a little more space from the rest.

Kas raised an eyebrow at his tone. 'Think you've just made it for me.'

'Balls I have. You think I trust Anatin either?'

'Anatin's loyal to his company. A prince-elect's agent like her has a master and a mission, and that's all that counts.'

'Anatin's loyal to you, mebbe,' Lynx said with a shake of the head, 'but not me. I've been around mercs enough to know loyalty to the new blood is thinner than water. You reckon he gives a shit about me? Experienced fighters he don't call friend are useful enough at a pinch, but my use could be dying as well as living. I knew that back in Grasiel – "pin it on the bastard from So Han" is a game I've seen played a few times.'

'We don't work that way.'

'You don't, he does. Man's got a cold heart – I ain't condemning him for it. You're a merc commander, that's the only choice you get if you want to last long. As for Teshen and Reft, they're a decent enough pair of sergeants, but the one who could be half Wisp is the more human of the two.'

'Pretty harsh verdict on men I trust my life to.'

'Pretty harsh world out there.'

'You think I don't know that?' Kas snapped.

Lynx opened his mouth to reply then checked himself. 'Aye,' he admitted, 'I know. Didn't mean it to sound otherwise.'

There was a long moment of quiet as they both chewed over their words. Lynx felt the familiar knot of anxiety tighten at the back of his mind, the thinning of the air in his lungs even though the current tunnel was still larger than any he'd known at the prison mine.

'Being down here really fucks with your head, eh?' Kas said at last.

'Aye.'

'Well – my point was this. Look at all of us around you; ask yourself who'd think longest about leaving you down here.'

Lynx didn't reply, but his eyes lifted towards Toil, leading the way.

'Aye, and that woman knows full well the effect she has on men. You can bet she's taken note of all the looks she's had in the last few days. I'm just saying watch yourself, in case she reckons she needs someone to do something stupid.'

'Been a long time since I needed help on that front,' Lynx reflected. He glanced over to where Sitain lay in the travois, clutching Reft's pack and gun while the huge man dragged her down the tunnel. Lynx had taken a turn earlier for an hour or two and was feeling the effects in his biceps now, but he could see Reft had appreciated the relief for all his size and strength.

'Good reminder right there,' Kas said. 'You did something stupid 'cos it was the right thing to do and they backed you up. Teshen was the first in line and much as I like the man, I'm willing to admit he's got a heart some way chillier than average.'

'Reckon he's not the greatest fan o' Militant Orders either, but point taken.'

'Good.'

'Still doesn't mean I'll do whatever a pretty girl tells me to.'

Kas smiled. 'Sure, you just keep thinking that.'

They lapsed into silence again, a short burst of effort diminishing the ground between them and the rest. For the tenth time Lynx tried to work out what the hour was, but the best he could guess was daytime. After another hour or two, at the next rest, Sitain announced she felt well enough to try walking. While the others sat and ate a morsel of their dwindling supplies, she tottered back and forth to try and regain her balance.

She was far from ready to run by the time Anatin decided it was time to leave, but the young woman managed to keep to the slower pace being set for an hour or so before being persuaded back into the travois again.

'I'm fine,' Sitain insisted as Lynx guided her back down.

'But you're weak still. No point exhausting yourself. Short bursts to start.'

'You can't drag me all the way across this city.'

'We're not far from the rift,' Toil announced, coming to join them. 'Save your strength for then, it's an open stretch of ground. Might be we need to run there.'

'She can't run, not yet.'

Toil shrugged. 'If we get ambushed, the slowest target's not going to have the best of days.'

'You think they're waiting for us?'

'Would make sense. We'll find somewhere to hole up and rest when we get there, assuming it's safe.'

'You don't want to get straight across?'

'Not in daylight. Besides, we've been underground a good while now. A few hours rest will do us good, a few hours of light too.'

Lynx scowled. 'Yeah, I could do with seeing the sun again. How is it this doesn't bother you?'

'I'm used to it,' she said with a shrug. 'But I can see you getting scratchier the more time we spend underground. Some folk go that way, the darkness gnaws at you and it's bad to ignore. Isn't a sign of weakness, just one the deep dark's not the place for you.'

'But you love it?'

Toil shrugged. 'Some of us learn to embrace the dark,' she said. 'Your friend Teshen's born to it, I reckon, but I had to learn.'

They all turned instinctively to look at where the long-haired Knight of Tempest lay, head propped up by his pack and eyes closed.

'Born to it,' Lynx said, nodding. 'Well, that's not worrying at all.'

'Hey, there are only three types of relic hunter in this world,' Toil said. 'Those who're born to the dark and those who learn to love it.'

'And the third?'

Her smile was cruel. 'Those who get lost to it. Doesn't matter how much you warn them, they'll wander off and get lost.'

'And which one am I?' Lynx asked.

'Only you can know that.'

With that, Toil sat down and pulled her necklace out from under her tunic. Lynx frowned at it through the twilight for a while before realising it was some sort of tooth or claw. Again he remembered the man he'd met years ago, the one who'd claimed to have travelled this way and wore a maspid tooth around his neck. A man whose mind had cracked after what he'd seen in the dark. Toil turned it in her fingers for a while, frowning as she did so, then tucked it away again.

'Souvenir from some past trip underground?' he asked.

She nodded. 'A memento. Reminder of getting lost.'

All too soon for Lynx's weary body, they were off again. It turned out to be a short trip, but one he still felt his feet to start to drag on. Tunnels became more like oversized corridors, the stonework better preserved or more carefully done. The script of the Duegar appeared more often; images of animals and plants too, but never themselves, Lynx noticed. They ascended stairways and crossed great conical-roofed halls. Empty rooms and large chambers adjoined their path, while the sound of water and life began to echo from different directions, startling the mercenaries after a day or two of near-silence underground.

And then it happened. A faint awareness of light that had Lynx squinting in muzzy confusion before they turned two corners and the world seemed to fill with the blaze of returning life. Shafts of crisp white light seared through mote-filled air while the brilliant green glow of leaves seemed to envelop them all. The rich, sharp smell of damp earth filled Lynx's nose like the flavours of a feast, the bright pinpricks of red and yellow flowers as warm as a fire on his skin.

For a moment he could only stop and stare as true colour returned to his world, rocking back on his heels as the light and scent filled his being. It was hard to look at but impossible to turn away as the dragging weight of darkness lessened with every breath and he felt he could at last stand straight again.

A punch to the shoulder drove him back to his senses, the beatific sense of wonder evaporating like morning mist as Teshen's face appeared right up against his.

'Stop fucking gawping and get your gun out.'

Lynx blinked in confusion even as his body obeyed and pulled his mage-gun from his back. He looked around and saw the others do the same as the Wisps held back, keeping to the shadows.

They don't like the sun, he reminded himself. *This part we'll have to scout ourselves.*

He thumbed open the breech to check it was loaded then snapped it shut again. Ashis and Reft moved right towards an open doorway, Teshen and Kas ahead to the arc of pillars that had once denoted the edge of the chamber but was now swamped by foliage. Toil headed left so he followed her with Varain, leaving Anatin to watch over Sitain.

A relatively low curved roof swept down to the pillars. Where chunks of rock had tumbled from a fissure lay a snaking mass of ivy trails. Toil picked her way past with professional caution, checking the open tear in the rock before moving on to the far end, obscured by sprays of yellowed leaves.

Eventually they found themselves at the end and headed on through a deep archway into a similar open arcade. This one was larger in every way with a small tower of stone in the centre, entirely choked by foliage. There were tunnels and large double- and triple-storey chambers off this, all apparently empty and bearing no sign of monstrous inhabitants, so they returned to where they had left Anatin and Sitain. The others had found similar; Teshen and Kas had seen nothing larger than a rabbit, while Ashis and Reft had found a network of chambers all dimly lit by long diagonal shafts cut through at intervals.

It seemed to be the best place for them to rest in safety so, with a pang of longing for the bright autumn sunshine, Lynx followed the others through a crescent corridor and into a broad room with a long pedestal and doorways leading off in three directions.

'Oh ye gods and evil biting fishes!' gasped Toil, trailing in last after thanking their Wisp guides. 'No one move.'

The mercenaries froze.

'What is it?' Anatin hissed, gently sliding his second pistol from its sheath.

'Tomb,' Toil said, by way of explanation. 'Give me a moment. Did you go all the way in?'

'Yes, the other rooms too.'

'You step into the light?' she said, pointing at the slanted column of sunlight that illuminated the centre of the tomb, directly in front of the empty pedestal.

'No.'

'Right then.'

She pulled a length of cloth from around her waist and balled it up before tossing it through the drifting shaft of sunlit motes. There was a bright flash as soon as it touched the light and a wash of flame swept down from the ceiling to catch the trailing end of cloth and set it alight. It fell to the floor, burning, while the mercenaries reeled back from the sudden, brief heat. Toil just nodded grimly to herself and reached out with her gun, reversed so the wooden stock touched the sunlight.

Nothing happened. She gave a satisfied grunt and withdrew the gun. 'A sunstore trap,' she commented to the others. 'Should be safe for at least half a day now.'

She edged forward towards the centre of the room and stood just to one side of the light, looking up and all around as though searching for something. Toil paused when she faced a jutting door frame but kept looking until she'd scanned the rest of the room before she raised her mage-gun at it.

'Ice anything that moves,' she said softly before taking another step. Two more paces took her just shy of the pedestal where she hesitated and turned back to the mercenaries. 'Reft, toss me an axe.'

The big man did as she asked and Toil caught the weapon, hefted it to check the weight then hurled it at the wall on the far side of the door frame. Nothing happened though she immediately had her gun up and ready to shoot. After a long moment she breathed out and visibly relaxed.

'Looks like we're okay.'

The mercenaries collectively gasped.

'What the fuck was that about?' Anatin demanded.

'This is a burial chamber; they're dotted all over Duegar ruins. I don't know why. Folk reckon they were dying out so towards the end they had all this space going begging. The oldest tombs are in the deep dark where you don't want to go, but since these are closer to the surface they got some nasty protections against folk like me.'

'Like curses?'

Toil snorted. 'Sure, I almost shit myself over a five-thousand-year-old scribble, not the bloody sun's rays stored and used to burn your face off.'

Anatin let the scorn slide, aware he'd sounded stupid. 'What else are we looking for, I mean?'

'All sorts.' She pointed to the jutting door frame. 'That's not a doorway there, more like a cupboard you really don't want to open. Things that look like ghosts and turn your blood to ice, crystals that'll blind you – I once saw a statue rip pieces off a man, just plucking away until someone hit it with an earther and almost buried us all. Don't walk into a light shaft unless it's been triggered recently, never stand on a slab of stone with a defined edge or it'll tilt under you.' She paused and laughed. 'And since you're mercs I should probably add – don't put your fingers *or anything else* in any holes you see, okay?'

'But no more here?'

'Someone's been here already, long ago most likely.' She shook her head and forced a smile. 'Should've guessed that really, this close to the open air there's little chance of a tomb that hasn't been raided. But a cautious explorer is one who's still got their head attached.'

'This has been raided?'

Toil pointed to the oval-shaped hole above their heads from which the fire had come and light still shone. 'Should be a sort of glass up there, sealing it tight – you can sell that to any princip in the world to use as a window strong enough to resist an icer. They've chipped the stone out around it.' She moved towards the pedestal and nodded. 'This has been opened too, seal's broken.'

'They put the stone back?'

'Nah, broke the clasps and levered it up, it'll hinge somewhere I guess. You let go of it and it'll slowly slide back into place.'

'So this is safe?' Ashis asked, looking around the chamber, wide-eyed. 'We ain't gonna get 'et?'

'Not by the tomb, anyway,' Toil said. 'Maspids I ain't promising about, but we'll rig up a grenade at the entrance in case anything comes our way. I'll check out the rest of the tomb while you do that.' She beamed suddenly. 'After that, a good long sleep!'

Teshen grunted. 'Sounds good to me. Kas, let's take a better look at the rift before we rig anything over the entrance.'

He nodded back the way they'd come and Kas followed him out, unshipping her bow as she went. Lynx watched them go as Toil headed off through one of the open doorways. He looked at Anatin who shrugged and slipped his pack off his shoulders.

'Toil's the expert,' Anatin commented, 'she can clear the damn rooms. I want a smoke.'

Lynx hesitated then settled down too, content to sit with a loaded mage-gun on his lap pointing towards the other doorway. The light filtering down through the rock was meagre, but after days in darkness he was happy to bathe in its welcome glow once he'd tested the safety for himself. Lynx sat in the centre of the room as Sitain got up and stretched her aching limbs, walking the perimeter while Reft and Ashis slumped with Lynx. Anatin struck a sulphur match and lit three tightly rolled cigarettes, passing one to Lynx and the other to Ashis.

Before long Toil returned, confirming the rooms off to the side were empty and safe. Lynx felt his eyes sagging before she'd even crossed to clear the other set, but as soon as she was gone from sight he made his gun safe and stretched out on the dry dusty floor. With his head propped up by his pack so he was looking straight at the shaft of light without actually being in the line of fire, he closed his eyes and felt the warm embrace of sleep settle over him.

*

Lynx dreamed of Govenor Lorfen again, as he knew he would. The time underground had scraped at the scabs of his memory, but Lorfen embodied the bandages Lynx had laid over parts of his soul that would never fully heal. He knew the prison had broken him, however much he pretended and lived his life as though it hadn't. The face he presented to the world was not just to protect himself from it, it was to contain the damage done. He had tried to return to a normal life, but had found he could not settle anywhere.

Employment as a scribe or a rich man's bodyguard, Lynx had tried both and more besides, and failed every time. Before long the walls started to look like a prison cell, those he saw each day became fellow inmates and at To Lort you trusted no man. The trusting died, only those who struck first survived and as much as he tried to be calm and joke his way through life, Lynx knew he would one day strike first.

Drunkenness was usually his path out. Picking fights with locals, bitter unpleasantness to the widows who'd thought him a gentle man, it didn't matter really. He couldn't contain the bubble of anger for ever, one day it would force its way out and he'd leave or be driven out. You chose the man you wanted to be and tried to live up to that, but a person's nature could never be denied fully.

'*Sleep here for the night,*' Lorfen had said one day as the sun dropped below the horizon and he was tidying his desk for the evening. '*The office's yours if you want it.*'

'You want to lock me in here?'

Lorfen shook his head. 'The door will only be locked if you lock yourself in and the windows aren't barred.'

'Why?'

'You don't return an animal to the wild in one day.'

'Calling me an animal?' Lynx said, hands tightening.

'We all are,' Lorfen replied calmly. 'We're all slaves to our nature, however much humans can strive to be more than that. You've made good progress these last few weeks.' He gestured to the papers on the table where Lynx had been working. 'I couldn't have trusted the man I first met to do scribing work, you were too far gone.'

'What, then?'

'On my desk there are your release papers, signed and sealed. A man could easily rob me and escape out of the window should he want.'

'I don't understand. Is this a test?'

'No. If you want to go, go. If you stay another two weeks, I'll give you clothes and a horse, a sword too.'

'Why not now?'

'Because I want to be sure you'll not be killed or hanged a few miles down the road. Best you get used to sleeping out of a cell before you head into the wilds by yourself.' Lorfen nodded towards the window, currently shuttered. 'Thought you might want to watch the dawn tomorrow, nothing like the darkness for making a man appreciate the sun's rise. If you're gone in the morning, it's with my good wishes – and there's nothing worth stealing in here that I wasn't going to give you anyway.'

Lorfen gave him a long, studied look while Lynx tried to think of something to say. Eventually it was clear the prisoner had no words so the governor simply shrugged and pulled a plain silver ring from his finger, pointedly setting it on the desktop.

'In the morning, I'll tell you what the ring means. Sleep well.'

He left, taking care to put the key in the inside of the lock before he went. Lynx stared at the closed door a long while after Lorfen had left before finally getting up to lock himself in. That done he sank down in the battered armchair that stood to one side of the desk, gnawing on one knuckle and staring for an hour or more at the ring in the lamplight. He slept badly, eventually making a nest of clothing for himself in the corner of the room. When he realised the first glow of dawn was creeping past the shutters Lynx wrapped Lorfen's cloak around his shoulders and dragged the chair in front of the window.

When it came, dawn was magnificent. The sun burst through the clouds lingering at the horizon, golden fire erupting up through the sky as the Skyriver's cold hue turned orange and pink. It wasn't just a new day to Lynx but a whole new world. Haloed in the soft yellow light of winter it seemed to suffuse his whole being, filling his body with a warmth he'd forgotten long ago.

Chapter 23

'Wake up, sunshine.'

The whispered words filtered slowly into Lynx's mind, at first coming in Lorfen's accent before they were repeated in a honey-rich woman's voice. Lynx wrenched around as panic flooded his body, hands flailing for a weapon only for his wrist to be grabbed in a strong grip. He hauled himself up, his free hand clawed and grabbing at his assailant's throat with such ferocity he slammed her backwards before his eyes could even focus.

Something jerked Lynx bodily back. He released the throat and tried to turn, but before he could a hasty punch rocked his head. Lynx blinked and realised it was Toil standing in front of him. He opened his mouth to speak just as Reft's massive arm slipped around his chest and hauled him up in the air, squeezing the air from his lungs, but Toil saw the change in his face.

'Reft, wait!'

The pressure on his chest lessened and Lynx wheezed. 'What's going on?'

'Oh yeah,' Kas said in a lazy drawl from behind Toil. 'I forgot to mention, Lynx is kinda twitchy in his sleep. You might want to be careful how you wake him.'

Despite everything, a wicked grin flashed across Toil's face. 'Hey, thanks for the warning. I'll watch out for that.'

Toil released her grip on his wrist and cocked her head at Lynx while Reft withdrew his arm. She pursed her lips and blew him a mocking kiss. 'Looks like you needed a proper wake-up anyway. It's time to go,' she said as she turned away.

Lynx looked around and realised the others were already pulling their packs on their backs. 'Gods,' he muttered as he scrubbed his hands over his face and fetched his kit, 'how long did I sleep?'

'Four hours,' Sitain said, offering him a weak smile. The young woman was looking far from hale, but there was some colour in her cheeks now and she was standing steady. 'Sun's just gone down.'

'You're good?'

She nodded and raised her borrowed pistol. 'Good enough.'

'Looks like the Charnelers got here before us,' Teshen announced as Lynx readied himself. 'There's a stretch more'n a hundred yards long that's been burned, recently enough that a few trees are still going. We didn't see anyone but couldn't poke our heads out far either and there's a couple of hundred vantage points round here. Might be they passed through, might be they're waiting. Rest of the ground's got decent cover, enough to get us across and cloud's coming over.'

'We go as one?'

'Pairs. There's wildlife all over the place, any sharpshooters won't want to reveal their positions shooting at the first thing that moves. We take it slow and make as little noise as we can.'

'And remember,' Toil broke in, 'the bad things mostly come out at night. First person to shoot might attract the worst attention. Leave the travois too, it'll make too much noise and we can't use it beyond the rift anyway. Anyone who falls behind gets left behind, that's the rule for relic hunters. Anyone doesn't like it can stay and die with the injured.'

'That's reassuring,' Sitain muttered.

'I never said this'd be fun, so watch your step and try not to get shot. I'll probably feel a little bit bad as I go on without you.'

They crept out as slowly as they could, Teshen dismantling the tripwire that had been laid across the doorway and pocketing the grenade once he'd deactivated it. Outside, the moonlight cast stark shadows, the jagged tangle of thick cover both worrying and reassuring Lynx. He knew how easy it would be to miss a Charneler or maspid ambush – hells, another of those damn centipedes could be lurking and he'd never see it – but at the same time, any watching Charnelers would be struggling to pick out details in the chaotic mass of shadows.

'Lantern,' Toil whispered back to Sitain.

The young woman looked alarmed for a moment then remembered she was carrying the small Duegar lamp the Wisps had given her. One brief twist and so far as Lynx could tell nothing happened, but Sitain looked satisfied with the result. He reminded himself the mage's eyes were far more sensitive to the strange light and concentrated on the matter in hand instead.

Moving to the edge of the arcade, the mercenaries peered out at the steep sloping walls of the rift. The long mournful calls of mountain owls drifted along the valley floor on a breeze that carried the bitter scent of ashes. Thin trails of smoke spiralled up from the scoured section, picked out by the light of the Skyriver. The mercenaries spent a long while standing at the edge there, letting their eyes acclimatise to the contrast of light and dark and watching for any movement or noise that might betray an ambush.

'Anything?' breathed Anatin to his scouts, who crouched just ahead of the rest.

'No,' they said in turn without moving. Both Teshen and Kas remained where they were a minute or so longer and clearly Anatin knew not to disturb them further. They would be satisfied when they were satisfied.

Lynx contented himself with looking at the path they would have to walk, leaving the sharper eyes to look up. They were no more than twenty yards from the edge of the burned stretch. Presumably because if they had to sprint it would be good to have more open ground near at hand. The stink of burned vegetation overlaid everything else there while the jutting bones of charred branches cast an ominous feeling over the ash carpet. From somewhere he thought he could detect the scent of night jasmine when the air stilled and the smell of ash receded, but it was too faint for Lynx to know if it was true or just wishful thinking. Or a rogue memory of the first time he'd seen Toil.

'You?' Teshen whispered at last.

'No,' Kas replied. 'Just those odd scuffs that could've been anything.'

'Agreed.' He straightened and turned to face the rest, hidden beneath the crooked branch of some sort of stunted pine. 'Kas and me first, follow where we go. Then Anatin and Toil, then Lynx and Ashis. Varain next with Reft and Sitain last since you're likely to make the most noise. If anyone starts shooting we'll do what we can to cover you – your choice on how fast you come.'

'But we know they've got grenades,' Toil added darkly. 'So if they start shooting, fucking run for it.'

That left a cold sensation on Lynx's neck, but there was nothing for him to do beyond watch Teshen and Kas creep forward through a meandering path of shadows. Trees and bushes both served as cover, and for one whole stretch they went on their hands and knees to keep inside the thick black shadow cast by an amorphous clump of bramble. Lynx found his hands tightening around his gun stock as he thought he saw a movement half a dozen levels above them, but before he could be sure of anything it was gone. Part of him wanted to raise his gun and fire, to send an icer into the black overhang, but not only would that announce their presence it would trace a line back directly to where he stood.

'They're there,' Anatin breathed, shifting position.

'Keep hold o' yourself a minute more,' Toil warned. 'Long and slow is how we like it, boys.'

She slipped her gun strap over her head and settled it behind her to be sure it wasn't going to snag on anything. At last she deemed it time to move and crept forward, just as quiet as Teshan and Kas, while Anatin moved slowly and steadily behind her. The ageing mercenary wasn't as stealthy as Toil, but was happy to let her get ahead and pick his path forward as silently as he could.

At last he made it across and again the next pair waited for their turn. Ashis's hand was twitching and Lynx reached out to take hold of it and remind the woman to keep still. He received a furious look in response, but she was enough of a soldier to recognise she had the jitters and try to control it.

After a longer pause she set out, walking hunched over to pass under the first few branches. Lynx allowed a fair gap before following, under the branches then across the madcap black lines cast by a spray of shoots growing from the base of a fallen tree. He avoided looking up, knowing his pale skin would catch the light, but saw Ashis take a few anxious glances. He hissed as softly as he could to warn her, but the woman didn't seem to notice.

Ashis kept going at a steady pace and Lynx was struck with a sense of foreboding as he followed. There was a mounting tension in her body that was making her heavy-footed – he had no choice but to follow her but he felt his heart quicken with every step.

It happened almost dead centre, as far from cover as it was possible to be. Ashis glanced up again as she moved out from under a tree and into the shadow of a high mound of grass. Her foot snagged a root as she went and the jolt twisted her round sideways.

There was a moment where everything paused. Ashis suddenly was in the full glare of the moon's light, her face turned up towards the sloped canyon wall, mouth open in a cut-off cry. Then her balance went and she toppled backwards, arms wheeling as she hit the ground with a clatter.

Lynx's hand went to his gun, but then he stopped. Returning fire from out in the open was a stupid waste of time. There was a long moment of quiet and for a heartbeat he thought they'd got away with it – that their caution had been unwarranted. Then the gunshots came.

The whipcrack of icers rang out from left and right. Lynx instinctively ducked down as the white trails lanced down from the slopes of the rift. The clutter of shadows ahead of him was slashed through by the icers' chill breath, four, then six then eight. Puffs of dirt erupted on all sides of Ashis as she threw herself over to try and scramble to her feet. As the first volley finished Lynx broke into a run, barrelling his way towards her and not waiting for Ashis to get upright.

She was on her hands and knees when he reached her. Lynx grabbed Ashis by the scruff of the neck and kept running. She yelped in surprise but kicked down at the ground as hard as she could to keep upright while Lynx dragged her along. Up ahead one of the mercenaries poked a gun barrel out of the shadows and fired upwards. A corkscrewing blade of light streaked down towards them as Lynx ducked his head and kept pounding onwards. The sparker was followed by two icers as more shots crashed down around them, then Lynx saw the blessed sight of Anatin lean out and level a mage-pistol.

Lynx closed his eyes just in time, but the searing light of the light-bolt cut a streak across his eyelids all the same. He stumbled forward, blinking at the phantoms of light and shade lurching before his eyes and barrelling on towards the sound of his comrades' guns. All around them the deadly whisper of icers flew, heralded by distant crashes. A smear of orange washed high across his vision and Lynx ducked instinctively. Panic filled his mind but the searing heat of fire didn't strike him and he realised the burner's power had faded before it could burst.

The range of the icers was another matter. Just as his eyes started to clear Ashis howled in pain and crashed to the ground. Lynx tightened his grip and drove on, hauling her bodily across the ground, a roar of determination welling up from his gut. Ten yards from safety, however, the injured woman was snagged on something and Lynx jerked to a sudden halt. His shout turned to fury as he heaved with all his strength to pull her free – just as Ashis slipped a knife and slashed at the bandolier that had hooked on a branch.

The two mercenaries flew forward and fell in an untidy heap. The ground where they'd been standing burst under the impact of three icers and showered them with dirt. Lynx found himself half-pinned by Ashis, who was gasping in pain. He realised she'd been shot in the foot, a tell-tale dusting of frost around the puncture wound that now started to leak blood.

Before he could fight his way upright and make a decision about leaving her, a great pale shape swooped into view, surrounded by shadow. For a moment he felt a surge of alarm, thinking it a Wisp hunter descending for the kill, then one of Reft's huge arms scooped Ashis up and barrelled on. Close behind him was Sitain keening in fear and Varain reaching for Lynx to help him up. A cloud of dark seemed to surround the young woman, the light of the Skyriver and moon dimming as Sitain slowed alongside Varain.

Lynx felt an immediate heaviness in his limbs and realised the danger. He shoved Sitain backwards and scrambled clear of her, trusting that shroud of night magic to make it harder for the Charnelers to get a clear bead on any of them. It took a long few seconds for Lynx to regain his balance, but then Varain was waving Sitain forward and together they raced for the cover of the far side. As they staggered into the darkness beyond, an ear-splitting boom rang out behind them and Lynx turned to see a writhing ball of light burst over the rift floor.

The mercenaries all scrambled back as spitting sparks raced in all directions, savagely lashing branches and casting a jagged light over everything. The spark-grenade's claws seemed to surge towards them, hissing and scraping all around the stone pillars they'd run between but falling short of catching the mercenaries themselves. The searing light convulsed in the way sparkers always did, seemingly fighting with itself for a while longer before it tore itself apart and the darkness rushed back in.

Panting, Lynx squinted through at the rift beyond. The light of Anatin's light-bolt still shone down from wherever it had struck up the rift wall, but he knew it wouldn't last long and not all of the Charnelers had lost their night vision.

'Up,' Anatin croaked, 'all of you, on your feet.'

'Ashis is hurt,' Kas said.

The Prince of Sun lurched forward and grabbed Ashis by her jacket, pulling her upright. 'You'll walk or you'll die,' Anatin growled, slipping an arm around her waist.

'I'll bloody well walk out of here,' Ashis panted. She gripped Anatin's shoulder with one hand and pulled her mage-gun free with the other to use as a walking stick. 'What're you all waiting for then?'

Toil activated her lantern again then looked around at the near-black hallway ahead of them. There were doorways leading off in several directions as far as Lynx could see, the vaulted roof highest over an overgrown statue or fountain in the centre. From somewhere he could hear a low babble of sound, a colony of bats he guessed. It wasn't the brief, specific sound of the maspids but a formless hubbub he'd heard before in their roosting sites. As though to confirm the thought, the sharp smell of guano drifted on the air towards them.

'Pick a door, any door,' Toil muttered, gun in hand as she looked from one to the next.

All three were the same size, about twelve feet high and almost as wide. Toil moved closer, her lantern swinging from her waist and, once she was just a few yards from the first, Lynx seemed to be able to see a faint outline of the room beyond.

'That one,' Sitain said, pointing a shaking hand towards the left-hand doorway.

'You're sure?'

'The rest are tunnels.'

Lynx raised an eyebrow then remembered how her eyesight was far better. 'Rig a tripwire here?' he asked instead.

Kas looked down at the doorway. 'Nothing obvious to hook it to,' she said. 'Let's not waste the time.'

Beyond the doorway was a tall tunnel with empty alcoves set at regular points along it and a pair of tiny side chambers exactly halfway down. They neared the far end and a sense of space and cool air seemed to loom ahead of them. The reek of droppings was a slap in the face now, the sharp-sour smell as harsh as vomit at the back of his throat. The crazed chatter wasn't so intrusive, but it made him worry for what it might mask.

'Shattered gods!' Ashis hissed, retching slightly. 'Filthy fucking flying rats.'

Varain hawked and spat. 'Aye, like Deern's here with us and brought his whole stinking family too.'

'Stow it,' Anatin said. 'Sitain, what do you see?'

'Huge chamber, lots of rubble,' Sitain whispered.

'There a way through?'

'I think. Watch your footing though, there's shit everywhere.'

Lynx experienced a sudden sense of foreboding. *Big chambers are crossroads here*, he thought to himself, *and we've just announced our presence.* Working by feel alone he slipped the icer from his gun and replaced it with a burner.

'Hear something?' Kas asked.

'Nope, not over all that, but . . .'

'Aye, me too.' She slid a handful of arrows from her quiver and nocked one.

Up ahead, Toil prowled warily in and Lynx felt the space open up around him as he followed. It was a massive chamber, a natural cavern perhaps from the irregular lines traced in the bare blue glow of rock, though the floor had been levelled out. He couldn't see much of the ceiling, it was too far off, but there was the whip of wings in the air and the sense of movement.

It's past dusk, Lynx realised, *most of the bats will be hunting. Gods, it must be deafening when they're all in here.*

A huge arched doorway opposite them was half-obscured by fallen rock, but there were several open exits left and right on top of a series of squared openings high above ground level. Almost obscured by the sound of their feet on the stone floor, Lynx heard some tiny noise away to the left. Before he could identify it some buried instinct was turning his gun that way. He was already pulling the trigger as he caught a faint flash of movement and orange flame exploded out across the room.

Angular limbs seemed to freeze in the burner's brief light, dark grey carapaces and eyeless heads. One was caught in the full force of the explosion and was hurled backwards, a whitened underbelly showing briefly as it pitched into the rock face behind, crumpled and broken. Up above the dark shapes of bats exploded into shrieks and clicks of alarm, corkscrewing trails of greenish fire winking up through the air from the piled guano.

Exposed and reeling in the light, the other maspids were peppered by shots. Lynx saw the nearest punched through, head and body, and fall immediately dead. Another two were winged and turned away, chittering frantically, while one more ducked low and surged forwards to attack. Pairs of legs drove it forward while its forelimbs hauled at the ground. A dark, blunt head jutted from its pony-sized body, interlocking sets of mandibles unfurling as it closed the ground and snatched with its forelimbs.

Toil leaped back from its darting attack, mage-gun held out in her left hand and a short-sword in her right. The maspid seized the gun, forelimbs hooking around each end and tearing it from her grasp. Its mandibles clacked down around the body of the weapon as Toil twisted and chopped into the side of the blade-like forelimb. The maspid flinched and tried to release the gun, but before it could disentangle itself Reft slashed at the other forelimb and almost chopped it in two. The creature wrenched itself around away from the steel bite, only to have Anatin shoot it point-blank with his second pistol.

The cold breath of ice brushed Lynx's cheek as the maspid's carapace crumpled under the impact and the rank smell of its insides followed a moment later. He was already tracking another target, sending an icer streaking past another maspid that had scrabbled halfway up the rock wall in search of cover. A moment later Kas sent an arrow into the creature's rear that seemed to catch a nerve and it held still, back legs shuddering, for a moment until Ashis hit it full on with a sparker. Bright lines crackled across the rock, snatching a second maspid in their jaws. They both fell, stone dead, and suddenly everything was still.

The light of the sparker faded and the last flames of the burner vanished, but even as he reloaded Lynx knew they were dead or gone.

'Gods,' Sitain gasped, 'where did they come from?'

'Reload,' Lynx barked at her.

With shaking hands Sitain did so, though it was a struggle for her to slide the new cartridge in and Lynx saw she didn't even stop to check what she was loading. It was an icer so he said nothing, but knew she'd not be loading by feel like the rest of them.

'You didn't see them?' Anatin asked.

'No! Lynx? How did you?'

'I didn't. Just seemed a good place for an ambush. Maybe I heard that damn clicking sound too.'

Toil exhaled heavily and clapped a hand on his shoulder. 'Good work, you probably saved us there. Calm yourself, Sitain – they're damn hard to spot at the best of times. Just fade into the rock when they're still.'

'But I—'

'You're alive,' Toil interrupted, 'so keep moving and stay that way.'

Before anyone could speak a distant booming rumbled up the tunnel behind them from the rift. Lynx turned and cocked his ear. It wasn't just a few remaining shots, there was a tiny tremble running through the stone as crash after crash echoed out. They all stood stock-still until the detonations petered out, trying to make sense of what they were hearing.

'Gods, that's grenades,' he said. 'Lots of 'em. Most o' the rift could be on fire after that.'

'More than you'd use to flush us out,' Teshen added. 'And too far away.'

'Reckon they got ambushed too?'

The cold-eyed man nodded. 'Hopefully they'll wipe each other out. Either way, let's get moving.'

'What about the pack that attacked us? Can we go on?'

'We got most of them,' Toil said. 'They're hunters, not mad killers. However many are left, at worst they'll just track us.'

'And pick us off if they get the chance?'

She gave him a wolfish grin. 'Not if I get them first.'

Chapter 24

Exalted Uvrel clattered into the huge hall she'd entered the city through, gun ready and a squad of dragoons on her heels. This time she didn't pause to marvel at the great constellation dome. Screams and explosions echoed across the empty stone hall. At the far edge where steps led up to the open sky she paused, bringing her gun up to sight for a target. Her troops charged up behind her a moment later and adopted a similar position, but there was nothing to see.

She pressed on, running lightly on the weaving grassy path until she had rounded the crumpled shell of a stone building, where she dropped to one knee. The others fanned out around her, but even the experienced dragoons faltered at what they saw. For a few seconds it was hard to make out, such was the chaos of the scene. Fires raged, flame coating the huge hollowed-out boulders that lined the road and casting a dirty smoke up into the darkened sky. Shapes moved in the jagged shadows; large angular bodies, while the great steps that led up to the enclosed pasture were washed in blood.

As they watched, a grey horror backed down the steps, a shrieking and kicking horse clasped firmly in its jaws. More of the monsters appeared, framed at the top of the steps, while the last cries of human voices were snuffed out. The maspids had their dead too – at least a dozen humped waves in a lake of fire, some still twitching. A knot of torn limbs and torsos lay at the base of the steps and a crater at the base of a fissured wall told its own tale.

'Grenades did their work,' said one of the soldiers behind her in a hoarse voice.

'Not enough,' whispered another.

Uvrel sensed heads turn her way as another two appeared at the top of the steps, feasting on the flesh of all they'd killed. That meant there were at least five left – most likely more, given the sounds emanating from further inside. What to do now she wasn't sure, there was likely no one left to save and most likely no horses either – certainly none by the time Uvrel could reach them.

It changes nothing, a voice whispered at the back of her mind. *The assassin is all that matters. The Hanese mercenary, the mage – neither matters in comparison.*

'Sir?' prompted the man beside her, a trusted sergeant.

Uvrel suppressed the urge to shoot the man and tried to take a breath despite the tightness in her chest.

'It changes nothing,' she said at last, willing herself to sound stronger than she felt. 'We came to find the assassin and avenge our brethren, now the walk home will just take a little longer.'

'You want . . .'

She turned to face him and the man's question went unfinished. 'We are the Knights-Charnel of the Long Dusk,' she said, speaking quietly, but the soldier's face made it clear her restrained rage was visible. 'Servants of the Gods and Custodians of Insar's Sacred Shards. These creatures of Banesh will not deter us from our sworn duty.'

'Yes, sir,' the man said, paling. 'What about the maspids?'

'Sir,' said one of the others – the young grenadier she'd kept beside her throughout the day.

'What?'

'There were two grenadiers up there,' she said, pulling from her belt a slim length of steel that looked like a broken club. 'Most likely on the stairs given there's no fire there.'

'And?'

'Dead man's pyre. If I drop a crackler on them, it'll set off any grenades they've got left.' The young woman's face betrayed no emotion despite the fact she was talking about her friends. 'We take as many as we can with us, that's our way. If we need help from our friends to do it, fine.'

Uvrel grunted in acknowledgement. 'Do it.'

The grenadier pulled a spark-grenade from her bag, priming it and fitting it into her thrower while the dragoons stepped back to give her room. With a calculating look and one step forward she hurled the crackler through the gloom of night.

'Come on,' Uvrel said, not bothering to watch it land. She turned and headed back to the rift, a great crack splitting the night behind her. More explosions followed, two huge roars that made the ground shudder underfoot as Uvrel broke into a run. She had seen a grenadier explode before; the eruption of fire and pain that resulted was a terror no professional soldier forgot. Uvrel bit down the bile that rose in her throat and ran as hard as she could to the steps leading to the gallery where one detachment of her dragoons waited.

'Move out!' Uvrel roared, shoving men out of her path, not wanting anyone to have time to think. 'Get across the bridge, all of you. Follow me!'

Every soldier had a single pack of belongings that they snatched up. Uvrel had prepared against this eventuality at least and they all carried food, ammunition and torches. The startled soldiers scrambled to obey. Within a minute the troop was making their way up a half-dozen short flights of steps which led to the enclosed stone bridge spanning the rift. Runners had been sent through the network of tunnels, stairways and galleries to the cavalry troop also positioned on this side and they soon merged into one stumbling, dark-stricken mass in the broad tunnel.

This high up the V-shaped rift, not too far from the top of the steeply sloped walls, the bridge was well over two hundred yards in length – long enough to feel constraining despite being ten yards wide. The darkness extended far ahead of them, punctuated by regular smears of ivy-strained moonlight, and even Uvrel felt her trepidation grow. When the pale faces among the sharpshooters appeared suddenly in the gloom, Uvrel felt a jolt of alarm and only just prevented the man beside her from firing on them.

They'd all glimpsed one unit of cavalry stationed on the far side be ambushed by maspids soon after their quarry had come into view. Uvrel had heard it more than anything else, until a cold-hearted dragoon higher up had fired a burner into the enclosed space where their comrades had been positioned. Their remaining icers had exploded and the burner's flames had washed through the gallery, scouring it of life. How many more maspids were stalking these halls, she couldn't tell, but Uvrel just had to hope their supply of torches could be rationed long enough to see them to the other side, even if they kept close to the surface.

If we can't see anything, we can't keep moving, Uvrel reminded herself as the sharpshooters snatched up their belongings and fell in. *And if we don't keep moving, they'll start to wonder how they're getting home.*

She gritted her teeth and upped the pace, pushing on to the far end as fast as she could. Sauren was positioned close to it with another unit of dragoons. She would push on to the grand avenue they'd identified earlier, a huge thoroughfare that looked like it ran straight across that whole section of the city. Sauren could gather the remaining troops and follow.

Uvrel would have to drop the pace but she knew she had to keep moving.

Give them time to think, to ask about the horses or where we're going, and someone will put an icer in the back of my head.

The realisation added a renewed clarity to Uvrel's usual sense of purpose. She would catch these mercenaries and secure retribution, information or both before she left this dead place of horrors. If they were forced into the bowels of the earth itself, burning the clothes from their backs as torches while maspids hounded their every step, Uvrel would do whatever it took.

Her god demanded nothing less.

*

The mercenaries left the cavern as quickly as they dared. Ignoring the corpses of the maspids, they made for the far side where Toil examined what remained of carvings on the wall. Choosing one of the exits, she led them into a low tunnel that set Lynx's teeth on edge before it opened out into a wider chamber.

A narrow channel cut across their path, most likely once a river since there was a stone bridge spanning it. After a cursory check, Toil crossed and went through a doorway outlined in the faint bluish light that, by now, was the only thing keeping the velvety dark at bay. After a moment she waved the rest forward, Ashis whimpering despite Sitain's efforts to dull the pain and flow of blood in her foot. The young mercenary struggled on as best she could, her unloaded gun a crutch while Reft all but carried her by her free arm.

They found themselves in a tall, open space dotted with individual stone formations – not dwellings, Lynx guessed, but something deliberately built all the same. The structures were low enough that most of the mercenaries could see over them and they made swift progress across, all of them watching for grey shapes and listening for pursuing footsteps. At the edges of sight they saw hunched creatures no larger than rabbits scrabble out of their path and disappear. The whisper of their feet soon vanished into the bowels of the ruin and as they moved further away from the jungle of the rift the signs of life vanished once more.

Beyond the strange formations they reached what seemed more like streets to Lynx. Toil confirmed as much. The hollowed-out spaces were smaller than most they'd come across, but contained house-sized stone blocks with open doorways, windows and walkways between many. The houses were all shells now. Anything not made of stone had long since rotted away or crumbled to dust.

They varied in size and number. Some chambers contained a dozen or more, but there was a familiarity to the regular, mundane shapes that both eased Lynx's anxiety at being underground and gave the place a dismal air. Lynx was struck by a sense that he was walking through the bones of some long-dead behemoth, the streets filled with a mausoleum hush.

They passed great stepped slopes that led both up and down, prompting Toil to explain that these residential parts could be on a dozen levels or more. She took them up one level after just a few minutes of walking, in case there were Charnelers pursuing them directly, but then they continued on for more than an hour without seeing anything else alive. Their path was mostly clear, occasional rock falls proving no great obstacle when most chambers had several exits and had been laid out in a relatively regular fashion.

By the time they stopped, Ashis was looking pale and weak. Kas removed her mangled boot to reveal a nasty wound that made Ashis moan with fear as much as pain. Lynx had seen all sorts of injuries over the years and knew Ashis wasn't going much further on that, but before the young woman could start to beg her comrades Anatin cut her off.

'We're not leaving you here,' he said flatly, 'even if we have to drag you by the hair.'

Lynx wasn't the only one to turn to Toil to see her reaction, but if the woman was angry she made no sign of it.

'I don't want to leave anyone behind,' she said simply. 'Just want to be clear you don't always get a choice down here.'

'Sure,' Anatin drawled, 'it's clear. I know us professional soldiers often need lessons in the hard realities of life.'

'She's your soldier, your charge.'

'And my choice, not yours,' Anatin warned. 'Just so we really are clear.'

Toil shook her head. 'No threats here. I'm walking that way,' she said, pointing. 'I ain't stopping for anyone who can't keep up, but I'm not cutting any throats either. What do you take me for, some sort of assassin?'

'Aye,' Anatin said, ignoring her attempt at humour. 'You're a killer; I've met agents like you before. Hells, I've been glad to stand beside one for years,' he added, clapping a comradely hand on Teshen's shoulder, 'so I know exactly what you're capable of. Sitain, time to earn a Jester's pay again, then, Kas, you bind it tight. Better the foot's never the same again than she falls behind out here.'

The pair set to work as everyone else settled down for another mouthful of water and hardtack. Lynx's stomach growled long and loud at the lack of a proper meal, but if anything the sound cheered the rest up in the face of dry, near tasteless food. By unspoken agreement they had stopped in the centre of a cavern where there was a broad crossroad offering a view of all four directions. Many of the others were tightly packed with free-standing stone shells in the centre, but they all realised the security of stone walls was a false one.

With the shocking power of their spark- and fire-bolts, they needed to see danger at a distance. For Lynx's part, he was doubly glad of that – their strange lanterns gave the darkness a meagre tint but it was enough for shape and size. Anything that reminded him the walls were a dozen yards away made the experience a little more bearable when the darkness was a palpable and oppressive thing.

After no more than ten minutes Toil pushed herself upright. 'All rested?' she asked, shouldering her gun.

'Already?' Kas groaned. 'What happened to resting?'

'We got outnumbered and a whole lot of grenades went off.' Toil extended a hand and the other woman reluctantly took it and allowed herself to be pulled upright. 'We want to be at the other rift before the Charnelers. We *really* want to get there first – as much as we want to get as far as we can from where those grenades went off.'

'Please don't tell me something nasty will've been attracted by the noise.'

'Okay, I won't.'

Kas hesitated. 'Shattered gods, you're joking right? More?'

'Let's move out,' Toil said, no trace of humour in her voice. 'Another few hours travel and I'll feel a lot calmer.'

'Another few hours? How big is this damned corpse of a city anyway?'

'Big – and you never make best time underground. Walk slow and walk soft. The hurrying man hurries straight to his death, so my first employer said.'

'And who was this wise old mentor?'

Toil's face darkened. 'Just some old drunk who fell screaming into the black on the first day. Probably couldn't call him a mentor, really. And the one who took over was a Knights-Charnel irregular who double-crossed us and left us for dead, so I don't feel much in the way of affection for him either.'

'Does that make us veterans then, given we've survived longer than most o' those who've gone underground with you?'

'It makes you lucky you've got me leading, that's all.'

The mercenaries set off and soon found themselves on a frustrating diversion lasting an hour or more. Lynx felt chilled at the thought of trying to do this without a guide, as Toil apparently had on her first expedition. A whole section of caverns were ruined and impassable so they had to skirt around it and rely even more heavily on Toil's compass to keep them in the right direction.

The Wisp warriors who'd guided them to the first rift had been very clear, according to Toil, of the direction they needed to keep to. Too far north would lead them directly under the spires and the greatest concentration of maspid dens, too far south and they would find that most paths just led deeper underground.

Exactly what had happened to the blocked caverns was anyone's guess; even Toil had been unsure about it. The scale of damage, the fallen sheets of rock and shattered edges of stone, suggested a medium-scale battle where earthers had been fired, but none of the telltale signs were visible and it could have just as easily been warring elementals or something entirely unknown.

An hour after they got back on track, Toil gave a soft hiss and raised a hand to call a halt. The mercenaries hunkered down immediately, guns raised and hearts hammering as they expected grey shadows to suddenly storm towards them. For a while they all kept perfectly still until Teshen edged closer to Toil and whispered to her.

'Think I see it too.'

'Good,' she grunted. 'Was worried it was wishful thinking.'

'What is it?'

'Light of some sort, up ahead.'

Lynx squinted the way she was pointing, as did the rest of them. 'Can't see a thing.'

'Me neither,' Sitain pointed out, 'and I can see better than all of you.'

'Not your sort of light, love,' Toil replied. 'This is real light, not shadow-cast.'

'The Charnelers got ahead of us?'

'With luck it's just another light-garden, but we're taking no risks.'

They crept forward as stealthily as possible and the barely perceptible glow slowly grew. It was nothing they could see by, really, but even Lynx soon could tell the difference as the darkness became less absolute, returning to a paucity of light rather than the utter and consuming black shroud of underground.

They heard the gunshot not long after first noticing the light – a distant, single echo coming from the same direction as the light. It was clear they weren't under attack themselves so the mercenaries continued forward and a quarter-hour later ended up crouched behind a ridge that overlooked a huge light-garden. From what Lynx had been able to glimpse there was a high roof studded with shining chunks of crystal, similar to the one they'd first encountered the Wisps in, but larger still.

More importantly, there were human sounds coming from somewhere not far beyond the ridge. With Reft and Ashis installed at a slight bottleneck to guard their rear, Toil took Kas and Teshen to scout the area briefly, but before long they returned and made it clear everyone should have their guns at the ready.

'What now?' Anatin whispered as the voices continued below.

'We wait.'

'Why?'

''Cos I saw a pair of maspids down that way,' Toil said as softly as she could. 'Those dumb bastards are in a whole world of trouble and we're going to sit it out.'

They poked their heads over the ridge to get a better view of below, an overhang of rock keeping the ridge in enough shadow that Toil deemed it safe. Almost a hundred yards away, voices carrying well thanks to their agitation, was a party of twelve Charnelers – all cavalry troopers by what Lynx could see. They'd managed to shoot some sort of creature, he couldn't tell what but something like a beaver by the size, and were in the process of skinning it while an argument continued over the building of a fire to cook it over.

The light-garden itself was a half-mile long, Lynx estimated, with a kidney-shaped lake visible in the furthest corner. Most of the rest was low foliage; waist-high clumps of reddish grass punctuating a meagre scrub that thickened and seemed to be more colourful the nearer it got to the water. The other principal large feature of the cavern was a huge, bifurcated stairway that rose up behind where the Charnelers were, as ornate as anything Lynx had seen up to now, while he could see five entrances to tunnels of varying sizes behind it.

As they watched, one of the Charnelers sat to relight one of the torches they'd discarded on the stairs, while several others started to wade through the undergrowth in search of fuel to burn.

'Oh, don't do that,' whispered Toil as two headed for a dip in the ground edged in creeper. 'Bye bye then, you're all dead.'

Lynx found himself holding his breath as the troopers started kicking their way through the undergrowth. They made some initial headway before grinding to a halt and cursing loudly as their boots got tangled. One bent down to rip away the creepers snagging his boot then cried out and snatched his hand back.

'What is it?' breathed Sitain.

'Tanglethorn,' Toil replied. 'Nasty stuff. When they fall the maspids will use the distraction. Won't pass up an opportunity like that.'

As she spoke, the man who'd cut himself on the thorny creeper began to thrash around, anger making his movements more pronounced, and in moments he tripped. Then he started to howl and writhe, but the spread of tanglethorn seemed to only contract and tighten around him. His shouts became screams and his friend tried to go to his aid only to trip himself. Then there were two of them vanished but shrieking as the thorns tore at their skin and half the remaining Charnelers ran to help them.

'Damn stuff just tightens around you,' Toil said, 'cuts everything it can and ties you up good. It'll end up a coffin of leaves if you keep fighting, closes around your chest and starts to bleed you as it puts a poison in your veins. They say you won't even notice as it starts to digest your skin, but I'd prefer a burner still.'

The shouts of panic were ringing out around the cavern now. Lynx was still watching the quickest would-be rescuer tug at the creeper trails when the first maspid came into view. It was a dark shape that moved with breathtaking speed, no less terrifying for being more visible now. Racing low over the ground, the maspid had a long grey body as thick as a pony's, but with a broad, fan-like tail behind.

The rapid clicks of maspid calls echoed around the cavern as it went, causing some of the soldiers to look in the other direction. It kept its wedge-shaped head low as it used its large forelegs to negotiate the uneven ground. The Charnelers didn't even notice its arrival until it exploded forward at the man lighting the torch, bowling him over with the force of impact. The man screamed as the maspid buried its mandibles into his neck, but two more were already leading the charge.

The officer managed to half-turn before one snagged his arm and wrestled him to the ground. The third maspid surged up under the gun of another trooper, cutting his shriek off as it bit into his face. Just as the remaining troopers scrambled for their guns another charged in from the other direction and bowled one soldier over as he swiped at another. One of their guns went off wildly, a white icer trail smashing into the rock ceiling, while another trooper pulled a pistol and shot the newest attacker in the side.

The wounded maspid reeled from the impact as the trooper drew his sabre and slashed wildly at it. His blows were glancing and in seconds one of the others abandoned its kill and snatched his left leg up in a lightning grab. The soldier howled and chopped at its flank as he was hauled around, the sabre biting deep and lodging in one of its legs. The maspid pulled him off his feet and buried its mandibles in his side, turning his shout into a scream before the first pounced and silenced him.

A gunshot echoed across the room. Lynx followed the icer's white path to where it punched clean through the body of the wounded maspid. Its legs collapsed underneath it, going still almost immediately while its forelimbs thrashed furiously at the corpse beneath it. The remaining pair turned towards the source of the shot, where a trooper was calmly backing off and sliding another shot into their gun.

'Poor bastard's only got icers,' Varain muttered from Lynx's right. 'He's not making it far.'

The soldier continued to back away as the other maspids went for him, his next shot bursting through the nearest's head and felling it. The other one charged into him and smashed him from his feet with one swipe, but then stopped dead. It darted sideways then retreated again as the soldier struggled back to his feet, one arm hanging limp and tanglethorn creepers already snagging his legs. The maspid tried to reach for him but the soldier flinched back out of reach and tumbled to the ground, disappearing amid the dark narrow leaves and only then bellowing in panic.

The remaining soldiers were unarmed and seemed frozen in fear. They turned and fled across the cavern and towards the mercenaries. The uninjured maspid darted after the soldiers with deceptive speed, three pairs of legs driving it forward with a lazy grace. Like a hunting hound it caught the first soldier and hooked her ankle with a practised snatch. It barely broke stride as she tumbled, screaming, and it half-clambered over her to continue its pursuit, plucking the other soldier from the air mid-stride and biting down into his neck to finish him.

Lynx nudged Toil's elbow. 'Now what?' he whispered.

In the cavern the cries had tailed off and the only sound was the maspid dragging the corpses of the two soldiers who'd fled back to the remains of its pack. Of those, the one shot twice had slowed to feeble twitches, its head drooping as its life ran out. Despite the sabre caught in its leg, the other injured maspid moved relatively well still and picked over the bodies to check they were all in fact dead before gathering one up to carry back to its nest.

'Couple more shots won't hurt,' Toil muttered, loading an icer into her gun.

Lynx and Teshen did the same, while Anatin slipped a burner into each of his pistols in case they missed and were charged. The three with mage-guns lined up their shots together, Lynx picking out the further of the two maspids and settling it in his sights.

'Ready on the rear one,' he said softly.

'Yes,' added Teshen a moment later.

'Good,' Toil said and pulled the trigger. The ear-splitting roar of three guns firing together hammered at Lynx's ears as he watched the icer trails cut a path through the air. Lynx's shot took the injured maspid just above the tail while Teshen and Toil both hit the other in the back. The creatures thrashed and beat at the ground, one faltering and collapsing a few moments later while Lynx's abandoned its prize and began to drag itself round behind the great stair.

'It's getting away,' Sitain gasped as Lynx calmly slid the spent cartridge bolt from his gun and replaced it.

'No it ain't,' he said, not bothering to line up another shot. 'Not dragging its back legs like that.'

'You're not going to finish it off?'

'It'll find some dark hole to die in,' Toil confirmed with a nod. 'No point wasting the ammunition.'

'What now?'

Anatin patted her on the shoulder and stood up. 'Now we honour the finest traditions of warfare.'

'Eh?'

'We go loot the bodies, lass. Say one thing about the Militant Orders controlling the continent's weaponry, it makes the bastards rich enough to pay well.'

'And they've standardised the size of cartridges,' Toil added, stepping over the rise so she could make her way down to the cavern floor, 'so once you kill 'em, you can use their own ammunition to kill their friends. Keeps it in the family and saves you money, so my daddy used to say.'

'No wonder you're so screwed up, then,' Sitain muttered. Before she could blink Toil had turned and grabbed her by the jacket, hauling her forward so their faces were almost touching.

'Keep a civil tongue in your head,' Toil said softly, 'there's a good girl now.'

Before Sitain could reply Toil released her and continued on down the uneven rocks, towards the corpses. Lynx watched her go for a moment then clapped a hand on Sitain's shoulder.

'Reckon you touched a nerve there,' he said. 'Best you keep as quiet as a temple mouse until your magic's stronger, eh?'

Sitain shrugged him off and made to follow Toil. 'I'm not the one scared of the bloody dark,' she said, scowling.

Lynx hauled her back and shook her hard enough to make her teeth rattle. The force would have pitched her down the slope of broken rocks if he'd not kept a hold of her arm, and left Sitain looking dazed as she tried to regain her balance.

'Enough from you, girl,' Lynx snapped. 'I ain't here to take your shit.'

Sitain fought to break his grip for a moment then realised how much stronger he was and gave up. Instead she pulled her pistol with her free hand and held it up to Lynx's face.

'Get your bloody hands off me,' she yelled.

Lynx looked down at the muzzle wavering beneath his nose. 'Put it away,' he said. 'You'll only get hurt.'

'Get fucked. You're not my da, you don't get to tell me what to do.'

He sighed. 'First off,' he said with as much patience as he could muster, 'I'm your superior in the company, so I can break your teeth for waving a gun in my face. Secondly—' He flickered his eyes slightly to the side, looking past her and Sitain instinctively turned that way.

Before she could realise Toil hadn't sneaked back up again Lynx had snatched the pistol out of her hand, two fingers wedged under the hammer in case she pulled the trigger. He clicked the hammer back to a safe position and tossed it behind him, trusting someone to catch it, then grabbed Sitain's arm again and shook her once more to make his point.

'Secondly,' he growled, fingers tightening on her biceps enough to make her squeak, 'I'm bigger and nastier than you – and so's the rest of us. You want to pick a fight, go for it. Just remember a veteran's someone who kills before they get killed. Don't come whining if they cut your throat without even thinking.'

With that he released her and stalked past, heading for the gruesome scene on the cavern floor.

'Kitty's got claws,' Toil whispered as he passed her, too quiet for anyone else to hear. 'I was wondering when I'd see those.'

She wore a small smile and despite everything the coquettish look Toil gave him made the breath catch in Lynx's throat. He kept his mouth shut, not trusting himself to speak any more, but still he felt his nostrils flare as he passed her, seeking the heady scent of her. Heart already pumping hard with anger, his blood seemed to jolt with renewed energy as he filled his lungs. If she noticed, she made no sign, but he felt her gaze on his back all the way to the first of the corpses.

Chapter 25

They stripped the bodies of valuables in silence, ignoring the Charnelers caught in the tanglethorns, and soon they were on their way. No more soldiers came down the great stairway to investigate the gunshots. Either their commander had assumed a maspid ambush and left them to their fate, or the squad had been sent down to try and flank the mercenaries as the rest went on ahead. Fearing that it might be the latter, the mercenaries didn't linger longer than a minute or so – just enough time to help themselves to food, cartridges, a few meagre coin purses and a couple of spare mage-guns.

Lynx ignored the rest of the group as he went about his task. Once he'd taken the icers from the first dead soldier, Anatin had told him to ascend the stair a little way and keep a watch. Lynx obeyed without a word, glad for the space it afforded him. While it was darker on the stair, slightly away from the diffuse glow of the light-garden, there was enough illumination. As he squinted up the stair, he thought he could detect a faint shine from far above. Whether it was the Skyriver, moon, or another light-garden Lynx couldn't tell, but there was no sound or movement the whole while so he found a precious few moments of peace. By the time they moved on his blood had cooled somewhat and as they entered the darkness of the tunnels beyond, Lynx was focused on the task at hand again.

They passed through a dozen more chambers of stone houses before the landscape of the ruin changed again. Larger tunnels appeared before them, ones that branched off towards grand facades built into the rock face. Ornate colonnades screened the shells of palaces or temples – strangely no statues, Lynx realised, nothing that might show the face of the long-dead Duegar race.

'Hey, Toil, you know what they looked like?' he called.

She glanced back then saw him nod towards the empty shells and shook her head. 'Nope. I've seen a few guesses – some educated, others not so much. Most reckon it was a religious thing, what statues they did carve were animals or plants. Enough of those survived that the lack of Duegar people is obvious. All we know is they weren't Wisps and the Wisps don't seem to know any more than us, but they give less of a damn about gods and the like.'

'What's wrong with a person statue?' Ashis asked.

'Ah well, there you've got me, but then I ain't some shit-brained priest with too much time on my hands and a towering sense of superiority.' Toil shrugged. 'Well, maybe that last bit, but I can prove most of it. If anyone knows what they looked like, it'd be the Militant Orders, but they're not the sort to encourage questions. Still a bit touchy on the subject of whether the gods were once Duegar.'

'They have statues, though, of the gods I mean.'

'Aye, but they all look different, don't they, and mostly are just human with some small addition. Each one's some symbolic aspect of the god, not the god's face itself. That's forbidden, folk like us aren't meant to see that.'

'How does that make sense?'

Toil laughed. 'A priest won't help you make sense of the world, only where they want you to fit into it. If anyone knows what the gods or Duegar look like it'd be the Charnelers. It's said they possess more god-fragments than any other Order – so either they don't want to tell us because it's hard to pray to something shit-ugly or they're too busy using the pieces to build an arsenal.'

'Enough o' that talk,' Anatin growled. 'I may not be the most gods-fearing o' men, but you're tiptoeing around blasphemy there, girl, an' we could use a little divine favour right now.'

If Toil had a response to that, she bit it back and they continued in silence. The ornate stonework continued, becoming more fluid and intricate in parts while even the high roofs of the caverns were smoothed over and often bore decoration. Lynx tried to imagine the number of stone mages that must have been required for all this work. Even if the construction had taken place over hundreds of years, the skill had to have been far more prevalent among the Duegar race than magery was in humans.

A while later they came to a huge chamber of worked stone, as big as any they'd come across underground thus far except for the natural caverns. Toil stopped them well short and the mercenaries hunkered down in the deep shadows as the distant, distinctive sound of metal on stone rang out ahead. Past Toil's shoulder, Lynx could see a huge, dimly lit space with what looked like tiers of steps on the far side and a double bank of pillars behind them, some larger than redwoods with a smaller set further up the stepped side of the huge hall. The source of light was hard to work out, a pale flicker weaker than the light-gardens – and those were gloomy by any normal standard.

'I think we're there,' Toil whispered to the rest. 'I'm going to have a look around.'

'You want us to wait here?' Anatin hissed. 'Think we're stupid?'

Her face tightened. 'Don't worry, old man. If I screw you over, you won't have time to see it coming.'

'That supposed to reassure me?'

'Fine, Teshen or Kas can come with me. Happy now?'

'Ecstatic. Teshen, go on. You'll be hardest for her to get a jump on without making a lot of noise.'

Toil nodded towards the hall. 'If it's all of them, there might be patrols too. If you're not here when we get back, we'll backtrack the way we've just come to find you, okay? Sitain, swap me your lamp, it's smaller than this.'

The woman shrugged off her pack too and slung her gun across her back, hanging Sitain's lamp from her belt. The pair set off without another word, walking almost silently until they were in the lee of a pillar and could check their surroundings a little more carefully. After a long, slow inspection Toil set off again and disappeared from view, whereupon they were forced to just watch the sliver of empty hall they could see and listen out for danger.

'Reckon she'll ditch us?' Sitain asked.

Lynx glanced her way but couldn't make out her expression. 'Doubt it'll be her first choice,' he hazarded.

'Lovely.'

'Don't worry, you've got her lantern. She won't want to leave that behind – even if we're expendable.'

They fell to silence again, knowing even whispering would carry in the echoing tunnels. The wait seemed interminable to Lynx as the minutes ground past, the shadows deepened around him, slowly tightening their elusive threads around his chest. He tried to put his mind elsewhere, to recall the places he'd seen and others he'd read about, but his thoughts drifted inexorably back to To Lort prison and the mines it serviced. The days of back-breaking labour in almost total darkness, the violence and abuse meted out by prisoners and guards alike, the sleepless nights because of hunger and fear.

It seemed more like a dream now; a nightmare he'd woken from but could never quite shake off and knew would be waiting when he slept again. The man he'd been then was both hardly recognisable and all too familiar. An ache began to build in his head, a sense of pressure. It was something he recognised well enough, the topography of fractures in his mind, as though a light could be shone through the fissures.

It had been a long time after Governor Lorfen had released him that Lynx had finally been able to recognise he'd been broken by the prison – that some fractures never healed. He could bandage and glue parts back together, create a whole again, but that wasn't the same as intact and perfect. There was no going back to that time, not after the things he'd seen during the war and after it, there was only struggling on with life.

He'd known men to lose limbs in battle. Some railed against the loss their whole life, others learned to live without the missing part of them, the bit that no longer existed. Lynx had learned from their example how to salvage what remained, to accept that some things he'd never be able to do again and set aside what was lost. It was why he wandered the Riven Kingdom so determinedly, never staying for long in any one place. So long as he knew and embraced his impulses and fears, he could control them.

Down here in the dark, those fears were starting to claw at the shell of his mind. The scratching he'd been able to ignore, but he knew it wouldn't be much longer before the demons started tumbling out.

After far too long, Toil and Teshen returned. Lynx felt a jolt in his gut as they suddenly appeared round the corner, so lost to his thoughts he had to blink several times before he could focus on their shadowed faces.

'It's the rift,' Toil announced quietly. 'But they got here first.'

'All of them?' Anatin asked.

'Looks like it, I never got a proper count. From the guard positions though, I reckon so.'

'So they outnumber us and are dug in? Any good news? Can we bypass them?'

'I don't think so. There's two bridges here, about two hundred yards apart and one a level lower. The Wisps said there are more below that but we'd be dead before we crossed. As for others, we'd need to work our way a mile in either direction.'

'We can't take either one; they could just drop grenades on us.'

'And fighting our way across won't be so easy anyway.'

'So we strike out for one of the others?'

'Ah, well, it never just rains, eh?' Toil said, chewing on a fingernail.

'What?'

'On the far side we've not many options to leave the city. We take a more southern bridge and we'd have to head back this way or take some real sketchy tunnels. Ones the Wisps reckon will fall on us if they're not already blocked. We go further north and we've got a long time underground, nearer the maspid dens.'

'How did the bloody Duegar live here with so few bridges?'

'Most likely they had wooden ones too, or cable cars to get across. Remember – all that's left of the city is what was formed seamlessly out of rock. Nothing else lasts for thousands of years.'

'So – what then?'

Lynx just made out Toil baring her teeth in a grin. 'Don't worry, I've got a plan.'

*

They split into two groups, Teshen leading Anatin, Sitain, Varain and Ashis left out of the tunnel to scout and ambush any patrols while Toil, Kas, Lynx, and Reft went right. The grand hall beyond was silent and empty but still they moved cautiously. Toil hadn't really needed to remind anyone that any sound could carry to where the Charnelers were stationed, but she'd taken the time anyway. They moved slowly enough that Lynx had a good look at what they were sneaking through. It resembled a stepped assembly hall; the double bank of pillars continued all the way around and half-hid five more tunnels just like the one they'd left, plus an open stretch in the centre through which he could just about see flickering lights.

The steps of the hall were tiers of man-high blocks, six in all, with the ridged slopes running down at regular points for access. Up above there was a strange gantry suspended from the ceiling. It was too high for Lynx to work out what exactly it was, but from the platform hung trailing fronds of some sort of plant, the flowers of which seemed to give off a pale cold light. A peppery blossom scent hung on the air, barely noticeable but a welcome variation on the damp stone and cold earth.

At the right-hand end Toil entered a smaller chamber and ascended a spiral of ridged slope to an upper chamber, then again to a similar one near the ceiling of the great chamber. There were no openings for Lynx to look down at the gantry, just a pair of deep, narrow slits flanking a broader space in the wall. Toil approached that cautiously once she'd turned her strange lantern off. The others followed suit, creeping through the black shadows to peek through openings. For a while Lynx couldn't make out much beyond until, with a jolt, the view resolved into something far larger than he had been expecting. A scuff of clothes and boots nearby told him he wasn't the only one to instinctively clutch at the stone as they realised they were looking out over a vast chasm – one significantly larger than the rift they'd crossed, if Lynx was any judge.

The darkness was profound and while the stone was still laced with a tiny bluish tint, there was little light to catch it.

The walls were so far away it was almost impossible to judge anything in the distance. He looked up instead towards the roof, but could make out even less and soon found himself tipping forward towards the void until he caught himself.

Somewhere further down there were torches burning – just the pinprick of distant stars in a night sky, but enough to add definition to the scene. There was a broad stone bridge spanning the gap, over a hundred yards long and leading to a wide avenue on the far side. The faint lines of stone suggested smaller roads both above and below that grand avenue, punctuated with regular gaps in the parapet.

Toil motioned for them all to retreat to the back of the chamber and kept her voice barely audible even then.

'There should be a ridge just below this,' she whispered, pointing where they'd been crouching. 'If it follows similar things I've seen. I'm going to head along that and see if there's anything we can make use of.'

'Like what?'

'Artefacts, mechanisms, traps – don't know yet. Point is, these parts may not have been explored so carefully. If there's anything, we might be able to put it to work for a distraction.'

'All of us?'

She shook her head. 'It'll not be an easy climb. Volunteers?'

Lynx looked at the others. Reft said nothing of course, while Kas shrugged. A sudden sense of distrust took hold of him at the tone of Toil's voice, however, and before Kas could reply Lynx spoke up. 'I'll go.'

'Sure?' Toil asked sceptically. 'She's a bit more limber than you, I'm guessing.'

'Reckon you won't find me lacking there, love,' he said, affecting a leering tone. 'Question is, can you keep up with me?'

Toil snorted. 'You'll be staring at my arse as I lead the way; men've done more for less I suppose. Come on then. You two, head down a level, keep a watch for patrols. We need to keep as silent as we can, right?'

She got two grunts of acknowledgement and then they were off, Toil and Lynx making their way to the edge and feeling around for a ridge beyond the lip. It turned out there was indeed one, but more than a foot below the edge of the opening and close to invisible. In the end Toil had to use Lynx as an anchor and dangle her leg out over the edge until her foot was securely placed. She crouched down on the ledge and slipped Lynx's grasp, tugging his sleeve gently to indicate he should follow her. Lynx lay flat on his belly, keeping his centre of gravity as low as possible. He knew as well as anyone that in darkness it was easy to lose your balance on level ground. Treacherous visions of slipping down on to the ledge then just continuing past it swam through his mind as he moved.

Eventually he made it down on to his hands and knees, reaching out for Toil only to find himself with a handful of buttock. The woman seemed to stifle a laugh and Lynx hastily withdrew, lowering his hand until his fingers rested on her boot. The pair shuffled on as quietly as they could in that fashion, Lynx doing his best not to hamper Toil's progress but not lose her in the dark. At one point he could have sworn she was messing with him, seemingly unaffected by the near-total dark, when she stopped so suddenly he almost went face first into her backside, but his reactions were good and he stopped just short. Refusing to be outdone he gave her a gentle pat and Toil started off again without another word.

The memory of her opening the door in Grasiel, naked and blood-spattered, appeared fully formed in his mind and Lynx cursed himself silently. Despite his tangle of anxiety and the current danger, keeping his mind on the job at hand wasn't somehow quite as simple as willing it so. This close to her, his nose was again filled by Toil's intoxicating scent. It turned out even his fractured mind preferred the memory of her naked over older ones. He had no idea how long that slow shuffle through the black lasted, but he was far from bored when at last Toil made a faint hiss and stood gingerly up.

In the black he could only just make out what she was doing and felt a moment of panic when she slid herself left on to some sort of platform. Lynx scrabbled to follow as Toil ran her hands around the sloped walls to make the dimensions out. He glanced warily back at the flickers of light on the bridge, a torch illuminating two figures patrolling the length of it, then pulled himself up beside her.

'Alone at last,' Toil purred in his ear.

Before Lynx could think of a clever reply she'd slipped away, further down the platform, the rasp of her hands on smooth stone just about audible. Apparently satisfied with what she saw she reactivated her lantern and the walls glowed pale blue once more. It was a welcome sight even if it wasn't anything close to bright. Lynx saw they were in a low attic-like chamber perhaps thirty yards across, with sloped walls. The rear wall was a featureless sheet of stone, while the few open yards they'd crawled through were repeated three more times down the bridge side.

'Well, shit,' Toil said, looking around the space as though the shadows might unfold to reveal rather more useful artefacts than the entirely empty chamber actually held. 'Ulfer's horn, this could've been more helpful.'

'What now?'

Toil was silent a while, long enough for Lynx to experience another sense of foreboding. 'Now?' she said eventually. 'Now it's time for plan B.'

'Am I going to like that one?'

'We're outnumbered ten to one in a place of near-total darkness,' she said, moving to the rear of the chamber in case the glow of her lantern was noticeable to those below. 'Not sure there are many likeable plans.'

'Not much of an answer, that.'

'What are you, my mother?'

Lynx shook his head. 'I'm a suspicious bastard who doesn't have a whole lot of faith in others. Certainly folk who're rather more devoted to a cause than the average mercenary.'

'Meaning?' Her hand didn't exactly hover over her gun's grip, but there was a stillness in Toil that spoke volumes.

'That I'd prefer to talk things through rather than watch you do something rash.'

'Me? Rash? I don't know what you're talking about.'

'No one told me about sending the Princip out the window like that. Reckon even Anatin got a surprise there and it made escaping a sight harder.'

Toil shrugged and seemed to relax a little. 'We couldn't have the Charnelers pretend like nothing had happened now, could we?' She took a step towards Lynx and her voice softened to a purr. 'Don't you trust me, Lynx?'

Inwardly he smiled. 'Not a whole lot.'

Another step, one hand holding up the lantern until the sloped stone above her face glowed enough to show off her eyes, wide and innocent. 'We need to trust each other if we're going to get out of Shadows Deep alive.'

'There I agree.'

She was inches away from him now and Lynx couldn't help but breathe in hard. His fingers tingled, aching to slide around her waist. 'So I'm in your hands as much as you're in mine,' Toil added huskily. 'A union, if you will.'

Lynx smothered an awkward cough, trying to ignore the sensation of being a transfixed teenage boy once more. 'Do you smell oil?'

'What?'

'Oil, can you smell it?'

'I'm trying to have a moment here,' Toil said sharply.

'I know what you're trying to do.'

'You're now adding insult to disregard? Can't a girl have an honest moment with the man in front of him?'

'Sure. Let me know when honest is happening and I'll brace myself.'

'Quite the fucking charmer, aren't you?' Toil tossed her head back and set the lantern down at her feet. 'Can't blame a girl for trying, though, eh?'

'Oh, I think I can.'

She went still again, just for a moment. 'I advise you keep any blame to yourself,' she said, 'in my line of work it's not welcome.'

'Fair enough. What now?'

'Now? Well, you have your misgivings about plan B, despite not having heard it, and you can smell oil. Or was that just bullshit to stink up the comradely mood I was trying to inspire.'

'Comradely?' Lynx had to fight the urge to laugh. 'Woman, I'll not hold it against you, but don't pretend you weren't messing with me there. Once we're out in the sun again and safe, I'll gladly and breathlessly assist any comradely mood you want to create, but until then don't you insult me either, eh? I wasn't born yesterday and I *have* seen a beautiful woman before, have been led a merry dance by one too.'

'You're not helping your chances there.'

He smiled in the dark. 'Reckon I am, if there really are any chances. Folk like you don't want simple and easy, you're not built for it. Being called on your bullshit works better'n getting your way all the time.'

He couldn't see Toil's expression now but felt a moment of satisfaction when she turned away and crouched at one of the central openings. 'Oil, you said?'

Lynx joined her at the edge, whispering, 'Can't you smell it?'

'Maybe. Your nose is sharp?'

'I ain't this shape because of beer.'

'Interesting.'

'What?'

She pointed down into the dark where one cluster of torches was, at the far end of the bridge. 'You see the shapes around those torches? Look like bowls?'

'I think so.'

'Oil burners, maybe.'

'After all these years?'

'I've seen the like before. Oil from way down in the rift, some sort of system that draws the oil up when it's burning. There won't be much there right now, but if the Charnelers think to light it, it'll start going. The Duegar didn't need the light, but this will have been an important crossing so a bit of drama isn't beyond them at all.'

'After all these years?'

'There's no mechanism, not in the ones I saw. Just stone pipes and engineering. Unless the pipe's broken it should have lasted the years. Not all will have, been a long time after all, but we don't need them all.'

'How does this help us?'

'Still working on that bit. They'll cast good light; maybe help us pick off soldiers while we're still in darkness.'

'Until they come and get us. We can kill five times our number and still get wiped out.'

'It's a start, isn't it?'

'Didn't you say we shouldn't have a gun battle near the rift?'

'True.'

'Well?' Lynx demanded as loudly as he dared. 'What's changed? Why're you so happy to do that now?'

'A lack of alternatives,' Toil said with a shrug. 'You got huffy with the idea of me coming up with a plan B on the fly, remember?'

'Right now I'm open to suggestions.'

'Fair enough.' She nodded back towards the rear of the chamber. 'Fetch me the lantern, would you?'

'Why?'

'Because I need it for something.'

Frowning, Lynx complied. He got half a dozen steps before a sixth sense prickled and turned him around. In the gloom he could just make out Toil on one knee, fiddling with something in her hands. Before he could move she gave the object a twist and tossed it out into the black beyond, out past the bridge.

'What in deepest black was that?' he hissed.

Toil retreated from the edge again, slipping past Lynx as he tried to grab at her arm. 'That was plan B,' she said simply.

From somewhere far below there was a deep shuddering boom.

'Shattered gods, a grenade?'

She fetched her lantern and extinguished its light. From the Charnelers below there came shouts of alarm.

'In the dark every army's the same size,' Toil said before crawling down to the ledge. 'Be as the lightning bolt under blackest night, my brothers – strike with fury and speed, let them fear what they cannot see and see what they fear.'

'Quoting the Shonrin of So Han to me is the fastest way to meet my nasty side,' Lynx growled.

Despite his tone, Toil made an amused sound. 'Glad to hear it. We've no time for good kitty right now. There's killing to be done.'

Chapter 26

They returned to the others as quickly as they could. As they crawled, Lynx's blood continued to fizz with the prospect of danger and memories of the speeches by the Shonrin he'd heard as a youth.

Not so much heard, he reflected with a sour taste in his mouth, *more like swallowed hook, line and sinker. Can still remember the fire in my belly when I signed up – that belief in our nation's destiny we all had with a fervour stronger than any drink. And it was a drink we gladly drowned in, killed the parts of ourselves that wouldn't butcher people and unleashed the rest upon the world.*

Lynx was silent for a while as he faced the others, composing himself. He knew Toil was playing him like a harp – the deft plucking of strings, confident in the result. Despite everything his old training came back to the fore – the need for swift action when the enemy was still uncertain. He hated her for it, but maybe the reminder wasn't so stupid a one.

'We need to move. They'll be wondering what's going on.'

'Retreat?' Kas asked.

'Attack,' Lynx replied with a shake of the head. 'I'm guessing Teshen will have heard that grenade and taken it as his cue.'

'Won't they hold back, just waiting for us to come to them?'

'They can't, they're running out of time. Whatever wood they've brought for light down here, they'll be running out of. Most likely they're going out of their minds trying to work out how we've kept going underground for so long. This darkness is a killer all by itself – without light you'll be lost down here until the wildlife finds you. They can't just hope we'll make a run for it, we've already proved better at this game than they are.'

Kas nodded. 'So you send out squads to sweep, at the first sign of enemy contact you bring the bulk of your troops into the fight. Leaving a few sharpshooters and grenadiers at each bridge to stop anyone who slips past.'

'So their superior numbers are split already; squads to sweep, rearguards on each bridge, support teams at each bridge. We pick them off and watch our backs, we've got a chance here,' Toil added.

Lynx sheathed his mage-gun on his back and drew his sword. 'First things first, we try to kill anyone on this side – silent until the first gunshots. Leave it to those on the far side to announce where the tasty maspid snacks are.'

The others nodded as Toil pulled swords, Reft his pair of hatchets.

Kas tugged a fistful of arrows from her quiver. 'Looks like I'm leading the way,' she announced, nocking one arrow while keeping the rest ready in her draw hand.

They went in near silence, following Kas down to the main bridge level. The open archways and chambers were a chaotic place in the dark – a place for hunters, not prey. Kas stalked through them with the confidence of a cat. Away from the wide avenue running down the rift edge it was a tight network of small chambers and short twisting tunnels.

It didn't take them long to track down the nervous whispers of a squad of Charnelers on their side. Carrying torches against the gloom they shuffled through open rooms, clearly unhappy with their orders, but not so frightened that they were going to refuse. With over-exaggerated gestures Lynx split his group up, sending Toil and Reft around ahead of the squad, while Kas and he slipped behind them.

They gave the other two a decent chance to skirt back round, whereupon an opportunity presented itself. There was a long blank wall of stone with a narrow opening that seemed a perfect ambush point and Lynx patted Kas's shoulder to signal they should go for it. When the squad was just reaching the opening Kas rounded the corner behind them and in the blink of an eye had shot the nearest two Charnelers.

Half-blinded by the torch their leader carried, the pair never saw the arrows strike them. It was only the tap of Lynx's boots on the ground that alerted them to the threat. Arrows zipped past his head as Lynx charged, fighting the urge to roar as he went. The torch tumbled to the ground and faces turned in the faint light – a glimpse of surprise as Kas let fly again and again and Lynx batted away a wavering bayonet before burying his blade in the throat of the owner.

Behind them, Toil and Reft appeared like demons from the dark, both wielding a blade in each hand and leaping into the heart of the soldiers. Lynx smashed a gun from one soldier's hand and as another raised his weapon an arrow took him in the shoulder. Then Reft was there, chopping at arms and necks with swift, brutal strokes and ploughing through the remaining Charnelers.

The man's power was terrifying to behold, even to a former So Han commando. Where Toil and Lynx slashed and stabbed with all the strength they could muster, Reft seemed to merely flick his wrists. Limbs were severed, blood gushed black in the sputtering torchlight, men and women smashed to corpses in his wake.

In moments it was over and Toil swiftly cut the throats of two squirming soldiers with arrows buried in their chests. Thanks to Kas's rapid shooting none of the soldiers had managed to fire their guns or even call out before being felled. Lynx wiped the blood from his sword, ignoring the hammer of his heartbeat in his ears, and bent to tug the cartridge case off the nearest soldier.

'Running low?' Toil asked.

He shook his head. 'Can never have too many,' Lynx replied, flipping the lid of the case open. He picked up the torch and held it over the case briefly, checking the contents, before dropping it on one of the corpses.

'Ten icers left here,' he commented, checking the next.

'Fewer in this one,' Toil said, doing the same. 'That could be good for us.'

'They don't want a long fight, that's for sure,' Kas said as she retrieved her unbroken arrows and wiped the worst of the blood off. 'Another reason to keep to the shadows.'

'Aye,' Lynx said, adding, 'damn good shooting there, Kas. Where'd you learn that?'

'That how they shoot back home,' she replied simply. 'Can't match a mage-gun for power or range, which is why most don't bother to learn, but my people are a stealthy lot and there's only so fast you can load a gun.'

'All done?' Lynx looked around at the rest.

Toil finished up emptying one cartridge case into another and slipping the strap over her head. She nodded and they moved out, Kas leading the way again. They were beyond the larger bridge now, working their way towards the smaller one the level below. Where the other group had got to was impossible to tell, but they both had the same goal in mind so Lynx put it out of his mind. Neither party was getting across either bridge until a lot more Charnelers were dead.

As though on cue, the crash of a gunshot rang out through the ruined city. The mercenaries all drew their weapons. It had come from somewhere up ahead; it hadn't sounded too close but the stone walls would play games with any echoes. There was a pause then a clatter of returning fire, three or four shots in rapid succession. The sound of screams added to the clamour, then more gunshots and the distinctive crackle of a sparker. After that it went silent but Lynx knew that wouldn't be the end of things.

'Get to the bridge,' he hissed. As one they raced towards the rift edge, coming out close enough that they could see the glow as tiny figures attempted to light the ancient oil lamps on the far shore. Lynx levelled his gun, careful to keep to the shadows, but he held fire, unwilling to reveal their position on a difficult shot.

'Toil, Reft – move closer and get burners ready. Hit any group trying to come across.'

'And you?'

'Kas will pick off anyone she reckons she can get. They won't have much clue where she's shooting from. When you start firing, retreat straight off. Head for the tunnel back the way we came. Most likely you'll get grenades coming your way so get gone as fast as you can. I'll shoot and move, give their sharpshooters no line to follow. We'll come up behind when we can.'

'And Anatin's lot?' Kas asked as Toil and Reft raced off.

She had laid her spare arrows on the ground beside her and now drew her composite bow full. As a torch started to bob up the side of one half-illuminated stone bowl near the middle of the bridge she let fly. The arrow clattered close, causing the Charneler to flinch and stumble – but clearly they had no idea where it was coming from. The second shot winged him and he fell, howling in pain, while Kas knelt to grab another arrow.

'They'll see what we're doing and go for the other bridge. After this push, all bets are off.'

'Aye, your friend's thrown a tiger among the pigeons.'

Lynx looked down. 'The grenade?'

'Fuck knows what lurks down there, but even she's worried by it.'

'I know. If something comes, run for the light-garden.'

She released another arrow at a squad of Charneler troopers creeping forward, guns at the ready, and turned without waiting to see it strike.

'Sounded like an order, that. We're not both running for the light-garden?'

'Maybe.'

'Kinda pessimistic by your standards.'

'Just got a bad feeling.'

'Someone walked over your grave?'

Lynx shook his head. 'Not quite. I'm just saying, don't wait for me. Most likely I'll be right behind you, but—'

He didn't get any further as the hush and dark was split apart. A great wash of yellow fire exploded somewhere above them, then a second. The forbidding gloom was nudged aside momentarily as flames spilled down in a sheet of light. A moment later a great crack and hiss accompanied a blinding white light, off towards where Reft and Toil had just been heading. Knives of lightning burst over the stone floor, cutting a jagged path towards them.

'Shit, crackler!' Lynx said, raising his gun.

'They're clearing their route,' Kas said, loosing another arrow. 'Don't want to be caught like rats on that bridge.'

Lynx grunted and fired, the sound of his icer rattling his head and cutting a straight white path to the leading Charnelers. One soldier fell but Lynx and Kas were already moving, scurrying away from their position just before a volley of icers gouged at the stone there.

'Retreat?'

'Check the others!' Lynx called over the roar of the flames coating the rift wall.

They raced on through a chamber of long shadows, into a second where Reft and Toil were huddled on the ground together.

'Shit!' Toil yelled. 'Get back!'

Lynx and Kas slewed right, suddenly realising they'd be visible to shooters on the bridge. A pair of gunshots followed but they were already behind cover and in moments they saw Reft and Toil crawling into the lee of a bulbous pillar twenty yards ahead of them.

'You hit?'

'Just caught the edge,' Toil yelled back. 'Few more seconds and that crackler would've got us!'

'You got a shot?'

Lynx saw her shudder and shake her head to clear it. They really had been lucky – the numbing claws of a spark-bomb stretched well beyond the area it killed in. Lynx had felt the fringes of such an explosion several times; a tingling scratch all over your skin, every muscle twitching madly. Still Toil levelled her gun around the edge of the pillar while Reft heaved great breaths of air as he tried to recover his wits.

Toil fired, a streak of yellow darting between pillars before exploding on the near end of the bridge. Lynx couldn't see the effect, but then an explosion followed it and he realised she'd hit someone – set their cartridge case off even.

'Let's go!' he yelled.

As he struggled up Kas stayed on one knee and fired again, but then she was following him at a running crouch back towards the hall with the glowing plants. Reft and Toil were close behind, the big man pausing to turn and scan with his gun raised before continuing on. They raced down one set of steps and up the opposite side as fast as they could. Sweat and nervousness prickled Lynx's neck as he realised how exposed he was, but there were no gunshots before he reached the further set of pillars. Just shy of the tunnel they turned, spreading a little wide and reloading.

For a moment nothing happened then the hammer of footsteps echoed up towards them. Lynx mentally checked himself until his instincts were screaming with panic. Then he dodged around the pillar and fired a sparker at the intemperate handful who plunged straight out onto the open slope. A moment later the enormous boom of an earther followed and a great chunk of stone on one pillar exploded, showering the more cautious soldiers with shards of stone. Toil followed it up with a burner and fire burst over the rear wall of the chamber, flowing right and left to engulf those near it. Kas let fly with three quick arrows before Lynx reloaded and fired another sparker.

An icer from Toil followed it and then Kas called a halt. Either they had killed all the Charnelers or they were about to get a savage response. Not wanting to see a grenadier get in on the action they ran for it, sprinting down the dark tunnel towards the dubious safety of the halls and tunnels behind.

*

Uvrel stared out into the darkness and shivered. Some part of her felt the void stare back at her; a cold and inhuman regard for its prey. She had halted at the centre of the bridge – occupying the very heart of the bubble of light and protected only by the threat of her sharpshooters. She had no idea how the stone bowls were fed, whether they would last untended for years or disappear in minutes, but they needed light. Now she had it and could glimpse the vastness of the huge underground rift, walls of stone and dark on all sides, she only felt more assailed, but for her soldiers to fight they needed to be able to see.

How the mercenaries had run around in the dark for days she couldn't understand. Whether by trickery, magery or something else, it was an advantage they possessed and she had to lessen that as much as possible. As vulnerable as it made Uvrel feel, the oil burned and the dark was pushed a fraction back.

The advance group had reached the other side and disappeared into the chambers beyond. Gunfire and shouts echoed back as the second wave reached the far side and moved on it. Had she bothered to look she would have seen a similar ripple of movement on the lower bridge – fifteen soldiers in each group, more than half of her remaining complement crossing. Fifteen sharpshooters and dragoons were stationed in various perches that afforded a good view of each bridge, reluctantly bestowed a couple of grenades by Oudagan to ensure any rush across was doomed.

'Exalted?'

She turned to see Lieutenant Sauren, face illuminated by dancing yellow light. Despite everything it was a welcome sight.

'Let's go.'

They advanced cautiously, though they could still see the last man of the second wave ahead. A handful of dragoons flanked her along with the lieutenant and a grenadier – all keeping a weather eye on the dark spaces on the sharply sloped rift wall ahead. The dragoons had their guns raised, ready to fire burners at the first flash of movement even if it wouldn't save their lives. The mutual assurance of death was as much as Uvrel could offer, but these were mercenaries. If they had a code it was no different to that of rats – fierce and remorseless in the advantage, but scampering, cowardly vermin at any other time.

As they reached the far side Uvrel couldn't shake the feeling of being watched, but no gunshots split the night – not at them anyway. Some brief battle had waged further ahead then fallen silent as the second group arrived as reinforcements, while sporadic shots continued to come from the levels below. She glanced behind at the far side where a huge archway and slope led directly away from the bridge, as though expecting the view to change and the stone walls would peel away to reveal the Skyriver.

If only we knew how far it was to the surface, she thought for the twentieth time since they'd reached the rift. A scouting party had been sent a short way, but reported no obvious signs of the surface so she'd not let them go further. The choke point of the bridges would have to do. Uvrel didn't know how many exits there were but she wasn't willing to risk her prey slipping past.

'Find them!' she said out loud, startling one of her hardened dragoons with the sudden sound.

Ahead of her she saw the faces of the dragoons in the second wave turn in the shadows, the rift-side avenue bathed in the great lamps' orange glow, highlighting the darkened swathes of stone, which had been scarred by the firebombs of the first rush.

'Sweep these chambers, root them out – keep pressing until they're dead!'

Insar guide us, Uvrel added in the privacy of her mind. *Lord of the Still Night, watch over us, Lord of the Quiet Dark defend us.* Exhortations of god on the battlefield was best left to frothing fanatics, in her opinion. She led men and women of cold pragmatism so while some might be comforted, more would be distracted.

Uvrel led her small group forward, following the soldiers past two scorched bodies into a large half-lit assembly hall. Some strange breed of plant that glowed with inner light had colonised the upper levels, so she didn't need the torches to see the bodies of her troops. Six – no, seven – dead just in here, the telltale scars of burners and sparkers marking bodies and stone alike.

At the far side the second wave were working their way forward, moving in pairs around the edge of the hall towards a tunnel mouth. Uvrel suppressed a scream at their caution, knowing the others had died because of intemperance, but also certain the mercenaries weren't waiting to spring a trap. She ran forward ahead of her escort with her gun drawn, up the slope to one side and fired a burner down into the shadows lurking within. Yellow light roared along the stone passageway, flames spilling out around the edges even as they were chan-nelled on down into the ruins beyond.

'Save your caution for the other end of that tunnel!' Uvrel roared, waving the dragoons and cavalry troopers forward. 'Find those creeping rodents. I want their heads!'

*

Sitain slumped to her knees, gasping for air. Her heart battered against her ribs, threatening to burst its way out, but the iron fingers of Teshen closed around her arm and hauled her upright.

'Keep going.'

'I can't,' Sitain wheezed.

She looked back the way they'd come, the curved tunnel marked with whorls of blue that followed the workings of the mages who'd carved this place. Her hands shook with the exertion of running up two flights of stairs and through a host of chambers with Teshen to rejoin the others.

Before he could reply there came more footsteps behind. The big man gave a short growl then, unexpectedly, tossed Sitain aside and turned on his heel. She fell with a thump, sliding over the smooth stone into a corner of the chamber while Teshen disappeared through a doorway ahead, making for the night-lit chambers beyond where the others lurked with Sitain's lamp.

The pain of striking stone wasn't enough to eclipse the panic in Sitain's heart. She fumbled for her mage-pistol, drawing it on the second attempt, but her legs refused to obey her and she could only sit huddled and pathetic as the boots drew nearer. Her eyes blurred at the heaving breaths she was taking, the room around her fading from view until a flash of movement made her bite her tongue in alarm.

A Charneler surged straight past her, his path lit by the flickering shadows of a torch carried by the woman behind him. That one also ignored her, failed to see Sitain in her quest to press forward, while a third seemed to stare straight at her with his gun levelled. Terrified, Sitain forgot all about her weapon, caught in a primal fear, and held her arms up across her face as though that might stop an icer punching through her body.

Something seemed to erupt from inside her. With her eyes screwed up in fear she barely saw the shadows wash forward over the soldier. He staggered as though dazed by a blow, wide-eyed and confused, then the haze receded again. He gave a wordless shout and raised his gun, while Sitain shuddered and stared straight into the depthless black of the gun's muzzle.

The shot never came. A dark glitter of movement slashed in through the air – sharp lines of deepest purple and black moving in staccato fashion. The Charneler saw something, but he never knew what as the mass of jagged movement darted past and left long, perfectly straight wounds in its wake. In the half-light he seemed to falter then fold as the thin lines of blood all over his body widened and became a torrent. Sitain shrieked at the tide of blood that washed towards her, hardly noticing the first two Charnelers who gaped at the death of their comrade.

Before the pair could recover themselves, Teshen was between them, lashing out at both in the same movement. The barrel of his mage-gun slammed into the woman's throat, the man had Teshen's dagger driven so hard into his chest that the force bowled him over. Teshen ignored the fallen man and slashed at the woman with his knife before she could even paw at her crushed gullet. Both died without a sound. Teshen paused for a moment with his gun levelled at the tunnel before relaxing as no more followed.

Sitain scrambled sideways as blood continued to creep towards her, forcing herself to tighten her grip on the pistol so she didn't drop it. Teshen pulled her upright once more and looked her straight in the eye.

'Spirits watch over you,' he muttered, his words sounding as much a blessing as an accusation. Sitain could only gape in response.

'Ready to move now?'

Before she could find the breath to speak, the air around her shuddered once more, light and dark turning in on themselves as movement too fast to follow swept left and right past her and out of sight once more.

Only an impression was left in her mind – not words, but sensations and that lingering memory of dark gems glittering at night, when the night elemental had visited her out on the road. The impressions they left coalesced into words in her mind.

Flee.

It hunts.

Chapter 27

Commander Quentes watched the flames dance below him and failed to dispel the image of funeral pyres from his mind. They cast a grainy yellow light over the rift that its great curtain of darkness seemed reluctant to accept. A small portion was illuminated, just enough to show how high the rocky roof was above them.

As for below, there was little revealed. A suggestion of depth, no more – but it reminded Quentes of the vastness of the ocean. A depth never fully seen, but one that always lurked beneath and impossible to ignore.

He found himself chewing nervously on a fingernail. The taste of grime and grit lingered long after he realised and removed the finger. It was a habit from his childhood, one he could barely remember now, but as he stared at that wall of dark Quentes felt his hand twitch once more.

No place for a soldier, this, he thought, mage-gun clutched tight in his hands though he saw no target.

Though there were guards on the stairs watching their backs, he couldn't help but regularly glance around at the shadows of the stairways behind him. He wasn't the only one – they all feared the maspids, though most hadn't even caught sight of one yet. They'd heard the screams or seen the looks on the faces of those who'd seen the aftermath.

The scouting party sent down to investigate that light at the foot of a great stairway hadn't returned. They'd just vanished into the bowels of this vast tomb and now Quentes felt a chill in his bones as though he was already dead.

A sound broke his brooding, one unlike any he'd heard before. So deep he thought it was an earthquake, rising up from the unknown depths of the rift below them. The sharpshooters and dragoons all looked at him with panic in their faces, but Quentes had no answers, only terror of his own. The air seemed to shudder as the sound grew – building from a distant rumble to the throaty roar of a lion as big as a mountain. Quentes felt his guts clamp at the sound, but he couldn't stop himself looking out over the stone parapet as one of the sharpshooters whimpered and pointed.

There was something moving in the void. Some sort of light shone there, ice white and describing a shape he couldn't make sense of. Then it moved and wisps of pale flame blurred the darkness. Quentes yelped and his knees gave out beneath him. He dropped down, distantly feeling his chin scraped raw on the stone as he hugged the parapet for support. The voices of his soldiers were incoherent noise, howls and shouts he couldn't understand. He couldn't move, his breath caught in his lungs – a veteran of a dozen battles, enfeebled by terror at last.

'Screw this place!' raged a dragoon beside him, grabbing Quentes by the shoulder and shaking him uselessly. The commander just stared back unseeing when the man hauled him around and yelled into his face. 'Orders? Sir? Fuck!'

The dragoon slapped Quentes around the face, rocking his head back but still unable to break the cage of fear. He released the commander and left him sprawling against the parapet. Quentes watched him with glassy incomprehension as the dragoon reached into a bag on his hip and pulled out a painted iron sphere. Into a small hole he inserted a mushroom-like plug, the stalk sliding most of the way into the sphere while the cap curved to match the outer shell.

'Not today!' the dragoon keened. 'I ain't dying today.' His breath was ragged and tight, his hands trembling as he struggled to even arm the grenade.

Eventually it was done and he gave the grenade's pin a twist before looking over the parapet again. Quentes lurched drunkenly to follow, gaze inexorably drawn down into the black. The light was still there, moving closer. Swift purposeful movements, angular lines painted in light and dark like some sort of huge infernal spider. He saw the grenade sail past him and plunge into darkness, vanishing from sight. His breath caught in his throat as the darkness consumed it and the horror below continued upwards – the light growing, the blur of flame and shadow pulling ever closer.

Fire exploded across it, a great cloud of orange that just for an instant illuminated some long dark body before enveloping it in flames. Quentes moaned as much in hope as in fear, blinking at the bright flash of flame, but then the fire fell away and the monster continued, the fires that shrouded it only renewed by the explosion.

'No!' howled the dragoon.

There were more shouts behind him, voices so stricken with panic they sounded like animals waiting for slaughter. Quentes could only watch. It was close now, perhaps a hundred yards below them, and the first of the sharpshooters found the courage to fire. More followed, the white threads of icers punching through the dark, followed by the spiky trails of sparkers and fat yellow burners. Some hit it, others failed, but it kept coming.

Fifty yards, twenty, the horror unveiling yet still shrouded in dark. Fires burned within a cloud of shadow, white flame shone up between great plates of stony armour adorned with spines. Gunshots rang out as it turned its misshapen head up and paused, long hooked claws caught on doorways and balconies. Long burning eyes ran from above a horned muzzle around the sides of its blockish head. Tusks jutted down from its mouth, illuminated by the fire within. Four crooked, spiked limbs extended from its sinuous body, each one trailing a tattered curtain of black, like wings.

The demon roared once more and the world shuddered around Quentes. His bowels loosened and the steel trap of terror tightened around his mind. Screams echoed in his ears – his own or those of others, he was too far gone to know. His bones seemed to creak at the force of its voice. His eyes blurred and felt ready to burst under the pressure. A wall of shadow washed over them like a sandstorm, dimming the light of the bridge lamps, and the gunfire stopped.

The dragoon beside Quentes faltered, half-fell on him and a second grenade spilled from his hand. It fell slowly over the parapet and the demon darted forward to meet it. White glowing threads lashed out from its mouth to catch the grenade before it hit the slope, a tongue of searing whips enveloping the iron ball and greedily withdrawing. No explosion met it, just a brief, intense burst of light as the horror's jaws closed around it.

The demon threw itself forward and for a moment Quentes looked it full in the face. Its head was the size of a pony, with greyish tusks bigger than his leg. A stink of sulphur and burning oil filled his nose as the heat of its presence scorched his face and knocked him back like a hammer blow. Through the madness of pain and fear Quentes saw shadow-wreathed claws gouge through the stone ceiling of their vantage point and sweep up a handful of soldiers. Their screams were short-lived as the foot closed around their heads and crushed the life from them, the demon snapping once, twice at the clawful of bloody, ruined flesh then discarding them with a flick.

Quentes scrabbled back along the blood-slick floor and felt a gun under his hand. He raised it and pulled the trigger, the searing heat of a burner striking the monster full in the face, but the flames just flowed around the demon as it turned to inspect him once more. Then the claws swept back into view, dark and huge. He felt it strike him. The world collapsed into blurring darkness and brief pain before it was all extinguished and the dark consumed him entirely.

*

'I hope you're happy now, Toil,' Kas hissed as they skirted the stone shell of a building to discover a slanted fissure in the rock ahead.

'Happy?'

'That gods-damned grenade!' Kas said. 'Looks like you got your wish.'

As though to emphasise the point another rumbling roar raced through the tunnels. Lynx looked past Kas at the fissure. It would be hard going to get through, but the sound had come from that direction. If they wanted to get back towards the rift and find the other group, they needed to head that way.

Toil went to the fissure mouth and held her lantern up high. The faint light of the rock around them illuminated how tough it would be. After a few moments she shook her head and pointed to the far end of the chamber where a small tunnel led out.

'Let's try another way.' She paused and cocked her head at Kas. 'Happy? Not sure about that, but if we find those Charnelers all dead, you'll owe me a drink.'

'You get us out of here,' Kas replied, 'and I'll stand you more'n one drink. That ain't the bit I'm worried about.'

'Come on then.'

It took them a long while to find an alternative path, during which they heard muted roars and explosions. By Lynx's estimation they had skirted back past the lower bridge, where

Sitain's group had been, but as they found a series of staggered ramps leading up they saw no one. It was a sapping climb and the sounds of violence had fallen worryingly silent again, but there was little more they could do without risking running into Charnelers. Finally they ventured to the outer edge of the rift wall and peeked out of a long bank of windows down at the fire-lit ridges below.

For a moment Lynx didn't see it, so staggered was he by the yawning chasm ahead. The great lamps only emphasised just how huge the rift was, each hundred-yard-long bridge looking small and fragile across that great space. Then a great shape moved on the far side, lit by fires of its own behind a veil of darkness. It was massive, that much Lynx was sure of, with four long limbs that resembled bat wings as it clung to the rift wall. A long glowing spray of tongues flickered out, questing into the burrows of great doorways and windows.

Inside those chambers, Lynx could see sparks and flickering lights as though the creature's tongues were sparker-trails. The unease that had been growing inside him hardened and he turned to Toil.

'You know what that is?'

She shook her head. 'Not really,' she whispered back. 'Beasts of the deepest dark don't have names, but it's assumed they're what are called golantha in ancient scripture. Most adventurers won't see one in their lifetime. Wisps refer to them as Darkest Lights if they have to mention them, but even they don't really know anything about them.'

'And still you decided to poke its nest?'

'Couldn't see any other way. You weren't volunteering alternative plans so far as I recall.'

'What do you know about them?'

Toil frowned at him. 'They're big and dangerous. What more do you want?'

He met her gaze for a while but either she was telling the truth or he couldn't tell when she was lying. His disquiet remained, however, an instinct he'd learned to trust in the dark of the To Lort mine – suspicion as a first resort, when it was dangerous to live any other way.

'What's it doing?' Kas whispered from her vantage point. 'Rooting for anyone left alive?'

As they watched, it paused and turned its blunt head. Lynx's heart seemed to stop for a moment as the half-hidden horror raised its tusked snout as though it had heard them. Then its mouth opened again and the long whips of tongue flashed out, probing like a snake. In its throat Lynx saw flashes of light, a gullet edged in curls of flame. But it wasn't looking up at the four mercenaries. Soon its attention was dragged down and the tongues quested towards the levels well below them.

'It's no elemental,' Lynx breathed, 'but that's magic still. Fire and lightning, night magic surrounding it too maybe.'

'So?'

Before he could reply, the golantha abruptly pushed off from the slope it clung to and threw itself across the rift. A powerful stroke of each crooked limb seemed to propel it a long way before it dropped down on to the bridge, covering forty yards in a single bound. The creature itself was twenty yards long from its broad head to stubby tail, but moved with remarkable agility and Lynx realised the blur of darkness trailing each limb was, at least in part, a leather frond of wing.

It ran with snaking speed along the bridge, ignoring the great stone bowls of fire, until it neared the far side whereupon it rose up and leaped, again beating at the air with all four limbs to hurl itself on to the rift wall above the bridge. There was a rumble and crack of stone as it landed, followed swiftly by a deafening roar, and they all reeled from the noise.

As the sound died away Toil looked out over the edge again, soon joined by the others. The slope was such that they needed to lean precariously out to get a good view. Now the ground did shake as the golantha ripped at a gallery with one sweep of its claws and screams came from within. The white flash of icers skipped off its body, making it flinch and snap at the source of the shot. The orange flower of a burner bursting over its forelimb it ignored, but eagerly lashed forward with its flail-tongue at the assailant. More icers struck its flank, prompting another roar. This time its tongue was wreathed in spitting arcs of lightning as it struck back.

'Burners don't seem to hurt it much,' Lynx muttered, watching the monster move swiftly across the slope towards the lesser bridge. A figure in black and white was still caught in its jaws as it went, shrieking madly until it bit down. There was a crash and a flash of light. For a moment Lynx thought the Charneler's cartridge case had exploded, but the body was not ripped in half nor the golantha injured.

'It's the magic,' he said with mounting certainty as the remains of the Charneler were allowed to fall, uneaten, from the crackling strands of tongue. 'That's what it's after.' He turned to Toil, anger mounting inside him. 'Did you know? Or suspect, at least?'

'Know what?'

'That it fed off magic – when you divided us up, did you mean to keep Sitain away from you?'

'Sitain's the only other one with a lamp!' she snapped back. 'We couldn't go together!'

'But you put her with the person we're most likely to leave behind and the hardest hearts in the company.'

'You've been underground too long,' Toil spat. 'It's messing with your head, making you paranoid.'

'You reckon?'

'Hey!' Kas shouted, stepping between the two of them. 'Now's not the fucking time for any of this.' A rumble of noise from Reft's throat indicated the big man agreed with her. Kas went to the edge again. 'More importantly, it does look like it's hunting someone down there.'

Lynx looked out. The golantha was working a diagonal path up the rift wall, away from them but ascending too. If it was after Sitain, it didn't look like she could get away from it easily. As he watched, it ripped away a section of pillars and drove inside, worming its narrow body into the space beyond. The sound of destruction continued and Lynx realised the interior wasn't as safe as they'd hoped. He looked around, realising the great support pillars and archways were well spaced – enough for even a large creature to get into so long as it could smash away the thinner parts.

'Let's go.'

'Go?' Toil said, astonished. 'You want to go and fucking fight that?'

'I want to see if the others need help.'

'You're mad! We've got to pull back, let it root out the Charnelers then make for the bridge once it's sated.'

'We're going,' Lynx stated, glancing at Reft. The big man nodded, Kas too. Toil looked from one to the other, her face tight with anger, but eventually she swallowed it and shook her head wearily.

'You people are mad. Deepest black, stupid and mad! Come on then, without me you'll be stupid, mad *and* dead.'

'That's the spirit,' Lynx said through gritted teeth.

*

They retraced their steps a short way, heading down with as much caution as they could muster. What had happened to the remaining Charnelers, Lynx couldn't say. Perhaps they'd all fled into the ruins, perhaps they'd stayed to fight and been massacred. Either way the sounds of gunfire had faded and the quiet was broken only by the occasional muffled crash of stone.

As they neared the sounds of its progress, Lynx realised the golantha had worked itself a long way into the interior now. The broad tunnels and grand scale of the Duegar ruin apparently worked in the monster's favour, easily accommodating its lithe body. Once they'd closed on it Toil led them deeper into the ruin, trying to skirt around the creature rather than attack it directly. Rounding one great natural pillar Lynx glimpsed a group of Charnelers on a high walkway, fleeing from the golantha.

He raised his gun, ready to fight, but only the last of the group spotted him. Instead of shooting he just yelled a curse and carried on going, no doubt saving his ammunition for the native horrors. Lynx was happy to do the same and followed Toil in a long arc around the monster. As they neared whatever it was hunting, he felt a jolt in his guts. The sound of gunfire rang out once more, this time from somewhere close at hand.

Rounding the next corner he almost fired at a figure across the chamber until Toil raised a hand in front of him. Lynx looked closer and realised it was Anatin, the greying mercenary commander bent over and exhausted. He was cradling his left hand, which looked like it was wrapped in a rough bandage.

'Where are the others?' Toil called.

Anatin yelped and looked up, clapping a hand to his heaving chest as he realised who they were.

'Fuck!' was all he said at first between panting breaths.

Lynx's eyes widened. Anatin's hand wasn't bandaged – the stump where his hand had once been was. A belt was tight around the arm, keeping pressure on it, but somehow the man was still going despite his injury.

'The others?' Toil repeated.

'Ashis fell behind,' he shouted with a shake of the head. As he made to continue, a larger figure appeared behind him, emerging silently from a tunnel; Teshen.

'About time,' he called as Lynx's group hurried over. They reached the pair just as Varain and Sitain also appeared, both looking exhausted but uninjured. 'Damn thing's chasing us.'

'Charnelers?'

'Sure, them too maybe. Didn't seem so important all of a sudden. One put an icer through Anatin's wrist as Ashis went down, but no one's so keen to stop and fight right now. A couple tried to pin us down and got munched for their efforts.'

'Ashis's gone?'

The man's face was blank and hard. 'We won't get back to her. Either the Charnelers have killed her or she's eating a burner right now.'

Lynx nodded, though he felt a sickened feeling in his gut. Seeing someone die was something he was used to, but leaving them to die alone in the dark cut him to the quick.

'Where is it?' he said, forcing himself to focus on something else.

Teshen pointed back behind them. 'We ducked through the smallest doorways we could find. It'll be looking for a way round.'

'It's not giving up the chase?'

'No chance.' He cocked his head in Sitain's direction. 'Reckon we've got something it wants.'

Lynx nodded. 'Looked that way from where we were; any magic it can sniff out.'

'So what's the plan?' Teshen looked first at Anatin then Toil, but neither spoke immediately.

'We give it what it wants,' Toil said slowly, looking straight at Sitain.

'You've got to be fucking kidding me,' the young woman gasped.

'Nope.'

'What? Tie me down and leave me like a sacrifice while you run for it?'

Toil gave her an evil smile. 'Could be worth a try. You a virgin?'

'We're not doing that,' Lynx broke in, half-afraid Toil was serious. 'But you're good bait, better than our cartridge cases even.'

'Plus we need those if we're to kill it.'

'I'm not sacrificing myself so you can get a clean shot! In case you'd not noticed, the damn thing's been shot at a few times anyway.'

Lynx shook his head. 'I'll do it. Burners didn't seem to have much effect so hand those over, they'll smell like magic all the same.'

He opened the looted cartridge case that hung at his waist and pulled a handful of icers from it. These he put into his own before swapping in most of his remaining burners and sparkers. 'Cough up all of you, burners and sparkers – grenades too if we've got any left. The golantha looks like it's made as much from fire and lightning as anything else under that armour. A bag of tasty treats for it might make me the best option.'

'Golantha?' Teshen asked as they all complied.

'Ask Toil,' Lynx said with a shrug. 'Mebbe another day, though. Let's move from here before it finds a way through, hey?'

'How's this going to help us?' Anatin demanded as they started walking. 'You're taking all our most powerful cartridges – icers aren't doing much more than beestings to the bastard.'

'Enough beestings and it'll go down,' Lynx said, 'but I'm not waiting for that. Can we lure it somewhere and collapse the roof on it?'

'I doubt it,' Toil said. 'The Duegar built their cities to last centuries. To take down a large stretch would be damn hard.'

'Okay, so we lure it out to a bridge, kick it back down the hole it crawled out of and hope the fall slows it up enough to get ourselves across. The Charnelers guarding the far side are dead I reckon.'

'Burners and sparkers don't hurt it,' Toil said, 'but earthers will. Nothing shrugs off the force of an earther impact easily. That's why icers sting it; it isn't the cold that hurts.'

'How many earthers do we have?'

Reft held up a splayed palm, Anatin volunteered two and Varain had another three. Like Lynx, the others didn't often bother with earth-bolts and they knew without looking that their plundered cartridge cases wouldn't contain any. He took one now, as did Toil and Teshen, one shot each proving scant comfort but better than nothing.

The group were walking fast through chambers, looking left and right as best they could to try and work out where the golantha was. There was no sound of breaking stone to follow. The halls here were larger so, while it might have been forced on to an oblique path by the odd bottleneck, it wasn't having to smash its way through.

'Shattered gods!' Varain yelled suddenly, pointing through an archway.

They all turned and froze as flickering light illuminated the far side of the neighbouring chamber. For a moment they just stared until dancing trails of light cut the gloom and the scrape of claws on stone seemed to fill the air. A dark, broad head with huge tusks rounded a corner and that broke the spell. The mercenaries all broke into a sprint in the other direction while a roar of fury boomed through the tunnels behind.

Lynx heard it coming but didn't pause to look back. It was large enough that it couldn't run through most tunnels and arches, but if it reached them out in the open he knew it would chase them down easily. Just as he thought that they came to a massive domed room, the Duegar lamplight picking out great friezes of geometric shapes and strange beasts soaring amid the clouds. The dome itself was specked with glowing shards of crystal, casting a clear-enough light over their predicament.

'Make for the far side and cut back,' Lynx yelled, glancing behind. He couldn't see the golantha yet but could hear it coming. 'I'll go this way, try and find my way to the bridge.'

'Follow the light,' Toil replied as the others fled without a second thought. She pointed through the archway he'd spotted, beyond which a faint glow gave some texture to the dark. It wasn't much, but the smooth floor seemed to gather all the meagre scraps of illumination available and he knew he'd worked long hours in no better.

'Head that way and let the bridge lamps guide you.' She paused. 'You sure about this?'

'We'll soon see.' Lynx's attempt at a smile became more of a grimace, but even that was lost to the dark. All the same, Toil gave him a slight nod before she turned on her heel and sprinted away after the rest.

Just as he was about to run Toil slewed left, away from where the others were making for. Lynx felt his heart stutter as he watched her head into the darker depths of the ruin's interior and soon become swallowed by Shadows Deep.

Away from Sitain, away from me. Oh, shattered gods, was this her plan all along? Were we the ruse?

Lynx felt his guts turn to ice as he stared after her. Ahead of him, the strange light of Sitain's lamp vanished as the rest of the mercenaries turned a corner and a wave of numbing, irrational terror struck him like a fist. He staggered back, gasping as the black closed in around him and his chest seemed to tighten with every feeble effort for breath.

I'm going to die in the dark.

The words seemed to float through Lynx's mind, a jack o' lantern that somehow worsened the darkness of terror enveloping him. Heart hammering, muscles wavering, he almost fell to his knees. Sour fear welled from his stomach to choke up his throat, his head swimming as phantom shapes twisted before his eyes. But, even as he felt himself stagger, a flame of rage was kindled, the shackles he fought every day to keep on it falling away. As the darkness tried to consume him, a blind beast reared up and faced it, aware only that what it hated was all around.

Somehow it gave him the strength to move, to fill his lungs and turn towards the scrap of light still visible, through the archway. As he did so, the menacing click of claws on stone cut through the air behind him, unmuffled by stone walls.

Lynx turned and saw the glowing strands of the golantha's tongue flicker at the edge of the chamber entrance, seeming to caress the corners of stone as it sought him. Fresh panic jolted him into movement and Lynx started off for the light ahead of him, barely remembering to pull a sparker from his cartridge case and drop it gently on the ground.

A trail of breadcrumbs! he thought, feeling drunk with fear. *Shattered gods, mebbe I've finally tipped over the edge.*

Hoping the monster would follow the scent, he fled down the short tunnel that led off in the direction of the rift. At the apex of the tunnel's curve he set another cartridge down just as the monster roared and set off in pursuit of him. A muted cracking sound followed and Lynx felt a moment of hope then a surge of panic as he realised it must have taken the bait of his discarded sparker.

Means a horror from the deepest dark is following you, he reminded himself, *so fucking run!*

It wasn't far to the rift, he soon discovered, a vaulted hall spanning most of the distance he had to cover. There was debris of shattered stone littering the floor of it, the thirty-foot-high columns that looked out over the rift mostly a brutalised mess now. This was where the monster had broached the ruin and on the periphery of his vision Lynx thought he glimpsed pools of blood and broken bodies.

He didn't stop to check. The imagined horror was enough to spur him on and ignore the stitch building fiercely in his chest – years of a generous appetite catching up with him again. The golantha was close behind and he hadn't reached the rift-side avenue on the other side by the time it forced its way into the hall. Lynx tossed the burner in his hand behind him as far as he could, hoping it would buy him a few more seconds. He turned the corner and started the sprint to the bridge, realising with a jolt it was only fifty yards off.

That was when he noticed the bedraggled squad of Charnelers – eight or nine of them, all with their guns pointed his way.

Chapter 28

'Run, you fools!'

Lynx sprinted towards them, yelling as loud as he could but not slowing when their guns twitched. If the monster hadn't roared as it entered the wrecked hall behind him, they would have likely shot him dead. As it was the Charnelers simply paled and looked past the running mercenary, frozen with fear by what was following him.

Lynx decided he didn't care and raced on, chest burning and knees screaming, but terror kept him moving. The light of the great oil lamps on the bridge shone out through the darkness, filling him with hope despite the fact they'd make him a clear target. He craved the light all the same, as much as he feared the shadows behind.

The Charnelers were close to the mouth of the bridge, just a dozen yards short of it, and Lynx gave them a wide berth as he ran past. His cartridge cases flapped madly at his side and he was forced to run with one hand holding them for fear of setting the contents off. Out of the corner of his eye he saw the Charnelers shrink back. A whimper escaped more than one as there was a thump and clatter of rubble behind him. The golantha heaved itself out on to the wide road leading to the bridge, scattering fragments of stone.

Mage-guns rang out almost as one great sound, the sharp report of icers echoing out across the rift as Lynx raced past. He didn't see what followed, but he heard the sinister rasp of the golantha's tail as it swept forward and a deafening roar of fury. He rounded the great pedestal that bore one stone lamp bowl and kept running, legs barely able to keep going as his strength wavered. The full expanse of the great bridge shone before him, bathed in yellow light. Had he had the strength, Lynx would have howled at how far it now looked to the other side.

One last shot cut through the air behind him then there were only brief screams, followed by the crackle of ice-bolts succumbing to the golantha's strange hunger. Lynx lowered his head and willed himself on, black spots appearing before his eyes as his lungs screamed for air. After twenty yards he could stand it no longer and tugged the spare cartridge case free, dropping it on the ground as gently as he could manage before running on. He hoped that would buy him time to get clear, time enough for the others to arrive and save him.

As he reached the dancing flames that marked the halfway point, something gave and Lynx tripped, flapping madly as his ankle seemed to fold underneath him. He twisted and hopped as momentum carried him forward, then flopped down awkwardly on to one knee before ending up sprawled on his back. Lynx looked up at the darkness above as pain flowered in hot bursts across his knee and he heaved for breath.

Behind him the golantha closed, its attention fixed on the cartridge case he had dropped. It prowled forward and Lynx felt a moment of sheer terror as the monster regarded him with what seemed a wary intelligence. It moved without haste but its long limbs swallowed up the yards as easily as its shroud of darkness blurred the flame-scars marking its body.

He somehow found the strength to get to one knee and fumbled with his gun, pulling a sparker he'd kept back. It was his last one. The rest were just icers, aside from his single earther, but he knew he'd get only one chance.

A sudden sense of calm came over him and his trembling fingers managed to slide the spark-bolt into the breech and close it in one neat movement. The golantha reached the cartridge case and paused, watching Lynx as he stood his ground.

It's expecting me to run – it's not used to anything facing it down.

Lynx dismissed the worrying thoughts that accompanied that and eased his gun up. The jangle of fear and simmering anger flowing through him had struck a strange balance and he knew he wouldn't run any more. If the others didn't appear he would stand his ground. He had made his choice and nothing would sway him. That resolve had been how he'd survived his years on the road. More than once he'd wanted to end it, to violently escape the crawling personal demons when drink had failed him. It had been obstinacy that had kept him alive, that much he could admit to himself. Not bravery, not strength of character or morals – the simple blinkered refusal to accept defeat that had stayed his hand when his mage-gun seemed so inviting. If this was the day obstinacy killed him rather than kept him alive, so be it.

There was a movement to one side as the others raced towards the bridge, but he kept his focus on the beast as though breaking eye contact would make it attack. In truth he knew it wasn't interested in him – the couple of dozen cartridges and two grenades in that case before it were far more attractive – but he still felt a surge of hope as it continued to watch him. Even if Toil had abandoned them the rest had appeared behind him and were cautiously making up the ground. If it couldn't really be hurt, it wouldn't care – kill him if he attacked it maybe, but otherwise ignore him. That it seemed to notice him, or perhaps his mage-gun, probably meant he was more than just an annoyance.

'Or mebbe you just guessed there's a plan here,' Lynx muttered, sighting down the barrel of his gun. 'There's always the cheery option I suppose.'

Slowly the golantha dipped its head, jaws open and snaking trails of tongue reaching for the cartridge case. Lynx let it curl one glowing thread around the case before he pulled the trigger. The mage-gun slammed back into his shoulder and the jagged sparker-trail slammed forward. It hit the cartridge case dead-on and burst into a ball of crackling light. An instant later the case exploded and everything went white.

Lynx was thrown back by the force of the impact, a blinding flash and roar of flames seeming to fill the world as he was hurled across the pitted stone of the bridge. He rolled, arms up across his face, and forced himself to keep going as a wave of heat washed over him. His ears rang with pain, the hurt spreading across his body. Finally he found himself face down on the cool stone, blinking at the crazed streaks of light and dark running across his vision. In the distance there was a roar – of anger or pain he couldn't tell – dulled by the peal of noise echoing through his head. He tried to look up, hand tightening around the stock of his gun, using it to push his body up.

Lynx flopped on to his back, unable to properly keep himself upright, but managed to jam an arm underneath himself. The dark of the rift and the orange of flames seemed to continue moving around him, swirling and shuddering even as he got his other arm around to support his lurching body. Legs splayed in front of him, Lynx tried to see what had happened further down the bridge, but all he could see were smears of light against the dark. The effort of looking was enough to make his head spin and his guts spew up what little remained in his stomach. The sourness of bile added to the dirty stink of burning oil at the back of his throat, causing his stomach to heave once more, but once that was done his wits seemed to return a fraction.

He dragged himself sideways towards the support of the stone wall running down the side of the bridge. The golantha, somewhere amid the chaos of flames, roared and thrashed at the stone beneath it. Lynx could feel the violence of its movements and guessed he'd really hurt it, but before his vision could clear enough to behold his handiwork more gunshots rang out.

He heaved himself up, propping his back against the wall before jerking the breech of his gun open. Moving mostly by feel he found the earther he'd taken from Reft and loaded it. He still couldn't see well, but he staggered forward towards the writhing, shadowy blur of the golantha. Finally he started to be able to see something and stopped dead as the monster whipped around, rear legs tearing furrows in the bridge's surface. Chunks of rock skittered past him, one striking him square on his injured knee.

Lynx howled in pain then the sound died in his throat as the golantha slammed its forelimbs down on the bridge and made the ground shudder under his feet. Its body still seemed to be traced in fire and lightning beneath battered stone plates, but now half the glowing trails of its tongue hung limp and dark. One great tusk had shattered, deep fissures running through the stub that remained. Its limbs were flame-scarred and bent too, one forelimb stiff and unmoving, the other curled inward and struggling to take much of the monster's weight.

Lynx set himself back against the stone wall and raised his gun again. He aimed at the largest part of the golantha, hoping his eyesight could be trusted, and fired. Lynx cried out at the impact on his shoulder, eyes blurring so he barely saw the furrow of the earther rip through the air. He would have fallen had he not had the wall behind him, and as much sensed as watched the monster reel under the impact.

Before the golantha recovered itself the pale, hairless head of Reft appeared on its right. The giant mercenary walked without haste, gun raised and waiting for his moment. Just as the golantha seemed to recover its balance from Lynx's shot, Reft fired and caught it in the side. The blow almost folded it in on itself and it was only the strength of its sinuous body that kept it upright. Then the others arrived.

Anatin's shot took it low in the hindleg and his earther knocked the armoured limb from under it. As it flopped to its belly Teshen caught it high in the back and threw it against the side of the bridge. The golantha's roars still ripped the night apart but now they were laden with pain as well as rage. Varain rocked it back again, Anatin pulled his other mage-pistol and added to the hammer blows, and then there was a moment of quiet.

Lynx felt the world go still around them as the crash and clatter of echoing gunshots faded and the golantha listed against the bridge wall. The mercenaries watched it waver then it seemed to find renewed strength from somewhere, lightning crackling out from its brutalised maw as it raised its body up again.

Reft never gave it the chance. As the golantha lifted up off the ground he raised his gun once more. Lynx found his chest tighten as Reft checked, pausing for two frantic heartbeats then pulling the trigger. The shot rocked him back as a dark stream of air punched into the golantha, but while Reft staggered the monster was smashed back. For a moment it didn't seem it was going to be enough, then the strength in its battered body failed it and the golantha fell with a hiss – toppling over the side and into the dark chasm.

They all stared, Lynx panting and wheezing, as there came a distant crash from far below. It seemed to drag out for an age, but eventually the sound was no more. Reft gave a grunt of satisfaction and flipped the breech of his mage-gun open, tossing the spent cartridge over one shoulder and sliding a fresh one in. Behind him Lynx saw Sitain and Kas. The former held a long mage-gun with little conviction while the latter barely glanced towards them as she guarded their rear.

'Gods,' Varain croaked, taking a step towards the half-demolished stonework before thinking better of it and turning towards Lynx. 'Fucker didn't go down easy.'

'I've seen fortresses take less of a beating,' Anatin added. 'Let's just hope that's the end of it, eh?'

They all stopped and looked his way, but the ageing commander just barked a laugh. 'Hey. I'm just saying the bastard crawled out o' that deepest dark once. I ain't going to hang around to see if it can manage it again – nor whether its got a mate and a squalling brood of little monsters with some pressing questions about what happened to Daddy.'

Lynx shook his head. He didn't even want to contemplate such a thing, but Anatin was right, hanging around was a damn stupid idea.

Before any of them could move the ground at Lynx's feet exploded into stone fragments. He flung himself sideways on instinct, the crash of gunshots ringing out from somewhere above. Above his head a yellow trail ripped through the gloom, streaking across the bridge and into the emptiness beyond. He gave a gasp, realising how close he'd come, then looked up to see a dragoon pitching forward over the edge of the gallery two levels up, an arrow protruding from his chest.

More icers crashed down at him and Lynx realised he was the easiest target, the closer mercenaries being at a precariously low angle. Kas continued to back up, firing until her hand was empty of arrows. Not bothering to grab more she slung the bow over one shoulder and swung up a mage-gun that she'd hung by the shoulder strap around her neck. She didn't fire, but kept scanning for a target as she retreated from the rift wall. As soon as they were clear enough to be safe Teshen fired a burner up at the gallery. Flames washed over the stone facing and momentarily obscured the recesses behind a sheet of fire, whereupon the rest also started to back away, loading as fast as they could.

'Spread out!' Anatin yelled. 'Don't give them a target! Varain, Reft, go!'

The mercenaries obeyed without a word. Lynx kept up as fast a rate of fire as he could at the gallery to give the others a chance to reach him. He wasn't shooting at anything, just trying to make any dragoons hesitate. It would only take one popping up with another burner to scour the bridge clean of life.

He dropped to one knee, barely trusting himself to walk let alone run, as Varain and Reft sprinted up to him. There they stopped and followed suit, firing icers as fast as they could and with no regard to their ammo count.

'Go!' Varain shouted to the rest, whereupon Anatin, Teshen, Kas and Sitain hurtled towards them.

Lynx kept his attention on his gun; open, discard, load, close. He raised it to his eye and— And the gallery exploded into flame. Fire burst out from inside it, spreading wide before it spilled over into the open air. Bodies came with it, dark shapes flailing madly amid the sea of yellow. Their screams were cut short, two then three falling out over the edge and dropping with a sickening crunch on to the ground below.

The mercenaries hesitated, all staring up at the blackened gallery as fire mushroomed out then melted away to nothing – starved of fuel. There was still a sound, though, Lynx realised. Something more distant, shouts and gunshots perhaps, then the clearer sound of running feet.

A figure appeared at the gallery and Lynx almost fired on instinct, but she came at such a breakneck pace surprise stayed his hand. It was Toil and she didn't stop when she reached the edge of the gallery but flung herself right over the edge. Gun in one hand and a drawn-out curse echoing across the rift, Toil seemed to hang in the air above a twenty-yard drop before gravity caught her and she began to fall.

Lynx blinked as she was jerked back, realising her free hand held a rope as her fall became a long arc swinging back into the high space of the great tunnel leading away from the bridge. Well clear of the ground she swung all the way in, disappearing into the shadows of the tunnel before it pitched her back again. Toil reappeared still howling the same word as she let the momentum propel her towards the bridge then let go of the rope.

It was a fall of several yards and she fell heavily, sprawling on her side and ending up on her back with the wind driven from her body. Even as she lay there and Teshen sprinted forward to help her, the woman rolled over and pointed her gun almost directly up at the gallery.

Nothing appeared behind her, but for a moment they were all transfixed by the sight apart from Teshen. Then the Knight of Tempest was at her side and pulled her upright, Toil's feet kicking in an effort to run before there was even stone beneath her.

Knew she hadn't just abandoned us. Lynx felt a wry smile briefly cutting through the fatigue and pain. *Didn't doubt her for a moment. Nope, not at all.*

'Maspids!' Toil croaked as though she'd heard him, stumbling forward. She straightened up as best she could and gave the mercenaries a crazed, unsteady grin. 'I ain't gonna lie, there's more'n a few of the little scamps back there.'

That jolted all the mercenaries back into action. While Teshen and Toil made up the ground the rest started a slow creep towards the other end of the bridge, guns directed both forward and back. The tunnel behind remained still and dark, but the whisper sound of movement emerged from its depths and built with every moment.

'Fuck,' Anatin moaned. 'This place ain't giving up, is it?'

Lynx glanced over at the commander and saw the man's face was pale, the shock of his injury finally setting in. How he'd pushed on this hard for so long with one hand blown off was astonishing, but if they didn't get out soon he'd have nothing left.

'Keep going, you old bastard,' Lynx said and was rewarded with a murderous look in Anatin's eyes. 'We're almost there.'

The mercenaries moved in crabbed fashion, watching the deep shadows for more of the swift hunters, but none appeared.

'We're in the light,' Toil huffed, visibly pained by her exploits but refusing to slow the others down. 'They're too clever to charge us out here.'

Lynx looked left and right as they went, trying to see beyond the bubble of light projected by the bridge's huge lamps, but it didn't extend far down the grand avenue running in both directions. 'Running out of light now,' he commented.

'Forget the rear,' Toil added, 'they won't cross that now.'

'Shitting gods!' Varain hissed and swing his gun left as they reached the end of the bridge.

A dark shape was moving stealthily towards them, but there was little cover for it. Once they rounded the lamp pedestal at the end they had a clear sight and Varain's icer punched through the maspid's head, felling it instantly.

Two more followed it, creeping through what shadows the avenue's low balustrade could cast. Lynx felled one while Sitain and Toil shot the other. Anatin gave a shout from behind them and fired on another pack closing from the other flank.

The mercenaries tightened into a knot, guns facing down each side of the grand avenue as half a dozen maspids braved the light. Lynx found his aching hands return to their old rhythm with mechanical precision – the steady crack of icers ringing in his ears until suddenly the maspids were dead or vanished. They stayed frozen to the spot for a long moment then the mercenaries let out a collective breath.

'Any more?' Anatin croaked.

'We're clear,' Teshen said, glancing left and right, 'but let's not tarry.'

They hurried on into the dark of the tunnel beyond, a grand vaulted space more than thirty yards high that ran at a shallow incline for further than Lynx could see. They trotted up it at a steady pace, not wanting to tire themselves any further, but not even Toil could tell how far it would be to the surface from there. The Wisps had told her it was close, nothing more, but right now not close enough. Behind them muffled gunshots and shouts continued sporadically.

They had gone only fifty-odd yards when a sudden shout from behind them stopped them all dead. Lynx hung his head for a moment, anticipating an icer slamming into his back, but then the voice shouted again.

'Turn around!'

Slowly they all did so, guns held low but ready. Behind them was a woman, her uniform battered and torn from what Lynx could see. She held a mage-gun aimed directly at them. There was no way to tell what was in it, just an icer or a burner that could kill them all, but Lynx didn't fancy finding out – especially this close to the kiss of the sun on his cheeks.

'Drop your guns,' the woman yelled.

'Really?' Anatin shouted back, somehow sounding wearily irate. As he spoke Teshen started to edge sideways but the woman wasn't caught out and jerked the gun towards him. Her uniform wasn't a standard one, Lynx realised, maybe a dragoon officer. Not someone who'd only carry icers anyway, so her threat was all the more real.

'Really,' she said, taking a few steps forward. 'I just want the assassin, trussed up and fingers broken. I'll kill the lot of you if you'd prefer – I will if that gun turns any further my way – but I just want her to interrogate. I'll leave the Hanese and the mage, I don't care about them any longer.'

Lynx heard Toil take a deep breath, ready to reply, but before she could the Charneler snarled and spun around, hurling herself backwards as she fired on a maspid charging at her. The sparker caught it dead on and ripped through to the second one following close behind. The pair convulsed under a shower of sparks then fell dead at her feet as she fell on her backside clear of the sparker's effects.

There was a pregnant pause. The officer looked down at her spent gun and heaved a sigh. She knew she couldn't reload in time, but just to underline the point Kas sent an arrow into the corpse of the maspid nearest her. The woman looked up with a defiant expression.

'Go on then,' she said. 'Get it over with.'

There was a faint creak as Kas held the tension on her bow a moment longer, but then she released it and shook her head. 'I ain't.'

Anatin nodded wearily and sheathed his own pistol, well aware Teshen had a shot lined up should it be necessary.

'What's your name?' he called in a weak voice.

'Uvrel,' the woman called, struggling slowly to her feet. She faced him down with a proud expression, unwilling to bow her head even in the face of death. Clearly exhausted, she stood tall and faced them down. 'Exalted Uvrel.'

'Ah,' Anatin said. 'You're in charge of that merry little band, then?'

'I was.'

Toil stepped past him. 'It's over, Exalted. No point pretending otherwise.'

'Then end it.'

'No,' Lynx broke in. 'Listen – you hear that? That's the

sound of what remains of your command getting taken apart.'

'I am well aware.'

He shrugged. 'I won't say I've got much respect for any Charneler, let alone someone from the Torquen. But that being said, I've never heard of an Exalted who was a coward.'

Toil moved up beside him, nodding. 'You've lost here, you know it, but you've got your honour still and it sounds like there's currently something left of your command. We won't stop you.'

Exalted Uvrel looked surprised. She glanced towards the arc of lamplight spilling over the stone floor from the bridge then back at the mercenaries.

'Just like that? A man who murdered Charnelers at the side of the road suddenly develops a sense of honour?'

'Was honour got me to that point. The girl begged for help and I couldn't walk away.'

There was a moment of silence before more gunshots echoed across the rift behind her and Uvrel started reloading her gun before she'd even thought about it.

'Careful now,' Anatin grunted. The strain was obvious from his sagging, but his voice remained strong. 'Best you hold off on that bit until we're out of sight. We'll not be taken by surprise again; our sharpshooters will take you down easy enough if you follow.'

'Go lead your men one last time,' Lynx added. 'We'll not leave that part out when we tell the tale.'

The Exalted nodded slowly, looking down at the maspid corpse at her feet then cocking her head towards the way they'd come. The bridge was empty from what Lynx could see and the gunshots were less frequent now. Still she hesitated before turning her back fully on the mercenaries, but eventually Uvrel accepted they were as good as their word. She started back that way, one hand slipping into her cartridge case to pull a fresh cartridge out.

The mercenaries backed away, Teshen keeping his gun level in case she turned, but Lynx knew she wouldn't. They were almost out of sight, up the slope, when she had loaded the mage-gun again and started off purposefully down the bridge. Holding the long gun one-handed she rested it on her shoulder as though at complete ease and out hunting.

'Luck to you,' Toil whispered as the woman disappeared from view. 'You won't make it, but all the same.'

Lynx nodded and turned away, looking up the slope towards where he hoped he might soon see the faint glow of daylight. 'Now let's find the sun again.'

She snorted quietly. 'It's night-time; dawn's a way off still.'

'Woman, I'm really starting to hate you.'

'Yeah, I know.'

Chapter 29

Toil led the mercenaries out into the chill night air no more than half a mile from the great rift. Not a word was spoken, but relief broke over them like spring rain as the Skyriver lit their path. They pressed on in the near dark to get clear of the city-ruin and dawn was a glow on the horizon before they stopped to rest. Anatin was suffering badly by that point, despite Sitain's best efforts, but he kept pace with fierce determination. They made a brief camp, barely speaking as the sun appeared over the horizon and the dull shine of the Skyriver faded, before pushing on once more.

The danger wasn't over, but Toil knew the worst had passed and the rest seemed to assume as much. The wild places that bordered Shadows Deep seemed to be bursting with life after those days underground. For most of that first day the mercenaries almost fired on every bird that broke from cover, the dark having marked them all in some small way. With food and water their biggest concern, elementals notwithstanding, they travelled as fast as they could towards civilisation. When Teshen found a stream and Kas felled a deer as the others replenished their waterskins, their supplies and spirits were restored so the miles passed as easily as could be expected.

It took three days of hard travel to find anything approximating a road, another two before they came across a village where they could buy ale and bread. By that point Anatin was close to collapse, but a combination of money and Reft's winning smile secured them a stringy mule to carry him.

The rest were forced to walk for another three days, mostly in bone-weary silence as even the hardiest among them flagged, but finally they found a town where horses and proper supplies were available. It cleaned them out of those small pieces of jewellery mercenaries carried for such an emergency, but the town traders assured them that the city of Chines was only five days travel by horse. They made it in four, arriving at that grand old city of towers and aqueducts as the first storms of early winter whipped up the waters of Parthain beyond.

It turned out the rest of the company was yet to arrive so the group gratefully settled themselves into a quiet corner of the city overlooking the famous Dragonbone Plaza. With funds secured from a bank of ancient and venerable name – the clerks and guards looking more than a little concerned by the battered group of mercenaries – they were free to enjoy the city in comfort while they waited. The fame of Chines's Dragonbone Plaza was in part down to every type of food known being available there, along with every type of beer, wine and exotic spirit, so their various hungers were soon sated. The upper levels of its southern aspect enjoyed a fine reputation for narcotics and Anatin was not alone in muzzily dreaming several days away until a loud, familiar squabbling cut through the hubbub of city life.

Toil dragged herself to a balcony to watch the mercenaries greet their comrades, Deern and Himbel putting their long-smouldering arguments aside to announce their astonishment at the others surviving. She kept herself clear of the boasting and clamour that followed, taking herself off for the evening while the company drank a tavern dry in celebration. The next morning she enlisted Teshen, Reft and Lynx to rouse the rest and herd them on to a wide, three-masted ship in the harbour while the crew partly disassembled and loaded their wagons for transport.

The weather had subsided in recent days and a brief sparkle of sunshine kissed the waters as they set out across Parthain. Once Chines was well behind them, Toil went in search of the captain and instructed the man of a change in destination. It caused some token consternation, but with a cargo of hungover mercenaries he chose not to argue about being compensated for the inconvenience. They expected it to be a week's journey across Parthain, whichever part of the far shore they headed for, and the wind remained behind them for most of the way.

Early on the sixth day they drew in to the port of Su Dregir, a city that rose in steps on the flanks of a hill and looked west across a crescent bay. Like Chines it was old and elegant; the entrance to the harbour ran beneath a great stone arch that spanned the gap between the shore and a small fortress island. One of the oldest settlements on the shore of Parthain, Su Dregir had once ruled the region and the Palace of the Elect overlooking the harbour was a testament to its past glory. The harbourside had three districts on distinct levels, each following the curve of the shore and each as notorious as the Dragonbone Plaza, while on the far side were the seven so-called daytime districts.

It was said that there were dozens of tunnels and hidden caverns cut into the hillside itself, but Toil had proved difficult to draw on the subject once the mercenaries learned their true destination. It was widely known, however, that there were three small rivers which cut through the hill, or had been built over, rather than followed channels in the uneven hillside. Few doubted that an adventurous soul might find passage through the dark, but the city's criminals were known to discourage investigation.

On the very top of the hill was the great lighthouse that guided ships into harbour and just beneath that stood the grand pale walls of the Palace of the Elect. As they neared the city and the mercenaries all piled onto the forward deck, Toil found herself alone and staring at the great green glass lanterns that topped the wall – the tines of the city's crown, they were often called. It was one reason why Su Dregir was often called the jewel of Parthain, a visual reminder to the other cities on Parthain's shore of its wealth and the proud, ancient families whose great houses dotted the far slope.

There was a sharpness to the air that Toil recognised, a promise that the weather would turn nasty, and soon. She had already given Anatin the name of an inn where he could billet the company. They would not be moving on from Su Dregir before the start of spring, long enough for her to see what further use she could make of the company. None of the mercenaries noticed as she caught a trailing rope on the island-side of the great arch and lifted herself away, possessions already packed and on her back.

It was not a route just anyone could use to avoid being challenged by the dockmasters, not unless a fortified guardpost was preferable to routine questions. Toil was challenged then allowed to pass by a grey-bearded guard who had her in his sights before she'd dropped inside the island wall. From there she commandeered a small boat and rowed herself to the opposite shore, far from where the Mercenary Deck would be disembarking.

Toil walked alone and unmolested through the less distinguished parts of her home city until she reached an ancient cut-away stretch of the high district that housed a tight network of mausoleums. Taking care not to be followed, she made her way almost to the furthest of those, where the rock overhung the oldest tomb, then put her shoulder to a slab of stone. It gave way easily and Toil found herself in a tunnel of rough-hewn steps that led steadily up into the cellars of the Palace of the Elect itself.

She tugged three times on a bell pull as she entered, hearing nothing of the result, then climbed up a long flight of steps and through a hatchway to find herself in a circular chamber at the rear of the Archelect's residence. Ten yards across, the plain room had thin windows well above head height and a pair of stone chairs facing each other in the centre.

There were no soldiers or servants. The room was barred from the outside and she heard no signs of life until the deep clunk of bolts being drawn back echoed dully through the stone wall. A masked face entered first, the gleam of a golden ceremonial faceplate illuminated in a candle's light.

The masked one stared at her, pistol extended for a while longer than was necessary, before the bodyguard withdrew and a small man entered. He had long greying hair tied neatly back to reveal the face of a man clearly not of the local aristocracy. His heritage was somewhere further south, golden tanned skin and black eyes. A heavy coat of black overlaid fine clothes, a belt of gold and a torc set with emeralds around his neck. Just by the way he walked it was obvious he was not a fighter, had never been one, but Toil still knelt with genuine respect.

'Sit. Speak.'

He didn't wait for her to respond before settling into one of the stone seats, grunting slightly as he shifted for comfort and rested his chin on his fist.

'It was as we feared, Archelect,' Toil said. 'The Knights-Charnel were poised to move.'

'No longer?'

'I killed the Princip and his powerbase in the Council of the Assayed was fragile. After so public a setback, the Knights-Charnel will be forced to withdraw. Their appetite for control doesn't yet extend to taking an inland city by force.'

The man sighed. 'But for how much longer? I fear we'll not be able to rely on that assumption many more times.' He pinched the bridge of his nose then straightened up. 'Did you encounter difficulty? Get away clean?'

Toil's face darkened. 'Far from it. We were lucky to escape at all.'

'We?'

'The mercenaries I hired to cover my escape. We were pursued through Shadows Deep by Torquen troops, all the way to the deep rift itself.'

'Explain.'

'An Exalted was on us from the very first moment.'

The Archelect leaned forward. 'Do we have an informer?'

'Not us.' Toil hesitated. 'I've yet to work out the details, but the mercenaries managed to get tangled up with the Knights-Charnel as they approached Grasiel. I believe the Exalted was pursuing a rogue mage who'd been taken from their custody – at first anyway.' She shrugged. 'I think I managed to catch her attention afterwards. But if she *was* after them, they were either extraordinarily unlucky or something rather more predict-able among mercenaries.'

'One betrayed their comrades?'

'It looks that way. I have a suspect. He'll be taken in hand before I risk using them again.'

The man looked surprised at that. 'You'd use them again after that?'

Toil hesitated. 'They have some interesting talents in their ranks,' she said after a pause, 'and we've been saying for a while that some trusted unaffiliated companies could be useful.'

'True. Very well. I defer to you on this subject.'

Toil almost laughed at that. Theirs might not be a trad-itional master-agent relationship, but the Archelect was not a man who deferred. She knew that wouldn't be the end of this conversation.

'And the traitor?'

'Might unbalance the company if he was murdered cleanly. I believe I can find some leverage, but if not, an accident or a random act of violence would surprise no one.'

He nodded. 'Two separate reports please; one on the Knights-Charnel, one on these mercenaries.'

'Yes, sir.'

'Good. And good work in Grasiel – I was sceptical at your assessment but you seem to have proved me wrong. It looks like we'll have a busy year ahead of us. I'd advise you to make sure you enjoy the winter festivals. You will be part of a busy diplomatic effort come the spring.' He cocked his head to one side. 'Not the diplomatic part, of course. Age has not entirely addled my mind.'

'I've been away for a while, sure there's some housekeeping to be done before I've time for festivities.'

'No doubt. Your pet scholar tells me the city has been some-what energetic of late. Which reminds me – he also informs me that his friend in Jarrazair is close to a breakthrough, so close I've suggested one, ah, relatively trustworthy mercenary company might find profit in wintering there.'

'*Relatively* trustworthy? Hmm, so long as you kept my name out of it. I don't fancy being the one to explain to my mother why her favourite son is away during the winter festivals.'

'Of course. Please do give her my regards when you see her for Ulfer's Feast.'

'Not Father?' Toil asked with mock innocence.

'Only once he's good and riled about something.' The Archelect laughed. 'I'd hate you to waste the moment. My children are looking forward to their next lesson, by the way. Some foolish servant has been filling their heads with rumours of the Red Lady and, well . . . they have drawn conclusions. We shall soon all be burdened by their intellect. You most of all.'

'I look forward to the challenge, Archelect.'

'So do they, my friend, so do they.'

Epilogue

Lynx opened his eyes and immediately regretted it.

His eyes blurred as a stabbing ache appeared behind them, dark shapes swimming in and out of focus somewhere ahead. He tried to open his mouth and found it half-glued shut by dried saliva, his lips chapped and raw, his tongue like sandpaper.

From nowhere an involuntary shiver ran through his body. The room seemed to wrench around him as the ache filling his head pulsed hard enough to make him whimper. A shuddering breath brought a little clarity and a lot of stink – piss, sweat and mud. He was cold, his fingers numb and stiff, but he couldn't yet summon the energy to lift his head.

Slowly Lynx began to make out details of the dark room. A high ceiling, pitch-coated timbers and filthy stone walls. Somewhere at the back of his mind an animal stirred then jolted awake as Lynx's heart began to hammer in his chest. Not the bunkhouse at the inn they had hired out when they arrived in Su Dregir, the city of Toil's employment. This was somewhere a whole lot worse.

Fuck's sake, not again.

It was a cell. An involuntary croak escaped Lynx's lips and seemed to startle other occupants in the room. Moans rose from either side of him as bone-deep fear started to judder through his body. He hauled his head and shoulders up off whatever he was using for a bed and tried to reach for a blanket. His head rang like a temple bell and the flesh of his back prickled fiercely in the cold. It took a moment of flailing to discover there was no blanket – worse, no clothes.

Lynx slipped one hand behind his head as he felt himself lurching back. All around him figures appeared, groaning like the risen dead. His head spun as he tried to make sense of everything, but the panic welling up from inside overrode his thoughts. His hands tightened into fists as growls of confused anger came from the other beds.

'The fuck 'm I naked?' muttered a figure. It turned, thin arms and pale flesh marked with scars. A dark scrappy beard and tangled hair, laced with white. Narrowed eyes lifted to stare at Lynx. 'Why the fuck are *you* naked?'

Lynx didn't reply, every muscle in his body tightening with cold and alarm. Nearby a massive lump of white flesh rolled over, moving groggily. Lynx sensed a building anger in the air and his heart started to pound so hard he could hardly hear anything as more voices spoke up from around the room.

'What happened?'

'Shitting prison? Again?'

The big man rolled back on to his bed and there was a squawk. 'Move you bastard lump! Reft – ah fuck! Hey, elbows!'

Lynx took a deep breath and prised his fists open, blinking several times before he could focus on the man in front of him. It was Anatin, the mercenary commander looking old and tired without his clothes on. The bandage on his stump hand and a leather cord bearing a grubby ring was all he wore.

'What're you lookin' at?' The less-than-princely commander glared at Lynx with bloodshot eyes.

'Ulfer's shitter,' croaked the figure behind Reft, 'what happened to my head?'

Deern sat up and scratched his head as he looked around the room. The latest set of bruises on the man's face were yellowed shadows, making his pale skin look even more sickly. 'Bugger me, it's too early for this many cocks in one room.' With that he crashed back down again.

'Too early for your noisy shite,' muttered another figure. Lynx blinked at the dark-skinned back until the man rolled over and Himbel's face became visible. The ageing battlefield surgeon was also completely naked. He swung himself around and sat up, idly scratching his balls.

'Gods, count 'em on your own time, Himbel,' Lynx grunted. 'Is this all your fault, Deern?'

'Me?' Deern spluttered. 'Fucking fuck you, gobshite son of a Wisp whore!'

'Hangovers bring out the poet in you, eh?'

'Enough,' hissed Anatin. 'Any more shouting and I'll dock all your pay. Or kill you. One or the other. Coldest black, my head feels like someone shoved an icer into each ear.'

Lynx looked around to see who else was there. Safir was propped against a back wall, his arm bound to his chest to support his injured shoulder despite the fact he was also naked. The wincing easterner gave him a mock salute, somehow contriving to still look mostly elegant and composed. Teshen was in the furthest corner, beyond Anatin, while Lynx realised with a horrible certainty he couldn't explain that the bony white arse beside Anatin was Llaith's.

Is that everyone we were drinking with last night? The men anyway?

'What happened last night?'

'We were celebrating, weren't we?'

Anatin sat up. 'Yeah, we got paid. Ah, shattered gods, what did I do with the money? Has it been stolen?'

'No one's stole from us,' Safir contributed. 'No matter how drunk we were.'

'How do you know?' Lynx asked.

454

'Look around,' he said. 'No one's burned. Our illustrious commander has a sixth sense for anyone about to try and roll us for our pay. He might be so drunk he can't see, but you touch his purse and that pistol is drawn as fast as Kas can loose an arrow.'

'Man's got a point,' Deern said, sounding slightly muffled from behind Reft. 'We'd all be crispy an' dead if someone tried it inside the pub.'

'Also we took it to the bank, remember?'

'Ah, yeah. That too.'

'So what?' Lynx said, struggling to string two thoughts together. 'We were celebrating, Toil took you to get our money right?'

'Oh, aye, there's a story for you later,' Anatin added. 'Made the deposit, noted the ledgers straight after 'cos your girl, Sitain, wouldn't leave me alone until she'd seen her money. Then what? We started drinking?'

'Celebrating, aye that's where I get fuzzy.'

'Lynx was going on about some roasted pig.'

'Damn good pig too,' Lynx added. Despite everything the memory of that spice-stuffed piglet made him smile. 'Even you admitted it was worth the walk.'

Anatin nodded. 'There was wine too. Then that whorehouse.'

'We got rolled by whores again?' Deern moaned.

'Nah, you picked a fight with Toil. Or Kas or someone.'

'The dockside bar,' Teshen said suddenly, 'that stuff made from apples.'

There was a collective groan.

'Then we left?'

'Barracks bar,' Lynx contributed. 'Some place Toil suggested.'

'Was that where you tried to get their champion to box Reft, Deern?'

'He tries that everywhere,' Anatin said dismissively. 'Never fucking works, but for the exact same reason it never gets us in much trouble either.'

'Then what? We drank more beer there, but I can't remember anything after Toil bought that round.'

Something clicked into place in Lynx's mind. For a moment he forgot the cold, the pain of his hangover and the discomfort of a rough pallet for a bed. The panic receded and in its place laughter bubbled up. He tried to contain it for the sake of his aching body but soon was shaking uncontrollably, choked laughter spilling out to the bemusement of his companions.

'Payback,' Lynx wheezed between laughs, 'oh, she's nasty.'

'What the fuck's happened to him?'

Lynx took a few heaving gulps of air and tried to dampen his slightly hysterical laughter. 'Shattered gods, that's a scheming mind she's got!'

'Who?' Deern said. 'He talking about that bloody woman he's been mooning over?'

Lynx was still laughing too hard to mind Deern's comment, but with an effort he swung his feet onto the ground and started trying to find his balance. 'Look lively, boys,' he spluttered. 'We're about to be on display. Guard!'

'Someone care to explain?' Himbel asked, standing and stretching his back.

'Don't worry, old man,' Lynx said, 'you don't seem to be the shy type anyway.'

'Eh? What are you on about?'

Lynx looked around the room. By the expressions on Teshen and Safir's faces, they had worked it out, but the others were all bemused. All except for Reft that was, but the giant had the physique of some hero's statue so, like Himbel, was perfectly comfortable being on display.

'Reckon that door's about to open.'

Lynx levered himself to his feet and swayed for a moment while his head lurched. Once it subsided he glanced down at his left hand, suddenly remembering the last time he'd been in a prison cell. His silver ring was still there so he kissed it in a fit of whimsy. That done he stretched his aching back, scratched his round, still-bruised belly and made a pantomime of flexing the muscles in his thick arms.

As he was done there came a deep clunk from the door as bolts were drawn back. Lynx shook his head and marched forward, Safir and Himbel following along behind.

The door opened to reveal beaming faces. Toil stood beside Sitain, one arm draped over the young woman's shoulders. The newly confirmed Jester of Sun looked little better than Lynx felt but there was still a smile on her face to go with the badge on her jacket. Behind them were more faces, Payl and Kas closest with the rest of the women of the company lining the corridor, waiting for their comrades to run the gauntlet past them.

Toil looked as stunning as ever, Lynx couldn't help but note, and wore the sort of wicked smile most men dreamed of waking up to. As the men of Anatin's mercenary company marched forward for their inspection, the women's eyebrows raised and their grins widened.

'Hello, boys,' Toil purred. She carefully looked each man up and down. 'We've come to rescue you.'

Acknowledgements

As always my thanks must go first and foremost to my wonderful wife, Fi, who's cheerfully weathered the eccentricities of being married to a writer and kept me on an even keel, in addition to more specific help reading and commenting as *Stranger* developed. Thanks to Ailsa too, for being a near-constant delight and unwittingly providing the odd line of dialogue.

Secondly, to my other beta-readers: my father and my big brother who have both been a huge support in so many ways over the years – the least of which being their willingness to read outside their preferred genres at the drop of a hat – and non-relation Rob who stepped up either because he's a great guy or can't pass up the opportunity to strenuously complain about a split infinitive. The collective effort at Gollancz remains a valuable constant for me too; I can't believe they've been putting up with me for more than ten years now and are still, astonishingly, listening to my opinion.

Finally, particular thanks to the two men who've worked so hard on this book and my continuing career. First of all a big manly hug goes to Simon Kavanagh for fighting my corner, and for his unfailing belief and encouragement. Secondly, a very British grunt and nod over a pint to Marcus Gipps, both for his work at Gollancz and efforts to point out all the times I've made myself look stupid so no one else got to see them.

Turn the page for a preview of Tom's exciting
eBook only novella set in the weeks following
Stranger of Tempest

Honour Under Moonlight

1

Lynx opened the door and hope died at his feet.

'Ah, shit.'

The gentle white glow of moonlight slipped past him into the room beyond. It was dark inside, but he could make enough out that he didn't want to see more. A sickle-shaped pool of blood gleamed blackly just past the door. Across it was an arm, outstretched towards him, fingers slightly curled. It looked to be both an invitation inside and a plea for help.

Lynx looked back down the steps to the cobbled courtyard, through an open archway to the street. The sky was clear and the moon sat behind the gauzy veil of the Skyriver. Tonight was the midwinter solstice, one of two nights in the year when the moon followed the Skyriver's path all night and had its light amplified by that great ring of dust and rock. There were plenty of people passing, most costumed and walking in pairs towards wherever they planned on enjoying the night's revelries. No one seemed to be paying him any attention so Lynx gingerly stepped across the threshold and closed the door behind him.

Without the moonlight it was hard to see, but the strip of light sliding through a pair of window drapes was enough to guide him towards them. He flicked the drapes open and skirted another corpse to reach a balcony door of paned glass, which he also uncovered. That done, there was more than enough light to see by. For half a minute he just stood amid a scene of bloody destruction, wondering what in the deepest black had happened.

The surprise was distant and fleeting. While a corpse or two was hardly a welcome sight, Lynx had encountered enough death to move rapidly on to how much trouble he was in. His fingers twitched towards his hip before he remembered he was also in festival garb – it was the reason he was here in the first place – so no sword hung there.

'Guess this costume wasn't such a stupid idea as it first sounded,' he muttered, looking down at himself.

Granted the red and white tunic was on the ridiculous side – and a white, wide-brimmed hat pinned with a long red feather skated close to daft if he was honest – but there were upsides. Traditionally the Knight of the Blood sported four diagonal slots for weapons on his chest – a pair of daggers on the left-hand side, a pair of pistols on the right. His hand went to his chest and thumbed open the clasp around the handle of one short-barrelled mage-pistol. Lynx flicked open the breech of the gun to be sure he'd loaded it before heading out, then closed it again and moved to inspect the room.

He twitched open a cupboard door that was ajar to check it wasn't actually another room, then stepped into the kitchen to confirm it was empty of assassins, living or otherwise. There was a narrow stairway that led up to a bedroom where the bed was neatly made and no one was hiding underneath, after which he returned to the scene of the crime.

He'd not been here before, had hardly spoken to the room's owner in over a week, but there were little touches in the room that spoke of her all the same. Her brass-bound, black-glass Duegar lantern sat on a shelf in the far corner, and a red and white costume that matched his own hung from a peg nearby.

Lynx looked again. It had to be said that the bloodied dagger rammed into the breast of the costume wasn't entirely part of the traditional get-up, but it still suited the room's owner. And he would be forced to admit the two dead assassins on the floor weren't beyond the bounds of things to expect around Toil either. Perhaps not on a daily basis, true, but death was more than just a passing acquaintance of hers. More of a close neighbour who often popped in for a glass of wine and a joke.

The costume on the peg was that of the Princess of Blood – whether it was a joke with herself or not, Toil was a cheerfully violent woman in some sort of clandestine employ of the Archelect of Su Dregir. She might not be an enthusiast of Tashot, the game that was a favourite among Lynx's mercenary company, but the Princess of Blood card was a widely known and powerful image nonetheless.

Her letter containing instructions to come dressed as the Knight of Blood had seemed as fitting as it was in poor taste, coming from a woman willing to enrage ancient monsters from the belly of the earth when it suited her. The Princess was the highest card in the suit of Blood, the Knight often called her consort.

He holstered his pistol and took a closer look around. There was a polished dining table between the kitchen and balcony door with half a dozen sturdy chairs around it. Unlit oil lamps hung from every wall and a fainting couch, of all things, stood to one side of the fireplace. Faint embers were all that remained in the grate, just the ghost of warmth lingering as the chill of winter intruded. It was a surprisingly refined room – leaky corpses aside – with a patchwork of thick, patterned rugs covering the floor and pictures on the wall.

The two largest of those were portraits hung together over the fireplace – the first of a middle-aged woman with a glittering smile Lynx recognised all too well. Alongside her was a great slab of a man painted warts and all, not to mention the scars, but wearing a roguish grin and a ruby at his throat.

Lynx breathed in deeply. The faint scent of night jasmine rose from the couch and some sort of sweet pork stew called to his beer-filled stomach from the kitchen, though the dead bodies added a less welcome flavour to the air. Upon inspection those also turned out to be a man and a woman, although probably not related to Toil as he was sure the portrait subjects were.

Curiously, both corpses were also in costume; black and white with thick black capes and hoods swept back. He would have assumed it was just to blend in on festival night, but it was strange for them to then both choose the same look. As for what the costume was, Lynx didn't recognise it so he crouched to inspect the badges on the chest of the nearest body. Simple diamond shapes; the first a black 2 on a white background, and the other a device he didn't know. It seemed to be a black moon, the lower half of which was crumbling. Something about that rang a faint bell, but Lynx couldn't place it.

Both assassins – assuming they were such, but they carried long-knives and pistol-bows, which were more conducive to quiet murder than extremely loud mage-guns – had died of knife wounds. One, the woman, had a hilt protruding from just below her jawline – driven with great force up into her head. The weapon didn't have a guard and all he could see was a rough, rounded wooden grip that made it probably a kitchen knife. Certainly it hadn't been worth retrieving by the killer. The other body bore long slash wounds that looked like they had come from a larger weapon, more akin to the short-swords Toil preferred.

Lynx walked around the room, picking his feet over the wreckage of a chair and a shattered porcelain bowl. A wine bottle lay on its side, spilling white wine across the table to drip down one side, the remains of a glass stem near the door.

She'd hurled the first thing she'd had to hand, probably inter-
rupted while fortifying her courage for a night in my company,
Lynx decided in a moment of black humour.

Opposite the front door was the doorway to the kitchen, one
window open to admit the cold. A butcher's block stood in the
middle of the kitchen, a fat cleaver resting in the centre. Buried in
the door jamb by his head was a short, blackened steel quarrel.

That window's how one got in then, he decided, looking down
at the bodies. The man was closer, but his money was on the
woman.

Hear her coming, stab her in the throat and use her as a shield
when you hear the front door give. Man at the door fires, misses.
You throw the only thing left in your hand, the wineglass, and shove
the dying woman into his way. That buys you time to grab your
short-sword and get to work at close range.

Did Toil run straight out of the door afterwards? Lynx wondered.
Unlikely, she's hardly one to panic.

He looked at the unused costume again. *And she had time*
enough to hammer that into the wall, or did she just miss a throw?
Not a blade you'd use by choice and it's in deep, dead centre. A
message for me? I was supposed to meet her here, after all.

'Hands in the air!' barked a voice, causing Lynx to jump.

Slowly he did so and edged around until he could see
the speaker. He gave a sigh of relief when he saw it was a
watchman, a short and round man with a fat moustache and
a mage-gun pointing at Lynx's chest.

His relief was short-lived when he remembered the bodies
on the floor and saw the calculating look in the watchman's
eye. Greying and fat he might be, he didn't look a fool or
remotely fazed by the sight.

'Ah,' Lynx began, keeping his hands up.

He was suddenly acutely aware his costume included promi-
nently displayed weapons. Being a mercenary, he'd replaced

the shiny stage knives and pistols provided by the costumier. In the bright moonlight, the watchman would be able to clearly see the scratched steel blades of the daggers and the all-too-real loaded mage-pistols.

'Yeah, these. I can explain.'

Toil, Lynx and the soldiers of Anatin's
Mercenary Deck are back

Turn the page for a preview
of the second novel of
The God Fragments

Princess of Blood

Interlude 1

(Now)

'So a pederast, an assassin and a convict walk into a palace.'

'Shut up.'

Lynx sighed. 'What? I'm bored.'

'I don't care.'

'No one's listening.'

Toil's voice lowered to the whisper of a razor being sharpened. 'What part of "I don't care" confuses you?'

'What's the harm in passing the time with a joke?'

'Because if you don't shut up I'll rip your kneecaps off and use them for earmuffs to block out your bloody whining.'

Lynx shut up and looked around at the grand hall of Jarrazir's Bridge Palace once more. It was magnificent, he had to admit. Jewelled light shone through a long bank of windows running almost the entire length of the hall. Dancing motes of emerald, blazing orange and glittering sapphire washed over the assembled crowd of Jarrazir's nobility. A spray of red carpet surrounded the pair of thrones at one end, all canopied by pristine white cloth bearing the symbols of the city and prayers stitched in red. Flanking them was a pair of stone urns, strangely out of place with only fragments of faded glazing and decoration until Lynx realised they were Duegar artefacts.

After an hour of the sight Lynx still felt it was all very pretty, but lunchtime was now fast intruding on his thoughts as the scents of spices and roasted meats hung thick in the air. As a portly and tattooed ex-soldier of a nation everyone hated, he was rather more noticeable than he liked anyway. Right then the great and the good were out in their finery to notice and be noticed, so unobtrusively sidling over to the buffet wasn't really an option.

Swan-necked maidens with bare shoulders stood like serene statues, or perhaps well-behaved cattle, while watchful matrons in silk headscarves fussed at their side. Prowling around the girls displayed like goods were knots of young noblemen, searching out both marriageable flesh and offence. Several had more than one glove tucked into their belt that did not match their clothes, proof of a duel to come.

Official delegations studded the throng, obvious by their matching clothing and uniforms, while members of the priest-hood stood out even more clearly. Just ahead of Lynx were the starkly austere priests of Insar, in plain white robes with heads cleanly shaved, while red and grey figures displaying the intricate braiding and geometric patterns of Catrac's cult loitered near the far wall. Lynx looked down at his own clothes. Fortunately the grey and green of Su Dregir's Lighthouse Guard was as understated as he could have reasonably hoped for. The fact he was in any form of uniform was a detail he remained unhappy about, but now wasn't the time for *that* discussion so he contented himself with not looking like an utter tit. This was Toil's business and he was just window-dressing for the hour.

Lynx felt a nudge from the man beside him.

'Tell me the joke instead,' Teshen said. 'Distract me from the urge to fire a burner into the roof.'

Lynx glanced up at the huge pale beams, so high the grain of the wood was invisible. Flags of every colour fluttered in the slight breeze, representing each of the city-state's several hundred noble families, while the beast emblems of Jarrazir hung over the empty thrones.

'It'd stop the boredom,' he conceded. 'Maybe even cook a dove or two if one is lurking up in the rafters.'

'You're not still bloody hungry are you?'

'I could eat.'

Toil turned round, eyes flashing with anger. Ahead of her stood the Su Dregir Envoy himself, chatting to a doughy old lady wrapped in purple silk like a child's sweet, the captain of his personal guard stationed between them. If either man had heard the conversation over the generally hubbub they chose to ignore it.

'Both of you, shut your traps right now,' she hissed. 'At least try to look like real guards.'

'Sounds like *someone's* a little on edge,' Teshen whispered primly once Toil had turned back. The tone didn't exactly match the man's dead-eyed killer look, but Lynx got the impression joining a mercenary company had forced Teshen to develop a light-hearted side, even if he remained firmly in the alarmingly lethal category.

'It's the dress,' Lynx opined, nodding forward. 'Maybe the heels. They don't look comfy.'

'Oh, I like the heels,' joined in Payl from the other side of Teshen. 'The poor bugger who had to buff her feet to make them presentable, however – now *they* have cause for complaint.'

Lynx smirked over at Payl. The woman was usually calm and professional – as second-in-command to a lazy, roguish drunk she had to be. That she'd joined in was a testament to the sheer boredom of standing amid that great crowd and waiting for the city's ruler to finish whatever it was that was taking so long.

'Was it you, Lynx?' Teshen asked. He was a burly man with long pale hair and under normal circumstances wore the Knight of Tempest as his badge – Lynx's direct superior – but today he was just another Su Dregir guardsman.

'Well I don't like to brag,' Lynx said. 'But I reckon I've a certain deftness with a pumice stone.'

It was just possible he could see the tips of Toil's ear turning scarlet with fury, but he knew she wouldn't give them the satisfaction of turning round again. Toil – ruin-raider, assassin, agent of Su Dregir, plus half a dozen other unsavoury things – had scrubbed up remarkably well, he had to admit. A layered silk dress in the Archelect's green and grey ran from calf to neck, following the Jarraziran form of leaving arms and feet on show, with her dark red hair in a complex triple braid down her back.

'Almost fell over with shock when I saw her,' Teshen said. 'Who'd have thought under those hobnailed boots was a pair of feet like that? Probably best Anatin didn't come with us; man's got a thing for a well-turned ankle. I know I'm new to this, but I'm guessing elite guardsmen shouldn't have a hard-on.'

Lynx had to agree, the feet really had been a surprise. Toil wore thin sandals – straps of grey silk exposing neat, un-callused heels and pristinely groomed, painted toenails.

'Are all you fighting women like this?' he whispered to Payl. 'All with your little beauty secrets?'

Payl snorted. 'My feet look like they got chewed on by feral dogs. Just as well I'm tall and no man ever bothers to look that far down.'

'I'll tell Fashail to report back next time he's hard at work down there,' Teshen said.

'The boy knows he'll get his nuts cut off,' Payl said confidently. 'As scary as you are, Teshen, he ain't that stupid.'

'It's the arms that get me, I reckon,' Lynx said after a moment's reflection. 'So she's secretly a delicate little princess when it comes to her feet, now we all know, but it takes real skill to pull off the arms.'

'Not so much,' Teshen said dismissively. 'I've seen Reft do it easy enough.'

'I meant, pull off that concealment.'

'Ah.'

While almost every woman not in fighting dress had bare arms, none sported the number of scars Toil did. A lifetime of fighting and clambering about the pitch-black caverns of Duegar city-ruins had done little to support today's role of bookish secretary to Su Dregir's official Envoy.

It had required a complex variety of ribbons, torcs, bracelets, painted charms and rings to distract from the battering Toil's arms had received over the years. Close scrutiny would catch her out still, but with luck few would be getting that close. Toil was a distractingly beautiful woman for those who would be distracted and physically imposing for those who wouldn't.

'How about you, Aben?' Teshen asked the last of the group serving as guards to the Envoy. 'Anything you'd like to add?'

Aben was new to their number, a bigger man even than Lynx, with tanned skin, an easy smile and neat black curls spilling out from under his official cap. Currently his face was scarlet and he seemed to be having some sort of silent shaking episode, possibly a coronary.

'You okay there, friend?' Lynx said with a nudge. 'Looks like something in your head just burst. Was it the feet? Does a well-turned ankle do it for you too?'

Aben's eyes swivelled in their sockets as though seeking an escape. He'd worked for Toil for several years now. She was *the boss* to him, a ruthless and remorseless figure within the Su Dregir underworld. She *wasn't* a person to be joked about in her earshot and *was* someone with a long and enthusiastically vengeful memory.

'Hey look, more people come to join the vigil,' Payl commented. 'And of-fucking-course it's the last bastards we want to see here, there or anywhere else.'

Lynx turned as Teshen voiced the words they were all thinking. 'Bastard shitting Charnelers.'

'Least all those who chased us will be dead by now,' Payl added quietly. 'Don't fancy getting recognised by anyone after Grasiel.'

'So – an assassin, a convict and a whole boatload of pederast shites walk into a palace,' Lynx muttered.

Toil spun right round, cheeks now spotted pink with anger. 'If they're here, you lot keep your mouths shut from now on, understand? No jokes, no witty asides, no. . .' Her eyes narrowed as she focused on the Charnelers and Lynx saw anger turn to murder in her eyes. 'Godspit and the shitting deepest black!'

Without warning she started off, shoving Payl out of her way. In his surprise Lynx barely noticed her slip a dagger from Payl's belt as she stalked forward.

'What? So it's alright for her to swear?' Teshen commented in a mock-hurt voice.

'I'm going to fucking gut you like a fish!' Toil roared across the great hall.

Lynx and Teshen exchanged looks while Payl and Aben started off after the spirit of vengeance. Ahead of Toil the crowd erupted into chaos.

'Well, that's the boredom part sorted out,' Lynx said.

'Should we. . .?' Teshen nodded after the others.

'If you like, but they can handle it I'm sure. And I'm damn sure Toil can handle herself. Not like I'm keen for her to win friends here anyway, given what she wants to volunteer us for. More importantly I've just spotted a roast pheasant that no one's watching. Reckon it's near enough lunchtime.'

'Is there beer?'

'Wine.'

Teshen shrugged as shouts filled the air. 'The sacrifices we must make. . . Lead on, my friend.'

Chapter 1

Three Weeks Earlier

A dusting of snow lay on the ancient city of Jarrazir as five figures hurried through the still hours of night. Every stone and tile sparkled in the silver glow of the Skyriver, every curl and twist of the bay's waters was limned in white moonlight. Statues of heroes and rulers watched from the great arc of the Senate wall, beneath which the Deep Market nestled. The market itself was a sweeping warren of walkways and arches, arcades and canopies, spread over three storeys in parts and bewildering in the detail and intricacy of its design.

The five figures kept silent as they wound their way towards the market's heart, the three who led moving with the confidence of familiarity. Jarrazir was a city of old names and older customs, one of which was a prohibition on alcohol so the night-time streets were empty and silent. The Deep Market in particular was deserted – the cold of winter and its unsettling, unearthly style meaning even vagrants kept clear at night.

Had she been alone, Lastani would have been apprehensive at best. She had lived her whole life in Jarrazir; a childhood of tales and superstitions not so long left behind for more academic pursuits. Only the reassuring purpose of Mistress Ishienne ahead kept her focused on the task in hand.

No, not quite. Not just that. She suppressed a nervous giggle. There was something more bringing her here, to the oldest part of an ancient city where even the light of the Skyriver struggled to reach. *There is the possibility of something quite wonderful too – a place in history perhaps, should we be successful.*

Lastani bit her lip and kept on walking. She would not be the one to draw Ishienne Matarin's ire this night, not at the culmination of all her teacher's work.

Let Castiere do that. He's incapable of keeping his mouth shut. Let him be the fool who sullies this night with some idiocy, I will be the perfect pupil at least this once.

As they rounded a corner and entered a small square cut through with jagged black shadows, she glanced once at Castiere as the slender young man drew level in his haste to get to the market's heart. He saw her looking and flashed Lastani a grin, his excitement bubbling close to the surface.

'Almost there,' whispered Mistress Ishienne, her voice carrying clearly in the hush despite the scarf across her face.

The words were unnecessary, perhaps an indication of Isheinne's own anticipation. This might prove a breakthrough in her work, the fruits of years of translating and deciphering a script thousands of years old. Lastani could not fault this one crack in her reserve, the scholar's detached calm that had been a constant during Lastani's four years tutelage.

She looked around as they neared the Fountain, as it was called. So many days spent here amid the bustle of humanity as wares were sold and all manner of services offered from dawn until dusk. Day after day of transcribing and sketching, measuring and dreaming – losing her purse twice, her heart once and her maidenhood along with it. But now it was alien and frightening here, scoured of life and the things of men. The stone mages who had built the Deep Market, hundreds of years before, had chosen the fountain itself as inspiration for their otherworldly craft and by custom, only stone remained here at night.

There, where the stall of kind Uslien normally stood, only bare and empty stone. Here, her dearest Lefaqe's tent of silks would be strung each morning – to see the space empty was to feel a curious hole in her heart. But no one would leave their belongings here, certainly not so close to the fountain that was at the heart of it all. The Fountain which was no fountain and no crafting of a stone mage – at least, no human one.

They turned the corner and stopped, Lastani almost running into Mistress Ishienne as the Fountain itself came into view. In the dark it was a forbidding, squat lump of stone almost invisible in the darkness of shadow, but somehow all the more chilling for it. In the light of day she found it fascinating – the intricacy and otherworldly beauty of the ancient artefact breathtaking to behold – but now it was profoundly disquieting.

A nine-sided stone block the height of a man was set within a trio of fat, sinuous serpents of some unknown metal. The Fountain was Duegar-made and the finest example of that race's artistry within a hundred miles. Every flat surface was covered with wind-scoured carvings and detailing of remarkable intricacy and complexity – a puzzle of knots and patterns that incorporated every face and facet of the fountain into one vast mathematical pattern. A domed stone canopy stood over it, perhaps twelve feet above the stub of its nine-sided apex, and it was this that restored Lastani's courage.

The Duegar script that covered the inner face of the dome was just as intricate as the decoration below, worked into a three-branched spiral that wound into the centre. And now, amid the blackness of night, the curling metal script was faintly glowing.

Lastani had always half-believed that to be nothing more than embellishment – a lie told in the assuption that no sensible person would attempt to refute it. But there it was; the star-script of the Duegar, almost as perfect and complete as the day that long-dead race had set it there. Two small pieces were missing; she had read the accounts of the enterprising thieves a dozen times or more, and the strange deaths that had followed under cover of this darkness. Lastani was still staring in wonder when a figure stepped out from behind the fountain and gave her such a fright that she squeaked in terror, breaking the reverential hush.

Mistresss Ishienne turned and fixed her with a stern look, unperturbed by the stranger's sudden appearance. Lastani covered her mouth and ducked her head, cheeks flushed with embarrassment. They were there on an errand of momentous and grave scholarly import, not to jump at ghosts. Lastani felt Castiere's patronising hand on her shoulder, the youth suppressing a laugh before he followed their Mistress's lead and bowed to the newcomer.

'Master Atienolentra,' Ishienne called through the still night, 'you are well met again.'

'Let's hope so,' the man replied in a deep, rumbling voice. 'You, Mistress, continue to be a delight on the eyes.' He paused. 'Your pronunciation less so, however. Perhaps best just call me Atieno.'

'My apologies,' Ishienne said, inclining her head. 'It seems I have spent too much time favouring dead languages over existing ones.'

With a start Lastani realised she had seen this man before, or glimpsed him at any rate. At a meeting Ishienne had taken, just a week beforehand. Lastani had been returning to the house when she saw Master Atieno leaving. Hidden from the faint shine of the Skyriver by his hood, she had only glimpsed the white threads of his neat, pointed beard, but it was enough.

With piercing light brown eyes against a dark face of crow's feet and prominent cheekbones, Atieno would have been handsome man but for the glowering severity he wore. His greying black hair was long and tied neatly back, his worn clothes kept clean and neat. In his fifth decade at least, he remained tall and strong-looking – a marked improvement on the handful of suitors who had attempted to woo Mistress Ishienne during the time Lastani had lived in her house. Judging by Atieno's words, the idea had crossed his mind too.

The last two figures of Ishienne's group stepped out from behind Castiere and eyed the man suspiciously.

'Who's he?' Bokrel demanded.

The mercenary fingered the rounded butt of his holstered mage-pistol as he stared at Master Atieno. Bokrel was a monkey-faced wretch with grubby cheeks, a scrappy beard and wandering hands. Right now there was a livid pink frost-burn down the back of his left hand, a testament to how slow the mercenary was to take a hint, but he was the brains of the operation compared to his rotund comrade, Ybryl.

'He, Master Bokrel, is a key component of what we attempt tonight,' Ishienne said sharply. 'Try not to shoot him please. I doubt it would end well for you.'

Atieno gave the two mercenaries a stern look then seemed to mentally dismiss them. He carried a large walking staff that looked like a weapon in his hands, but like the mercenaries he also had a mage-pistol in his belt. With stiff movements that spoke of a lame leg, he walked around to the face of the fountain that was, by common agreement, the front.

'You believe you can do this?' Master Atieno called.

Ishienne gestured to the swirls of script glowing above them. 'I have seen it in the stars,' she said with a small smile.

'That, I have heard before. Rarely has it inspired confidence.'

'The difference, I suspect, is that I've had to understand enough to teach my pupils.'

Lastani took a step forward. 'Mistress Ishienne translated the Duegar script, but the riddle within has been something we have all devoted our lives to unpicking.'

'The young say such things so easily,' Atieno said with gentle mocking. 'They've had less to devote thus far.'

'*I* have given it enough years for all three of us,' Ishienne declared, 'and my assistants contributed several of their own on top. The sacrifice has been shared, and now we must see if it was in vain or not.'

'Where do you want us?' Bokrel asked abruptly.

'At the edge of the dome,' she replied, pointing to the arched gaps between the dome's stone supports.

'And then what?'

'Keep guard,' Ishienne said simply. 'We must not be disturbed. Most likely you need do nothing to earn your pay, Gods grant. I require you only to be awake and ready in case anything. . . unexpected, occurs.'

'Like what?'

'If I knew that, I would expect it. Come now, Master Bokrel, you led me to believe you were an experienced soldier and had explored Duegar city-ruins.'

Ybryl snorted at Bokrel's side, causing the man to glare at her. 'We ain't explored the damn things.' Ybryl chuckled, not noticing the look Bokrel gave her. 'We ain't that stupid.'

'What then?'

'Guard duty, escort,' Bokrel explained reluctantly. 'Let the other damn fools go underground an' play with monsters.'

Ishienne hissed in irritation. 'You have combat experience at least?'

'Yeah, we've been in a few fights.'

'Good – in that case keep your eyes open and your guns loaded, your mouths shut and your wits primed.'

Before Bokrel had a chance to object Ishienne turned away and gestured to her two charges. 'Come, take your places.'

Lastani and Castiere ducked their heads in acknowledgement and went to stand beneath the nearest two snake mouths, peering up into the dark, toothless maws that looked down on them.

'And I?'

'Just as you are, Master Atieno,' Ishienne said, making her way around to the last of the snake mouths. 'Yours is the most complicated of tasks I'm afraid.'

'It always is,' he said. 'Firstly, your powers though. What are they?'

'Does it matter?'

'It does.'

Ishienne frowned. 'Very well, but I will be doing the sculpting of magic – you need but echo my workings. I am a stone mage, Lastani an ice mage, and Castiere fire. Does that meet with your approval?'

'It does,' Atieno said with a nod. 'There are powers that my kind will not work with. The risk is too great.'

'And those are?'

'Not stone, fire or ice.'

After a moment it was clear he would say no more on the subject so Ishienne gave a cluck of the tongue and went back about her task.

'For the first stage, you are not required, Master Atieno,' she informed him. 'The job is ours alone.'

At her nod, Lastani stretched up to the mouth of the metal serpent above her and opened herself to her magic. A faint white haze appeared around her hand then she felt the bite of cold on her skin – not painful to her, just different, for all that it would freeze the skin off any other human in a matter of seconds.

A soft crackle from the far side told her that Castiere was doing the same, sending magic up into the mouth of the serpent with all the control he could muster. Ishienne was silent, but Lastani could just see her out of the corner of her eye and the woman was reaching up also. She concentrated on the task at hand, allowing the magic inside her to flow out through her fingers and coil up into the snake.

All this they had expected. The months of deciphering and research meant she could quote the words above by rote, but still Lastani felt a thrill at it working. The fountain was drawing her magic, not greedily leeching off her but gathering all that she released into the belly of the earth. Mistress Ishienne had described it as a votive offering, something that had made poor pious Castiere wince, but Lastani saw now how right she was. They were giving the fountain something of themselves, a trace of their power, to prepare the way for what would come next – what they would ask of it.

The flow of magic steadily grew and Lastani began to be able to sense the others, the heat of Castiere's magic and cool weight of Ishienne's. There was a balance in what they were offering and Lastani knew not to over-tax herself in this initial stage, but still she freed a little more of the clean, cold bite in her bones to more closely match Castiere.

Their powers were to be most obviously in balance, as they often had been in Ishienne's library while debating the grand puzzle of the Fountain. Whether by chance or consequence of their magic, the two thought in entirely different ways. Sometimes Castiere's dancing focus would alight on the path, sometimes Lastani's careful method would instead.

'Enough,' Ishienne called and the trio cut the flow of their magic.

Lastani stepped back so she could see her teacher's face. Though the woman's expression was hidden in the shadows, years in her company told Lastani that Ishienne was satisfied with the first step.

'Now we wait,' Ishienne added for the benefit of Atieno. 'There is a precise order to this ritual that must be followed.'

'You are confident in your interpretation?' Atieno replied in a voice that betrayed neither scepticism nor belief. 'Many have attempted this.'

'And many have got this far,' Ishienne said. 'This pause is the first test, your presence another, the details of the crafting a third. A plain translation of the text above your head will get you no further than this.'

'And a mistranslation would see Lastani dead,' Castiere added drily.

'Now it is your confidence that concerns me,' Atieno declared. The man leaned heavily on his staff as he spoke, but made no effort to move away from the fountain.

'Our confidence is well-founded,' Lastani found herself saying. 'The work is a puzzle, understanding that is the crux of Mistress Ishienne's breakthrough. By mirroring the decoration on the fountain—'

'I'm sure Master Atieno isn't interested in the details of our research,' Ishienne broke in. Lastani couldn't tell whether that was through a desire to preserve her secrets or impatience to be getting on, but she shut her mouth with a snap and tried not to picture Castiere's smirk.

'Research is not where I excel,' Atieno agreed sombrely, 'so I will take your word as though it were scripture.'

'Would that the Book of the First Sun could stand up to such rigour,' Castiere muttered.

'This is not the time, Castiere,' Ishienne reminded him. 'Now, are you both ready for the second phase?'

Lastani nodded and stepped forward, opening herself again as Castiere did the same. This time they let their magic only gently bleed out and Ishienne, controlling something within the fountain itself, regulated the magic in a precise pattern before both assistants threw one long, sustained burst of raw power in. When Lastani stepped back again, she was light-headed and suddenly weary, but there had been no apparent effect on the fountain.

'Now you, Master Atieno,' Ishienne said, stepping to the side until she could see the man. 'Palm against the middle panel, please. Let the stone draw your hand in and take your magic. I will guide you as best I can, you must mirror my workings as you sense them.'

'Have a care,' Atieno warned her as he stepped forward and placed a hand against the stone. 'Tempest is unlike your magic. There is cost and wildness other mages do not know.'

Despite everything, Lastani felt a shiver down her spine as he said the word. The mages of tempest were so rare most considered them a myth, their magic not of elements but of change. The Militant Orders had no use for them and struggled to control them, so they demonised Atieno's kind and killed them when they could. It had taken Ishienne's extensive contacts and several bribes before she had found Atieno and convinced him to come.

'I understand,' Ishienne said calmly. 'A trace of tempest is required, nothing more. It is the key, not the shoulder to the door, and I know you pay for every drawing.'

'Not only me,' he said. 'It would twist every strand of magic it touched, if you tried to draw much, and turn your power against you. It cannot be controlled – refusing to accept that has killed more of my brethren than the Militant Orders ever managed.'

'Your warning is appreciated, then,' she replied. 'Should anything more than the tiniest amount prove inadequate, we will break off and reassess.'

A grunt was all Atieno replied with, but he set to work without hesitation. Lastani resumed her place, hand stretched up to offer a steady, modest flow of power. The mingling she had sensed within the Fountain remained, but she could not feel any of the tempest magic within that blend. Only by the sound could she tell the carved face under Atieno's hand had opened under Ishienne's stone magery and closed again around it.

At first there was nothing, no indication that the magic was affecting the fountain at all, but eventually she began to feel the ground faintly tremble. Carefully regulating herself to match Castiere, she touched one finger to the metal snake. It was doing the same, a tiny shudder running through the entire Fountain and deep underground.

Off to her right there was a slight gasp from Ishienne, then a sound of satisfaction. Lastani could not tell that anything had changed until she heard a telltale grind and the whisper of stone on stone – Ishienne forming and shaping the very structure of the Fountain. It was a Duegar construction, designed with magic in mind and made to respond, but still Ishienne moved slowly.

Lastani saw the brief flourish of surprise on Atieno's reserved face as the stone began to move towards him, freeing his arm and allowing the man to take a laboured step back. The fountain continue to move, petals of stone peeling organically back under Ishienne's deft touch until the stone had folded right back to the metal snake-shapes on either side.

'There,' Ishienne declared, releasing her magic and stepping back. 'It is done.'

Lastani smiled and moved to do the same when with a jolt she realised she couldn't.

'Ah, Mistress?' called Castiere from the other side. 'I've got a—'

Either he didn't get any further or Lastani didn't hear him. The mouth of the snake snapped shut on her fingers and for a moment there was only the white-hot pain of crushing. From the howl that broke through it, Castiere had experienced the same. Lastani had time for one brief flash of fear before the snake began to feed savagely on her magic and all rational thought vanished from her mind.

She wailed and hauled at her trapped fingers but her muscles had turned to jelly, her mind a cold void as the trickle of magic was turned to a raging torrent. The air whitened before her eyes as her ice magic turned the chill night freezing. Within moments she couldn't feel her body except the unremitting pressure on her fingers, everything else subordinate to the wild plunder of magic.

Her eyes blurred and a veil of darkness started to descend. Lastani barely noticed hands on her body, the shouting voices. Even when the hands began to pull then frantically haul at her, it was distant and unreal. The pain receded, the world around her darkened and contracted to a single, diminishing point of light before everything snapped back with terrible force.

Lastani took one ragged breath then screamed with all her might as something gave in her fingers and she was dragged away. Shrieking, she curled over her injury but strong hands unpeeled her fingers and roughly stretched them out.

'The other one! Go!' roared a man above her, just a dark blur through her tumbling tears.

She fought him but could do nothing against the man's strength and with perfunctory jerks he yanked one finger then the next straight. Each movement sparked another shriek from Lastani, but afterwards the pain dampened and her wits returned. Her vision cleared a fraction to see Atieno and Mistress Ishienne staring down at her bleeding, pinched but no longer dislocated fingers.

'He's on fire!' roared a voice from behind Atieno, prompting the man to turn with a snarl on his face.

'Cut the hand!' he roared, rising. 'Get him away or he'll die!'

An orange corona lit the inscribed canopy above and haloed the fountain. Lastani couldn't see Castiere from where she lay, but she knew how the fire mage would be looking if he was trapped as she had been – surrounded by the unchecked ferocity of his magic.

There was a grunt and a wet crunch. The light vanished and she heard a weight fall to the ground, but not the screams of a man whose limb had just been severed.

'Castiere!' Ishienne yelled, running past the open face of the fountain towards her pupil, but never reaching him.

A flash of pale grey light darted out towards her, as fast as a striking snake, and snatched the woman up like she was a toy. Lastani screamed in terror, Ishienne's cry cut off in the same instant it began. Impaled on blades of shining mist, she hung helpless – her mouth open in a silent scream – as an indistinct nightmare hauled itself out of the darkness inside the fountain.

Long, slender limbs unfolded, two, six, eight – the ghostly creature seemed all limbs and no body, just a knot where the joints met, but it moved with fearsome purpose and speed.

A great detonation crashed against Lastani's ears. She reeled, eyes watering and barely registering the taste of ice magic in the air. Atieno had fired his mage-pistol, but though the horror flinched there was no damage Lastani could see.

Wailing in terror, the two mercenaries backed away. Bokrel had his gun out, wavering uncertainly in the apparition's direction, but when he fired the white trail went high and out into the night beyond. Ybryl hadn't even got her gun out, the woman just quivered and wailed quietly as the horror turned their way. It dropped Ishienne and she fell limp, a dead thing on the floor. That was enough to make the mercenaries turn tail, but before they could get a step or two it slashed forward and tore furrows down their backs.

The mercenaries fell, their cries cut short as the horror stabbed forward to dispatch them with perfunctory savagery. Lastani was paralysed with fear as she watched them die, unable to run while she had the chance. When it turned towards them she still couldn't move, a leaden chill filling her body.

Atieno growled a curse and pulled something from his waist – small, just the size of a hazelnut. Lastani barely saw anything of the dark object as Atieno hurled it towards the ghostly spider-thing. The small shape landed at its feet. The ground seemed to shudder and twist, the horror somehow tangled as Atieno dragged Lastani upright and started hauling her away.

'Come on!' he roared in her ear, slapping her face to jerk her back to her senses. Lastani gasped at the impact, her head rocking back, but then some trace of her strength returned and she found her feet again.

'Move!' Atieno roared again, leaning heavily on his staff with one hand and the other gripping Lastani's arm so tight it hurt. His bad leg dragged heavily underneath him, but still Lastani would have fallen behind without his hold on her.

Together they fled as fast as they could, not daring to look behind in case the creature was right there. Only at the edge of the Deep Market where they were surrounded by dark empty silence did they pause and check behind. There was nothing there – all was still and silent. No screams of the dying, no darting movements of whatever had attacked them.

'Ishienne,' Lastani gasped. 'Castiere?'

'They're dead,' Atieno said gruffly, 'and we're not out of danger yet.'

'What? How do you know?'

'I don't,' he snapped. 'But I ain't a man to gamble on his own safety. I don't know what we just unleashed, but I for one won't hang around to see how far the danger goes.'

'But. . . what do I. . .?'

His face softened. 'Come, girl, we need to keep moving.'

'Where?'

'Your teacher's house. Your home. You need to pack your belongings.'

Lastani stared up at him with incomprehension. 'But. . .'

'Come on,' he urged, pulled her along with him as they headed for the coiling ramp that led up to the inhabited part of the city. 'Folk will have heard the gunshots, they'll fetch the watch.'

'I should stay.'

'Not a good idea. At best they'll find some brutally murdered people, at worst. . . well, you don't want to be anywhere near the fallout and I need to get paid.'

She gaped at him. 'Paid?'

'Aye.' His face hardened again. 'My fee. I ain't so rich I can afford to go without that. I did as your Mistress asked and I need to pay for food somehow. Compassion doesn't help there. And you – you don't want to be at her house when some angry watchmen come looking for answers. Asking why some monstrous ghost just got set loose in the city. Take what you can without it looking like you've killed and robbed her.'

They started up the slope, Atieno's face taut with apprehension. Lastani followed without willing it, her body just obeying even if her mind couldn't comprehend his instructions.

'What then?'

'After that is anyone's guess.' He paused and frowned at her for a moment before seeming to make up his mind. 'Come with me if you want, lay low a few days and let the worst pass. After that. . .' he shrugged and started walking again, labouring up the slope until they were at the top and he could peer suspiciously around. There was no one in sight so he waved Lastani onward and pressed on to the cover of the nearest side-street.

'After that, let's just hope what we did doesn't come back to haunt us.'

TOM LLOYD was born in 1979 in Berkshire.
After a degree in International Relations he went
straight into publishing where he still works. He never
received the memo about suitable jobs for writers
and consequently has never been a kitchenhand,
hospital porter, pigeon hunter, or secret agent.

• • •

He lives in Oxford, isn't one of those authors who
gives a damn about the history of the font used in his
books and only believes in forms of exercise
that allow him to hit something.

• • •

Visit him online at @tomlloydwriter or on facebook.

MOON'S ARTIFICE

Book One of Empire of a Hundred Houses

Tom Lloyd

Tom Lloyd kicks off a spectacular new fantasy series!

In a quiet corner of the Imperial City, Investigator Narin discovers the result of his first potentially lethal mistake. Minutes later he makes a second.

After an unremarkable career Narin finally has the chance of promotion to the hallowed ranks of the Lawbringers – guardians of the Emperor's laws and bastions for justice in a world of brutal expediency. Joining that honoured body would be the culmination of a lifelong dream, but it couldn't possibly have come at a worse time.

On the cusp of an industrial age that threatens the warrior caste's rule, the Empire of a Hundred Houses awaits civil war between noble factions. Centuries of conquest has made the empire a brittle and bloated monster; constrained by tradition and crying out for change. To save his own life and those of untold thousands Narin must understand the key to it all – Moon's Artifice, the poison that could destroy an empire.

• • •

'A hugely assured modern fantasy novel' *SFX*

THE STORMCALLER
Book One of The Twilight Reign

Tom Lloyd

In a land ruled by prophecy and the whims of Gods, a young man finds himself at the heart of a war he barely understands, wielding powers he may never be able to control.

Isak is a white-eye, feared and despised in equal measure. Trapped in a life of poverty, hated and abused by his father, Isak dreams of escape, but when his chance comes, it isn't to a place in the army as he'd expected. Instead, the Gods have marked him out as heir-elect to the brooding Lord Bahl, the Lord of the Fahlan.

Lord Bahl is also a white-eye, a genetic rarity that produces men stronger, more savage and more charismatic than their normal counterparts. Their magnetic charm and brute strength both inspires and oppresses others.

Now is the time for revenge, and the forging of empires. With mounting envy and malice, the men who would themselves be kings watch Isak, chosen by Gods as flawed as the humans who serve them, as he is shaped and moulded to fulfil the prophecies that are encircling him like scavenger birds.

• • •

'The world is beautifully realised, the battles suitably grim and the dragon, when it appears, is magnificent' *Guardian*

'Fantasy with a magnificence of conception, a sense of looming presences whose purposes are not ours to apprehend' *Time Out*

'Gallops along with scarcely a dull moment' *The Times*

'Lloyd creates a vivid world . . . he echoes writers such as Moorcock and Gemmell' *Interzone*

ABOUT GOLLANCZ

Gollancz is the oldest SF publishing imprint in the world. Since being founded in 1927 Gollancz has continued to publish a focused selection of bestselling and award-winning authors. The front-list includes **Ben Aaronovitch**, **Joe Abercrombie**, **Charlaine Harris**, **Joanne Harris**, **Joe Hill**, **Alastair Reynolds**, **Patrick Rothfuss**, **Nalini Singh** and **Brandon Sanderson**.

As one of the largest Science Fiction and Fantasy imprints in the UK it is no surprise we have one of the most extensive backlists in the world. Find high-quality SF on Gateway written by such authors as **Philip K. Dick**, **Ursula Le Guin**, **Connie Willis**, **Sir Arthur C. Clarke**, **Pat Cadigan**, **Michael Moorcock** and **George R.R. Martin**.

We also have a strand of publishing in translation, which includes French, Polish and Russian authors. Gollancz is home to more award-winning authors than any other imprint, with names including **Aliette de Bodard**, **M. John Harrison**, **Paul McAuley**, **Sarah Pinborough**, **Pierre Pevel**, **Justina Robson** and many more.

The SF Gateway
More than 3,000 classic, rare and previously out-of-print SF novels at your fingertips.
www.sfgateway.com

The Gollancz Blog
Bringing you news from our worlds to yours. Stories, interviews, articles and exclusive extracts just for you!
www.gollancz.co.uk

GOLLANCZ
LONDON